ESC   Escandon, Maria Amparo

L.A. weather   DISCARD

12/10/2021

L.A. WEATHER

L.A. WEATHER

L.A. WEATHER

MARÍA AMPARO ESCANDÓN

THORNDIKE PRESS
A part of Gale, a Cengage Company

Copyright © 2021 by María Amparo Escandón.
Thorndike Press, a part of Gale, a Cengage Company.

ALL RIGHTS RESERVED
This is a work of fiction. All of the characters, organizations, and events portrayed in this novel are either products of the author's imagination or are used fictitiously.
Thorndike Press® Large Print Basic.
The text of this Large Print edition is unabridged.
Other aspects of the book may vary from the original edition.
Set in 16 pt. Plantin.

LIBRARY OF CONGRESS CIP DATA ON FILE.
CATALOGUING IN PUBLICATION FOR THIS BOOK
IS AVAILABLE FROM THE LIBRARY OF CONGRESS.

ISBN-13: 978-1-4328-9304-0 (hardcover alk. paper)

Published in 2021 by arrangement with Flatiron Books

Printed in Mexico
Print Number: 01   Print Year: 2022

For Marinés, the girl I gave birth to
And for Zooey, the woman she became

CONTENTS

CONTENTS

I believe Icarus was not failing as he fell,
but just coming to the end of his triumph.

— "FAILING AND FLYING,"
FROM *REFUSING HEAVEN*
BY JACK GILBERT

2016
JANUARY

Sunday, January 10th

The twins were here one minute, gone the next. Conceived in vitro, Diana and Andrea had enjoyed the care, nurturing, and love that their parents selflessly offered in abundance after having birthed them under such desperate, artificial, anti-natural, miraculous, controversial, and diabolic (as Aunt Belinda had pointed out in a hush-hush tone outside the delivery room to her friend Bertha, who heard nothing since she'd forgotten her hearing aid at home) circumstances. And so, over their three-year life span, the girls had accumulated a wide array of colorful beach balls and inflatable cartoon characters that were kept in their grandparents Keila and Oscar Alvarado's oversize, kidney-shaped pool. This kind of swimming pool was a near-mandatory feature in almost every West Los Angeles backyard, but regrettably, due to a state of

11

neglect that had lasted well over ten months, it was filled with greenish, standing water up to four feet deep, in which colonies of mosquitoes and other winged and long-legged insects thrived with no reason to envy life in the humid thickness of the Amazon rain forest. Permanently suspended on a blanket of rotting leaves from the sweet gum trees that lined the yard, the half-deflated toys had developed layers of slimy mold. But still, the girls loved their toys and knew where they were, even in the after-dusk darkness. And so, Diana tried to reach a mermaid and Andrea a hippo, and both girls fell in, one right after the other, while Grandma Keila opened the door for the pizza man. It was 6:48 P.M.

Holding the large deep-dish pepperoni and anchovy pizza warm in its box, Keila called her granddaughters for dinner, searching for them in their secret hideouts around the house. Not quite sixty, she moved about the rooms with the agility she had perfected over years of yoga practice. Her complexion showed barely a wrinkle, mostly ironed out with a little Botox here and a little filler there. A meticulously selected strand of gray hair fell on one side of her forehead; the rest of her soft-curl bob, she colored dark brown.

She first went out the back door to the end of the yard and checked in the detached garage, home to everything but cars. Oscar had used the right side of the space as a gym before he acquired the habit of watching the Weather Channel for eight hours at a time. Now, the dumbbells, the Nautilus, the treadmill, and the Soloflex were under a tarp, waiting for the next guilt-driven exercise outburst, which would not come. Oscar's lack of interest in things, especially his inattention to the backyard and the swimming pool, had been gradual but complete. Her husband of thirty-nine years — a passionate, entrepreneurial, honest, faithful, charming, thinker and achiever — was no longer himself and so her vagina became off-limits to him at the same time the backyard went feral.

Next to the exercise equipment were three bikes last ridden twelve years ago. The blue one belonged to Claudia, Keila's firstborn. The pink one was Olivia's, her second daughter and mother of the twins. And the red one with the basket was Patricia's, the youngest of the three.

To one side of the bikes, a file cabinet, which Oscar kept under lock and key, acted as a partition wall. Its top drawer contained folders and more folders filled with love letters postmarked in the seventies by the Mexican and the U.S. postal services, organized chronologically. The second and third drawers stored tax returns going ten years back, just in case; the birth and marriage certificates of Oscar, Keila, and their three daughters; school diplomas and special papers and projects; old insurance policies; and anything else from the past that might be needed in the future. Kept in an acid-free envelope was Keila's U.S. Certificate of Naturalization, along with an American flag no larger than a handkerchief and a welcome letter signed in facsimile by President Reagan. In the bottom drawer, the original grant deed of the family home in Rancho Verde (owned free and clear since day one) had developed a slight musty smell caused by the humidity that seeped from a slowly leaking pipe below.

Next to the cabinet, an artificial Christmas tree, divided into four sections carefully wrapped in heavy-duty trash bags for protection from dust and vermin, was leaning against three large suitcases from the pre-wheels era. Two of them were packed with ornaments and lights and fireplace stockings and a Nativity complete with the Holy Family, shepherds, sheep, an angel, and the three Wise Men mounted on their elephant, camel, and horse, respectively. The third suitcase contained a menorah, a box of candles, honey jars, Seder plates, and other celebratory Judaica. To the side of the door, in the most accessible area, were the earthquake survival kit with enough emergency supplies for the entire family and the fire-evacuation suitcases ready to go at a moment's notice. "Be prepared, always prepared," Oscar would often tell his wife and children. Keila, now a bit annoyed, called out to her granddaughters again. They were elsewhere, definitely. It was 6:53 P.M.

Her next stop was her art studio, adjacent to the detached garage. The door, featuring a colorful mezuzah attached to its frame, was ajar, so the girls could well have wandered in, even though they'd been instructed not to. The place wasn't large. A turntable, a stool, a worktable, a toolbox, a gas kiln, and various buckets of different sizes and colors with dry and hardened glazes, slips, and clay were spread around haphazardly, making the room seem even smaller. At the far end was a shelf with several boxes marked with art piece titles and dates, but the absence of new work was evident, and more so to Keila, who ran her hands over the smooth surface of the empty table and sighed. She had stopped creating her coveted stoneware sculptures of nude couples for the Brik & Spiegel Gallery in Mexico City as part of her Crossed Legs Strike, a protest against Oscar's apathy. She missed the feeling of her fingers squeezing the malleable clay into bodies that burned with desire. Her last series conveyed the opposite: lack of interest.

The girls were obviously not in the studio, so she continued her search in the house. After making a stop in the kitchen to leave the pizza on the counter, Keila went upstairs, to the bedroom that had once been Olivia's, the twins' mom. Two pink blankies were tossed on the unmade bed where the girls had taken a nap that afternoon. The winter sun had set a while ago, but the moon was bright among gray clouds and offered Keila enough light for a quick search behind the couch, in the closet, under the bed. She wondered why she had agreed to babysit the twins again, after the last scare, when Andrea had put a pinto bean up her nostril and she'd had to pull it out with a pair of tweezers, the toddler kicking and squirming in her arms. She looked in the other bedrooms and went downstairs. Maybe the girls were exploring the forbidden forest, the once-dazzling backyard's landscaping, now in full deterioration.

16

It was now 6:59 P.M.

Two minutes later, Keila heard Olivia calling her. She and her husband, Felix Almeida, were back from their lunch at the Marina — a six-hour affair at Vittorio's involving altogether too many hugs and kisses and promises to schedule future get-togethers with friends they hardly ever saw, following the baptism of the Donosos' forty-seven-foot-long Hans Christian Offshore Explorer sailboat, the *Ugly Duckling*. Keila came out of the shrubs, annoyance gone, frustration vanished, and now quite a bit worried.

"I can't find the girls."

Olivia dropped the doggie bag with quail egg ravioli in saffron cream sauce and shaved Parmesan cheese leftovers and yelled to Felix, "Look in the pool!"

It was 7:03 P.M.

Olivia jumped in and sloshed in waist-deep murky water looking for her girls among plastic hippos and mermaids and rotting vegetation. Keila and Felix waded in behind her. The moon was no longer sharing its light with the early evening, so they had to rely on what their feet could sense, a frenzied search for bulk, a body. Olivia bumped into something. A bucket. Keila's leg got tangled in kelplike weeds. A timid

17

drizzle announced an overnight downpour, a cause for celebration, given the drought. But no one was celebrating. Not in that pool. Before he knew for sure his twins had drowned, Felix dialed 911 on his cellphone and yelled incoherent sentences, like "They must be in the water!" and "Get here now!" until the operator managed to obtain enough information to dispatch an ambulance. Dragging their feet, the three combed the bottom from the shallow side to the deep end.

In the same high-heeled shoes with which she'd accidentally put a tiny scratch (unnoticeable, really) on the *Ugly Duckling*'s polished deck that afternoon, Olivia was now frantically kicking decomposing debris around the pool where she'd learned to swim, barely a toddler, thirty-three years ago. Until she found Andrea. Then Felix found Diana, a few feet away. They pulled their daughters out onto a lounge chair and began mouth-to-mouth resuscitation. Keila ran to open the front door for the paramedics, two young men loaded with rescue equipment who ran straight to where the girls were, no need for directions, as if they'd performed previous drills in that particular house. The twins were hastily resuscitated. Both coughed up water and began to cry almost simultaneously. "A miracle," cried Keila. It was 7:12 P.M.

Olivia rode in the ambulance and Felix and Keila trailed behind in her Jaguar. While the paramedics worked on stabilizing the girls, who were now wrapped in thermo transport cocoons, Olivia compressed herself into a corner so as not to get in the way, nauseated and half listening to the EMS responders talk about a certain condition, the diving reflex, some medical explanation of the girls' impossible survival. Was she making this up, or did she really hear it? She blamed her mother for her unfit, careless babysitting, blamed the Donososes for buying a new sailboat, blamed Felix for having talked her into going to the Marina, and most of all, blamed herself for insisting on having babies when not just nature, but the entire cosmos, had been against the idea. She wished she could blame God, but all of a sudden she doubted He existed.

Once the girls were rushed to the ER, Olivia, Felix, and Keila were guided to the waiting area, where what seemed to them hundreds of hours went by. Olivia's wool dress, Felix's slacks, and Keila's sweatpants dried while they paced around. Felix held Olivia's hand tight and looked out the window, as if he were about to jump off a cliff and drag her with him into the void.

A janitor came by to mop the little puddles of muddy water that had been dripping off their clothes. That's when Olivia noticed that she'd torn a strap of one of her fuck-me-now shoes, as Felix called them. She never wore high heels to work. She spent most of her days walking around dusty construction sites full of obstacles in houses and small apartment buildings she bought to flip and sell. High heels were for weekends, not scaffolds.

"How did you know to look in the pool?" asked Keila, breaking an hour-long silence.

Olivia could not answer Keila's question. Her jaw had become locked and her teeth ground against each other as if trying to block her rage from escaping in the form of words. But her attempt at keeping the situation civil failed as she let out a loud, injured-animal-like squeal.

"I'm never, ever letting you watch the girls again! Never! And Dad? Where was he?"

Monday, January 11th
Oscar's chair had developed a concave shape over the years, like a hammock, punished by his persistent weight. He had logged several hours in front of the TV in the sitting area outside his bedroom without

20

minding the fact that it was turned off. He'd do that sometimes, more so lately. He'd spend the entire night staring at the dark monitor before making a decision. Eventually he'd point the remote control and hit the power button.

The skies had no intention of clearing up. The Weather Channel said so. Though the much-announced thunderstorm had become a broken promise, an upper-level trough of low pressure was expected to close in on the Pacific Northwest, pushing a deep marine layer over Southern California's curved coastline. Oscar leaned forward to get a glimpse of the sky through the window, his personal corroboration of the forecast. He scratched his head and squinted to focus. People marveled at the fact that at sixty years old he still had a headful of hair, albeit completely gray, to which he always replied, "It's a Mexican thing."

The light of day, although shy and dreary, was starting to creep into the sitting room adjacent to the master bedroom. The house was quiet. Keila should be up, he thought. Every day at six in the morning she'd pick up the *Los Angeles Times* from the sidewalk and bring it inside to read over breakfast. Before, they'd share it, splitting the sections in harmony and then swapping them. Lately, she'd only read the comic strips. He'd read the obituaries (always with a faint fear and desire all at once of finding his own). But now, not even reading about people's passing entertained him.

He got up from his chair and peered into his bedroom, where he found no sign that Keila had slept there. The bed was made. Her clothes, her shoes, were not scattered all over the floor as usual, haphazardly, in the manner of obstacles for him to trip over. Standing at the top of the stairwell he listened for noises downstairs in the kitchen — perhaps the twins had stayed overnight and were getting their Cheerios, their strawberries with yogurt — but he heard nothing. How could he? The girls were barely breathing through respirators three miles away, no one knowing for sure if they were going to survive without permanent damage.

"Where is everybody?" he wondered aloud into the empty house.

It was 7:12 A.M.

Claudia Alvarado kept her maiden name after she got married because she was famous. She had invested thousands of hours building her reputation as a chef and creating a persona under this name and was not willing to lose that asset just to comply with tradition. She and her husband, Gabriel Breene, had been together only long enough to still be trying new sex positions. Had she not married him two months after they met at a party that she'd catered in San Marino, she'd still be living in the world of singledom, or *singledoom,* as she jokingly said in her speech at her wedding rehearsal dinner, which she also catered. Her crème-fraîche-white gown, no frills, no lace, no bulk, just silk, smooth and fluid like a waterfall sliding down her skin in slow motion, only accentuated her tall, thin body. Who can trust a skinny chef? That was the predictable question frequently asked by her unoriginal nemesis, a rival cook who used her blog to attack Claudia and turn her readers' attention to her suspicious waistline, partly a gift from nature and partly a result of her habit of running marathons.

It didn't matter to Rancho Verde that she had her own cooking television show, *La Cocina de Claudia,* with great ratings according to Nielsen, by the way. It wasn't significant at all that her business was reviewed in most food magazines, that her television show had millions of viewers, and that her two cookbooks were among the favorites of every Mexican-food enthusiast in the country, both those who sought traditional recipes and those who ventured into the cultural mix that was Angeleno cuisine. What everyone talked about was the fact that at her ripe age of thirty-six she hadn't found the man of her life, and even her most beloved relatives, like Aunt Belinda, agreed that the longer she waited the slimmer her chances would be to bless the family with a child.

But when she married fashionista Gabriel, with a taste for pink shirts of all shades, patterns, and textures, even Aunt Belinda raised her eyebrows and proclaimed, "Well, there," agreeing with everyone that it had been worth the wait. Never mind that he presented his credentials to no one; his pedigree, as Oscar would refer to any form of résumé or proof of a particular social status, remained unknown. The fact that Gabriel spent a great deal of time comparing Los Angeles to New York, where he was from, puzzled most of Claudia's relatives, who had no interest in the subject. What gained him immediate access into the family was that on his first date with Claudia he came bearing two dozen red roses for Keila. Soon he asked Oscar for his daughter's hand in marriage in a rather pompous ceremony considered by all who knew about

24

it as a bit much: the mariachi serenade below Claudia's window and the professional photographer who recorded the entire event and produced a video that went live across social media that same night. Before long Gabriel had moved in with her, bringing along no more than a couple of suitcases and his Russian Blue cat, Velcro.

But that morning, when her nieces Diana and Andrea were being kept in a hospital across town, Claudia did not wake up to the thought of her marital status, as she had for years. The call came when she was sitting in her kitchen in her pajamas, perusing the ashtray she'd lifted at the party she'd catered Saturday night. It was not fancy, quite the opposite. No one would miss it and that bothered her. Why would she bag an ordinary, square glass ashtray, the kind that, if you came across it in a roadside motel room, you'd throw in a drawer just to get it out of sight? She'd eyed a box of Riedel wineglasses in her client's pantry and could easily have packed them in her van along with her chafing dishes and taken them home without anyone noticing. But rather than making thoughtful decisions in such circumstances, she inevitably acted on impulse. This habit of hers, this need to accumulate other people's possessions, was not something she could or cared to explain. As she considered returning the ashtray to its owners before Gabriel discovered it — anonymously of course, say, dropping it in their mailbox in the middle of the night — the phone rang.

"The girls? Where?"

The cheap ashtray's image, bird's-eye-view and sideways, remained in Claudia's mind, looping intermittently with other loose, random thoughts, during the entire drive to the hospital. While zooming down the freeway, she imagined a gigantic glass ashtray filled with water and the lifeless bodies of her nieces lying at the bottom. Surely Olivia would kill herself for having lost her daughters in such a careless way.

Why was her sister's life like a soap opera while hers was so predictable? "Wait a minute," she said aloud. "Soap operas *are* predictable." Where did the difference lie, then? Perhaps in the fact that Olivia's life happened to her, while Claudia planned her life and accomplished her goals. She promised herself to revisit this insight some other time when she wouldn't have to pay attention to the road. She'd already missed a few exits, and that set her back ten minutes.

As she corrected her route, she wondered if she'd have the strength to cater the funeral, God forbid, and concluded that she would. In situations of deep grief people tend to get busy and helpful as a way to alleviate sorrow, and she knew that's what she would do. She quickly put together a menu of finger foods and stored it in her memory, just in case one or both girls did not make it. She'd avoid the chicken taquitos with guacamole held together with a toothpick, a greasy cliché. She'd also stay away from the tortas ahogadas. A dish with the word "drowned" in its name could not be part of the menu. Instead, she'd serve the small squash-flower tamales. Edible flowers were sensitive and appropriate to the occasion, she thought. Then she'd add to the menu the grilled lobster tail skewers with tamarind dipping sauce, the silver-dollar quesadillas with chilorio, the scallop ceviche tostadas from Culiacán smothered in lime juice, plenty of tequila to drown the despair, and she'd also bring a sample of fine wines from Baja's Valle de Guadalupe, smuggled through Tijuana to avoid the excessive export tax.

She stepped on the accelerator and jumped into the car-pool lane. She knew she could get fined, but ever since she'd allocated a budget to pay for this kind of ticket a few years back, she'd only gotten

27

busted four times, which proved that she didn't overuse this self-awarded license. Her strategy had been so successful that in the past year she had saved hundreds of hours of dreadful Los Angeles traffic at a very low cost, considering that her tickets averaged out to just a few dollars for each time she sped along the car-pool lane with no companion in the car.

"They're in stable condition," Keila told Claudia as she walked into the waiting room of the Pediatric Intensive Care Unit, where the girls lay in adjoining beds. "Olivia is inside. We're only allowed to go in one person at a time."

Claudia didn't seem to hear the last part. She rushed past Keila and Felix without offering a greeting and went straight to the unit, opening random doors along the way until she found Olivia. Seeing the girls hooked up to respirators and tubes and monitors finally made the crisis real. I will never have children, she vowed to herself.

Olivia hugged her long and tight. "Thanks for coming, sis," she whispered. "They're going to be fine."

Claudia clearly heard "They're *not* going to be fine." She could always tell when her sister said words to convince herself of anything she didn't really believe. It was the

28

nearly unnoticeable tremor in her lips, the way her voice struggled to find its way out of her mouth in hesitant little bursts that told her the truth.

"The doctor said they're doing more tests to check for any brain damage, and there's a possible risk of infection, since they inhaled a lot of contaminated water, but I'm praying, we're all praying," said Olivia.

"Is there anything I can do before I go?"

"But you just got here," Olivia said.

"I have to run to the fish market, but call me with any news."

Truth is, fish was not on Claudia's menu that day, but watching her nieces in such a state provoked a feeling of hopefulness that she tried to repress, as in her view resorting to hope meant she did not have control and that angered her. Regardless of how much she loved those girls, there was nothing she could do to save them. She measured life's events on a scale of hope versus control. The less control one had over a certain situation, the more hope one needed to face it. Once, when she was illustrating her theory to Olivia, she used a medical example: one had to have much more hope for a positive result when afflicted with terminal cancer than when healing a scraped knee. To her, that was the core principle of hope: people turn the management and resolution of a situation over to a higher authority — whether it's a doctor or God himself — when they are incapable of handling it directly, therefore demonstrating the need for high hopes in desperate situations. Because she refused to relinquish her power to third parties, she left vowing never to set foot in a hospital again.

Patricia, the youngest of the Alvarado sisters, learned about the accident in Minneapolis, where she was visiting her client, Target, at their headquarters, as she did every other Monday. Known in her industry as the Social Ace, she used digital media to connect brands with their audiences at their deepest emotional levels. There was no consumer want or need that she didn't know how to identify, address, and help her clients satisfy with products and services. "I don't tell my friends about your brand because I like your brand, but because I like my friends." This was her ultimate rule of engagement when posting messages and ads on her clients' behalf on digital platforms.

Keila had called Patricia in the middle of a meeting where she was discussing Target's social presence at the upcoming Billboard Latin Music Awards, and Patricia had ignored the call, as she always did. Several text messages later, finally responding to her cellphone's nonstop vibrations, Patricia excused herself from the conference room to call Keila back.

"The twins drowned in the pool and were resuscitated." Keila's voice trembled as she delivered the news. "We're at Cedars-Sinai. Olivia is undone."

Patricia left immediately, promising her client she'd work on the awards' social strategy over the weekend, and got on the last flight out of Minneapolis before an impending blizzard shut the airport down. A savvy economy traveler, she preferred a bulkhead seat or an emergency exit to have more legroom. Clients didn't always pay for business-class tickets. But this time she didn't care that she was sitting in a middle seat — the only one available for her last-minute booking — two rows from the back of the plane, where people wanting to use the bathroom congregated to fart. All she cared about was that she had been able to get out before the storm hit and was on her way to comfort her sister. But the ride was a bumpy one and she felt nauseous and weak. She wondered if it was due to the plane shaking or a genuine physical reaction to the emergency. Being on day seven of a

31

juice cleanse probably didn't help either.

She tried to distract herself with work, but couldn't. Somewhere over Nebraska she caught herself praying to a God she did not believe in, asking the clouds that swelled outside in the big void to spare her sister yet another tragedy. Everyone knew how much of a mother Olivia was, how much she had wanted those babies, and all she went through to have them, but no one talked about the miscarriages and disappointments. It was as if they had never happened.

What was so mysterious about suffering? Why did people avoid talking about misfortune and grief? Except for a few death announcements and surgeries, people didn't discuss pain or hardship. She had made it her mission to address the good and the bad, to share the joy as well as the drama and bring out into the open the full spectrum of human emotions and experiences — "the open" being social media. But at that moment, on the plane flying over Colorado, she tried to take her mind off her anxiety, so she focused instead on purchasing a hot meal from the flight attendant, resigned to go through one more dreadful airline-food experience. Maybe it was time to take a break from the juice cleanse and eat something solid. This time she got a plate of chilaquiles, but could have sworn it was vomit. She thought about shipping it to the airline CEO in a refrigerated container for him to taste, but instead took a picture with her phone and made a note to herself to post it across all the social platforms on her dashboard as soon as she landed.

It was clear to Patricia that she and Olivia had a bond that didn't exist between her and Claudia: motherhood. Even before Olivia married Felix, a rather mediocre Realtor who sometimes irked Patricia with his sexist jokes, and started fertility treatments, she had demonstrated her maternal instincts by helping Patricia raise her son, Daniel, while she, Patricia, the teen single mother, finished high school, dated boys, got drunk, used drugs, crashed the car, fucked guys, went to traffic school for speeding (twice), broke up with boyfriends, bungee-jumped, skydived, went to college, traveled abroad, got summer jobs, crashed another car, changed majors, graduated, got more jobs, and married Eric Remillard on a whim.

"Infinite Text" was how she titled the story of her life with her husband. She lived in Los Angeles, Eric was based in San Francisco, and they both had busy business travel schedules. They had agreed to live in different cities, but they managed to spend every weekend together, here or there, or wherever they happened to be. Texting was their preferred way of communicating. They sent each other selfies, links, news articles, ideas, GIFs, memes, and everything that might help keep them in the same realm. This arrangement allowed Patricia to be close to her parents, and more important, to Olivia.

As a sign of her profound appreciation for her help with her son, Patricia had built her sister a social presence as @theothermother_sis, regularly posting and praising Olivia's motherly accomplishments. What would she post now?

During the Uber ride to the hospital, Patricia was able to talk to Olivia on the phone and piece together the details of the girls' accident and what the doctors were saying in terms of their recovery. She had time to google the particulars of the diving reflex condition in which, in rare instances, a child who drowns in cold water experiences a decreased heartbeat and less need for oxygen and stands a chance of surviving if she's resuscitated within forty-five minutes and tweeted this important piece of information to her thousands of followers. As her Uber sped down surface streets, she cherished the sight of mini-malls with nail salons, frozen-yogurt joints, laundromats and hole-in-the-wall ethnic restaurants — surely family run, surely immigrant owned. She felt at home. The Los Angeles afternoon light — with its oranges and reds overly saturated like a bad Instagram filter — bounced back a distorted reflection of her face in the window. At twenty-seven, she had a complexion devoid of imperfections, except for a zit on her cheek that she'd squeezed during the flight. "You're the spitting image of your great-grandmother," Keila would tell her oftentimes, showing her a faded photograph of a young woman whose days would soon end in a concentration camp in Poland. She sighed and went back to her phone. There was a text message from her client Benjamin.

Everything all right?

No. More later, Patricia replied quickly as the car pulled up in front of the hospital.

Visiting hours were in full swing. The line to get on the elevator seemed too long for Patricia to wait, so she climbed the seven flights of stairs to Pediatrics, skipping steps (remembering as she stepped on the last landing that she'd forgotten her carry-on suitcase in the car) and running until her sister was in her arms. All of a sudden, with no offense to Keila, she wished Olivia had been her mother.

Tuesday, January 12th
The twins went home after infections were ruled out. They were to undergo brain function as well as cardiac and vascular tests periodically throughout the year, but the overall prognosis was positive. "A miracle," the doctor had proclaimed upon delivering the good news, implicitly diminishing his own accomplishment in bringing the twins back from the dead. Keila, who had been camping out in the waiting room since the first night, leaving her seat only to use the bathroom and make short trips to the hospital's cafeteria, continued to nurse her guilt, a weight on her chest that would limit her breathing capacity for the rest of her life.

In the car ride back to Rancho Verde, she turned off the radio, rolled up her window, and as she drove down the palm-tree-lined streets of Los Angeles, where the homes' front lawns were screaming for water, she allowed herself to think about Oscar. She fanned her disappointment in the way he had handled the situation into a spiteful rancor. In fact — she corrected herself — he hadn't handled anything at all.

Had the twins' accident happened two years before, Oscar would have taken charge of the emergency with authority and intelligence. Throughout their marriage Oscar had proven to be an astounding problem solver and fast thinker — like the time when Olivia, then nine years old, had played with a neighbor's puppies while visiting her grandparents in Mexico City, only to find out two weeks after she'd returned to Los Angeles that the entire litter had contracted rabies. At the time, the vaccine was not easy to find in the United States, as the disease had been eradicated, so Oscar flew with Olivia back to Mexico to get her the painful shots. And what about the time when the earthquake destroyed the bridges along the 10 Freeway back in 1994? Repairs would take over a year. His daily commute to the office would increase to an hour and a half each way, maneuvering through crowded detours, so he temporarily moved his office to a nearby executive suite and subleased his own office to someone else. When Patricia became the victim of a rape that resulted in a pregnancy at age fourteen, Oscar immediately had her identify the boy, report the assault to the police, and press charges. He had found a therapist for her, removed her from school to protect her from potential peer scorn, hired a tutor, and when she decided she wanted to keep it, provided the best possible medical care. When little Daniel was born, he welcomed the baby into the family; a true Alvarado. But now Keila expected to find Oscar where she left him: sitting in front of the TV watching the Weather Channel, oblivious to the crisis that had unfolded around him. She had spent hours wondering what could possibly have changed in Oscar's life, but nothing came to mind. His descent into apathy had been dizzying and inexplicable. It was then that the word "divorce" intruded in her mind like a YouTube ad that could not be skipped.

When Keila arrived home, she did not find Oscar in front of the TV. Instead, he was looking out the window with mild curiosity and said without taking his eyes off the cloudy sky: "El Niño is about to drop four inches of rain in the wrong place, right in the middle of the city."

"Are you even aware of what's been going on? I've been gone two days and you haven't noticed? I could have been dead, decomposing in some ditch."

"Where were you? I was looking for you."

"You mean since Sunday night? Weren't you worried about us? I waited for your call."

"I did call. You left your phone on your nightstand. I figured you were with one of the girls."

He was right, but instead of acknowledging her error, she attacked: "Your granddaughters almost died right in front of you while you were staring at the wall! We've been at the hospital all this time."

"What do you mean? What happened?"

"You just won't see what's in front of your nose."

"You should have called me! Olivia surely had her phone with her. Where are the twins?"

"What do you care? You're not even present in your own life, let alone anyone else's. I have no idea what's going on with you. Why are you giving up? Look at you!"

Oscar scanned his clothes: an old coffee stain ran down his pajama pocket and his sleeve had a tear at the elbow. His tongue felt acrid. Had he brushed his teeth? He didn't remember the last time he'd gotten a haircut or clipped his fingernails. He scratched his overgrown beard and wondered if the pang behind his sternum was a new, undiagnosed health issue, or even worse, shame.

"I want to divorce you, Oscar." Strange words to say after thirty-nine years of marriage, Keila thought as she said them. But there they were, her feelings turned into words that floated listlessly in the air trapped in the room.

Oscar sat down in his chair and said nothing at first, but then in a rush of strength he was able to whisper, "You do what you have to do."

Wednesday, January 13th

El Niño did not deliver the much-needed rain that evening, as expected. Palm trees wilted from thirst. Isolated fifty-five-mile-per-hour gusts of wind pushed small cars out of their freeway lanes, like tumbleweeds, across western portions of the San Fernando Valley. Dangerous eight-foot sneaker waves along the Santa Monica coastline were expected due to elevated surf. They were known to wash people off of beaches and rock jetties. Rip currents could pull swimmers out to sea. Surely the ocean would claim the life of another surfer. Surely Keila would follow through with her threat. Or not.

■ ■ ■ ■

Saturday, January 16th

What is there to say to your spouse after learning she doesn't want you anymore? Oscar walked around the house as if spooked by some demon, looking over his shoulder, hoping not to bump into Keila. She'd return home from her multiple errands — supermarket, cleaners, pedicure, art store, and maybe coffee with one of her friends from book club — and he would run to lock himself up in the smallest and darkest closet among coats and pants as self-punishment. He was well aware of his guilt. She had a solid reason to leave him. But later at night, when the house was finally quiet, he'd go to bed, lay down next to Keila facing the wall and pretend to be asleep.

Friday, January 22nd

Keila called for an emergency family meeting. Claudia, Olivia, and Patricia were to come to dinner without their husbands or children. To their surprise, Oscar was sitting at the head of the table, his beard shaven and his fingernails clipped. A tiny round Band-Aid on his cheek revealed his inability to pay attention. The three sisters had noticed Oscar's obsession with the weather and his languor when it came to almost anything else, but all three of them were too busy with the business of life to be concerned and they dismissed his behavior as a temporary eccentricity. Only Patricia sat next to him, holding his hand and staring at the turned-off TV for a few minutes before moving on to more interesting activities, like perusing people's profiles on OkCupid (oh, the little cybervoyeur). She thought of discussing the lethargy she sensed in him, but decided just to give him signs of love as she always had, without questioning him.

Keila opened a bottle of prosecco and passed out the glasses without asking if anyone preferred something else. The seating arrangement at the family table had been unalterable since the girls could remember, so each found her assigned spot in strict birth order, sensing some sort of momentous announcement.

"I'm sure you can guess why I called you. There's not much to say," said Keila. She took a deep breath.

"I hope you called us to apologize for your stupid carelessness," said Olivia, measuring her words, trying, unsuccessfully, to control the volume of her voice. "What was so important around the house for you to ignore your granddaughters? And you, Dad, was the blank screen of the TV more entertaining than watching the twins?" She slammed the table for emphasis and went on, "How many times have I told you, have we told you, Claudia, Patricia, that the pool is a hazard? If you'd fixed it and put a fence around it, this accident would have never happened. That's city code, for God's sake! How can I ever trust you again?"

Her eyes welled up as she sat down. She'd said it all and yet she still felt a lump inside her rib cage, as if she'd swallowed a pillow.

"I am very sorry, Olie," said Keila, breaking a long silence. "I'm sure you'll find in your heart to forgive me someday, even if I don't deserve it, because that's just who you are. But I know I will never forgive myself."

"I may be able to, Mom, but I don't know if I'll ever trust you with the kids again. Do you have undiagnosed ADHD? You're always thinking about something else. You can't leave two three-year-old girls to wander around a house by themselves with an abandoned pool filled with water festering with bacteria," said Olivia, then turning to Oscar, "And you, Dad, snap out of it. If that pool is your way of telling us you've checked out, I hope you learn to tell us in a safer way. You don't need to take us all down

43

with you. Just look what happened! Dad, say something, Dad!?"

Oscar opened his mouth but couldn't say a word. His cheeks reddened with shame. That was all he could express.

Claudia took a sip of prosecco and got up to leave.

"I'm really not hungry anymore. Mom, do you want to tell us why you called for this dinner before I go?"

"I'm sorry, sweetie, it's not the right time now. Why don't you all come back tomorrow and we can talk about it?"

"Fine," said Claudia, and headed for the door.

"I'm sorry I ruined your dinner, Mother," said Olivia, finding a level of sarcasm that she didn't know she had. She left without touching the warm chayote in butter.

Saturday, January 23rd

A bang and a rumble woke Oscar up at 6:00 A.M. He found his robe under a pile of clothes on the chair and went out to the yard to find that a crew of workers had taken down a portion of the fence; three of them were already busy emptying out the pool with submersible pumps. They had also brought concrete chisels, jackhammers, shovels, and wheelbarrows. A dump truck waited in the alley to haul away the rubble and debris.

"What's going on?" he asked one of the workers. But before he could get an answer, Olivia walked in through the opening on the fence.

"It was obvious last night that you weren't going to do anything about this," she said. "I had to pay them extra for the rush job. This can't wait a day longer."

"I'm so very sorry, Olie. I was there, too. I could have watched the girls. I could have fixed the pool and installed a security fence around it."

"You could have. But you didn't."

She turned away and addressed one of the workers. "Gracias por venir tan pronto, Miguel."

She had worked with them in the past whenever she had to demolish a pool for a client. They were part of her trusted crew, her guys. In spite of the tense moment with Oscar, there was still a sense of camaraderie with the workers, who called her "Archi." Once they finished draining the standing water, they were to demolish the side walls and prepare the hole to backfill it.

Oscar stepped aside and watched from the yard's portico. Keila came out followed by Daniel, Patricia's twelve-year-old son, who

45

had also woken up with all the noise, to look on.

"We deserve this," she mumbled to Oscar, and went back into the house.

"Why is Aunt Olivia doing this, Grandpa?" asked Daniel.

"We don't want the twins to have another accident," Oscar explained, trying to sound calm.

"But why is Bubbe so upset? Is she mad at Olie for destroying the pool?"

"On the contrary. She, well, both of us, feel very ashamed for failing to take care of Diana and Andrea. We got distracted and look what happened."

"That sucks."

"More than sucks."

That evening, after the workers had left and the pool was a dark hole in the middle of the yard, a grim reminder of the twins' accident, Claudia and Olivia arrived for the emergency dinner that hadn't happened the night before.

"Good call, Olie," said Patricia when she came downstairs to meet her sisters. "Nobody was going to remove the damn pool if you didn't do it."

"You're welcome to come over and use mine. I keep the water at ninety degrees," said Claudia.

46

"Dinner's on the table, girls," yelled Keila from the dining room.

After everyone sat in silence at their habitual places, Keila passed the reheated dinner from the night before, poured prosecco from a new bottle, and said, bluntly:

"The reason I called you for this dinner is to announce to you that your father and I are divorcing."

Claudia had just taken a sip of her prosecco, but was the first to reply, in shock, after spilling part of her drink on the tablecloth. "I thought you were going to tell us you're selling the house."

"I don't get it. You've been married, what, thirty-eight years?" said Olivia, the devastating consequences of the news not quite registering.

"Thirty-nine."

The second after Keila corrected Olivia, all thirty-nine years — her romantic evenings with Oscar, their children's births, their family vacations, the school carnivals, their days at the beach, their fights and disagreements — popped out of her memory archive, reminding her of something she wasn't willing to admit. She pulled up her sweater's sleeves, a habitual tic, and took a hefty swig of her prosecco.

"Why bother? You've hung in there for so

long, why give up now?" said Patricia in a broken voice, her eyes a dam about to break. "Is it because of the twins' accident?"

"No, it is not, but that didn't help. Listen, I don't know who this man is, but he's certainly not your father. The man I married vanished last year and I've got this sad avatar instead."

Oscar flinched and went back to staring at his empty plate. His daughters' voices seemed to fade, becoming a mumble of fright and disbelief.

"Dad is probably just going through some strange phase. What are you going to do later, when you're old and alone?" asked Patricia, drying a tear with her napkin.

"I'm not thinking about that now," said Keila. She tucked her signature strand of gray hair behind her ear and refilled her glass of prosecco, hoping no one noticed that her hand was shaking.

"We might not be around to keep you company. I might move away," said Olivia in a futile attempt to dissuade her mother.

"Can't you make up? Can't you get over whatever you two are going through?" asked Claudia.

"I've made my decision and it is final."

Patricia tried unsuccessfully to hold her tears as she stared at the platter of chicken

48

in almond and chipotle sauce with rice — one of Keila's famous recipes — that sat untouched at the center of the table.

"And what do you have to say about all this, Dad?" she finally asked Oscar, who seemed to have been invisible to everyone until that moment.

"I have no say. Your mother is determined. You know how she is."

During the long silence that followed, Patricia asked herself how she would give the news to Daniel. Her parents were his de facto parents, as they helped raise him along with Olivia while she finished school. And once she turned on the question faucet, a steady flow of unknowns overcame her. How would Daniel take his grandmother's decision? Would he neglect his studies like that other sixth grader whose parents had split a few months before? Would he start acting reckless and withdrawn? Would there be any more Sunday family dinners? Would Keila keep the house and Oscar have to leave, or the other way around? Of all their friends, who would side with Keila and who with Oscar? Was one of those friends the cause of the breakup? Could it be an affair? Surely not, at their age. Irreconcilable differences would be a ludicrous reason after so many years of marriage. But then, what did she know?

Suddenly, their family home began to look more like a house. A Spanish Revival–style house just like any other in Rancho Verde, just like any house featured in any given real estate app, a house divested of all meaning, staged for the listing photos: 4 bed/4 bath, den, enclosed courtyard, tiled roof, faded mustard-yellow stucco walls, arches everywhere, a generous portico, detached garage with adjacent artist's studio and maid's room common in Los Angeles homes of the era, kitchen fitted with state-of-the-art appliances and a service door to the backyard that seemed an afterthought, a typical feature in houses built in the 1920s, when the area behind the house was used only to hang the laundry out to dry in the sun and let the kids get their clothes dirty. Suddenly all the improvements lovingly done by her parents over the years seemed to vanish in her mind, an involuntary defense mechanism of sorts. If her home was lost, none of the renovations would have any meaning: the family room addition, the pool (now in the process of getting demolished), the brick patio with the big table to accommodate their friends on endless weekend lunches and barbecues where everyone raved about Keila's cuisine, the lavender that surrounded the pergola leaning against the garage, the succulents, the sage, the California fuchsia that grew along the west fence, and the painstakingly groomed ficus hedge in the back by the sweet gum trees, all carefully selected to be water-wise and fire-safe to reduce the risk of propagating fires in the wildland-urban interface where Rancho Verde had been developed.

Claudia's questions were of a different sort: Who would keep the house? Would the assets be split fifty-fifty? What about the house Keila had inherited from her parents in Mexico City? Would a divorce affect the family trust? Why were her parents doing this to her?

"You won't survive by yourselves," said Claudia, raising her voice.

"I'm not going to accept this," said Olivia, not knowing where that reaction had come from.

"Aren't you going to defend yourself, Dad?" Patricia asked, now seriously concerned about Oscar's ennui, or was it preemptive defeat? He surely was not quite in the room, and the fact that Claudia and Olivia didn't seem to notice irritated her to the point of wanting to get up and leave, but she stayed out of solidarity with her father.

Oscar shrugged and looked at Patricia intently, as if he needed to reveal a secret to her but couldn't.

Keila refilled her glass of prosecco again, opened a new bottle, and looked at Oscar, hoping to see him differently, perhaps with enough compassion to make her change her mind. The lines across his forehead seemed more pronounced now. The skin of his eyelids draped over his eyelashes like warm blankets, but there was no warmth in his gaze. He seemed focused on the curtain, or maybe it was the windowsill. She imagined herself making scrambled eggs with matzo and strawberry jelly for breakfast and having no one to share it with. At first the idea seemed attractive, but projecting it into a distant future, she wondered if she would enjoy the solitude, or if it would become a painful loneliness impossible to cure. She lacked the vision needed to foresee the details, and this caused her to feel an overpowering discomfort.

"This is what you will do," instructed Claudia finally. "You will find a couples therapist and will give yourselves one year before making a decision. Promise us. Now."

Claudia's command took Keila by surprise. The fact that her daughters were adamantly rejecting her decision to divorce Oscar was incomprehensible to her. One could imagine this kind of resistance in small children, still vulnerable and depending fully on their parents for their well-being. She would never have left Oscar while the girls were growing up. She'd had no reason to; life had truly been blissful. The most distressing event she could think of in her thirty-nine years of marriage was when Oscar sold the last remaining piece of the ranch in the Santa Clara Valley in Northern California. Rancho Horno Caliente, a thirty-eight-thousand-acre spread of rolling hills, creeks, natural wells, and warm breezes, had been in his family since before Mexico lost California to the United States, back in 1848. The great Don Rodrigo Alvarado and his wife, Doña Fermina de la Asunción Ortega, had received the rancho's grant from Governor Figueroa himself on the recommendation of the reputable Don Juan Bautista de Anza back in the early nineteenth century. The land was awarded to them since they had proved to be seasoned rancheros. It was there where the couple raised their twelve children and bred fine cattle. But over time Oscar's grandparents, parents, and uncles divided the land and sold most of it to developers. The pastures where horses and cows once roamed happily unattended was now the land where tech industry behemoths thrived. Apple, Netflix, eBay, and Roku had built their headquarters there and transformed the placid family rancho into what is now known as Silicon Valley. Keila never forgave Oscar, not for selling the last lot, as the transaction had proved to be a successful business decision, but for not asking her first.

Now that the girls were married and settled, she had no reason to endure Oscar's descent into the puny little man he'd become. Worse, even, he was like an anvil tied to her neck. She felt as if she were sinking into a bottomless underwater cave, the kind she and Oscar had once explored while scuba diving near Tulum. On the other hand, she thought, feeling averse to Oscar did not grant her the right to make such a drastic decision without giving it at least a second thought. She couldn't ignore the conspicuous opposing forces in her mind: What kind of example would she give the girls by divorcing their father? Her single war cry when it came to marriage had always been: "Stick it out!" So now, precisely because her daughters were married and settled, she'd have to make good on her position and drag the anvil around another year.

"Fine. Get me a referral. You girls must have quite a few friends in therapy."

Sunday, January 24th
Keila canceled the family dinner.

Oscar spent his day just like any other in the past year, except for the fact that his wife of thirty-nine years had just announced to his children that she was calling it quits. He'd watched Keila throw some reusable grocery bags in the trunk of her car and drive off, possibly to shop for produce at the farmer's market, a passion of hers. He'd helped Daniel with his math homework, always a mystery subject for the boy. He'd called Olivia about the twins. Perhaps he could visit them later? Would Olivia allow him to be near them again after his devastating failure to watch them? He'd brought a blanket out to the patio, bundled up, and sat under the pergola. What his feelings were as he watched an empty nest about to fall from one of the nearby gum tree's branches was anyone's guess. If only he weren't so successful at hiding his pain, if he could at least confide in Patricia, his chamaquita, the anguish that was consuming him. But instead, he pursed his lips and stared at the nest, not quite understanding it as a metaphor.

Demolishing her parents' swimming pool turned out to be hard work. Still exhausted, Olivia paid a visit to Lola, her childhood nanny, in Highland Park, a historic area in Northeast Los Angeles, where she'd lived since she could remember. Traffic was light coming from Santa Monica, where she was renovating an apartment building, so she took the 10, then zipped right through Downtown on the 110 North toward Pasadena, the oldest freeway in the city and the one with inexplicable tunnels with no reason to exist as they held nearly no soil overhead. She knew the area well, having flipped a few houses there in the past couple of years.

"Mi niña adorada!" said Lola as she saw Olivia standing at the door. "What a surprise! What are you doing in this neck of the woods?"

A wall-to-wall collage of picture frames — crooked from so many minor tremors — hung behind the couch, filled with family portraits: A young couple with two little boys appeared in several of the photos,

Lola's older brother, Sebastian, and his wife and sons. There were a few older ones in black-and-white of another family, this one with the parents and an older boy and a baby girl. That was Lola's parents with Lola and Sebastian. In another photo, Lola, a teenager, smiled, embraced by her nephews. She recognized a photo of her and her sisters, Claudia and baby Patricia, as little girls sitting on Lola's lap in their backyard.

"So, how's your brother? It's Sebastian, the one in this picture, right?" asked Olivia, pointing at one of the photos.

"They're still in Australia. Melbourne. These days I only see him and the boys on FaceTime," said Lola with a hint of sadness in her voice. "But tell me what's new with you? Do you have any pictures of the twins?"

Olivia pulled out her cellphone to show Lola, Diana and Andrea dressed in identical party dresses, smiling at the camera in the arms of Olivia and Felix. Lola adjusted her reading glasses on the tip of her nose and took a closer look.

"A true miracle. I'll tell you all about that," said Olivia.

"We can't let so much time pass by. It has been what, five years since we actually saw each other? Next thing you know I'll be dead and gone!"

"Don't even say that! What's going on with you? Have you retired?"

"Oh, no. I'll never retire. You mean, am I still working for the Haldipurs? Their kids outgrew me a couple years ago, but I stay busy with some stuff in the neighborhood. And you? How's the architecture business going?"

"Two of my projects have been featured in design magazines. Many are old properties, neglected rentals. I did one recently on Hub Street, actually, right around the corner. Maybe you've seen it — it's the house with the second-floor addition."

"I see."

"You've really kept your house as beautiful as always! I can see the love on the walls," said Olivia, pointing at the picture frames.

"A house is all about the love you put into it."

Olivia looked around at Lola's home. Small but perfect.

"Look, Lola, I'd love for you to come and help me with my twin girls. Please consider it for old times' sake. I've been relying on my mom, but she's just too distracted. You know how she is. To be honest, it's been a disaster."

■ ■ ■ ■

Monday, January 25th

"My mom canceled family dinner last night. That's how bad it is," said Patricia.

She was with her husband, Eric, in a hotel room near LAX.

"Oh, Pats, I'm so sorry to hear that. You must be feeling awful. What are your sisters saying?" said Eric in a French accent he'd continued to cultivate, even after living for twenty-one years in the United States and after having earned his U.S. citizenship in an emotional ceremony with four thousand other immigrants waving little American flags.

"We texted this morning. Claudia asked what we expected, considering Mom just announced to us that she wants to divorce Dad. Olivia says it's the beginning of the end. And I haven't told Daniel. I'm afraid he's not going to take it well. I guess he'll have to find out if things continue to deteriorate. I hope Mom and Dad really do give themselves a year to make up."

"Twelve months is a long time; I'm trusting your parents will deal with whatever is going on," said Eric, holding her hand. "Have you talked to your dad about all this?

59

Something's happening to him. I feel it."

"Of course something's wrong, I feel it too, but it's not the threat of divorce. He's been weird for a while, but he won't say anything, I've tried. It's so damn frustrating."

Patricia turned over to face the nightstand, hoping the conversation with her husband would stop, and adjusted her pillow to rest her head. She hadn't slept much and — even worse and unheard of — had declined to have sex with Eric the previous night.

"How can I cheer you up? Do you want to do anything special for your birthday tomorrow? I can stay in town, work from the hotel. Let's go out to dinner."

"No, that's okay. I'm in no mood for birthdays."

Tuesday, January 26th
Oscar didn't come home to sleep.

After dropping Daniel off at school, Patricia, concerned, texted her sisters for an emergency breakfast at John O'Groats, one of their favorite weekend dives, never mind it was Tuesday.

"Dad's disappeared. He didn't sleep at home last night. His suitcase is gone, his car's not in the driveway," she said as soon as her sisters sat down at the table. "I already left several messages on his phone. Nothing."

"He's never done this before," said Olivia. "Has Mom said anything?"

"She wasn't home either when I left this morning," said Patricia.

"Maybe they left together," said Olivia, hopeful.

"You must be kidding. The way things are right now between them? Call her," said Claudia.

Patricia hit the Mom contact in her list of favorites and activated her phone's speaker so her sisters could hear as the waitress brought three plates with eggs and bacon and a side of English muffins.

"Mom? Where are you? Dad didn't sleep at home last night," said Patricia.

"I know," she replied dryly. "But don't worry. He'll come back sooner or later."

"Have you reported him missing?"

"Why would I do that? He's not lost. He left of his own will, on his own two feet. And happy birthday, by the way. Is Eric coming down to L.A. to celebrate with you?"

"No. I'll see him over the weekend. Bye, Mom."

If Patricia's cellphone had been a landline

telephone, she would have slammed the receiver. Unfortunately, with these new technologies it was hard to express anger, unless she resorted to using emojis, but this was a call, not a text, so she was left with her feelings, a mélange of annoyance, frustration, and fear, wondering how to proceed. She suddenly hated her mother's lack of concern.

"Of course," she said to her sisters, enraged. "She's mad at him. Why would she be worried?"

"Some birthday you're having, Pats," said Olivia. "Are you doing anything interesting?"

"Not really."

"We can take you out for drinks tonight, if you feel like it."

"I know a new bar downtown," said Claudia.

"Thanks for the invite, but I can only think about Dad. I hope Mom's right, that he just left and is coming back soon, that it's only a tantrum."

"I'm sure it is," said Claudia. "So, no drinks?"

"Not tonight," said Patricia.

After she dropped off her sisters and called her office to request a flex day off work, Patricia drove to Eagle Rock in Topanga. She'd hiked the Musch Trail many times before and knew she'd have a decent phone signal in case Oscar tried to reach her. That was the birthday gift she wanted: to spend this perfect seventy-two-degree day by herself, walking among chaparral and sagebrush, admiring the Santa Monica Mountains in the distance and thinking hard about the state of things among the Alvarados. As her legs negotiated the uneven and sometimes dodgy climb along the dirt paths, her mind kept going back to a single question: How had her family become so disconnected? She remembered the days when everyone knew where everybody else was, what everybody else was doing. Every year, color-coded calendars were posted on the fridge and were updated daily by all involved. A tin can with markers sat on the countertop: yellow for Oscar, green for Keila, blue for Claudia, pink for Olivia, red for Patricia, orange for Daniel, and black for family events. It was all there: Daniel's chess club and swimming competitions, Keila's mammograms and gallery openings, Patricia's parties and weekend trips, Oscar's multiple errands around town, Olivia's school presentations, Claudia's marathons. Birthday parties, quinceañeras, bat mitzvahs, weddings, holidays, vacations. Everything was shared. A rhythm, the way the Alvarados moved along the hours and days and weeks of those calendars, year after year, had served as a thread of sorts that tied her family together. But by the time her older sisters had gone to college in New York and Miami and had gotten married and moved to their respective homes, something had broken. The calendar had ceased to exist years ago; the markers, still in the tin can, had dried up and were now relegated to the top shelf with the sous vide cooker, the ice cream maker, and the crème brûlée set still in its original box, aging undisturbed. It seemed to her that each member of her family was a top spinning on a surface by itself, unencumbered by what the other tops were doing or where they were going. What surprised her the most was the fact that they still met for Sunday family dinners, rain or shine, with or without husbands, with or without the twins. But people sitting at a table don't make a family. Monologues don't make a conversation. Even the most delicious meal meticulously prepared by Keila didn't inspire anymore. And in the past year, she'd watched her father descend into apathy. She didn't rule out depression, but she was more inclined to believe something was bothering him. Had she done enough to figure out what it was? She thought not, and this upset her. She wished she could pry open his mind and extract his pain, his worry. Or was this deterioration part of the process of aging? She wondered if all families went through this emotional separation as the children grew up and the parents got older. Perhaps she had a heightened sensitivity to what was going on because she lived with Oscar and Keila and could see the day-to-day decline in their care and affection for each other. Why did she live at home anyway? Was she hoping to hang on to the thread of days and weeks that connected her and her parents and sisters in the family calendar? She decided to ask her loyal Twitter tribe.

Am I suffering a bad case of millennialism, or am I justified to be comfortably living at my parents' house at twenty-eight? Share your thoughts.

She posted her tweet but deleted it almost immediately, suddenly feeling ashamed of herself at the thought that she might be closer to people she'd never met than to her own blood.

■ ■ ■ ■

As Lola drove up and down the hills of Highland Park, the neighborhood she'd lived in for the past thirty-seven years, she could easily distinguish which houses had been bought and renovated to be sold at twice the price and which ones hadn't yet: that one over there still had its patina, the charm of an old garden populated with gnomes and swans and Catholic saints, a wrought-iron fence and lightly chipped paint on the walls. That other one with the Tesla parked in the driveway sparkled with newness, surrounded by a water-wise garden, a bright red front door and a fence built with horizontal cedar slats. She wondered which of those new houses Olivia had transformed, sending the longtime tenants to live where the wind faded into oblivion, the only place where they could afford rent.

As she drove down the main drag, Figueroa Street, she counted the few landmarks and establishments that had survived — for the time being — her neighborhood's dizzying transformation from a quaint old Latino enclave into "America's hottest neighborhood," at least according to *L.A.*

Weekly. She found a parking spot in front of the flower shop and squeezed her bright yellow, lightly dinged Honda Fit in the small space and waved at her friend Susana, the florist, through her storefront window. She'd babysat for her years ago. Five boys; all grown, but still to this day one or another would stop by and bring her gifts, like a live turkey that instead of food became a pet, a sack of yams that she gave away, a fuchsia rebozo that she loved and used only on special occasions. Susana opened the door and yelled, "Lola! Come over for dinner tonight! The boys are in town and will want to see you. Seven o'clock?"

"I'll bring tamales costeños," shouted Lola as she walked past. Her meeting with a Legal Aid lawyer was only a few blocks away, so she headed down Figueroa in the direction of York Avenue, walking past La Fuente restaurant (their sopa de albóndigas was a dish she'd raved about on Yelp). She never ordered delivery; she preferred take-out just to have a chance to get a glimpse of Chicken Boy, the old, bizarre statue towering over the street, perched on the next-door neighbor's rooftop. It always made her smile, all the weirdness that L.A. had to offer, if you knew where to look. She wished Chicken Boy would stay there forever. But she knew it was doomed: prospectors, speculators, flippers, and developers were quickly taking over her neighborhood right in front of her eyes. It was becoming a playground for affluent hipsters: there they were, eating at Martita's, her favorite taco place, or spending their money at Verde, the organic juice bar, or at Vegan-O, the vegan restaurant next door. She'd seen a new bookshop right next to a 99 Cents Only Store, and Our Daily Bread, a bakery that sold croissants for four dollars. At least that place had preserved a famous mural of the Virgin of Guadalupe painted years before on its storefront. She had fought for that. Forcefully. Not that she was religious. It had been a matter of principle.

And now she'd learned that Olivia, the little girl she had helped raise, was contributing to the assault. How could she? She'd always come to her, not her mother, for comfort, until she went to college and Lola moved on. It was painful to accept that the sweet little Olie of her memories had turned out to be — well, the enemy. *La pinche enemiga!*

She felt light-headed. As she tried to hold on to a lamppost she almost got knocked over by a young man gliding by on a skateboard.

When she arrived at Kindness & Mischief, one of those new coffee shops, Kamirah Jones, flaunting a burst of curls the color of raven wings, was already waiting for her. Kamirah was a fierce pro-bono human rights lawyer specializing in eviction defense. She and Lola had become friends years before when Lola first went to seek help at Legal Aid on behalf of one of her neighbors.

"I almost got run over by a man-bun-wearing torpedo," Lola said, still stunned.

"I'm not surprised. Those people!" said Kamirah, offering Lola a cup of drip coffee and a poppy-seed muffin to calm her down. "I got you the same as last time."

Both women sat to discuss a new case that Lola had brought to her, a ninety-two-year-old widow who'd gotten an illegal eviction notice and had nowhere to go. In the middle of the conversation, Kamirah asked, "You seem upset. What gives?"

"Remember that family I used to nanny for — on the Westside?"

"It was quite a few years ago, right?"

"Right! I used to love working there. They spoke Spanish and cooked Mexican. And the middle girl, Olivia, she was my favorite." Lola looked guilty for a moment. "I wasn't supposed to have favorites, but she just won me over on day one when she put together a welcome-to-our-family bouquet from her mother's roses. I'll always remember the mom's face when she recognized her flowers, *my* flowers! But now this girl is all grown up. She's an architect, one of those people destroying Highland Park! I only know because she showed up on my doorstep the other day, asking me to come back to take care of her twin girls. Who almost drowned! That's what you get for having a swimming pool. A goddamn rich people accident," Lola said. "That would never have happened on my watch!"

"And so?"

"It's bothering me like a stone in my shoe!"

"Does she know you're an advocate with us?"

"No."

After her meeting, Lola drove home. Her house was on Range View Avenue, a hilly street with a partial view of the city sprawl. She'd been able to buy it outright years ago thanks to a settlement from a bus accident in which her parents were killed. She arrived at the precise moment when the afternoon sun bathed her avocado-colored house and made the color pop. Shadows danced on the walls as the branches of her

70

sycamore tree swayed in the mild breeze. It was as if the entire house glistened with joy. She walked through the wrought-iron gate onto her patio, where she had planted two rows of corn and a patch of serrano peppers, tomatillos, and epazote to give away to friends. Once inside, she dropped off her purse, plopped down on her couch, and took her shoes off. Her two-bedroom house was small, but it was hers. Lola owned it free and clear and she wasn't going to let anyone make her move out, not for a million dollars.

Thursday, January 28th

"I bet your dad is in some hotel room, sulking," said Gabriel, sipping his morning coffee.

"He's not with Aunt Belinda. We already checked. He didn't go to Mexico; Patricia says his passport is in his closet. He's never done this. Never. I've been leaving voicemails on his cellphone and nothing. What if he kills himself? He's been in a weird funk forever," said Claudia.

"He'll turn up. I'm sure of that."

"No, you can't be sure, so stop invalidating my angst."

"I'm just trying to be supportive. He's probably regrouping, considering his situation, and wondering how he's going to save his marriage. People do this sort of thing. They step aside, away from the trouble zone, so they can think things through. I would certainly do something like that."

Claudia got up behind Gabriel's lounge chair and squeezed his shoulders, massaging deep.

"How long are you staying?"

"I'm off to New York on Sunday. I've got back-to-back meetings all of next week."

Claudia lifted her hands off Gabriel's shoulders. She might never get used to Gabriel's nonstop travel. It maddened her. Suddenly she felt an urge to run to the bathroom and shower off his sweat from the night before, and that's exactly what she did.

Sunday, January 31st

"Have you tried calling your dad again?"

"For the millionth time," said Olivia to Felix on their morning walk. "He's not answering. And on top of it all, my mom canceled family dinner again."

"Why don't we go for tacos tonight, then? The twins could use a little outing, and so could we."

Olivia was eager to normalize their family life after the accident and had even organized a playdate with a neighbor's toddler the day before to test the girls' tolerance to activity. Perhaps these efforts to get back to life could help her shake the feeling of inadequacy as a mother that still loomed over her.

"He's probably teaching your mom a lesson. He wants her to miss him," said Felix.

"Personally, I think it's rude of him to have us all worried."

"I'd stay out of it."

"I can't talk about my parents and their idiotic fight right now."

Olivia accelerated her pace, leaving Felix a few steps behind.

"Hey, wait up," he said, out of breath. "Stop right now!"

But Olivia pressed on, risking an explosive reaction of foul temper that turned Felix into a basilisk for little or no reason. Fortunately for Olivia, that night he was more interested in Oscar's disappearance than in picking a fight over anything that made her feel inadequate (*You put a ding in the car! You lost the keys again!*), so later that evening, having decided against tacos, they stayed home.

"What if your dad just takes Prozac? He's obviously depressed," said Felix, continuing their conversation from that morning.

73

"I'm not sure that's going to solve their issues," Olivia said, already irritated, knowing where the conversation Felix insisted on having was going. She quickly turned toward Andrea. "Sweetie, don't spit out your chicken. If you want me to cut it into smaller pieces, ask me."

"How can you be depressed when you have so much money?" Felix said with sarcasm and a sprinkle of bitterness.

"He sold the land in the Santa Clara Valley way back in the eighties," she explained, annoyed. "Who knows if he still has all that money? He might have spent it."

"Hence the blissful life."

"Well, it doesn't seem so blissful now," she said as she grabbed Diana's plate. "Want some more nopalitos con huevo, honey?"

"Mommy? I'm tired," said Diana, rubbing her eyes.

"Let's go brush your teeth, sweetie," she said, picking her up. "You too, missy," she said to Andrea, dragging the girls away and leaving Felix alone at the table.

After everyone went to bed and the house was quiet, Olivia went to the kitchen, poured herself a cup of tila tea, and sat on a stool to think. Where was that feeling, the untamable beast that she called love, just to give it a name? Olivia had never been able to describe what she felt for Felix, not since the first day they met at a TED Talk about sustainable architecture. Three months into the relationship, love's impact was already unfathomable. She was all Felix ever wanted and he told her so, every day. She felt desired, essential. She couldn't decide which god to thank, so she thanked Cupid for shooting her through with an AK-47 instead of an arrow.

But then there was the other side of Felix, the "door-slamming" side. She also called it the "coffee-mug-thrown-out-the-window" side, the "walking-out" side, the "mirror-smashing-with-his-fist" side, the "grabbing-her-by-the-blouse-collar-and-rattling-her" side. It wouldn't take long after Olivia delivered a beautifully remodeled house to its owners, or landed a new project, that Felix would react in an incomprehensibly nasty way in an unrelated situation, usually one that he used to make Olivia feel inadequate, dumb. "There you go again," he'd say. "You forgot to buy eggs! Seems like there are never eggs in this house! You keep fucking it up!" And she endured it.

FEBRUARY

Tuesday, February 2nd

While Punxsutawney Phil back in Pennsylvania forecast an early spring, Oscar, the weather expert at the Alvarado household, was still gone and Keila didn't seem concerned. So, Claudia, Olivia, and Patricia decided to invite themselves for dinner at Keila's to confront her.

"You just don't give a shit if Dad is dead or alive," said Patricia, trying to control her fury.

"You can go on hating Dad, that's okay, I understand, whatever he did to you, but not caring about his well-being?" said Olivia, staring at Keila with piercing eyes. "He's our father!"

"Tell us the truth, now. Did he cheat on you? Did he hurt you? What atrocity has he done to you to deserve this kind of anger?" demanded Claudia.

"Just so you know, Mom, I already filed a

missing-persons report before coming here. Expect a call from the cops. They'll want to talk to the whole family," Patricia warned.

Keila slowly poured herself another glass of wine and sat at the kitchen peninsula, taking in her daughters' emotional blackmail.

"I know exactly where Dad is. You don't need to come here and ruin my dinner with your Jewish guilt," she said.

"Oh, yeah? Care to share this information with us, his daughters?" said Patricia, about to burst with the ire of an ill pachyderm. "You've been keeping us out of this, as if it didn't affect us!"

"It doesn't take a detective. I've been monitoring his activities on our credit card app. He drove to Florida, slept at roadside motels, got gas and ate all along the 10, then stayed at a hotel in Aventura. He's on his way back; don't worry. At his driving speed, he should be getting home around Sunday. So, cancel the silver alert."

"I reported him as a regular missing person. He's not senile, Mom," said Patricia.

"He could well be. A senile zombie."

"Why have you been keeping us in the dark? What kind of twisted person have you become, Mom? Did you enjoy inflicting this torture on us?" said Patricia, scraping her chair back from the table.

"At least you should have told us he was safe!" said Claudia, following Patricia toward the door.

"I just did."

"This is so mean, Mom. Who are you?" said Olivia, picking up her purse and following her sisters. And, since she was the last one out, she got the privilege of slamming the door.

Wednesday, February 3rd

With Gabriel back in New York for a few days, Claudia's house was entirely available to the three sisters to vent and scheme. As the sun set across the ocean, they sprawled on the king-size bed. Patricia rubbed Claudia's back, and Claudia rubbed Olivia's, like when they were little. Some leftovers they'd scavenged from the fridge were on a side table, still in their Tupperware containers. Velcro, Gabriel's cat, joined the pride on the mound, finding a warm little corner next to Olivia.

The twins had tried playing with him, but the cat ignored them, so they sat near their mom and reluctantly played with a couple of toys. Their latest babysitter had quit abruptly (boyfriend trouble, what else?), so

Olivia was forced to drag the twins around town enduring fit after fit: the one over not being allowed to play with the workers' power tools at the jobsite in Santa Monica; the next one at the grocery store where both wanted to ride in the shopping cart; then the one in the car where Andrea insisted on unbuckling her seat belt as Olivia was speeding to get on a freeway on-ramp. And now, here they were, fighting over Velcro at Claudia's house.

"At least now we know Dad is okay," said Claudia.

"Why wouldn't Mom tell us?" asked Olivia.

"I don't want to hear a word about Mom," said Patricia.

"Maybe she was afraid we would tell Dad that she was tracking his whereabouts and then he'd stop using his credit card," said Claudia.

"You've watched too many TV series. I think Mom is just furious with him for leaving and not doing what he promised us, which is try to mend his marriage," said Patricia. "And she just dumped it all on us!"

"Whatever it is, we need to sit down with Mom and sort this mess out. We can't just stop talking to her," said Olivia, ever the conciliatory one.

"I can't. Not just yet," said Patricia. "Can I sleep over again tonight?" she asked Claudia.

Not far from Claudia's Malibu house, Keila sobbed in her own bed. How could she have been so selfish, so cruel? It was one thing to be angry with her husband. It was another to make her daughters pay for it. She squirted a few drops of CBD tincture under her tongue to calm down and called Patricia.

"Can I talk to you?"

"Not now, Mom."

"Are you coming home later?"

"No. I'm at Claudia's."

"Listen, I was a jerk. Can I come over to talk to you girls? Please?"

"Olivia has to put the twins to bed. She's leaving now. And Claudia has to go to a wine tasting."

"How about tomorrow? Can you all come over tomorrow for dinner?"

A silence came back to Keila on the receiver. She waited.

"Hello?" she finally said. "Patricia?"

"All right, Mom. We'll be there."

Thursday, February 4th
Reconciliation had always been easy among the Alvarados. Most disagreements, dis-

80

putes, and fights were short-lived, resolved without major drama. In the end, most were irrelevant. But Keila's behavior had crossed that invisible line of deceit that everyone in the family knew about even though it was never explicitly stated.

On the way to meet with her — Claudia driving down PCH from her Malibu house in her Audi TT and Patricia following her in her Prius — they put their phones on speaker so they could talk from car to car.

"You do the talking. I'm afraid I might insult her and take this fight to the point of no return," said Patricia.

"Just think about the amazing mother we've always had and rule this out as a crazy odd stage she's going through. She's not this sinister, never has been, really," said Claudia, surprised at herself as she wasn't known for being empathetic.

"He's given her no reason to leave him."

"How do you know?"

"I live with them. I'd notice if there was something weird going on."

"C'mon, Pats. Men are so good at hiding their shenanigans. I'm not saying Dad is doing anything wrong, but in general, I mean."

"She can't deal with his downer mood. He needs help."

"Well, then, have you tried to help him?"

"He won't open up. You just missed the California Incline exit, by the way."

"Shit. We'll have to take the 10."

Claudia glanced at her rearview mirror to make sure Patricia was driving right behind her and sped on to take the freeway.

"Can you connect Olivia?" she asked.

Patricia added Olivia to the call without taking her eyes off the road.

"Hey, are you on your way to Mom's?" said Olivia on the speaker.

"Where are you?" asked Patricia.

"I'm almost there. I had to leave Felix in charge of the twins, but he's showing a house in West Hollywood, so I need to hurry up. I'll wait for you outside."

When Claudia and Patricia arrived at Keila's, they jumped into Olivia's Honda Odyssey minivan — dubbed "Homer."

"Damn, this car is bigger than my apartment when I went to NYU!" said Claudia.

"Focus, please, we need to decide how we're going to handle this."

Nearly an hour after the sisters parked outside Keila's house, they walked in the door with heads full of words. Keila was in the kitchen juggling pots and pans.

Olivia had been picked as the designated spokesperson, so she cleared her throat and delivered the message: "You'll get your turn to speak, Mom, so please don't interrupt. If you have a problem with Dad, don't drag us in. You two deal with it. We can offer support, but we're certainly not going to be the recipients of your anger. This stops today."

There. Short and to the point. Olivia would have never spoken with such aplomb to her mother (or anyone other than random flaky subcontractors working with her at her architecture studio) if she hadn't worked on the message with her sisters and rehearsed it thoroughly.

"Well said, Olie!" Patricia chimed in, happy to realize that writing up the message to her mother as if it were a PowerPoint slide had proven to be successful. "You can speak now, Mom."

Keila took a deep breath and slowly made eye contact with her three daughters while she figured out what to say to them. Her hands hovered over the pipián con camarones she had been making.

"You're right. What's going on between your dad and me is not your fault. I will never direct my frustrations against your dad toward you; I promise. Will you forgive me, girls?" asked Keila in a small voice.

"You'll have to prove it to us, Mom," said Patricia. "Now, could you look on your credit card app to see where Dad is right now?"

Keila launched the app on her phone and showed her daughters.

"He just checked into a Motel 6 in El Paso. I'm sure he'll be heading this way next. It's pretty much a straight shot on the 10 all the way to Rancho Verde. He'll surely stay overnight in Phoenix and be home by Sunday."

And just when Patricia was able to release the tightness in her chest, Keila snapped: "But I still want to wring your father's neck!"

Sunday, February 7th
Oscar parked his SUV on the driveway and rolled his carry-on suitcase into the house. No one was there to greet him, or to scold him for that matter. He was well aware of the apprehension his careless disappearance might have caused. He deserved it. They're probably watching the Super Bowl with friends, he thought. He walked around going from room to room, exhausted from the trip, and wondered what his life would be like if everything around him suddenly vanished. He ran the palm of his hand on the surface of the walls, caressing them, as if they were in danger of extinction.

Outside, the unusually warm day — eighty-four degrees was his guess, as opposed to the historical average of sixty-eight for that day of the year — bathed his skin. Not thinking that the strange February heat could be an effect of climate change, he stood at the edge of the dirt hole that was no longer the family pool, half filled with a slurry mix of portland cement and plaster sand. Henceforth, the kidney-shaped cement patch in the middle of the backyard would be known among the Alvarados as "the keloid scar." An excavator was parked to the side and two soil compactors leaned against the fence. To anyone watching him from the other end of the yard, he would look like a creepy version of a David Hockney painting: a wretched figure, hunched over from self-pity and a mild scoliosis that had been diagnosed late in life, moving his head this way and that, following the path of an imaginary swimmer. Where was Keila? Where were the twins? Where were the girls? It was supposed to be Sunday family dinner, but the house was on life support. Or was it him?

Monday, February 8th
"What kind of idiotic tantrum was that?" Keila yelled at Oscar from the driver's seat

of her car. "The girls were worried sick!" she added, carefully wording her recrimination to leave herself out and at the same time administer to Oscar a dose of guilt.

Oscar, in the passenger seat, looked out the window, wanting to jump out into the Mulholland Drive abyss. There were still a few minutes of enduring Keila's rage before they arrived at Olivia's house to visit the twins. He acknowledged Keila's reproach and felt a pang in his chest. His wife was right. What kind of man was he becoming, not to have given the slightest consideration to his daughters' feelings?

"I just needed some space." Oscar's voice was barely audible.

"You really have to come up with a better explanation when we see the therapist this week. You're not even good at disappearing! I knew exactly where you were."

"I wasn't trying to disappear. I had to get away to collect my thoughts. This thing, what you're doing to our marriage, to our family, is cruel and uncalled-for."

Keila stepped on the accelerator and took a curve a bit too fast. Someone in the oncoming traffic honked their horn.

Oscar kept his hand on the door handle, and when they finally parked, he got out of the car and rushed to the entrance, as if by going into his daughter's house he would be protected from the savage creature his wife had become.

But something unexpected happened as soon as they went into Olivia's house and found the twins in the den smearing Play-Doh on the shag carpet. An unspoken truce was suddenly called and both of them got on their knees to play with their grand-daughters, relieved to see them quite recovered. They each knew that the year ahead would likely prove difficult. They might not succeed in mending their marriage. But sitting on the floor, helping each other try to remove the sticky red paste from the teal carpet, they each silently vowed to try.

Wednesday, February 10th

Olivia and her sisters had been raised both Jewish (for Keila) and Catholic (for Oscar). To avoid confusion, Oscar and Keila had defined the Old and New Testaments to their daughters as the Movie and the Sequel, creating for them a fluid, hybrid faith that ultimately boiled down to the celebration of all holidays indiscriminately, without giving their religion any further theological examination. Hanukkah was the time to light up the menorah, Christmas was when the tree was decorated and gifts were given and

87

received, and that was that.

On this February morning, Olivia drove to Death Valley to celebrate Ash Wednesday by herself, as she had done for the past five years. It wasn't that she was devout, although the holiday's message of mortality was clear to her more than ever before. She sped down Highway 14, hurrying past lines of semitrucks and slow-moving cars. She had an appointment with her other babies, Sarah and Elias, and wanted to get there early enough to spend the day with them. No one goes to Death Valley on a weekday, so she knew she'd have the whole desert to herself. She had expected to see the grays and browns of its perennial texture, the rocks and sand of the badlands and cracked silt on the playa's surface, a sight she'd grown familiar with after years of visiting the park. But instead she found herself surrounded by a sea of yellow. Desert gold and gravel ghost flowers looked toward the sun among many other varieties that she could not identify, boasting petals in purple and pink and orange. She remembered her father telling her about a rare Death Valley superbloom he had witnessed as a child during a family vacation, and here it was again many years later. How ironic, she thought, that as the lush gardens of Los

Angeles died out, starved by the drought, the driest place on earth was now blooming exuberantly. Could it be an effect of El Niño, the weather phenomenon her father talked about, or was it simply a gift of nature to ease her pain? She slowed down her car to take in the view. It seemed to her as if a blown-glass rainbow had shattered into millions of pieces and fallen to the ground. Farther down, the mild wind blew little sand clouds off the dunes' crests, whitewashed by the sun. She had climbed up those dunes and had rolled down the soft, sandy inclines many times when she was younger, but these constantly moving mountains meant a lot more to her now; now her children had become part of them.

She parked on the curb along the road, right ahead of Zabriskie Point, a geological formation of rocks that had inspired a scandalous movie in the early seventies whose setting Olivia could not comprehend: Why pick such a rough spot to have wild sex and run around barefoot and naked? She grabbed her backpack and started her trek along a narrow trail that disappeared and reappeared as the desert reconfigured itself.

Olivia and Felix had decided to go through with in-vitro fertilization after failing to achieve a pregnancy with the aid of other kinds of treatments and methods, including seeing a shaman from Tucumcari, New Mexico, who claimed to have operated on Olivia's Fallopian tubes without having to cut her open and proved it by showing Felix a cotton ball with a drop of blood after the so-called surgery.

"Don't lift anything heavy in the next couple of days," he'd advised.

Of the thirty-six eggs that were harvested from Olivia's womb at the Manhattan Beach Fertility Institute, twenty-two, the strongest ones, were fertilized with Felix's sperm. Of those, ten did not make it past day three. Twelve had been frozen and of those, six were thawed and transferred into her uterus in sets of two over three years, but all of them ended in early miscarriages. Of the last remaining six embryos, two had become Sarah and Elias, two were Diana and Andrea, and the last two were indefinitely cryopreserved at the fertility lab.

After the three consecutive miscarriages, Felix had pleaded to Olivia, in exhaustion, "Can't we forget about all this and go back to enjoying life?"

"You mean sex?" she'd asked.

"Yes, sex, I want our sex-for-fun back, but I want everything else, too. Life. This obsession is killing me."

"It's killing me, too, but we have six more embryos waiting in the lab. Let's go again, once more, please."

She thought about those days, five years ago, when six months out the cramps and the bleeding announced the beginning of Sarah and Elias's end. That pregnancy had been the one that had given her the most hope, the one that had lasted the longest. She had even allowed herself to feel enough optimism to buy cribs and baby paraphernalia, against Felix's cautious optimism. But during a long weekend in Acapulco her cervix had begun to dilate ahead of time and the fetuses had caught an infection from the ocean water that had made its way into Olivia's uterus. Felix had taken her to the local hospital, where the nightshift ER doctor gave her sedatives and painkillers and whispered to her that everything would be all right in a trembling voice that lacked conviction.

There weren't any available beds or delivery rooms, and Olivia lay panting on a gurney parked in the hallway next to a drunken woman who had wrapped her car around a palm tree and destroyed her face. Ignoring the other patients, the doctor filled up a latex glove with saline, like a water balloon, and inserted it into Olivia's vagina.

"Hopefully this plug will delay labor," he said.

He then tilted her gurney down so her head was lower than her feet, in hopes that gravity would do its part to keep the babies from coming out. This angle allowed Olivia to see the underside of the neighboring gurneys, one of which had a blob of chewing gum stuck to its rusty frame. It was that kind of hospital.

It took her several hours of intense effort and pain. No Lamaze training, no epidural, no IV, no hope. As the years went by and the freshness of the agony subsided, she had come to accept the fact that she wasn't the only mother in history to deliver stillborn babies, but on that night, at the crowded Acapulco hospital, she believed that some otherworldly being had chosen her and only her to bear this eternal suffering.

The commotion around her gurney hadn't subsided yet, the doctor was still stitching Olivia up, and the nurses were hurriedly clearing the area when she realized that another nurse had whisked the tiny bodies away.

"Follow that nurse and get my babies back!" she wailed to Felix.

He hesitated for a moment but then ran

off after the nurse. When he disappeared among the crowd that milled about in the hallway, Olivia closed her eyes, nauseous from the painkillers, and cupped her breasts with her hands, gently, as if she were holding chicks that had fallen from their nest. She could feel the milk inside wanting to infuse life. Her nipples ached and swelled with the wish to feed. But no one would latch on to her with tiny lips; there would be no children to nourish.

In the morning, when Olivia woke up, alone, she had been transferred to a more private area, a corner behind a curtain. She noticed a clean gown and robe at the bottom of the bed. With a great deal of exertion, she took off the bloody hospital clothes and changed. She lay down again, still tired from the toil of labor, and stared at the ceiling. A gecko crawled into a crack as if it owned the place.

"Are you Mrs. Almeida?" a voice called out as the curtain was brushed aside to reveal a short and heavy man, ready to burst out of his guayabera shirt, each button a potential projectile. "I'm here from the funeral home."

He opened a shoebox and pulled out two small, red satin pouches no larger than a pair of socks with a golden sash tied around each one, and gave them to Olivia. Each weighed only a few ounces.

"I don't know which is the boy and which is the girl. I'm so sorry."

Olivia took the pouches, soft and supple to the touch, like stress balls, and put them in the pockets of her robe.

"Could you finish filling out the death certificates? Nobody could tell me what the babies' names were. Your husband wasn't sure."

Olivia took the pen and wrote Elias on one certificate and Sarah on the other.

"Is this paid for?"

"Yes. Your husband already took care of it."

When she returned the pen she hugged the man from the mortuary as if he had been a dear relative and wept on his shoulder.

"There, there," he comforted her in a professional manner before he excused himself. He had to leave, on to his next grieving person.

When Felix got there, he leaned against the bed and dried the sweat off his forehead.

"Any news from the mortuary?"

"They came out to get the paperwork signed," she said, but failed to mention the pouches in her robe pockets. She wanted to be the only one to touch them, to feel their warmth fading against her body.

"What about the babies?"

"I asked them to discard the ashes."

"I suppose it's for the best. We'll have to move on. Let's go home, I'm exhausted," said Felix, stroking Olivia's shoulder. "We can plan a memorial, something small, intimate. Just for us."

Now, standing at the top of the dune in Death Valley, on the very same spot where five years ago she had come in secret to scatter her children's ashes and tiny bone fragments, she wondered if she could reconfigure the facts into a different shape, another reality, like the sandy desert, changing its story at the slightest breath of wind. But she couldn't. Her story seemed to have been written on another part of the desert, chiseled on the solid boulders of the mountains that surrounded the valley. Those, she thought, haven't moved and never will.

Thursday, February 11th

Dr. Feldman must have had eyebrow reshaping and microblading, an eyelid lift, and definitely a good dose of Botox. That was Keila's impression as she sat on the couch in front of him. Having developed a radar to detect these cosmetic procedures as her friends went through them over their menopausal years and then denied it, she was able to draw her conclusions from his supple cheeks, glossy forehead, and expressionless face. He'd also had a less than successful hair-transplant procedure along his receding hairline.

She wondered if it had been a good idea to choose this therapist on Claudia's recommendation. "No other Beverly Hills therapist could have gotten my friend Giorgio out of his depression when his restaurant lost the Michelin star," she'd said. "Chefs commit suicide for this sort of thing." But now, sitting across from Dr. Feldman, she regretted having rushed into making an appointment. Celebrity therapists dealt with narcissists, mostly, not people like Oscar, with depleted self-esteem. She could have gone with Olivia's choice: "He's a pothead with Buddhist inclinations, Mom, you'll love him. He treats his clients outdoors, in Echo Park right by the lake, and after the session he teaches them tai chi. Wear something comfortable."

Oscar sat at the other end of the couch, quietly listening to Dr. Feldman's questions, the first one asked point-blank.

"So, tell me, why are you here?"

An unavoidable feeling of importance

96

flooded Keila. This was her opportunity to tell her story. She could go back, way back, to her single-cell-organism ancestors, but because she knew they had limited time, she decided to start when she was born.

"First of all, thank you for seeing us on such short notice," said Keila. "To answer your question, I had a happy childhood, if you ask me."

Dr. Feldman did not raise an eyebrow when he heard Keila's statement, but she sensed he wished he could.

"I see you want to tell me your life story, but when you're done I need to hear why you're here. You're in the hot seat now, and I'm not letting you off the hook," he said with half a smile, as if trying to break the ice.

Oscar crossed his arms and his legs, clearly expressing his reluctance to be there.

"My grandparents were killed in a concentration camp in Poland, but my parents avoided the Holocaust when they were shipped to Mexico as young children," she continued, now in possession of the podium. "They were cousins. A couple from the synagogue who couldn't have babies raised them. There aren't many Mexican Jews, so it's a very tight-knit community. I was particularly fond of Bubbe Myriam. Because

I was my parents' only child and my grandparents' only granddaughter, I had all their attention and love, just for myself. You can imagine what that does to a girl. The search for relatives in Mexico, Europe, the U.S., and even Argentina, following dead-end leads, was a constant in their lives until they passed away a few years ago, within two months of each other. They never found anyone except for an aunt they recognized in a photograph at the Museum of Tolerance.

"I could have married someone in the Mexican Jewish community. I had good prospects, great ones, in fact. But I married Oscar instead. Why did I marry a Catholic? Well, he wasn't much of a Catholic and I wasn't much of a Jew. Don't ever tell that to my parents. Religion wasn't an issue for me. It was the fact that Oscar is an American. He will say otherwise, that he is Mexican even if he was born in Los Angeles. But I'm not here to tell you his story. I moved to L.A. with him, very reluctantly at first, knowing it would kill my parents, but the decision wasn't so hard. We had a good marriage. We have three daughters, very lovely girls. Actually, everything was lovely — with a few bumps, why not say it — until something happened to Oscar last year. I don't know what. But now he just sits there, like right now. Look at him! It's as if someone had stuck a vacuum cleaner in his mouth and sucked out his soul. That's why we're here. I want to find out if this marriage has any hope of surviving."

"Would you like to say why you're here, Oscar? It's Oscar, right?" asked Dr. Feldman.

Oscar sat up straight and ran his finger along the inside of his shirt collar as if stretching the fabric.

"Keila is upset with me," Oscar said in a barely audible voice. "She wants to get divorced, but we don't get divorced in our family."

"Can you elaborate?"

"It's not an option."

Those were the last words that Oscar uttered in the entire session, which was mostly taken over by Keila, who expressed in various ways her own thoughts on the matter.

"Why perpetuate something that isn't working? People change. Our time on earth is limited: we should choose who we want to spend it with. Divorce is an option when no other options are available."

Dr. Feldman glanced at the little clock on the side table and handed Keila a tissue.

She wasn't aware she had a tear on her cheek.

"I'd like to hear more about Oscar's reasons to be in therapy, but our time is up for today. Would you like to come again next week?" he asked, pulling out his calendar.

"Yes," said Keila.

"No," said Oscar.

Captive in the car, Oscar endured Keila's rage as she maneuvered through the Sunset Boulevard traffic.

"Don't waste my time or the therapist's. If you're not doing this, say it now."

"I don't see how this is going to help."

"Got a better idea?"

"I'm fine, Keila. I've been worried about the drought, like every other sensible person living in Southern California, that's all."

"Why? We already replaced our toilets with the water-saving ones. And look how long we had our pool half filled! And the trouble it brought us! We almost lost our grandchildren! And now Olivia had to take matters into her own hands because you wouldn't do anything about it. It's so embarrassing."

Oscar closed his eyes and thought about their latest visit with Diana and Andrea. Olivia had allowed him to hold them, five minutes each. He'd felt an almost imperceptible vibration coming from Diana's chest, perhaps the activity of her immune system fighting infections, her frail little body recovering slowly, a good sign of health for someone else, but for him it was not. He couldn't stop imagining the girls in tiny caskets, no matter how much they wriggled and fussed in his arms, proving that they were very much alive and well.

"They're fine and that's all that matters," he said, contradicting his thoughts.

"Are you coming to therapy next week or not?"

"Don't you have to be in Mexico City to meet with your gallery people?"

For someone so oblivious, Keila realized, Oscar was quite aware of her work commitments and travel schedule. He also kept a mental chart of the daily temperature and humidity in the city and could recite it effortlessly as if he had a built-in barometer. She hadn't found his underwear in the freezer or had to run out on the street to look for him half dressed and disoriented. A fear that she had subconsciously been battling against suddenly leapt into view, but with these observations about Oscar's behavior, she felt she could rule it out: Alzheimer's. It couldn't be.

"You're right. I'll schedule a session for

later in the month."

The sun had long set over Sunset Boulevard, honoring its name as it did every day. Dusk had draped its indigo light over the endless lines of cars filled with people trying to get home on a Thursday evening, and the rows of low buildings, many of which had the blinking neon signs of fast-food restaurants and stand-up comedy places, or larger-than-life billboards advertising clothing brands, upcoming movies and television series, or celebrities with no apparent talent endorsing their own perfume brands. Latinos from across the diaspora — Mexicans, Hondurans, and Guatemalans — waited for the bus in loosely arranged lines, most of them heading to their second or third job. Oscar looked up and recognized Venus, the only naked-eye planet that could upstage the permanent glow of the city in the February sky, and wondered if there would ever be a cloud over Los Angeles again.

Friday, February 12th
Early that morning, Patricia found Oscar in the toolshed by the pool heater, reading the newspaper, uncomfortably sitting on the bench.

"Here you are! I was looking for you," she said, putting a cup of coffee she'd brought for him on the worktable. "You should have worn your robe. It's sixty degrees. Want to come back in the house and have breakfast with me?"

Oscar took off his reading glasses, put them in his pajamas' shirt pocket, and gave a long look at his daughter before answering.

"I'd rather read the paper here, mi chamaquita. It's quiet."

"Are you avoiding Mom?"

"What? No. Of course not. I just like to be by myself to collect my thoughts," he lied.

Patricia, disappointed, gave him a kiss on his forehead and turned around to leave.

"Just know that I'm here for you, Papi. You don't have to endure this alone, whatever it is."

On the way back into the house she felt an ache in her chest that she explained as a longing for Oscar's warmth. She needed the loving father she'd always had, but at the same time, it was clear to her that right now he needed her more, even if he wasn't ready to acknowledge it.

Sunday, February 14th
Claudia's Valentine's Day gift to herself was to run in the L.A. Marathon that morning.

Every year, she'd choose three of the most challenging races and train for them religiously. No matter the blisters, to hell with the cramped quads, damn the bloody armpits. She'd run the San Francisco Marathon with its intimidating hills, the Big Sur Marathon where she sprained her ankle at Hurricane Point, and the ever-ascending Grandfather Mountain Marathon in North Carolina. The L.A. Marathon was easy in comparison, but on that morning, around twenty minutes into the race, she quit and went home to sleep. Anyone who knew her would have been shocked. "Why? She's not a quitter," they'd say. But she just drifted back to her bed without giving it even the tiniest thought.

Tuesday, February 16th

If Keila hadn't inherited artistic genes (who knows from whom, as neither one of her parents could draw a line on a piece of paper) she'd never have met Simon Brik, owner of the well-established art gallery Brik & Spiegel in the posh neighborhood of Polanco in Mexico City. She'd never have had to decide whether to betray Oscar or not, in response to Simon's insistence. But there she was, sitting across the desk in his gallery, avoiding his profoundly blue eyes

104

while he laid out the details of her upcoming show.

"We could go with the couples fucking inside the glass bubbles. It's really your strongest series right now," he proposed, looking at several photographs spread over the desk. Hyperrealist, high-fired, polychrome ceramic sculptures, no larger than twelve inches tall, depicted several naked couples embracing in assorted sexual positions — men with women, men with men, women with women — each couple suspended inside a glass-blown balloon.

"I also have the anti-spooning series, it's the latest one. Don't you like it? Go to my website," she said, hoping to steer her show toward a less romantic theme.

"I saw it last month, when you uploaded it."

Simon clicked on Keila's website and the computer screen filled with images of sculptures of couples in bed, their backs turned against each other, their eyes open, staring at the emptiness, every one of them looking deep in thought.

"I'm drawn to the drama of this series, but right now I'm more in the mood for spooning," he said.

Over the years Keila had been subjected to plenty of men's advances. She had developed an ability to shrug them off by using a moral compass of sorts that worked quite effectively: she'd imagine Oscar standing right next to her. This gave her the power to express an absolute lack of interest that men quickly interpreted as thanks, but no thanks. Usually that would be the end of it. Simon was the only man who had persisted. For twenty-three years. He was still married when they met at a gallery opening. He pursued her, at first professionally, inviting her to have a solo show at his gallery. Then things began to get more personal. She stopped him immediately, but every so often Simon would bring out his feelings for her and put them on the table, usually a restaurant table, which was Keila's preferred setting for meeting with him. Neutral. Public. Safe. The answer was always no, but this time was different. Being at odds with Oscar had weakened her resolve. She had to imagine Oscar kissing her at that moment, although she wished it were Simon.

"The spooning series, then," she said, pretending to ignore Simon's obvious pass. "I'll have them shipped on Thursday."

She left the gallery with a wrung-out heart, wishing to get into bed and dream something, anything, instead of going back to her parents' house, which she had inher-

106

ited and kept in her name after their deaths. She decided to go to the cemetery to visit their graves. The two-hour drive allowed her ample time to think about what had just happened at the Brik & Spiegel Gallery. Her sudden attraction to Simon was a natural reaction given the state of affairs with Oscar, but if she were to continue with her commitment to try to rescue their marriage, she'd have to kill her feelings immediately. "Stick it out!" she shouted as she parked her rental car.

The Panteón Jardín, one of the largest cemeteries in Mexico City, had been sold out for years. "We've got a full house," the director would tell potential customers, but new burials were conducted daily in any remaining nook and cranny, letting no space go to waste. When relatives did not meet their perpetuity contract obligations, corpses were readily exhumed and placed in common graves to allow room for new tenants, many of them buried in recycled coffins that were still in good shape. There were several smaller cemeteries side by side within the walls of the Panteón Jardín, perfectly separated by wrought-iron fences, to house the deceased depending on their religion or other form of affiliation. Nowhere else was it so true that even after death segregation was still an issue, Keila thought. She walked past the mausoleums of notable Mexican families that still held on to expired and useless titles of nobility, past rows of plain graves painted in bright colors and decorated with virgins and crucifixes and wilted flowers in plastic vases, past the Water and Power Union cemetery, past the Mexican Social Security Institute cemetery, and past the Rotary Club cemetery, until she arrived at the Panteón La Fraternidad, the Jewish cemetery. She opened the gate and went straight to the far end. A small stone she'd left on her father's headstone years ago was still there, untouched. The thoroughly washed and wrapped bodies of her parents peacefully decomposed underneath the soil in simple pine caskets.

"I told you not to marry Oscar, but you wouldn't listen. I'm convinced you did it just to hurt us. He's not even one of us! He'll never understand. And I told you he was going to take you to live in Los Angeles. Look how long you've been gone," Keila almost heard her mother complain. Then she went on to hear her moan, as when the girls were little, "Now you have the three girls. Who's going to help you raise them? Now you've made your decision and we will just rot here by ourselves until we die and then we're going to rot some more in our graves. But that's all right. You go on and live your life without us. It's okay."

This guilt-inducing spiel was not new. In fact, Keila's mother would inflict it on her every time they spoke on the phone, even past the girls' teen years and into adulthood, and she would endure it stoically at the other end of the line. But now, at the cemetery, the spiel resonated more. It hurt. It was too late to fix the abandonment she had imposed on her parents by leaving for Los Angeles, even though she went back home to visit several times a year, but she still had the chance to recover what she had worked so hard to attain. Her marriage to Oscar against her parents' wishes had quickly morphed into a family, her own. It happened subtly and without her full awareness when she heard Claudia's first cry in the delivery room. This moment was followed by never-ending lessons that taught her not just how to be a mother, but how to be an American mother: Soccer mom? *You must mean soccer dad.* Why do I have to volunteer at the school carnival? *My mother didn't even know where my school was.* Your friends are hanging out at our house and plowing through our fridge and they don't even say hello? *Manners are strictly enforced in Mexico and parents always call the shots.* What? Your boyfriend is sleeping over? *Not until you're married, missy.*

Confronting and adapting to the way people raised their children in the United States had been Keila's major challenge and an unbridgeable divide that separated her from the other moms. It didn't help that with every new situation, whether it had to do with schooling or social life, Keila would hear her mother's voice inside her head giving instructions that contradicted what everyone did around her: *"She can't go to coed sleepaway camp! God knows, hormones can unlock every dorm door, get past every counselor supervising those kids!"*

Still, Keila persevered by purposely betraying her own upbringing time and again throughout the girls' growing years until she convinced herself that she'd finally obtained the Great American Mom title. But this notion had lasted only until it was time for Claudia to go away to college. Why she'd decided to go to NYU, all the way on the East Coast, with so many fine universities to choose from right in town was a mystery to Keila. But more important, why did she trade her beautiful bedroom with a walk-in closet in Los Angeles and her mom's daily affection and off-the-charts

110

gefilte fish for a cramped, dirty dorm full of New York cockroaches, a broken-down microwave oven with burnt pizza drippings, and four smelly roommates she didn't even grow up with? Not just that, as if four years of absence hadn't been enough, right after graduating she'd gone on to culinary school somewhere inaccessible by plane in upstate New York.

And why did Olivia go to the University of Miami at the other end of the country to go through a similar experience? At least she had benefited from better weather than Claudia. Had her daughters decided to go one step farther away from her, they'd have fallen into the Atlantic Ocean. Only Patricia had stayed home and enrolled at UCLA to be close to little Daniel. Keila ached every time another mom would say "Good riddance!" and quickly redecorate her child's empty bedroom to become a studio, or worse even, a guest room. Then there was her mother's voice, "You see Keila, Keilita? Now you are living in the same hell you put us through." Her children leaving for college had indeed been punishment for having left her parents in Mexico. Keila was sure about that and she endured it accordingly: payback time.

She sat up, dusted herself off, and left the

cemetery, quickly stopping by the grave of the late Mexican singer and movie idol, Pedro Infante. He was still so famous that every year for sixty years, right on his birthday, even if it fell in the middle of the week, the management had to remove three tons of trash left by fans who came to bring flowers, have a picnic, sing his songs, and celebrate. How odd is transcendence, Keila thought. In a hundred years — not even a tiny blink in the history of humankind — no one would remember or care about her ordeal. It was important to remain humble and small. Having been an only child, she had to remind herself that not everything was about her. She felt an urgent need to go home.

Friday, February 19th

Patricia slowed down her Prius and glanced at her phone's screen. It was a text from Eric.

client not buying the idea

She waited to reply until she stopped at the traffic light.

Fuck.

have to stay in seattle till monday. need to rework the forecast

She looked up to check if the red light had turned green.

Want me to fly over there?

busy with the team. let's hang out next weekend in sfo or la, schedules permitting

The line of cars started to move, so she accelerated with the traffic.

K. Cool.

She wrote the last text driving at eighteen miles per hour and quickly put away her phone just before a police car sped past her, beacon flashing, siren blaring. She was relieved when the officer stopped another motorist. She'd been fined before for using her cellphone while driving but, like every other Angeleno, she could not abide by that particular law. It was impossible to be out of touch during the long periods of drive time. This rule would have to be updated to meet the changing needs of society. Either that, or technology would have to hurry up and deliver the much-anticipated self-driving cars, not just for the elite, but for the masses, so people could focus on other tasks while getting from one place to another. This was, of course, a not-so-novel concept to people who lived in cities like New York, where public transportation had allowed multitasking since way before the tech boom. She envisioned a fast-arriving future where transportation would become on-demand driverless-car services owned by fleets, corporations, not by individuals. You could call a ride through an app and get a driverless vehicle to suit your need at that particular moment: one passenger, two, four, or more. Are you hauling something large? Are you going long distance or just a few blocks? Privately owned cars would be as obsolete as typewriters. Parking lots would be converted into apartments, since cars would be operating 24/7 with no idle time. She wondered what Eric would have to say about her ideas.

Eric lived in the future. He enjoyed an ultra-fine-tuned gut feeling that allowed him to predict consumer trends for brands and corporations. Chief culture officer was his title at Avenir, the trends and strategy company he'd started with his best friend from middle school. His routine involved dissecting every other newspaper, magazine, and blog, no matter how mainstream or

114

obscure, how well established or under-ground; talking to people in bars, restaurants, clubs, schools, galleries, and at events; watching broadcast television, streaming and binge-watching digital content, listening to radio talk shows, stalking shoppers at grocery stores and passengers on planes to ask them questions about their purchasing habits. He conducted focus groups on all kinds of themes, fact-checked current research, and examined the competition. He then met with CEOs to discuss his vision of things to come. He braided together what appeared to be random social facts, interpreted odd consumer behaviors, discerned patterns that no one saw, and delivered stories about the destiny of products and services to bigwigs in boardrooms around the world. He sometimes got involved in the nuts and bolts of the operations; for instance, as Patricia sat in her car that day, Eric was at a client meeting in Seattle working out some logistical details for Flying Burrito, a start-up company he was helping launch, which would deliver fast food to college students via drones. That's what Eric did. "I see things coming," he'd joke.

Eric and Patricia met when she attended a panel on career opportunities in the tech industry for graduates at UCLA, which he moderated.

"Just be aware," he told a group of female students when they approached him with questions after the panel ended and most people had left the room. "Women are outnumbered by men in the tech industry four to one. They get bypassed, isolated, pushed out. It doesn't look like it's going to improve much in the next few years. You're a new generation; I hope you can change that."

It might have been his directness, or perhaps the way he pointed his big Frenchman's nose straight at her, that made Patricia invite him for drinks.

"I don't see an obstacle," said Patricia later that night after she took a swig of her mezcal, her eyes fixed on Eric's nose as he tilted his head to allow his shot glass to reach his lips. "You think women are not prepared to fight that battle? Just try us."

Dazzled by Patricia's assertiveness, Eric proposed within two months and the two were married despite Keila and Oscar's dismay.

"Why so soon? Can't you just wait to see how the relationship evolves?" asked Oscar, puzzled.

"We're fast-tracking it. It's going to evolve

116

as we go. He already accepted my one major condition, which is that I stay in L.A. with you and Mom. I can keep raising Daniel here, with your help. Eric really doesn't envision himself as a father figure anyway, so he's going to keep living in his Queen Anne landmark house in San Francisco. That's where he likes to manage his virtual office. I'll fly up to visit him on weekends. It's going to work out fine, Papi. Don't worry."

Patricia parked in front of Claudia's house and texted her.

I'm here.

Coming!

Hurry up. I hate parking on PCH. It's a fucking racetrack.

Take it easy. We're just going shopping.

After fifteen minutes, during which Patricia sorted out a client emergency, replied to three emails, jumped into a conference call that she had previously excused herself from, and added a coat of fresh nail polish to her manicure, Claudia emerged from her house with a wrinkled Barneys New York

117

shopping bag, apologizing (but not really) for being late.

"I don't like where this is going with Mom and Dad," said Patricia while speeding down Pacific Coast Highway. "They barely talk, they haven't scheduled another therapy session, and Dad just wanders around the house, or he drives off and doesn't come home until late at night."

"Maybe he has a lover," said Claudia as she rolled down the window to get a whiff of sea breeze.

"Why would you say that? He's never given a hint."

"Then where does he go? With Aunt Belinda managing the finances, he only has to go to the office once a week."

"Somewhere dusty," said Patricia, wondering if that was some sort of indication of her father's strange behavior.

"How do you know?"

"I've noticed dust on his car. He hoses it down right away when he comes home. I've seen him."

"Oh, look at you, the little gumshoe! I'm going to start calling you Philip Marlowe," said Claudia.

"I'm just saying."

"Everyone washes their car at least once a week," Claudia said, as if there was nothing

118

unusual about that practice, even in the middle of a drought. "Lover. I'm telling you," she added a couple of minutes later.

At the store, Claudia went straight to the designer dresses department.

"I want to return this item," she said to the salesperson behind the register, taking a black dress out of the shopping bag.

Patricia pulled Claudia aside and whispered in her ear, "Didn't you wear that to Mom and Dad's dinner a couple of months ago?"

"Of course not. You're confused, little Marlowe. I have many black dresses," Claudia mouthed back.

"This is too embarrassing. Text me when you're done."

Patricia was familiar with Claudia's long-standing habit of returning clothes she'd already worn. She'd keep the tag attached. She'd wear the clothes only once. She'd refrain from using any perfume. She'd bring them back quickly and exchange them for something else. She'd only select items that were under eight hundred dollars, preferably at Barneys or Bloomingdale's, and would never, ever return anything at Neiman Marcus. For Patricia this behavior was consumer abuse of the worst kind, a betrayal of the retailer's trust, and she sided with the retailer. She wandered off to the shoe department to distract herself. She tried on a pair of Louboutin ankle boots that she had added to her shoe board on Pinterest. John Varvatos had some nice ones, too. She finally picked a pair of studded, laceless Sartore boots, perfect for her boyfriend jeans. She wasn't much of a shopper. Her trips to the mall were mostly for work, when she needed to do store checks or observe certain consumer habits. When she wanted to buy something, she'd shop online, but mindless shopping at the point of purchase was an ideal activity that allowed her to think about other issues, namely, her parents' possible divorce. Did her father's behavior deserve such drastic retribution? Or was it something else? She wished he wouldn't be so hermetic, so like a Tupperware container. She needed to find out what it was that hurt so much. After all, *she* was his chamaquita and believed she had a better chance of succeeding than her sisters.

Claudia was trying on sunglasses when Patricia found her.

"I've been looking all over for you. Don't you check your text messages?"

"I'm here, right? Let's go," Claudia said, and grabbed her handbag and shopping bag from the counter and headed for the door.

"You know, dust on the car doesn't rule out the possibility of a lover," she added, picking up the conversation where they'd left it earlier.

"Oh, stop it. What's the likelihood of either of our parents taking a lover? And I thought you weren't returning worn clothes anymore. We talked about this already," Patricia said as she followed her out.

"Stay out of this, Patricia, or I won't invite you shopping anymore."

"Oh, what a loss. I guess I'll have to miss the excitement of watching my sister trick the store."

As soon as they reached the exit and pushed the door that led to the parking valet bay, two security guards (who surely also worked as nightclub bouncers in the evenings) surrounded them.

"Please come with us. You're being detained for shoplifting," said the bigger man, looking Claudia straight in the eye.

"This is ridiculous! I'm a frequent customer!" said Claudia, raising her voice.

"You have a pair of sunglasses on your head that you haven't paid for."

Yes, that was the tactic. Patricia had seen her sister steal glasses before, cheap ones, nerdy reading glasses that she didn't need, at the drugstore. She'd try them on, pull them up like a headband, and try other pairs. Then she'd walk away wearing her own glasses with the stolen pair still on her head. Why didn't she notice she had two pairs of glasses on her head? She instantly regretted not being more vigilant of her sister's schemes.

"I swear it was a mistake," said Claudia. "I really thought they were my own glasses."

That argument was crucial, as it released Claudia from culpability and positioned her as just an absent-minded shopper.

Still, both sisters were taken into a back room where a young manager in a suit waited at the desk, his eyebrows carefully shaped.

"You're lucky the merchandise you were trying to steal is under five hundred dollars. It qualifies as a misdemeanor, but you'll still have to go to court and pay a thousand-dollar fine."

"Why are you being so hostile? I'm a longtime Barneys customer and a huge fan!"

"But Barneys is not your fan anymore, I'm afraid. In fact, you won't be able to come into the store or any other Barneys anywhere in the world ever again. If you do, you'll be arrested," said the manager. "All of this will be spelled out to you by our attorneys."

"With this attitude, you're going to go out of business!" Claudia warned.

After two hours in the room, where both sisters were searched and frisked by the guards, interrogated by the manager, and kept locked up until the police arrived and filed the report, they were finally let go.

"Listen to me," exploded Patricia when they were finally back in the car. "I'm never, fucking ever, going out with you if you steal again!"

Sunday, February 28th
Felix kept making up excuses to get out of watching the twins. Patricia was swamped with work. Claudia wasn't an option. Keila and Oscar, forget it. One babysitter bailed at the last minute: *"Sorry, I just dropped my phone in the toilet!"* The other one showed up but had to leave as soon as she arrived: *"Oh, my God! My tattoo is oozing!"* So, weathering another heat-record-reaching ninety degrees in the middle of February, Olivia dressed the twins in their Sunday best, secured them in their car seats, and drove in intolerable Friday-afternoon traffic down the 134 past Universal Studios, Warner Bros. Studios, the L.A. Zoo, Glendale, and Eagle Rock straight to Lola's house.

"Who in the world are these two sweetie

pies?" Lola exclaimed as soon as she opened the door. "Come in! I have some cookies."

"We're here to say hello," said Olivia. "I wanted you to meet Diana and Andrea."

Lola squatted to see the girls at eye level. "Are you Andrea?"

"I'm Diana."

"Ah, so she's Andrea! Who is older?"

"I am," both girls chimed in at the same time.

Lola produced some sheets of paper and a box of crayons and sat the girls down at the table to draw. "I always have these around for little visitors. Keeps them out of my cabinet with the porcelain dolls," she whispered to Olivia.

"I went home very sad the last time I saw you. I really thought I could persuade you to help me with the twins. You didn't give me a reason."

"I don't know if you'll understand."

"Try me."

Lola knew she was better at showing than explaining, so she turned to the twins. "Who wants ice cream?"

The twins yelled in excitement.

"Let's go to Scoops!" said Lola.

The shop was a few minutes away, but Lola, in the passenger seat of Olivia's car, took the long way, asking Olivia to meander around the neighborhood as she pointed at newly remodeled houses.

"Do you know how many friends I've lost because of people like you? See that house? My friend Elsa lived there for years. She got evicted and now lives in Victorville, where she can afford rent. I haven't seen her since she left."

They passed in front of another house, this one with a modern façade. "See that one? That was Rosario's. She's way out in Hemet now. And that one on the corner? That was where David lived. An old flame. Gone from my life. It's hard for me to put that aside and come work for you."

Olivia was silent all the way, taking in Lola's point, but after they ordered their ice cream and found a little table to sit at with the twins, she said, "I understand, Lola. I haven't been paying attention. I see a house where others see a home. I am very sorry."

Lola adjusted Andrea's bib and said, "Don't eat so fast, mi niña." She sat the girl on her lap, took a tissue out of her purse, and wiped her mouth. Then she reached across the table to roll up Diana's dress sleeves and to wipe up a spill of ice cream on the table. "Careful, sweetie," she said. "You don't want to get your pretty dress all dirty."

Olivia thought about the innumerable moments when she'd found warmth and safety in Lola's arms. First came the scraped knees, the bee stings, the lost toys. Then came the girlfriend fights and the boyfriend betrayals, the parental punishments, and the constant bullying that Claudia inflicted on her.

"I will take care of these girls for you," Lola finally said. "But you need to promise me something."

"Just ask."

"You won't flip anything east of La Cienega."

MARCH

Thursday, March 3rd

The promise of record-breaking rainfall in Southern California, courtesy of El Niño, had been keeping Oscar awake at night. During the day he'd search on the internet for any news quoting celebrity forecasters from NASA, AccuWeather, and the Weather Channel. They all agreed with the National Oceanic and Atmospheric Administration that March was still too early to tell how much water the climate phenomenon was bound to deliver by the end of the year, but they were already calling it the Godzilla of El Niños. At night Oscar would shuffle downstairs in his pajamas and slippers and sit on the portico to wait for raindrops; even one would keep him hopeful, but as the dry months went by he'd begun to wonder if the much-anticipated monsoon would ever happen.

In his recurrent nightmares all he could

see was smoke, smelly, orange smoke, the sign that the fire was near and it was time to run for your life. On this particular evening, he woke up with a start, overcome by a vision of his house engulfed in flames, his grandson, Daniel, barely escaping collapsing beams, rolling on the dry lawn in a futile attempt to put out the flames scorching his pajamas, his hair. This is what the drought in March meant: fires in September. Every plant and tree was tinder in the making. He tried to calm down, but the anticipatory dread would not go away. He walked to Daniel's room and the sight of him placidly sleeping helped. What awaited them in the coming fire season? Would their house in Rancho Verde survive another year? Living in the wildland-urban interface, that zone where nature and city cohabited (or collided?), where your surveillance camera could spot a mountain lion roaming in your backyard while you slept, where you needed to keep your pets inside at night or they could become dinner for a pack of coyotes, where the birds nesting in your trees were falcons and owls, where you could discover a deer and her fawn just a few feet away from the eight-lane 405 freeway, was both awesome and terrifying. He could not stop thinking that it was this unashamed human encroachment into nature that was causing so much destruction.

Whenever he succumbed to despair this way, he resorted to his own escape: he tippy-toed to the driveway careful not to wake anyone up, got into his SUV, and drove out of the city. He headed north on Interstate 5 for two and a half hours, got off the freeway, took a side road and then a dirt road, deep into Kern County. Lit only by the head-lights, small cloudlike clusters of white flow-ers hanging on low almond tree branches seemed to welcome him into the darkness. He parked a safe distance away from one of many beehouses he'd seen along the rows of trees and got out. Those bees were brought in every year for pollination just before the bloom started. Winter downtime was over. Soon the almond shells would harden and the kernels would start to form. He knew all this because he owned the land he was standing on. He had bought Happy Crunch Almond Orchard a few years ago on impulse and no one, not even Keila — especially Keila — knew about it. Only Aunt Belinda, his father's sister, was in on the secret, since she was in charge of the fi-nances of the business, as Oscar's father would have wanted.

In the eighties Keila found out Oscar had

just sold the land in Santa Clara to developers. Why hadn't he told her about his intentions to sell it? Had he been afraid she would oppose his idea? Or was it because of the prenup that cut her, his lawful wife, out of his trust? In order to inherit, the heirs to the fortune of the great Don Rodrigo Alvarado and Doña Fermina de la Asunción Ortega had to sign an agreement by which their spouses would not be included in the inheritance. To wed a member of the family, a bride- or groom-to-be had to accede to this. No one in the family knew why their ancestors wrote that particular clause. Some speculated that perhaps they had envisioned a future in which most marriages didn't last long and their fortune would ultimately end up in the hands of ex-spouses. Others didn't give the issue much thought. But for Keila this requisite had been a thorn from the start. She'd gone from questioning if it was even legal to exclude spouses from the Alvarados' fortune to acceding to that ridiculous, archaic, never-heard-of-anything-like-it demand as a way to show Oscar that she loved him in spite of being treated as a second-class family member, as proof that she wasn't marrying him because of his money.

Oscar's failure to discuss or at least inform

Keila of his plan to sell the land only made the distasteful nuptial agreement more odious to Keila. It was the one thing that had made her hesitate when Oscar proposed.

After Keila finally agreed that the sale of the land had been for the benefit of her family and he promised to include her in any future business decision, Oscar spent years searching for an opportunity, but every time he came to her with a proposal to buy this or that piece of property, Keila would turn it down flat.

"We have all the money we need. We could just live off the interest and not even touch the capital. Why go through the risk and trouble of starting a business? You can relax now. Think of yourself as retired."

Like many entrepreneurs, Oscar had never considered retirement. He had always had visions of himself dying at his desk, a ninety-year-old man who could barely keep his head up or hold a pen in his shaky hand, his reading glasses hanging from the tip of his nose, and his long-nailed, cadaveric toes sticking out of a hole in his worn-out socks. He had imagined he'd be closing his eyes for the last time feeling the satisfaction of having multiplied the value of his inheritance twentyfold. But it wasn't so much the financial accomplishment. His intent had always been to pay tribute to his ancestors' heritage, their profound pride and respect for this land of promise and possibilities. Millennia after the first indigenous Californians settled along the coast and inland all the way to the Sierra Nevada, Oscar's grandfather, Don José, married Doña Peregrina, the daughter of Don Refugio, who had received as grant the rancho next to theirs, Rancho Peñék, named after a legendary cat that had been spotted roaming the area. Both families thrived side by side, raising cattle and sheep and selling hide and candles. Two generations later, Oscar inherited a small fraction of this bountiful land, what he believed was an honor and a fundamental responsibility. He was sure he'd make his ancestors proud, if they could only witness his success.

When the proceeds of the sale of the land in Santa Clara hit the bank, he came to Keila with the idea of buying old houses in Venice and repurposing them into retail space.

"Who would want to shop on Abbot Kinney when there are plenty of nice shops on Wilshire? Furthermore, who would want to lease retail space in Venice, where it's full of stinky, aging hippies and derelict-sofa-cluttered alleys?" Keila was quick to answer.

Oscar dropped the retail-space idea, but then, while exploring the area even further, he walked along the Venice canals and imagined an exclusive neighborhood with multimillion-dollar homes overlooking a pristine waterfront.

"You must be joking! Why on earth would people want to live on those canals, with bad access, condemned sidewalks, and stagnant water filled with mosquitoes and floating dead rats?"

Another opportunity rejected by Keila was the purchase of industrial buildings in Culver City, to be renovated as workspaces.

"There's nothing in Culver City, not even a McDonald's. And the movie studios already have their own buildings."

Then there was the garment building in downtown Los Angeles, which could be converted into live-in lofts.

"You're in L.A., you want a nice big house with a backyard and a pool, not a clothing factory pretending to be a living space next to Skid Row. Want that? Go to New York!"

And finally, before he gave up presenting business ideas to Keila, who, after all, was an artist and what did she know about real estate, anyway, came the suggestion of buying homes to renovate and flip in Silver Lake.

"Do you really believe anyone would look out the window at a fenced-in cement reservoir and see a lake, and a silver one, for that matter?"

Now, years later, flanked by rows of trees, Oscar walked in the dark, dragging his slippers in the dust. He suddenly realized that he might not be able to die proud of his work. He regretted having listened to Keila. Over time, his real estate ideas had proven to be not just right, but visionary. Had he invested in all those properties, he'd be a wildly successful landlord; he'd be a true Alvarado. But he wasn't. Instead, he'd bought a water-guzzling almond orchard right before the worst drought ever recorded in the history of California, and now all he cared about was saving it without telling Keila he owned it.

He broke a twig off a low branch, one with tiny buttons of bloom, and bent it just a bit to check if it was pliable, a sign of life. When it didn't snap at the pressure of his fingers, he smiled, walked to his car, and returned home with a mix of renewed hope and fear of Keila finding him out.

Monday, March 7th
Armed with hopeful umbrellas after an inconsequential morning drizzle, Olivia,

Felix, and Lola drove to the pediatrician's office at the hospital to get the twins checked. Follow-up visits were not as frequent anymore, and this one would be the last regarding the pool accident after the doctor gave the girls a clean bill of health.

"We'll go for tacos afterwards," Olivia promised the twins.

Lola was quickly settling into Olivia and Felix's home — she got the guest room with a view, flex days when she needed to work at Legal Aid, and time off when she wanted as long as Olivia could cover for her — and while she was happy to see that her little Olie was now a mom in her own right, she found Felix abusive and arrogant, just the type she'd always despised. If it weren't for her love for Olivia and now the twins (who had instantly populated her heart), she would have left, gone back to Highland Park, and been done with the nanny business.

"We're running late," said Felix, irritated, as he trailed a line of cars sluggishly rolling down Vermont Avenue. "And it's your fault," he snapped at Olivia. "I can never get you out of the house on time. Why the hell did you have to change the girls' clothes right before we had to go?"

It was clear to Lola that Felix was itching

for a fight. A petty one, again, like the others she'd witnessed since she moved in the previous month. She reached out and quietly pinched Olivia on the arm. Olivia found Lola's eyes in the rearview mirror and knew not to answer Felix's question.

"There's the Children's Hospital. We're almost there," said Lola to diffuse the situation.

As she waited outside the pediatrician's office while the twins got checked, Lola remembered the promise she made to herself to always stand her ground, to never be like her wimpy, submissive mother always bending to her father's will. Such a sick macho. Perhaps that was the reason she never found a suitable husband. And now here she was, saddened to watch Olivia endure this man's temper and foul mood. Suddenly, she felt a pressing need to defend her.

On the way home, Olivia noticed in the rearview mirror the girls in their car seats talking with Lola, partly in Spanish with a few English words thrown in, and partly in their own toddler language. She had been adamant about educating the girls not just bilingually, but biculturally, with a little dose of Jewishness: pork carnitas tacos from Porkyland, a Jewish-owned Mexican food joint in El Monte, were a favorite meal; she, Oscar, and Lola spoke to them in Spanish, Keila spoke to them in Hebrew or Yiddish; and salsa, merengue, boleros, cumbia, and reggaeton filled the rooms in the afternoons.

When Felix married Olivia he had promised to learn Spanish, but had never gotten around to doing it.

"Make an effort. Spanish is not that different from Portuguese," she'd say, reminding him how well he spoke it with his mother, back in Lisbon.

"Portuguese is my native language just as Spanish is yours. Why don't you learn Portuguese?" he finally snapped back one day.

He had a point, Olivia thought. Language had been a delicate issue between them, "delicate issue" being the precursor of "taboo subject" in the context of spousal arguments. And just before it turned into a full-blown battle, Olivia decided to stop insisting, focusing on the twins' education and ignoring Felix's.

Wednesday, March 9th
After making her weekly stop at the Zen car wash (Claudia loved going in the meditation room while her car got cleaned), she went for Korean tacos. It was her hope

never to eat the cleansing kombucha probiotic amazon elixirs, matcha chia puddings, turmeric-infused kale and supergreens smoothies, massaged avocado and Inca spirulina algae salads, gluten-free baked goods, bland egg-white spinach omelets, God-help-us protein bars, or the vegan whatever-it-was that pretended to be something else, say burger meat or cheese, that was ubiquitous in Santa Monica, Westwood, Culver City, West L.A., Venice, Silver Lake, Echo Park, Silicon Beach, Koreatown, West Hollywood, Los Feliz, Brentwood, well, she might as well just say "everywhere." As much as those culinary clichés had traction among certain Angelenos (Patricia, for instance), the reality of the city's gastronomic landscape included ingredients like boar's ears, quail gizzards, kid goat testicles, octopus smothered in its own ink, corn fungus, ant larvae, toasted grasshoppers, and Palos Verdes rooftop salt. Claudia integrated in her recipes any herb and spice that she found and smelled with pleasure, no matter whether it was part of the Mexican repertoire or not, as she felt guiltlessly free from the weight of authenticity enforced on cooks in other parts of the world. Grains of paradise, asafetida, kaffir lime leaves, hoja santa, pasilla chiles, achiote, chepil, or epazote; she had everything she could imagine. With so many farmers' markets, smugglers, and specialty suppliers, there was nothing beyond any chef's reach. Except foie gras, a decadent extravagance. "There are limits to condoning inhumane behavior; no duck or goose deserves such cruelty, just so people can enjoy their grossly fattened liver," she'd tell other chefs. Thankfully the government had banned its sale (on and off over the years, but, oh well). After all, this was California, and she respected the law (sometimes).

By the time she reached Vermont Avenue — every other storefront posting signs in Korean and Spanish — she had vowed never to use such overused and inaccurate words as "fusion," "global"/"local," "syncretistic," "niche," "assimilated," "mash-up," and, worst of all, "California cuisine," which was so broad and overused it meant nothing anymore. In her perennial search for the best foods regardless of cuisine, exploring the vast cornucopia at her disposal, she'd realized that the little mom-and-pop restaurants in the mini-malls were where she found the mother lode of deliciousness. Why? Because immigrants operated them. They had brought their homeland's flavors in their suitcases and were adding them to the never-ending gastronomic experiment that took place every day in Los Angeles. She loved to observe, but more important, to participate in the frequent overlap between different cuisines, resulting in an endless continuum of delight and surprise. Multiply that by more than one hundred and fifty countries and you had yourself Angeleno cuisine.

Claudia had considered opening a food truck, but developed a TV show and a catering business instead. She'd done sold-out pop-up experiences whenever she found a suitable location, but mostly she poured her passion into her cooking show, damn the Michelin stars.

She left her car with the valet, sat at the farthest table, her preferred spot right near the kitchen (to better smell the aromas that spilled out into the dining room), and ordered plain old short-rib tacos with kimchi. She moved the napkin aside (according to Keila, true foodies didn't use one; they licked their fingers) and rearranged the condiments on the table, a habit of hers. But when her meal arrived, she was, curiously, fast asleep, her head resting peacefully on the table by the Tsang stir-fry sauce and the bulgogi sauce.

■ ■ ■ ■

Thursday, March 10th

Avoiding each other around the house became a contactless sport of sorts. If Keila was in the kitchen, Oscar went to the living room. If Oscar was in the backyard, Keila stayed inside. If they crossed paths on the staircase, they'd turn their backs to get past, like people do in an airplane's tight aisle. Oscar had refused to move to another room, so Keila put a pillow between them at night, like a barrier, a symbol of her Crossed Legs Strike. At the table, Keila would ask Patricia, sitting next to Oscar, things like, "Please tell your dad to pass me the salt."

"Is this how you're working on mending your marriage?" Patricia would ask, irritated. But neither of her parents would reply, seemingly stuck in a rut.

Most times, Oscar would drive to Happy Crunch Almond Orchard and come back late at night. If he stayed home, Keila would make up endless errands around the neighborhood, schedule lunches with her friends from book club, or get spa treatments at the gym.

That night, in bed, as Patricia observed how the rhythm of the house had changed, she wondered if she was witnessing, up front and in real time, her parents' marriage implode. She buried her face on her pillow and wept.

Friday, March 11th
Felix forgot it was Olivia's birthday. She didn't remind him.

Sunday, March 13th
Oscar had two watches. The nice one and the one he wore whenever he traveled with Keila. "If I get mugged, I won't be sad to lose this cheapo," he'd say, proud to outsmart the crooks.

This morning, he adjusted both watches to daylight saving time, wishing he could advance the hands all the way to harvest season and skip the complication of watering his almond trees during the summer months.

He went to the toolshed by the pool's heater — a useless piece of junk now that there was no pool to heat — and sat at the worktable to study and prepare. The next day he'd be attending an Almond Field Day and there was much to learn.

Monday, March 14th
Early on this chilly sixty-two-degree morn-

ing, Oscar drove along Highway 33 in Lost Hills, where the Almond Field Day sponsored by the University of California Cooperative Extension was being held. Armed with a coat, hat, sunscreen, and good walking shoes, he parked his SUV and made his way along the rows of trees showing off their full bloom to where the group of growers was already listening to the experts give their talks in folding chairs. These were UC Davis professors and soil conservationists. Him? He was a good student, exemplary, if anyone asked. As he listened to the panelists discuss highly technical topics like integrated crop pollination, or the latest in blue orchard bee research, he realized how much he'd learned about almonds since he first set foot on the land that was now Happy Crunch Almond Orchard, and how much he had yet to understand. He remembered when years before, looking on LoopNet, a commercial real estate website, for a property to buy, he'd come across an almond farm for sale. All the previous options he'd considered had been properties in the city: office buildings, apartment complexes, interesting ideas, yes, simple business opportunities, but nothing that made his heart leap. But when he saw the pictures of rows of almond trees in bloom he felt an unexpected closeness to his Mexican grandfather, Papá José, and his grandmother, Mamá Peregrina. He imagined the soil under their fingernails; their skin, sunburnt; their callous hands from working the land. How could this farm not be his calling? He'd bought it within weeks and started not just his new endeavor — a natural way of life for a true Alvarado — but a family secret that tore his heart in half: the left ventricle filled with joy, the right with dread.

When the panel ended and the growers clapped and walked over to the panelists to ask questions, he checked his own fingernails and there it was: dirt.

Tuesday, March 15th
Destroy? Donate to science? Cryopreserve? Give up for adoption? The letter from the fertility lab came on a day when Olivia was in Montecito delivering a home she had just finished remodeling and Felix happened to open the mail. It was a routine notice that was sent every two years to couples who had embryos in cryopreservation, to find out if their decision had changed since their original consent. Demand was high in those days. The labs would have a better use for embryos idly sitting in the freezer. Fertility

tourism had increased from countries where in-vitro fertilization was illegal. Desperate couples came to California to adopt embryos and get implanted, going back home with the promise of a family. As the field of human genetics advanced, people with hereditary diseases could now choose to adopt embryos with healthier genes to avoid passing down their illness to their offspring.

When Olivia came home that evening, Felix presented the options to her, with his final choice.

"Destroy them, of course."

"There's no way we'll kill our last two embryos. They are babies in the making, like Diana and Andrea."

"And how do you envision making those babies?"

Felix's stinging words sent her straight back to the day Diana and Andrea were born. Placenta percreta was the name given to her condition. Thirty-two weeks into her pregnancy and not able to continue to term, she was rushed to the hospital hemorrhaging severely. The two placentas that enveloped her babies had grown hundreds of veins and attached themselves to her uterus, causing intricate ramifications in her entire reproductive system, like the thirsty roots of a tree, and had ventured into her bladder.

This was her body's answer to how much she wanted to hang on to her children.

The C-section had turned into a slasher-movie scene, with doctors and nurses splattered with blood, surgical instruments flying around, gauze after gauze ending up in trays that were replaced at high speed, and plenty of instructions yelled in foul language. As soon as Diana and Andrea were pulled out of Olivia's womb, she lost consciousness and didn't realize that she had delivered a set of healthy twins until six days later. The girls were hastily taken to the crib to get stabilized while the doctor removed Olivia's uterus. Blood donors lined up, mostly family members with matching blood type, and a few other visitors who were later given chicken sandwiches and juice boxes and sent to sit in the waiting area to recover while the doctor tried to save Olivia. By the thirteenth hour, the doctor gave up on his race to cauterize each vein in order to stop the bleeding and called a team of gastroenterologists preparing to perform a gastric bypass surgery in a nearby operating room and asked for help.

After several days of touch-and-go recovery, Olivia was finally allowed to see her daughters for a brief moment.

"I can't think of a happier time in my life,"

she said to Felix, teary-eyed, as soon as the nurse took the babies back to the crib.

Felix shook his head in disbelief, thinking about the painful and scary details of Olivia's ordeal, and suddenly felt severely shortchanged by Nature for not giving men the ability to bear children.

Now, with the form from the fertility lab in her hands, Olivia realized that Felix was right, as he put it bluntly: "No factory, no product." How could she bear more children with nothing left of her womb but a hole impossible to fill?

Felix broke into her thoughts, bringing her back to the letter from the fertility lab still in her hand. "I'm sick of the drama our parenthood has brought us. Miscarriages, stillbirths, surgeries, treatments. I'm done!"

"But look at what we *do* have! Two beautiful girls! Wasn't it all worth it?"

"My decision shouldn't be a surprise. You know how I feel about all this. Those embryos have no chance anyway."

He pulled a pen out of his pocket, took the form from Olivia's hand, checked off the option to destroy the two remaining embryos that were in cryopreservation at the lab, signed at the bottom of the page, and slid the letter across the kitchen table for Olivia to sign above her name.

"I'm not signing this. We made the choice to preserve when we first started the treatment and I'm not changing my mind now."

"This letter is going to stay right here, on this table, until you sign."

That was the table where countless conversations between Olivia and Felix had taken place. Witness to their angst and desperation to create a family, the table sat in a nook adjacent to the kitchen, withstanding tears, fist slams, laughter, and screams throughout the years. The anticipation before a result, the disappointment that came afterward, the exhaustion of it all bounced back and forth across the table, like a ball in a tennis match. To anyone else, this was a typical mid-century modern teak table with four chairs designed by Hans Olsen in the fifties. Beautifully round. Well kept. Barely a scratch. Many a knockoff had been built over time, but this was an original. Olivia had found it during one of her frequent rummaging excursions to thrift shops around town. Immediately recognizing it, she bought it for next to nothing and rejoiced all the way home, with the chairs barely fitting in the minivan's back seat and half the table sticking out of the open back door. But objects are known to change meaning, and this table, now, was a landscape of discord.

"Just leave the letter there. I'll take care of it when I'm ready," said Olivia, and left the kitchen, accidentally banging her hip against the countertop.

Once in her bedroom, she texted Patricia.

I need you.

Patricia was on a flight back to Los Angeles to meet Eric for drinks and a fuck at their usual hotel right outside LAX before he got on a later flight to San Francisco, so she didn't see Olivia's text until eight seconds after the plane's tires touched the runway.

What's going on?

Felix wants to get rid of the embryos.

Can I come over later?

No. He's home tonight. I'll come over tomorrow after work.

During happy hour — Negroni for Eric, mezcal for Patricia — she kept thinking about Olivia, and continued to throughout her lovemaking session with Eric. But toward the end, with her inner thighs pressing against Eric's ears, and just before she felt what she later qualified as a monster orgasm, she switched her thoughts from Olivia to Benjamin, her client at Target. This unwanted thought was becoming more frequent, and more so when her clitoris was being stimulated. Why was Benjamin intruding in her intimate life with Eric? It wasn't even a sexual image, just flashes of Benjamin rapping his fingers on the conference room table, or Benjamin checking his phone and typing away with his thumbs, or Benjamin looking into Patricia's eyes and saying, "You're so right." She pushed him out of her mind and focused on the moment. Her time with Eric was a scarce commodity and she had to maximize every minute of it. During their after-sex routine, she cuddled in his arms. It was the wrong time to find gaps in their calendars where they could coincide somewhere, but they did anyway.

"I want to tell you something that's been on my mind," said Patricia.

Eric put his shirt on and grabbed his pants.

Patricia felt compelled to disclose her thoughts about Benjamin, but instead delivered a different one, a suspicion that she had been nursing for a while.

"I think Daniel is gay."

150

"Are you sure? How do you know?"

"I don't. I'm just guessing."

"Has he said anything about being gay?"

"No. I wish he had. He seems more irritable and restless, even tired. He complained that some kid at school called him 'bean queen.' I got the kid's name and told Mrs. Rodríguez. She demanded he write Daniel a letter of apology, but Daniel is still undone. Any thoughts? How should I approach this?"

"I'm glad you told on that stupid kid. I can't stand demeaning slurs. What a little asshole. He should have been suspended."

"I know. What an asshole."

"As for Daniel, if you want my opinion, I think it's healthy to be open on the subject for all involved. Just ask him directly. I don't know."

Patricia had hoped Eric would give her a bit more moral support. But what she usually got was stern words directing her relationship with Daniel at every turn. "Where's his homework? You let him play video games again!" he'd snap.

Over time she'd become aware of his inability to get emotionally involved, especially when it came to Daniel. Perhaps it was a result of Eric's strict French education at the Lycée Français, always focused on

151

emphasizing failures as opposed to praising accomplishments. Quite the opposite of what she'd experienced at her Montessori school.

"That's my thinking, too," she said, resigned.

She thanked Eric, and after a hug and more kisses, he hopped on the airport shuttle and Patricia drove home wanting more from her husband, but not really being able to pinpoint exactly what.

Wednesday, March 16th
The most loved space in the Alvarados' Spanish Revival–style home was the living room, designed to welcome large groups of guests who gladly sank into the comfortable sofas sprinkled with cushions of various sizes and fabrics. A small collection of Latin American and Chicano art decorated the walls. Among Oscar's favorites were a Linda Vallejo painting and a small Carlos Almaraz drawing, but it was mostly art pieces created by Keila that were the highlight — couples in love, couples in distress, all in high-fired polychrome ceramics. But Olivia and Patricia were not sitting in the living room that evening. They preferred the kitchen counter, perched on stools, each drinking a beer straight from the bottle.

"Don't sign it, just leave the letter where it is. He'll forget about it and one day it'll be gone."

"Impossible. He's going to insist until I drop dead from old age."

"He can't make you destroy the embryos and he can't make a one-sided decision. If you don't agree, you'll have to lawyer up."

"What? No! He's my husband. I want us to agree on our own, but I'm afraid it's not going to be possible. The best I can do is procrastinate. He did say he'd wait. Maybe he'll agree someday."

Patricia nodded uncertainly.

"Look, all I want is to hold on to the embryos, to keep them right where they are. They are a possibility, a promise," continued Olivia.

"Not to give Felix any credit, but he has a point. There's not much you can do now, after what you went through during Diana and Andrea's birth. Why keep them?"

Olivia was silent for a moment. She played with the beer bottle cap and looked out the window not registering that the sun, in its daily act of setting, had just painted everything orange.

"They're mine," she said, loud, clear, for the world to listen.

Patricia realized that Olivia would not give in.

"If that's your final decision, how can I help?" she asked after a long silence.

"Just hug me."

Patricia reached over to Olivia and put her arms around her. "Forever, sis."

And in that embrace, the memory of so many colorful family calendars that had been posted on the refrigerator year after year noting everyone's comings and goings popped into Patricia's mind. The kitties calendar, the puppies calendar, the Provence calendar, the Disney characters calendar — all of them thematic and showing different pictures every month. She realized that there was a strong thread of unity with Olivia, and this made her hopeful for the rest of her family. She thought about her parents' commitment to try to repair their marriage but couldn't come up with any visible effort. And just when her hopes were about to dissolve, Keila came into the kitchen looking for scissors to cut ribbons for the Easter baskets she was making and found her daughters in mid-embrace.

"What's going on?"

"Felix and I got into a fight," said Olivia, half whimpering. She'd never dare worry her family with details of Felix's impulsive behavior and nasty reactions, his aggression against her, thankfully always stopping right before committing battery.

"Come on, sweetie. No man is worth your tears."

"This is my husband, Mom. And it's not the first time I'm crying because of him."

"I'm only trying to be supportive. It's all right if you feel you need to reject my advice. I'm not worthy of your trust," she said, thinking about the twins' accident under her watch.

"Mom, please, that's an entirely different situation. Focus on the issue here: Felix wants to get rid of the two leftover embryos."

Still a bit hurt after not hearing Olivia say she'd regained even a sliver of trust and at the same time understanding the crisis at hand, Keila shyly volunteered: "Why? Is it the money? I thought you were paying for the storage."

"I am, but that's not it. I don't care about the money. He's just fed up with the problem. He believes that this whole process damaged our marriage."

"I get why you want to preserve the embryos indefinitely. I can only imagine your pain at the thought of destroying two potential little people. I'm surprised Felix doesn't understand this. They're fifty percent his!" said Keila, trying to move past her sudden outburst of guilt-triggering behavior.

"I'm starting to think this whole thing is doomed. I'm so tired of all the fighting. We bicker for no reason since the twins were born."

"There's always a reason, but sometimes we don't see it," said Keila, tiptoeing around the subject so as not to upset Olivia even more.

"I know the reasons, but what I mean is that they're not terrible enough to justify a big fight. We argue over which school the girls will go to, the color of the bedroom drapes, which days of the week Lola gets off, if I use the towel next to the shower, or if I wear my hair up in a bun. I give in most of the time and I'm exhausted. Come over here, Mom. Let's not hurt each other."

Olivia extended her arms and Keila joined in the embrace. To a stranger, these three women might have looked like a tightly twisted human Oaxacan cheese ball of compassion, but to Keila, the gesture was a vivid demonstration of her profound motherly love for her daughters. She felt a snippet of hope for reconciliation, a first step toward forgiveness. She thought that a future series of sculptures could depict this very moment of familial solidarity, a knot of arms, legs, and torsos exuding love, and came up with the concept for a couple of pieces in high-fired clay right on the spot.

"I know you'll find a way to resolve this situation with Felix. Your brilliant mind is already at work. I can hear the gears clinking and clanking in your head." Changing the subject to lighten the moment, she said, "Are you all coming to the egg hunt on Easter Sunday?"

How could they miss it? Easter celebration was one of their most cherished traditions. They regularly skipped Mass and went straight to the champagne brunch and egg hunt in their backyard, the latter being, according to Daniel, the best part.

"I tried calling Claudia to see if she can bring dessert, but she's not answering her phone. Do you know where she is?"

"Definitely not at Barneys," said Patricia.

Friday, March 18th
When Oscar arrived at Happy Crunch Almond Orchard, Lucas, his right hand, was waiting for him under the shade of a tree.

"I'm glad you came to watch the beekeepers move the colonies away," said Lucas, pointing with his gaze at four men loading

157

beehives into a truck, not far from where they were.

"Of course. I'd thank each bee, if I could, before sending them off."

"They're taking them to Idaho this year. They'll be back in California in November."

Lucas had worked the orchard along with his cousins Mario and Saúl, Los Tres Primos, as they were known, since Oscar had purchased the land. He'd arrived years before from Tulancingo in the state of Hidalgo, deep in Central Mexico, a city famous for being the birthplace of El Santo, the legendary wrestler. Lucas had immigrated young and hopeful, knowing nothing and owning less, and thanks to his drive to succeed he had become an authority in all things almond farming. Not just Oscar, but neighboring growers went to him for his advice.

"They're going to want the balance when they're done," said Lucas.

Oscar knew that once the check he was pulling out of his billfold cleared, he'd have near zero funds left. He'd need to get another loan. He wiped the sweat off his forehead and gave the check to Lucas.

"I hope the amount is correct. Here, you pay them, please. Make sure you get a receipt."

Oscar didn't wait to watch the bees start a new journey. He got into his car and drove back to Los Angeles, imagining the disastrous scenario of running out of money and not being able to pay Lucas, Mario, or Saúl, his guys, his team, his beloved people.

Sunday, March 20th

When she first met Gabriel, Claudia was not as wildly fascinated by his gym-toned body, or by his exceptional abilities between the sheets, as she was by his line of work. He presented himself to her as a story hunter, launching her imagination into worlds of cultural espionage and discovery that she had never visited, let alone inhabited. As a chef, she mostly lived in kitchens among pots, pans, and ingredients, dealing with male cooks in cramped spaces, wielding sharp knives, and yelling expletives in Spanish. She spent hours on end catering events, shooting her TV show, and writing recipes for her cookbooks. She'd always considered her job to be exciting, but when Gabriel described his business to her she concluded that his was the most exotic profession she'd ever heard of, even more than that of arctic explorers, astronauts, or circus acrobats. Gabriel sensed her interest and played it to his advantage during their brief dating period, to lure her into marriage. To anyone else who heard him, he sounded cocky and conceited, but not to Claudia, who had quickly become smitten with him.

"The most powerful thing that can be traded among people, more valuable than gold or painite, is a fucking good story," he told Claudia on their first date.

His pitch went like this: "Literary scout is an incomplete title. My job is to search for, find, and broker stories between authors and movie studios, TV networks, streaming platforms, and publishers. I know that the best stories may be in a secondhand bookshop in Prague, or the attic of a long-dead writer in Mississippi, or in the backstory of a YouTube sensation, or even in the fading memory of an old war hero succumbing to dementia. My work is part detective, part cultural anthropologist. I am a spy, a researcher, a negotiator, a trendsetter, a socialite, and a dealmaker. This is the reason I own this one-man niche. I supply the world with the most brilliant stories in adrenaline-packed adventures concocted by writers, stalkers, hackers, and odd characters, and then produced and marketed by heads of studios and publishers who come to me with preemptive offers. I have the power to turn someone's obscure dream into one hundred TV episodes, then syndication. I can find a screenplay written in film school and turn it into a blockbuster. That's why I have open doors to every Hollywood studio executive and New York publisher's office."

During the three years Claudia and Gabriel had been married, he'd found stories that had become improbable hits, like the voluminous and mesmerizing sci-fi trilogy written and self-published online by an unknown young Mexican author who had taught himself to write in English. The books had morphed into box-office-record-breaking movies, and a much-anticipated TV series spin-off was underway. During a subsequent Oscar party, to which Claudia wore a Chanel dress that she returned intact to the store the following day (not even a little champagne drop), she realized that Gabriel was a celebrity in his own right and that there were several people who'd be happy to have a piece of him, some of them men climbing the Hollywood ranks, but in particular a blonde with fake breasts that spilled out of her plunge. And by the way, wasn't her dress a Valentino from last year? It was hardly vintage, and that gave Claudia self-assurance, but still, as prevention against a potential hostile takeover, she held Gabriel's hand tight for the rest of the evening, except when she had to abandon her cocktail or greet the CEO of a major movie studio.

Gabriel's regular trips back and forth across the country and the fact that he owned an apartment overlooking Gramercy Park in New York and lived with Claudia and Ramsay, a yappy Yorkie, and Velcro, his cat, in her beach house in Malibu, qualified him as a bicoastal creature. "It doesn't matter if I fly east or west, I'm always heading home," he'd say.

"I'm struggling with all his absences," Claudia confessed to Patricia one afternoon while shopping for jeans on Melrose Avenue. "When I see him packing his suitcase I get flaming heartburn. How can you stand living apart from Eric?"

"Your situation and mine are complete opposites. You didn't ask for Gabriel's constant travel. It just fell on you to endure. In my case, I negotiated with Eric so I could stay in L.A. with Mom and Dad and Daniel. See? I want it, you don't. Take charge, Clau!"

Patricia was right. To Claudia, Gabriel's eastbound flights felt like a sword slicing her life in two: with and without Gabriel. She resented the fact that she had been forced to withstand his weekly absence, even though she knew from the beginning that his nomadic life was part of the package. On most weeks, he'd go to New York from Tuesday to Friday. He'd set up breakfasts, lunches, cocktails, and dinners with an assortment of industry people that Claudia had never met. "I can't talk now, I have back-to-back meetings," he'd tell her in the blunt, demanding, tough New York mode that he adopted when he was there. Successful bicoastal navigation meant more than just ping-ponging between coasts. True bicoastalites knew that they needed to morph into New Yorkers or Angelenos as they flew in each direction.

To illustrate why he chose to conduct business on weekends by the pool when he was in Los Angeles, Gabriel once told Claudia, "In New York, you brag about pulling all-nighters. You take your laptop to your Bahamas vacation and boast that you had conference calls every day. You self-exploit, you wear the bags under your eyes like badges of honor, and you erroneously believe that Angelenos are laid-back and lazy. In Los Angeles people are like ducks on a pond. They glide effortlessly on the tranquil surface, but when you go underwater you can see that they're frantically paddling along. They just won't admit it to anyone. You think they're just walking the dog at eleven in the morning, but they're really making some deal on their cellphone. Don't be misled when you see two women chatting over manicures. They're actually negotiating a contract. To survive you have to keep your cool. Angelenos only sweat in public at the gym."

On the days he was in New York, or wherever his story hunting took him, Claudia stayed back in Los Angeles, ate avocado-and-bacon tacos, refused to make her bed, binge-watched TV series on her laptop, and didn't shave her legs. She rarely went to New York with Gabriel, except when going on a gastronomy trip to peruse the ever-changing restaurant scene. The six years she lived there when she was a student were not enough to get used to the Manhattanite tone and manner of speech. Oblivious to her own habitual rudeness, she often ended up getting her feelings hurt by random people, mostly obnoxious waiters and disrespectful cabdrivers who had obviously adopted the prevalent stance.

The Sunday before Easter, when Claudia missed serving a catering event at the Skirball Cultural Center (an unheard-of over-sight), Gabriel did not hear Claudia's assistant's frantic voicemail: "She never told us about this event!" He was in New York having brunch with his Simon & Schuster contacts to discuss the true story of a musician who had voluntarily gotten crucified, so he found out about his wife's crisis only that evening when there were no more flights available to come home. By the time he came back to Los Angeles on Monday, the situation had been sorted out, except for a lawsuit the Skirball Center was threatening to file.

After Claudia had failed to answer calls from her office on Sunday afternoon and Gabriel could not be reached, her assistant called Olivia for help.

"She was supposed to be the star of the luncheon. They had to cancel and send everyone away. There was no food whatsoever."

Olivia drove to Malibu in the hope that she'd find her sister at home. Her house was a skinny one, sandwiched between others like it in a long row that separated the Pacific Coast Highway from the ocean. The façade was not impressive in any way: a garage door, a front door, and three trash bins, a blue one for recycling, a black one for regular garbage, and a green one for garden trimmings. There was barely a space to park and no sidewalk to protect pedestrians from cars barreling down the road.

Olivia parked her minivan next to Claudia's Audi TT, picked up the spare key tucked in a downspout behind a flowerpot, and went into the house, calling her sister. Ramsay greeted her with little jumps, and for a second Olivia thought he wanted to tell her something important, but he just looked her in the eye and barked and ran to the terrace.

Claudia was lounging by the pool in her bikini, a spread of gossip magazines by her side on the deck floor, Velcro rolled up by her feet, and an empty glass of wine on the side table.

"Where have you been? You missed the Skirball Center's event. Your staff didn't even know about it."

"Yikes."

"Yikes is all you're going to say? Everyone's been calling you. Where's your phone?"

"It might be out of juice. I haven't heard it."

Olivia walked to the edge of the terrace, leaned on the handrail, and looked out at the Pacific Ocean in front of her. Its undulating surface shimmered in bright oranges and reds, sequins in a drag queen's gown. This was a light — a hyperreal, Technicolor light — that existed only on celluloid and in Los Angeles. She wondered why Claudia didn't seem to care about having missed a catering event. It was so unlike her. Under normal circumstances she would have jumped out of her lounge chair and initiated immediate damage control. In fact, under normal circumstances this would never have happened to her sister. She wondered if Claudia was drinking too much.

"How did this happen? Didn't you have the event on your calendar?"

"I haven't checked it lately."

"Wasn't the Skirball Center in touch with you, especially right before the event? Didn't your people know?"

"I'm not sure I ever told them, so don't blame them. The event might have just slipped my mind, or something. Stop asking me all these questions!"

"Look, I have no idea what's happening here, but it's your business. You'll have to deal with it. I just came to see if you were all right."

"I'm fine."

"Are you sure? You don't sound like yourself."

"I'm just chilling here, can't I?"

Olivia couldn't conceal her concern. She worried that Claudia would catch her and start mocking her, as she always did.

"See you at Mom and Dad's next Sunday, then," said Olivia.

"Yes, I'll be there."

Claudia took her sunglasses off and picked up a magazine, waving her sister good-bye.

"Promise?" Olivia looked her sister in the eye in search of a nonverbal commitment and noticed that her pupils were unusually large. Maybe it wasn't alcohol. Was she using drugs?

"I'll be there, I said."

On her way out, puzzled by Claudia's lack of reaction to the situation, Olivia stopped in the kitchen to get a bottle of sparkling water for the road. She sensed a faint smell of gas in the air and noticed that one of the stove's burners was slightly on. She turned it off and opened the window to let the stench out. She then refilled Ramsay's empty water bowl, fed Velcro, and drove home.

Lola was bathing the twins when Olivia arrived. Felix had arranged a twilight open house in the Hollywood Hills, an ever more frequent practice among Realtors like himself who wanted to show the property for sale in all its dusk glory, and would not be home until later that night. He hadn't landed a deal in months and his foul mood was beginning to irritate everyone around him.

Rolling up her sleeves and kneeling in front of the bathtub, Olivia joined Lola in the soapy procedure of getting Diana and Andrea clean. As a result of the swimming pool accident, Olivia had asked Lola to fill the tub with as little water as possible.

"I think you're exaggerating. The girls don't seem to be afraid. Look at them, so happy in the water!" said Lola.

"It's really just me. I'm scared of going through another accident," Olivia told Lola.

"There's more, Olie. You're sad, worried. What is it?"

There was no point in trying to hide her anguish from Lola.

"It's about that letter in the kitchen, am I right?" asked Lola, knowing the answer.

"Felix wants me to tell the lab to destroy the embryos, but they're my babies too, Lola. I can't obey him."

"He plays games with you all the time, Olie. He knows you're a better mother than he is a father. He is jealous of your success, but he wants you to make money for him. He wants to be the boss, but he can't and

169

he is bitter because of this. That's why he's torturing you."

"I want to divorce him, Lola."

Olivia went to bed without waiting for Felix to come home, as she always did. She heard him walk into the bedroom in the dark and pretended to be asleep. She heard him bump his foot against the ottoman by the armchair, and heard him brush his teeth in the bathroom, before she felt his body by her side, under the sheets.

Monday, March 21st

Who cares if they won't approve another loan? thought Oscar.

"I'm so sorry," the bald branch manager had said. "We have to decline this application. In fact, any future applications."

"But why? I own my house free and clear. I've never filed for bankruptcy, never had a foreclosure, you can see my record: not a single delinquent payment, ever!" Oscar said, exasperated.

"You've reached your limit, at least with us."

"Fine, then. I'll take my business to another bank."

"Suit yourself. And good luck."

Oscar walked out of the bank holding a

170

thick manila folder in his hand. With so many financial institutions out there, he didn't need to worry. It was just a matter of finding the right one. His trees would be getting water no matter what. He'd find the money to pay for it. He owned the property free and clear. Perhaps an equity loan? Or a mortgage? Would he get approved with the amount of debt he'd accumulated? As he picked up his SUV from the valet, he began to wonder if he should have worn a suit instead of his preppy casual attire. In a city where the big shots were capable of wearing flip-flops, shorts, and baseball caps to important meetings, he had assumed that dress codes were irrelevant when visiting the banker. He tried to shake the feeling of self-doubt, straightened up in his seat, drove home, and sat in front of the TV for a half hour before he turned it on.

Wednesday, March 23rd

Precisely at 10:47 P.M., Patricia went outside to smoke a joint, her path lit up by the full moon. She lay on one of the lounge chairs around the cement keloid scar, bundled up in her adored, old, comfy Mexican wool sweater from Chiconcuac, the kind that Marilyn Monroe used to wear, and looked up to the sky. What was that longing she felt? It seemed to her that Eric had a very limited bandwidth when it came to feelings: he was basically transactional, so that she sometimes felt life with him was like having a sexual relationship with her bank teller, if she ever dealt with one anymore, as she banked only on her phone these days. Their intellectual and sexual connection was satisfying, but his emotional byte count was low. She felt shortchanged by the universe, and looking up at the moon only made it worse. Why did Earth only get one moon while other planets had so many? And why didn't our moon have a sexy name, like Elara or Ananke? Just Moon. It was like having a dog and naming him Dog.

Friday, March 25th

Good Friday wasn't so good for Oscar. He woke up trying to remember the last time he'd been to church, but drew a blank. Someone's wedding, perhaps. Or when his mother died, maybe. He'd been a good Catholic boy, attending Mass without question or complaint, terrified by the statues of multiple saints bleeding and in agony, and wondering if martyrdom would be his destiny. Unable to see the altar due to his childhood stature, he'd avoid looking at the gore that surrounded him by focusing on the only other thing he could see from his vantage point: the behinds of the women standing in the pew in front of him, which oftentimes tempted him to delicately free their dresses from the crack between their glutes' cheeks.

Having married a Jew was not why he had drifted away from the Church. His disillusionment happened much later, after he'd heard so many stories of children molested by priests. Now he was too far away from his faith to ever come back, but if asked he'd always answer that he was a Catholic, which meant to him that he had lost his religion but not his identity.

As he got out of bed and brushed his teeth, he realized he was on his own, with no god to ask for help. How would he solve his troubles with Keila? He took her toothbrush between his fingers, smelled it, then tasted it and sighed.

Sunday, March 27th
By Easter Sunday Olivia felt better about her decision to leave Felix and had already concluded that for the sake of the twins she would not make a fuss until it was a done deal. No one had to know. Not yet.

The reason why Easter was a much-preferred holiday over Passover was obvious to everyone in the family: What was more fun, hunting for Easter eggs and eating chocolate bunnies or spending hours at the Passover table and eating matzo? But the Alvarados still celebrated both holidays, as was their tradition, and on that chilly, sixty-three-degree, cloudless Sunday the family gathered in the garden wearing their spring best to roll around in the grass and dig dirt out of the pots and planters to find the coveted candy eggs that Keila had spent hours hiding early in the morning.

"Where is Claudia?" asked Patricia.

"Someone call her," said Oscar, a bit worried.

Olivia dug in her purse for her phone and called her, but again, there was no answer. Was something wrong with her sister?

APRIL

Saturday, April 2nd

Truth is, Keila never really left Mexico. Often, say, once or twice a day, her mind would leave her body in Los Angeles, zoom past San Diego, jump over the rickety border fence, fly over the Sonora Desert, over the state of Durango, the Sierra Madre, Zacatecas, Guanajuato, and helicopterland right on top of the roof of her house in Mexico City, all in a split second. When she was barely a toddler, her parents had bought a home too large for her three-member family, right on the main drag of Polanco, the affluent Jewish neighborhood, on Avenida Presidente Masaryk. Why a street of such importance in Mexico City would be named after a Czech politician remained a mystery to Keila, one that never piqued her curiosity enough to research, even years after she'd moved to Los Angeles.

Every time Keila transported her mind to

175

the rooftop of her house, she scanned the neighborhood and checked what had remained and what had changed. To her disappointment, much was different. Barely anyone lived on Masaryk Avenue anymore. Over the years, most of the mansions where her childhood friends had lived had been converted into flagship stores for brands like Chanel, Prada, and Gucci, where salespeople earned a fraction of the price of a single garment in an entire month. The streets on which she rode her bike as a child, carefree and unsupervised, now were blocked by traffic gridlock, but crowds still flocked to the high-fashion mecca to window-shop, as most people couldn't afford anything these boutiques had to offer, and those who could would prefer to take a quick weekend flight to Houston's Galleria and save, even after paying for travel expenses, as most clothing brands were pricier in Mexico, with no thanks to NAFTA.

But shopping wasn't everything. Keila was delighted by the fact that the neighborhood had also become a hotbed for gastronomy, where celebrity chefs reinvented Mexican cuisine for demanding patrons. She considered herself a curious foodie, but it bothered her that boutique hotels with no remaining trace of Mexican architecture had popped up everywhere. You could go into any of those hotels, all of them designed in a new minimalistic, sleek style, and feel transported straight to New York, London, or any other metropolis in the world. There was no uniqueness anymore. Gone was the influence of the famous Mexican architect Luis Barragán. No more colorful walls, monumental geometric spaces, and wood beams. Keila missed the charm of the old California Spanish Revival carved stone façades, now replaced by double-height storefronts of glass and steel. But she also understood the pressing desire Mexicans had to be perceived as cosmopolitan, to project their country into the global landscape. Sacrifices needed to be made, elements of national identity had to be lost, and architecture was one of them.

This time Keila was actually there, in the flesh. Not on her home's rooftop, but in her parents' bedroom, now hers, getting ready to meet with Simon Brik later at his gallery to finalize details of her show. She resisted applying more makeup than usual. She put her hair up in a ponytail, and although she'd brought a low-cut blouse, she kept it in her suitcase and instead wore a black turtleneck sweater, knowing how frequently Simon's eyes wandered in the direction of her breasts.

To avoid spending hours looking for a parking spot, Keila took an Uber to the gallery. Simon waited for her at the door.

Aside from a last-minute removal of a piece Keila despised (it wasn't representative of her feelings at the time she created it), Simon's sculpture selection remained unaltered.

"I sense you're not fully comfortable with the show. Is there anything else you'd like me to change?" asked Simon, preoccupied, as he paced around the gallery's main room.

"You can't change what I want changed."

"Try me."

"It's not related to the show."

"Is it about us?"

"There are so many questions I need answers to before I get to the subject of us."

"I can help. Let me. Please."

Simon put his hand on Keila's. She withdrew it quickly, as if pressed by a hot iron.

"I'll wait. I'm the champion of waiting. Just be open to the idea," he said.

"I'm dealing with issues at home, and I need to go through it alone."

A spark of hope lit Simon's face.

"Let's focus on the show," said Keila, to shift the topic before she regretted confessing any more details of her angst.

Most of Keila's friends, collectors, art junkies, and people looking to score a free glass of wine went to the show that evening. At least a couple hundred, according to Simon. The unwritten dress code that encouraged people to wear black to gallery openings made it difficult to distinguish the event from a funeral, more so if one noticed Keila's somber expression, as Simon did when he found her hiding in the back room instead of mingling with her fans.

"You could be the widow at a wake," said Simon in a soft voice, out of respect for a nonexistent deceased person. "We just sold the seventh piece. You should be happy."

"I'm very pleased to see that the show is going well," said Keila as she took a swig of wine from a plastic cup. "Look, I'm sorry for spoiling the evening."

"How long have I known you? I'm a Keila expert by now. I could swear this doesn't belong here," said Simon, tracing Keila's frown with his pinkie, barely staining the tip with her deep red lipstick. "That smile of yours, always there, even when you've delivered to me your worst statements of rejection. Where is it now?"

"Buried in a crisis that I can't confide to you, not just yet."

"Is it Oscar?"

"It is, but it's not the Oscar I've loved for so long. This Oscar is different," she said, wondering which was the real one, scared of admitting she'd made a mistake, a life-wasting judgment error.

"Go home, Keila. You have to."

Sunday, April 3rd

Sixteen of the eighteen pieces sold during the show. Keila went back to Los Angeles with jumbled feelings. She had never been so close to keeping her hand under Simon's and accepting his caress, but later she approved of her instinctive retreat. She acknowledged her sense of accomplishment for selling almost her entire inventory. Of course, she still had the other series of couples in conflict, but Simon had a fierce aversion to it. "All that back-turning in bed, it's such a put-off," he'd told her. She could start a new series, but she reminded herself of her Crossed Legs Strike in protest of Oscar's odd behavior. Was she punishing herself? Although she missed working in her studio, she knew she'd only produce work depicting anger and disillusionment. That's how revealing her work was about her state of mind.

Oscar greeted her with his decision not to

go back to therapy, as soon as she prompted him once again, as she'd done for the past few weeks.

"There's no point," he said, sitting on a lounge chair facing the kidney-shaped cement patch in the middle of the lawn where the pool once sat, the infamous keloid scar reminding both Keila and Oscar of their near-fatal carelessness.

"So you're giving up. One single therapy session was enough? You're done with our marriage?"

"I'm done with therapy. You're the one who started this nonsense! I'm happily married!"

" 'Happily' doesn't describe who you are these days. Don't try to sell that one to me."

"Let's try on our own. I really want to."

Keila went to her studio and locked the door. She lay down on an old couch, her beloved red love seat, and forced herself to calm down, counting slowly to one thousand.

Wednesday, April 6th

Ever since she met Felix, Olivia had been the victim of love's contradictory forces, hostage to bouts of joy, melancholy, misery, humiliation, and violence flooding her entire being all at once, leaving her spent, and now

181

the scrambled feelings had hardened into a single one: rage.

Searching for the original sensation, she dug deep into her well of shit, the one that doesn't show up on chest X-rays but everyone has, right behind the sternum, and came up with the terrifying realization that the most perilous thing she'd ever done had been to kiss Felix in the TED Talk auditorium parking lot. That act was still reverberating. It would never be over.

Olivia sat in front of the form sent by the fertility lab, now wrinkled around the edges and stained with coffee and still unsigned. Felix stared at her across the table, his lips tight, as if trying to prevent his mouth from spewing a vicious insult, but if that was the intention, he didn't succeed.

"I have no reason to bring to the world more people with your genes and mine. It's like trying to mix oil and water."

Something happened when Olivia heard his rejection. The crack inside her was subtle but final, announcing that the accumulation of hurt had reached its limit. There was no point in wishing that Cupid had missed the shot. Life had happened and there she was, at her kitchen table, facing a truth she'd tried to reconfigure over the years into some fanciful myth of harmony and bliss that she could believe and bear to live with.

"I don't love you anymore, Felix."

Olivia couldn't tell by Felix's expression, which was devoid of emotion, whether he had been expecting a blow of such magnitude or if it had caught him by surprise. He slowly got up, picked up his car keys from the kitchen counter, and headed for the front door.

"I'm moving on," she said, waiting for the door to slam, but it didn't.

Olivia wondered if Felix's final exit from her life would be as quiet and smooth, but in a flash she acknowledged this was not the way he operated. She began to imagine the turmoil and pain that she had just unleashed. He would force her out of the house. He'd take the girls, not out of fatherly love, but out of spite. He'd fight for the embryos just to destroy them. She feared that he knew how much she wanted them and he was not going to let her succeed, even if he lost, too.

She ran outside and banged on Felix's car's windshield just as he was pulling out of the driveway.

"Felix, stop!"

He rolled down the window, unmoved.

"Whatever we do, whatever happens between us, please don't hurt the girls. Keep

183

them out of this," she pleaded.

"You and I have nothing else to say to each other. Expect a call from my lawyer. And, just so you know, he's a monster and he's going to crush you."

As he drove off, he ran over a toy grocery cart that belonged to Andrea. Olivia picked up the broken pieces of yellow plastic scattered on the driveway, put them in the trash bin, and went inside.

Teary-eyed, she went to Lola's room and knocked on the door. It was late at night, but she knew Lola stayed up to watch *Corazón de Oro,* the hit prime-time Mexican soap opera on Univision that she was also hooked on — a story of betrayal, revenge, secrets, horrible sins, a blind character, and another one forever dying in the hospital.

"It's happening, Lola. We're divorcing."

"Have you both made the decision?"

"I made the decision."

Lola rubbed her face, as she did whenever she heard disturbing news. At the same time, she was glad to see that Olivia was gathering the courage to separate from Felix.

There was only one thing more permanent than marriage and it was divorce. All of a sudden the weight of this realization pressed against Olivia's chest and she began sobbing again. She would always be divorced from Felix and there was no way to get out of it unless they remarried each other or one of them died. There was no divorce from divorce. No exit clause in that contract. She was ending a temporary relationship to begin a permanent — and acrimonious — one with the man she was beginning to loathe.

"Come to me, let me hug you."

Olivia let Lola envelop her, like when she was a little girl. She whimpered slowly and used Lola's pajama sleeve to wipe her face. In the background, the actress playing the lead role in the soap opera on Lola's TV set whimpered, too.

That evening, Olivia watched Felix come in and out of the house carrying suitcases and boxes packed with clothes, shoes, and books and loading them into his car. Without saying a word, he walked around taking pictures of silverware, artwork, furniture, rugs, kitchen appliances, and utensils. Clearly someone had started advising him while she had buried herself in her bed, incapacitated by grief. It took her over a week to meet with her friend Carolina Donoso, who was in the process of divorcing. She was hoping to get some pointers.

Monday, April 11th

After shooting one of her cooking shows, Claudia drove home to Malibu, but ended up in Redondo Beach, one hour and twenty minutes in the wrong direction. What was she doing there? How had she gotten so lost? As she turned around and jumped in the car-pool lane, now going north, she ruled the confusion a freeway oddity, the hypnotic effect of a road that turned drivers into mindless automatons. When she finally made it home, she walked inside, leaving the keys in the car and the front door open. Thankfully, Ramsay followed her into the bedroom and jumped into bed with her and Velcro, thus avoiding venturing outside and getting squashed by a speeding car on PCH.

Wednesday, April 13th

"If his lawyer's a monster, then yours must be a fucking T. rex," said Carolina with a sense of authority. She and Olivia lay on towels spread over the deck of the *Ugly Duckling,* moored in the Marina.

"I'm keeping this boat, you know. Just to fuck him over," she continued.

"I'm sure in time you'll develop a taste

for sailing." Olivia wished she had her friend's malice and ability for revenge. She surely could use it now that she was about to start a cruel battle against Felix.

"Very unlikely. But it makes a nice hiding place when I want to be off the grid. It doesn't even have to leave the dock, ever."

Carolina turned over to expose her belly to the sun and took a sip of her Arnold Palmer. It was one of those days when the marine layer had dissipated earlier than usual and people basked in a mild mid-morning sun.

"He's keeping Fang, the asshole. Just because he proved he's the one who walks him and picks up his shit. Yes, of course, while I'm busting my ovaries at the office making the money. I wish I'd married someone like me."

Olivia drove home with a page of notes and advice, as well as the T. rex's contact information. The 405 Freeway, packed as it was with cars sluggishly moving along, gave Olivia ample time to distill her conversation with Carolina. Definitely, she thought, God had invented traffic so people could slow down and think. In evaluating the conse-quences of the divorce process, she had to rely on assumptions, friends' anecdotes, celebrity gossip in tabloids, and a wide variety of films, telenovelas, and books that explored the end of love. She knew she was not prepared for battle and would have to learn quickly.

Protected by her minivan's bubble, she sped home, determined to be swift and smart from that moment on, to remove all passion and lock up her emotions during the ordeal. She'd have time later to grieve and smother herself in her unfulfilled longing for a big and happy family. This divorce would be a business negotiation, and she and Felix and the twins would all win. Her motto would be, "This wineglass shattered; nobody got cut."

A call from Patricia distracted her for a second, but she waited to call her back until she reached her driveway off of Mulholland Drive.

"Can you help Mom with Passover? She needs a lot of stuff and Claudia is not picking up," said Patricia.

"Is she even in town? I haven't heard from her. What are you up to this weekend?"

"I'm off to Coachella with Eric. LCD Soundsystem and Calvin Harris are headlining this year."

"Lucky you. I haven't been to the festival in at least five years. I'll call Mom. Have fun."

"Just don't get that dreadful rabbi-gourmet wine we had to drink last year."

Olivia got out of her car, walked past her garden populated by cacti, and stood in front of her door. How many more times would she be able to open it and enter the house, her house? She and Felix had been looking to buy one. During an intensive and dizzying week, they'd toured dozens of homes in every L.A. architectural style: Spanish Colonial Revival, craftsman bungalow, English and Tudor Revival, hipped-roof cottage, Egyptian Revival, even one Châteauesque in Los Feliz. Finally, a Realtor friend of Felix's had said he'd take them to visit a fixer-upper with potential, but as soon as Olivia walked around the rooms and the yard, it became clear to her that this property was practically a teardown, a hopeless dump. It didn't need tender loving care, as the listing ad cheerfully stated; it was desperate for resuscitation. She immediately fell in love and bought it for half its value; it had been sitting on the market for nearly a year. Bringing this midcentury house back to life had been her masterwork. Rather than renovating it she set out to restore it, using original materials and regarding the floor plan as if it were the Ten Commandments. She researched the records at the building department to confirm her hunch: this was indeed a house designed by the famous Los Angeles architect from the fifties, Jerrold Lomax, and she owed him veneration. Every morning she'd stand by the full-height window to watch the sun peer behind the San Bernardino Mountains slowly waking up the Los Angeles basin. The feeling of openness, of a seamless affair between indoors and outdoors provided by the architectural expressions of modernism in Los Angeles, was what fueled Olivia's passion for finding houses in need of love. She'd renovate them with absolute respect for the initial idea, albeit with modifications to improve the lighting, create more storage space, and update kitchens and bathrooms. That's what potential buyers always looked at when considering making an offer. Over the years she had gathered a crew of loyal and excellent workers, all Mexican, to help her knock down walls, build new ones, rip up floors and carpeting and wallpaper, gut rooms, paint, and landscape. There was Sergio, the drywallero. Tony, the tilero, who worked with his two brothers laying tile, creating little masterworks in kitchen and bathroom floors around the city. Then there was Mauro, her electrician; Javier, her plumber; and Roberto, her rufero. They were her brothers in arms, her second family. And she'd even had the pleasure of attending a few naturalization ceremonies over the years.

At Felix's insistence, she had reluctantly agreed to have smart devices installed around the house: speakers, sound system, security cameras, thermostats, lights, doorbells, burglar alarm, irrigation, and digital locks.

"All those gizmos and blinking lights everywhere disrupt the clean midcentury design. Those things don't belong in a house like ours" was her argument, but ultimately she caved in, fixing one more issue with Felix by being submissive and hating herself for it.

Olivia's latest project had been to convert her garden into a water-wise space. She had removed most of the plants and replaced them with indigenous succulents and palms: a Joshua tree at the edge of the cantilevered terrace, a golden snake next to it, a patch of fishhook, foxtail, and strawberry cacti mixed with different varieties of tall grasses, like the dwarf pampa grass she loved, where the lawn used to be, and her favorite, a young saguaro planted outside the twins' bedroom that would become, in time, a sentinel looming over the house, its arms spread upward to protect the dwellers, when it had reached its full height.

Olivia went in and checked on the twins, who were with Lola in the playroom. When they asked about Daddy, Olivia told them he was on a trip, but then she thought about the latest news she'd heard about him: Carolina Donoso had seen him enjoying the tasting menu with a woman at Providence. She wondered if he had found someone else to latch on to, a successful partner to admire and loathe at the same time. Her stomach churned, so, for her own mental health, she forced herself to think about the innocent bystanders. She knew she'd have to tell the twins eventually about their parents' separation. She wanted the news to be the least harmful to the girls as possible, so she had picked up a couple of books on the subject and highlighted them so thoroughly that most pages were entirely bright yellow.

Since the pool accident she'd been looking for anything odd in the twins' performance, per doctor's orders. Were they slow to react? Did they focus on tasks? How was their balance? Did they awaken easily? Did they look pale? They seemed fine, but she didn't trust her observations, so she took them to the pediatrician regularly for proper checkups, even after they were given a clean bill of health.

After watching cartoons on her tablet for a while with the girls, she went to her bedroom to review her divorce notes. She called the T. rex and explained the situation.

"I've worked very hard during this marriage. I've contributed far more than half of our assets. My husband is a Realtor, but he doesn't make much money and it's not steady at all. I'm assuming I could get half of what we own. What do you think?" she asked on the phone.

"You could have been eating bonbons all day in your bed watching TV, never worked a day in your life, and still get half. It's the law."

"Can I get custody of my girls?"

"That's going to be a problem. Visitation rights. It's always a problem, a big one. Don't think you'll negotiate this one easily. The girls almost drowned in your care. He'll use that against you. You might lose, understand?"

"My mother was babysitting, not me. Does it matter?" Olivia sank in her seat a bit more.

"You left them in your mother's care."

"What about the house?"

"You'll need to fight for that. Most likely you'll have to sell it and split the proceeds."

"And the embryos?" she asked in a raspy voice, the words struggling to make it out of her mouth.

"That will depend on how aggressive we are, but I don't see how you can win this one. It'll be up to the judge."

"How do you know it's going to be so difficult? I haven't given you all the details of my situation yet."

"You don't need to. I know how this is going to go."

He seemed to Olivia to be the kind of lawyer who inflames the spouses just to complicate and prolong the process, taking the case to court rather than opting for mediation. He had said the word "judge," hadn't he? She'd heard of cases that had gone on for years, depleting the family's assets to cover legal fees, and she wasn't about to go through such an absurd scheme. She explained to the second lawyer on the list, a woman, that she wanted the divorce to be quick and fair. Carolina had recommended this lawyer for her swift negotiation skills and strong hand, and Olivia thought she seemed less nasty than the first lawyer. She agreed with Olivia and spoke at length about ways to separate from one's spouse without anyone getting hurt. She considered herself an expert in amicable divorces and shared a couple of cases — without revealing clients' names, of course — that could have gone quite wrong and that she had masterfully steered toward a better outcome.

After Olivia hung up she felt her head throbbing as if a reggaeton rave were in full swing inside her skull. Suddenly, a heavy blanket of sorrow suffocated her. Perhaps there was still time to ask Felix if they could make peace and try to mend the marriage. Divorce was not in Olivia's vision of the future. She felt for a moment that she was living someone else's life and pulled herself back from the dark room her mind was entering. Would hiring a less bellicose lawyer be a mistake? She had promised herself not to hurt anyone, but Felix's threat had scared her. If she wanted to keep the girls and the embryos, she'd have to go with the T. rex.

Thursday, April 14th
Early in the morning Olivia took the girls to Mommy and Me class at a nearby nursery school for two hours of structured play in the sandbox. Lola had business at Legal Aid and was out until the afternoon. Of the

eight moms present, two were discussing their divorces, but Olivia felt unprepared to share her story. Not yet, perhaps never. So instead, she told them about the girls' accident and how they had recovered fully thanks to the pediatrician's thorough care. All the other moms were surprised to learn about the diving reflex and went on to discuss cases they'd heard of drowned children and careless moms who couldn't be trusted with their kids around swimming pools. This conversation sank Olivia into her most self-punishing thoughts, the place in her mind where she questioned her ability to raise her daughters. She realized her guilt was still burrowed deep inside and wondered if she'd ever forgive herself.

After class ended and she changed the twins' clothes, breaded in sand like chicken breasts, Olivia drove them home to Lola and headed back out to buy a set of Passover Seder plates that Keila had seen in a Judaica shop in Westwood.

"Make sure it's the one with Hebrew and English names for each food," Keila had told Olivia on the phone that morning. "I can't find your bubbe's plate set for the life of me. I'm sure it was in the Jewish suitcase in the garage. I even looked in the Catholic suitcase. It was an antique!"

While looking for street parking around the shop, Olivia made a note of future errands. Later in the week, she'd have to buy all the needed groceries: walnuts, apples, wine, pears, horseradish, bitter herbs, and a long list of other items that she still hoped Claudia would take care of, if she turned up. She had no way to confirm her suspicion that Claudia might be overusing prescription pills, or drugs, or alcohol, or all of the above. She'd have to confront her. Then, in the middle of this scary thought, finally, a parking spot, a beautiful one half a block away from the shop, became available.

Luckily, the full set of plates was in stock and Olivia could drop it off at Keila's later on.

"I'm sorry," the saleswoman said, "your card was declined. Do you have another one?"

Olivia scrambled to pull out a second card, which was declined as well. She looked for the credit card that she used for her business, but remembered she'd left it at her desk.

"Maybe there's something wrong with the machine?" she asked in disbelief. "I still have at least two weeks before payment's due."

"I just ran another card for someone else

and it went through," said the saleswoman, tired and annoyed.

"I'll be right back." Olivia went to her car to check the credit card apps on her phone and gasped when she realized that Felix had been staying at the Peninsula Hotel in Beverly Hills. At eighteen hundred dollars a night for a Superior Suite, plus room service, plus charges in an array of famous chef restaurants. Her stomach churned again, but now she could even hear her intestines rumbling. Out of curiosity she checked the balance on their joint bank account and was shocked to discover that thirty thousand dollars had been withdrawn. Her immediate reaction was to call Felix.

"What a small and ineffective way to get your stupid revenge," she yelled at him on her cellphone.

"What are you talking about?"

"The credit cards! The money! You depleted our bank account! You think the judge is not going to notice? If you were trying to shrink me to size, to make me feel powerless, you failed! *I* left *you.* Remember this."

Here was the ultimate conflict avoider shedding her conciliatory skin to reveal her new self. Gone was the era of Felix trying to make her feel like a lesser being. No more put-downs! Armed with unheard-of self-assurance, she called the T. rex to report the incident. As for the Seder plates, she'd have to pass on the task to Patricia.

Friday, April 15th

"We're going to have to cancel our trip to Coachella," said Eric on the phone. "So sorry, Pats." It was right around the time he should be boarding his flight to Los Angeles.

"Why? Are you working this weekend? We got tickets, everything's packed."

"Did you check the weather? It's like a desert storm out there. The winds are knocking down power lines, trees are toppling, and tents at Coachella are blowing away. That's no way to enjoy a music festival. We'll go next year. Promise."

More than the tents, what seemed to be blowing away was Eric himself. Opportunities to meet were getting scarcer these days. This or that got in the way. Plans changed. The client; the partner; the flight; the wind. It was the wind changing direction. She launched the weather app to make sure it was a climatological event and not a metaphor of her marriage.

"All right then, I'll take Daniel hiking," she said, resigned.

■■■■

Saturday, April 16th

Unbeknownst to Olivia, a coyote ate her next-door neighbor's cat at 3:38 A.M. right below her bedroom window. The following morning she'd find some of the remains on her driveway and the rest among the cacti and grasses she loved so much.

Sunday, April 17th

After posting a series of angry messages denouncing anti-vaxxers in support of World Immunization Week, Patricia prepared lunch and drove west with Daniel.

She parked near the trailhead at Los Liones Canyon in the Santa Monica Mountains. It had always bothered her to have to live with misspelled names of places and towns. The early Spanish-speaking Californios, who named and renamed most of the places in the state, would surely flunk out of even the easiest of spelling bees today: Los Liones as opposed to Los Leones, La Cienega as opposed to La Ciénaga, Calabasas as opposed to Calabazas, Garvanza as opposed to Garbanzo, La Jolla as opposed to La Joya. She could go on, as she had a hefty collection of examples, but chose to focus on Daniel.

"We can go up in less than two hours if we keep a good pace," Patricia told Daniel. "Then, we can have lunch at the Parker Mesa Overlook and be home way before dinnertime. Okay with the plan?"

She ruffled Daniel's caramel mane, a mop of hair that had once been home to a colony of lice that he'd caught at the school's swimming pool.

"Okay with the plan!"

They walked along a mildly graded path with patches of shade, avoiding the occasional spiderweb and the chaparral branches hunched over from thirst. In other times, the canyon floor would be covered with wild lilacs and the spring bloom would burst with color, but these were times of dust and death on the Earth's skin. She knew well that she was walking on a bed of matchsticks, a highly flammable landscape that could turn into an inferno at any moment. She could see burn scars from old fires on the surrounding mountains and made a mental note to review the contents of her go-bag. She hadn't updated it since the last evacuation and couldn't remember if she'd packed cellphone batteries, or if they were in her earthquake survival kit.

They stopped at a clearing on a ridge to

drink from their canteens and to get a view of the Santa Monica Bay, not quite a thousand feet away beyond the mouth of the canyon.

"I'm glad Bubbe didn't come with us. She'd slow us down!"

"Don't underestimate your grandmother. She may seem old to you, but she's super strong."

"She said we might adopt a cat, but you'd have to say it's okay."

"We'll have to discuss that with her. By the way, did you save the coupon to buy the trekking shoes you want?" she said, steering away from the cat issue, as she wasn't a fan of felines.

"It's going to expire next week."

"Well, then, let's go shopping tomorrow."

Patricia paused for a minute before finally guiding the conversation to what was on her mind.

"So, whatever happened with that kid who called you bean queen?"

"He's still harassing people, but not me, at least not to my face. I know he talks about me behind my back. He's a stupid jerk."

"Are you still upset?"

"It makes me mad. Now other people think I'm gay."

"And how does that affect you?"

"I don't know. I'm angry, I guess. What do they care if I am or not?"

"Would it be a terrible thing for you if you were gay?"

Daniel kept quiet until they reached the top of the trail. They faced the enormity of the Pacific Ocean shimmering in front of them. Both took a deep breath at the same time.

"Would it be terrible for you if I was?" asked Daniel finally.

"Of course not," said Patricia in her most determined voice. "I accept you and love you no matter what. I will always protect you. I'll be your forever fan. I will turn into a vicious panther to defend you. You know that. If we were living in the eighties I'd be worried about your health. If we lived in a repressive country where being gay is illegal, I'd be worried about your safety. There will always be people who have a hard time accepting what's only natural. But here we are in twenty-first-century California. It can't get more progressive than this. What do you think?" she said, feeling discomfort deep inside, knowing that even under those favorable circumstances Daniel would eventually endure expressions of hate one way or another. But she wasn't about to discuss that with him, not just yet.

"I don't know, Mom. I guess it would be okay. Bubbe always tells me that you have to be true to yourself. Does that include being gay?"

"It sure does," said Patricia, silently chuckling at Keila's predilection for quoting self-help books.

"But how do I know if I'm being true to myself? I don't know if I'm gay."

"What would be the signs?"

"Maybe that I like a boy?"

"Do you?"

"Yeah, this one kid in swim team, but I'm not really sure. There's also a girl. Sometimes we swap our lunch. Her mom's a really good cook."

"I suppose your true self, as Bubbe says, will reveal itself eventually. I have gay friends who have always known, with no doubt whatsoever. For other people it's a process. I don't think there's a right or wrong way. It just happens. Why don't you take this one step at a time?"

Daniel flung a stone down a small ravine. In the distance, the ocean, contained by the bay, minded its own business, oblivious to the momentous conversation that had just taken place.

"We can always talk about this again, you

know that, right?" said Patricia, hugging Daniel. This time, he didn't wiggle out of her embrace.

Monday, April 18th

After Daniel finished his homework, after he played a video game, after he went to bed and turned the lights out, he hugged his pillow and thought about the boy on swim team.

Saturday, April 30th

Passover was always at the Alvarados'. They owned the holiday as if they were observant. It didn't matter that they weren't. No one really cared. It was all about tradition. Thirty or so family members and friends gathered every year to conduct the same rituals, sing the same songs, and eat the same food.

They all sat around the same three rental round tables for ten settings laid out on the patio, served by the same waiters, and catered by someone other than Claudia, who refused to cook Seder food. Did they talk about the same issues? Yes. Did they tell the same jokes? Yes. Did they feel they were stuck in a comfortably predictable loop, repeating the event over and over, in which whatever happened the rest of the year was just the in-between? Of course, except this time it was different for two reasons.

First, Olivia had to make up an excuse for Felix not being at the dinner. As with most lies, hers was convoluted: "Felix went to pick up one of those trees the city was giving away for free today. It's a program around Earth Day, you know. They're handing out free trees. He was planting it in the canyon and he threw out his back. Nothing serious. But he's in bed, watching TV."

Second, and most important, at least for a family who didn't much care about Felix's absence, Prince was dead. The entire Alvarado clan, as hard-core fans of his music, spent a good portion of the dinner talking about crying doves and purple rain. They discussed drugs and brought up names of other celebrities who had died of overdoses in the past couple of years.

"We're losing all the talent to drugs," sighed Patricia.

"And what about the thousands of people killed with illegally exported American guns in the Mexican drug wars, many of them innocent bystanders?" said Keila, whose indignation rose to red-flag levels every time she watched related news on Univision.

"I'm glad none of you girls has ever used

drugs," said Oscar, with 100 percent certainty.

An awkward silence fell over the group. Patricia picked up her cellphone, casually avoiding looking directly at her father. Olivia was about to say something when she felt a kick under the table. Since she was sitting between her two sisters she couldn't tell who had warned her to shut up. Claudia behaved as if she weren't there. She took a not-so-enthusiastic swig of wine and with her fork dragged the food around her plate, perhaps hoping to improve the taste.

Keila had noticed Claudia's enlarged pupils. She hadn't said a word throughout the entire dinner. She seemed distracted, like a teenager in a school test who doesn't know the answers and, defeated, decides to daydream instead until the bell rings. Keila knew that there was plenty of drug abuse among chefs. She had known a friend of Claudia's who had overdosed and died right in the middle of his restaurant kitchen. To her knowledge and contrary to the trend among cooks, Claudia had no tattoos and had not become addicted to any substance — but looking at her now, in her high heels, her slinky dress (was that a price tag peeping out from under the armpit?), and her normally perfect hair now in disarray, she wondered if she had missed a sign that could have helped Claudia remain clear of the danger.

As Keila tried to shoo away negative thoughts about her daughter and instead focus on the rituals of the Passover dinner, Claudia suddenly got up, clumsily knocked her folding chair to the ground, and wobbled toward the house, zigzagging erratically across the patio until she reached the cement scar in the middle of the lawn, where she collapsed facedown.

Sunday, May 1st

There is nothing benign about a benign brain tumor. Even a small one the size of a blueberry can cause irreparable damage. Keila wondered why people always compared tumors to fruit: it's the size of a grape, the size of a kiwi, the size of a lemon.

"Claudia's tumor is the size of an orange," said the neurologist the day after Passover, when he explained the results of the MRI to Keila and Oscar.

In the immediate confusion, after Claudia collapsed, Aunt Belinda had poured a pitcher of ice water on her head, thinking she had passed out from alcohol ingestion. Someone took her shoes off. Someone else loosened her belt. A third cousin even slapped her in the face repeatedly until Oscar made her stop. Eric shouted orders in French that everyone ignored, but Claudia remained unresponsive. Keila desperately shook her and yelled, "Stay with me!" This was the only phrase she could think of, a catchphrase characters in TV series always seemed to say to a victim who has been shot and is about to die.

In the chaos of the emergency, no one realized that the paramedics who responded to the 911 call were the same ones who months before had rescued little Diana and Andrea from the pool. With such knowledge of the terrain, they deftly whisked Claudia away and rushed her to the hospital. Several friends of the family, each in their own car, followed the ambulance, forming a procession eerily similar to those of funerals, only at twice the speed. Needless to say, the party was over.

Once Claudia was admitted to the ER, a number of tests were performed, a process that lasted well into daybreak. The MRI revealed a monster meningioma situated where Claudia's right frontal lobe should have been. The tumor had pushed the brain back to make room for itself, proving once again the undeniable law of physics: no two objects can occupy the same space at the same time. And since there was only so much space inside Claudia's skull, the right side of her brain had been wrinkled into a smaller area behind the tumor, causing all kinds of consequences that would surface later, if she survived the surgery.

Monday, May 2nd

Gabriel, who flew back from New York as soon as he heard the news and went straight from LAX to the hospital, missed the initial chaos, but he had been filled in by Patricia while in transit, thanks to the in-flight Wi-Fi. By the time he arrived in the hospital Claudia had already been sedated.

"It's going to take a few days to assemble and prepare the team of surgeons for Claudia's operation," said Patricia.

"I want to know who these doctors are, what are their credentials," said Gabriel, who as Claudia's husband felt entitled to start making decisions on her behalf.

"One of them will fly in from Phoenix. The others are local. I'll give you all the information so you can take over."

"Email me everything," he said, using his executive voice. "What are her chances of survival?"

Patricia struggled to answer, her mind shifting from scenario to scenario, all of them devastating, until she finally gathered strength and said, "Slim."

■ ■ ■ ■

Tuesday, May 3rd

On Keila's orders, Olivia and Patricia went to Claudia's house to pick up pajamas, clothes, makeup, and sundries in anticipation of their sister's recovery, or would it be her burial? God forbid.

After they parked on the narrow driveway and got out of the car, they noticed the first obvious sign of their sister's illness (not that there hadn't already been plenty of overlooked signs): the overstuffed, neglected mailbox. Those brochures, catalogs, magazines, and unsolicited preapproved credit card applications that did not fit in the slot anymore had been stacked on the entrance steps, some held together with rubber bands, clearly the work of a tidy and dutiful mailman. Because of Gabriel's two-week trip to New York to close a large movie deal, it had been up to Claudia to bring the mail in, but she didn't bother. Olivia sorted it on the spot, keeping the bills and throwing away the junk mail in the recycling bin at the end of the driveway. Once they were inside, Ramsay and Velcro greeted them as if they were goddesses from another dimension. Olivia fed the starving animals and filled their empty water bowls, while Patricia went to the bathroom to gather Claudia's shampoo and creams. The toilet wasn't flushed. The shower dripped steadily, which might have saved the dog and the cat from dying of thirst. Several turds of dog poop were sprinkled around the hardwood floor and the rugs. Olivia had to carefully skip around so as not to step on them. The kitty-litter box overflowed with little brown sticks resembling Tootsie Rolls peeping out of the sand. It seemed as if Claudia had gone on a trip and abandoned her pets for several days, but it couldn't be. When Olivia had asked her at Passover dinner where she'd been, since she hadn't answered her phone, she said she had spent the last few days at home. And then, what about the other signs of neglect? In the bedroom, clothes, shoes, and towels were strewn about. Uneaten food lay on plates and on the floor, probably dragged away by Velcro. Ants crawled in a trail over the armchair, hauling tiny bits of wilted lettuce. A glass of wine had been spilled on the bed, the stain now dry. How long had their sister been holding on, trying and failing to lead a normal life?

"How the hell did she manage to drive to Mom and Dad's for Passover?" said Patricia aloud, shocked by the utter chaos.

"Uber," Olivia yelled from the kitchen. "Her car's outside," she said, proud of her detective ability.

Then came her strange discovery: "Come here! The whole place smells of gas."

Olivia turned off one of the burners on the stove that was slightly on and opened the window.

"How did she not notice this stench?" said Patricia.

"How did we not notice that she was so sick?"

"I feel awful."

"We're not doctors. How could we know?"

"It's all so obvious now. She was practically screaming at us that she was not well. We just didn't want to hear."

"Let's not blame ourselves. It's not going to help her now."

"What if she dies? We should have seen what was going on."

"We could have caught the tumor when it was the size of a cranberry."

"Or a wolffia."

"A what?"

"Google it."

"You don't have to get so snippy!"

"Sorry, I just feel like a live wire right now. It's the smallest fruit there is."

There was so much to take in and under

stand about Claudia. So many questions about her recent behavior had been answered just in the past few hours, since they had learned her diagnosis. It seemed years since the family had gathered for Passover dinner only a few nights before. Her enlarged pupils. Her lack of interest in daily duties. Missing appointments and deadlines. Falling asleep everywhere. Not answering her phone. Not feeding her pets! She picked up Ramsay and hugged him tightly. She tried to hold back her tears but something inside, perhaps where sisterly feelings resided, seemed to burst. She walked outside, to the deck, and the sensor lights came on. The lit-up pool water lay still. The ocean waves could barely be heard slapping the beach below. She wished she could stay there forever, feeling the nearly imperceptible breeze on her face, but she had to gather Claudia's things, drop off the pets at her house, and return to the hospital.

In selecting a few clothes and pajamas from Claudia's closet, it was no surprise for Patricia to find several dresses with tags on, mostly from Barneys and Saks. But wait a minute, wasn't that sweater hers? She remembered losing it at a dinner party that she and Claudia had gone to together. Looking further, she found a shoebox full of sunglasses, many of which she recognized as hers, lost here and there over a number of years. Then she dug out another box filled with knickknacks that Claudia would never have bought or owned, at least rightfully, like one of the Emmy Awards for Best Actress given to Claire Danes for *Homeland.* This discovery of the coveted statuette led Patricia to inspect the entire closet. What else had her sister picked up from celebrity parties around town? Among all sorts of chef's uniforms, clogs, and Crocs were stilettos, designer sandals, and a large collection of jeans and bikinis, many of them surely bought (or stolen) at sample sales at Dover Street Market New York, one of her favorite shops. Claudia favored quirky fashion and had the model's body to show it off. Patricia wondered how someone dedicated to making food for a living could remain a size 2, but there it was: Claudia was not only thin as an asparagus, but surpassed her two sisters in height by several inches, and might be dead by forty.

If Claudia died, would it be Patricia's duty to return all the unused clothes to the stores? Would she and Olivia pick out some of the remaining clothes to keep, or would they donate the entire wardrobe to charity? Would she be the one to return the Emmy to Claire Danes? She had a legitimate reason to meet her in person and apologize for her deceased sister's theft. She'd also congratulate Claire for *Temple Grandin* (fuck, she was so good at playing personality-challenged characters). And *Romeo + Juliet,* well, that was her masterpiece, right up there with *Little Women* and *The Hours.* Patricia was definitely a fan to the core, but suddenly stopped herself, ashamed to be fan-girling as her sister fought for her life.

"Pats! Get over here! Look at what I found in the scullery!" yelled Olivia.

And there it was, in the small room adjacent to the dining room along with all the china and table linens, neatly stacked right on the shelf: Keila's mom's Seder plate set.

Friday, May 6th

As in the preamble of a joke, a priest and a rabbi walked into the hospital's waiting area. In light of Claudia's emergency, Keila and Oscar had called a truce and joined forces to help their daughter, harnessing the fullest range of celestial support on her behalf.

"Thank you for coming, Father. Thanks, Rabbi. As I told you on the phone, the tumor is the size of a grapefruit. They're operating now."

Oscar silently wished Keila's description of the tumor's size would go in the direction of smaller fruits, like figs, apricots, or better yet, blueberries, but she had the habit of exaggerating when she was worried, and he feared she would eventually compare it to cantaloupes or even watermelons.

For a change, Oscar wasn't thinking about the chance of thunderstorms predicted for the San Gabriel Mountains. He didn't pay attention when the National Weather Service warned about the risk of dangerous lightning, flash flooding, gusty winds, and hail. Possible mudslides in areas deforested by previous wildfires were not on his mind that morning. It was Claudia, his girl, his firstborn, who occupied his thoughts.

After saying a few prayers, both priest and rabbi settled side by side in a far corner of the visitor room to soothe anyone who might need comfort. Olivia and Eric sat with them for a while.

"It's been several days of tests and preparation. One of the surgeons flew in from the Mayo Clinic's Phoenix campus yesterday. The prognosis is bleak. She has a ten percent chance of coming out of the surgery alive. And if she does, there's a ninety percent chance of her never waking up from a coma." Olivia's voice sounded shivery and brittle.

"We should be prepared for the worst," said the priest, a man in his sixties with a bald head as polished as a light bulb, who for sure knew better than to resort to a heavily overused, prefabricated phrase that meant nothing.

By midmorning, after four hours in the operating room, the two surgeons came out and gave the Alvarados a quick update.

"We've managed to block the artery that was irrigating the tumor. That saved us about eighteen hours of surgery. Still, we're just getting started. We're doing everything we can, but we should be prepared for the worst."

Olivia had heard this nonsense enough times that day and felt sick to her stomach. She called Lola to check on the girls and followed the surgeons, who were heading to the cafeteria. Perhaps some chamomile tea would help her feel better.

"I'm sorry to ask you this, but if you're out here, who's driving the car?" she addressed the doctors in the elevator.

"We're estimating this surgery to last at least until midnight. We need to take bathroom breaks and eat," explained one of the doctors, the good-looking one with the goatee. He did seem a bit famished.

"I'm afraid you'll say yes if I ask you if the hood is open."

"It is. Your sister's brain is exposed right now, but it's all under control. We're in a super sterile environment. An infection is the least of our worries at this point."

As the doctors made their way to the grill bar to order bacon cheeseburgers with fries, Olivia felt her nausea intensify as she imagined Claudia's bare brain throbbing with diminishing energy, getting accustomed to the unremarkable endeavor of expiring.

Hospital cafeterias weren't precisely adequate environments to foster profound thoughts, and yet, in a perverse way, they were. Olivia sat down alone at a sticky Formica table. In front of her was a paper cup filled with weak tea, bathed by an excess of fluorescent lighting. She wondered if her sister had a list of unfulfilled wishes and desires. Had she ever wished to travel to Antarctica? Perhaps get breast augmentation? How about the desire to have a baby? Take up hang gliding? Win a marathon? Travel to India for yoga camp? Knowing she had a tumor growing inside her skull, would she have taken more risks, say, going on a bungee-jumping spree, or parachuting out of airplanes? Or was that too predictable and boring? Perhaps she had aspired to snatch a kayak out of a sporting goods store in plain sight.

These ludicrous ideas were only proof to Olivia that her sister had been immensely accomplished in the goals she had set for herself, goals that really mattered, for instance becoming a celebrity chef, achieving financial independence early on in her life, and living in an enviable marriage. Gabriel had proved to be a loving, dependable husband, from what Olivia could see; a fact that stung deep, now that her marriage was unraveling. Would Felix have flown back across the country like Gabriel did if she'd been the victim of a tumor? Unlikely.

In the past few hours Gabriel had been helpful, sorting out all the matters that no one else in the family had a level head to do under the circumstances, like dealing with the insurance paperwork. He had brought the notarized advance directive to physicians expressing Claudia's wish not to be kept alive by artificial means, like respirators. It seemed to Olivia that making himself useful was Gabriel's way of dealing with the crisis, giving orders and not even trying to control a nervous tic she'd noticed before in which he constantly rubbed his right eyebrow.

The waiting area benefited from the quietness of the afternoon. Most relatives and friends of patients undergoing surgery or in recovery had left to go about their business in the world of the healthy. The priest and the rabbi had gone to their respective church and synagogue a while ago. Eric had spent the entire day camping out in the waiting area — pale yellow vinyl chairs in facing rows — texting or stepping aside to the elevator lobby to make business phone calls, but he'd left earlier to catch a flight back to San Francisco. As for Felix, no one asked why hadn't he gone to the hospital to be with Olivia. No one really expected him to, the family outsider. The surgeons had returned to the operating room to continue their attempts to save Claudia.

Oscar sat by the window and looked out now and then, perhaps hoping to grow wings and escape into the thin atmosphere. Keila, Olivia, and Patricia discussed with Gabriel the updates they were provided by the surgeons, who came out to the waiting area at intervals. Every time the doors swung open the entire family would get up from their seats to surround the doctor.

"The good news is that Claudia's vitals are fine. The chance of uncontrolled hemorrhaging is now minimal," said the surgeon.

When the Alvarados went back to find their seats, Gabriel said quietly, "She always told me she wanted to be cremated. I'm looking into a couple of funeral homes."

"Aren't you getting ahead of yourself? Last I heard she was still alive," said Patricia, suddenly incensed.

"I'm just trying to be practical. Does anyone here really believe she's going to make it? I almost wish she won't. She might end up paraplegic, or God knows what else. What kind of life is she going to have?"

"What kind of life are *you* going to have, being forced to care for her? Is that what you mean?" snapped Patricia, now visibly angry, the Kleenex in her sweaty hand torn to shreds.

"Stop this nonsense right now," Keila insisted. "We're all very worried and short-fused. Let's not start insulting each other. We need to stick together."

"For the record, and you all know it damn well," said Gabriel, "there's no one in this world I love more than Claudia, and if she lives I will take full charge of her recovery and care, whatever it takes. What I said had nothing to do with my quality of life, but hers."

"She's going to live. Don't you know my sister?" said Patricia.

"Be realistic, for God's sake!"

"I really don't think you know my sister better than anyone in this room," said Olivia, immediately thinking about Claudia's list, the contents of which she couldn't start to imagine. Did she indeed know Claudia better than Gabriel? She bit her lip and headed for the hallway.

Patricia caught up with her by the elevators.

"Let's get some fresh air."

They walked along Burton Way toward Beverly Hills. This two-mile stretch that started near Cedars-Sinai Medical Center was one of the few streets in Los Angeles with a wide, grassy median, and possibly the least traffic in the entire city.

"I never see anyone on this street," said Patricia.

"There's a nanny with a stroller over there."

"Okay, one person."

"And the baby."

"That makes two, and us, that's four. We should have gone to Beverly Center instead and gotten a drink. Now I'm going to get a blister on my foot with these not-meant-for-walking shoes."

Patricia took off the spaghetti-strap sandals she'd worn to a meeting early that morning, but obviously the wrong choice of shoes to wear during what turned out to be hours of waiting and pacing around the hospital corridors, and walked barefoot on the dried-out grass. The city had shut down irrigation of all parks and public spaces to set the example for citizens to do the same in their backyards, and the once-green landscape was now a sea of dead shrubs.

Olivia called Lola to fill her in.

"What a relief. I'm sure she's in good hands. These doctors are the best in town," Lola said upon hearing the news that Claudia was alive. "I'm thinking about her, you tell her that."

"You'll be able to tell her yourself. I'll stay with the twins sometime next week while you come down to visit her. How are they, by the way?"

"Andrea is taking a nap. Diana is drawing. Don't you worry about them. And if you need me to watch them on my days off, I'll do it. I know you want to be with Clau."

Olivia hung up, overcome by sadness. A gentle, warm breeze swayed the palm tree leaves like hula dancers in slow motion on a car's dashboard.

"Have you ever wondered what might be on Claudia's bucket list?" Olivia asked Patricia.

"I haven't thought about it."

"We'll have to wait for her to recover so she can tell us herself."

"That's right."

"I don't have a bucket list. Do you?"

"No. When do you start thinking about these things?" Patricia asked.

"When you realize your time on earth ends at some point, so you pick and choose the few things that you most want to do before you kick the bucket. You're under thirty. You're probably still thinking you've got the Unlimited Minutes Plan, but look at what's happening with Claudia."

"She's going to make it."

Olivia's eyes moistened and she quickly dried her tears with her sleeve, hoping that Patricia wouldn't notice.

"Hey, trust me, she will pull through."

"I know. It's all of it together." Olivia took a deep breath, stopped walking, and looked Patricia in the eye. "I can't keep this from you any longer. I'm leaving Felix. We're done."

Patricia stopped, the dry grass making her bare feet itch. "Whoa. So, you're really doing it. It's about the embryos, right?"

"It's an accumulation of things. I'm so tired of his temper and his meanness."

"He's not the most likable person, you

226

know how we feel about him, but I didn't think he was that awful with you. You never tell us."

"It is awful, and has been for a while. I've never wanted to worry you. In the end it came down to the battle of the embryos. It's my fault."

"Can't be."

"Can too. I just killed my marriage."

As Olivia explained the situation to Patricia, they reached the end of Burton Way, where the street merges with Little Santa Monica, the commercial district of Beverly Hills, and walked toward Wally's, a wine shop and restaurant that Patricia wanted to try.

The scene at the bar was loud and happy in the middle of, well, happy hour, so the sisters had to raise their voices to hear each other.

Olivia signaled the waiter, and with a couple of words and restaurant-friendly nonverbal gestures indicating wine being poured into a glass, the sisters got their drinks within minutes.

"It's not your fault," said Patricia, catching the attention of a couple sitting next to them. "Yes, you pushed the fertility issue a bit hard, and yes, Felix participated in the plan, humored you when you kept insisting, and was with you all along the way, crisis after crisis, miscarriage after miscarriage, but he reached his limit with the remaining frozen embryos and that pushed you over your own limit. So, whose fault is it? All parties involved, or no one at all. But who cares? I'd say, stop the blame game and focus on divorcing quickly. And, look, if you're really set on salvaging those embryos, whether they live forever in the freezer or they find their way into the world, I'm with you. I'm sure you have your reasons."

"You know what the reason is. We discussed this already."

They ordered two more rounds while discussing strategies to save the embryos, some feasible (take Felix to court), some outlandish (misplace the embryos), and others outright illegal (steal the embryos). After an hour of scheming, Patricia got a text from Keila.

Where are you? Gabriel is being unreasonable. I need you here now.

Alarmed after checking their watches, Olivia called an Uber and, tipsy as they were, they returned to the hospital to find a full-blown fight between Keila and Gabriel, who were yelling at each other by the nurses' station.

"But why the fuck do you bring out Claudia's last will at this point?" yelled Keila, who was holding a document in her hand.

The fuck? Olivia had never heard her mother curse. She looked at Patricia, puzzled.

"What's going on?" she asked.

"Gabriel wants to make sure we're all aware that he is the sole heir to Claudia's assets, so he's brought her trust papers to the hospital to rub in our noses."

"I'm sorry. I didn't think this would be insensitive. I'm just trying to take care of the practical stuff," he said.

"Insensitive? Did you say insensitive? It's insulting!" Keila was clearly undone and in need of backup for words, so Patricia stepped in.

"Look, Gabriel, we don't give a shit about Claudia's will. If she's leaving everything to you, fine, but don't come here anticipating her death because she's not going to die!"

"Face the inevitable, Patricia."

Enraged, Patricia went for Gabriel's shirt collar and rattled him with unfamiliar strength, and just short of the aggression becoming an assault, Olivia and Keila pried her away. Two of the nurses who had been

229

watching the fight escalate ran to get a security guard.

"Where's Dad?" asked Patricia, sobbing. "I need Dad."

"I'm right here, chamaquita," said Oscar, who had just arrived. He grabbed her and held her tight against his chest. This was the embrace she had been longing for. This was the love she had missed so much in the past months. She took it in, wrapping her arms around Oscar's shoulders.

"You're all going to have to leave right now," said the security guard as he arrived.

"Look, sir, I just got here. I haven't seen my daughter," said Oscar.

"Everyone out or I'll have to restrain you!" They all left the nurses' station quietly, and each drove away, alone in their own car. Something had broken between the Alvarados and Gabriel. Olivia could almost hear it crash on the floor. She realized she had never fully trusted him, but made the effort to be amicable because she knew how much Claudia loved him, and after all, once he was married to her sister, he was family. Maybe he was right. Maybe they were denying the painful reality that Claudia was dying.

■ ■ ■ ■

Sunday, May 8th

No one remembered it was Mother's Day.

Monday, May 9th

These were the permanent water-conservation measures imposed by the governor: a ban on irrigating lawns within two days of a rainstorm; no more hosing down driveways; restrictions on offering water to hotel and restaurant guests; and other extreme measures, such as flushing toilets only when solid waste needed to be drained. Although Northern California had recently enjoyed some wet days and its reservoirs had been replenished, still more than 90 percent of the state was in its fifth year of severe drought.

Oscar welcomed the conservation news. He was a faithful follower of the famous "If it's yellow it's mellow; if it's brown flush it down" refrain whenever he used the toilet, in spite of Keila's complaints. She had yet to acknowledge the new normal, in which water was scarce and needed to be used sparingly, instead of lingering in the shower and keeping the faucet water running while she brushed her teeth.

But as Oscar drove to the hospital determined to camp out until Claudia recovered, no matter what the security guard ordered, he realized there was a far more life-changing new normal awaiting the Alvarados.

Wednesday, May 11th

"You need to go home and shower. You've been here since Monday."

Keila sniffed Oscar's shirt collar. He pulled back, startled by her proximity.

"Claudia is not going to recover because you wander up and down the hospital hallways all day. She's in stable condition and that's the great news we need to hold on to."

"It's her birthday. I can't leave her alone."

"Get some rest. I'll be here."

"Fine, and I'll bring back a cake. We'll blow out the candles on her behalf."

Oscar held his gaze on Keila a bit longer, turned around, and went home.

Friday, May 13th

Twice in the same year is more than enough, thought Daniel on the way to the hospital. He'd visited his little cousins, the twins, when they nearly drowned, and now his aunt Claudia. Sitting in the passenger seat next to Patricia, he wondered in silence if the family was cursed. It seemed to him that all of a sudden they were going through emergencies and crises on a monthly basis. He realized it was Friday the 13th and his stomach churned. Was this a bad omen?

"She's still in a coma, so she may not know you're visiting. It hasn't been long enough since the surgery for her to be awake. But feel free to talk to her in case she's listening. I'm sure she'd be very happy to hear your voice," said Patricia.

"Could she die while we're with her in the room?"

"Yes —" She paused before continuing. "— she could die at any moment, but right now I've heard from the doctors that she's stable. Since they disconnected the breathing machine, she's been hanging on, so I wouldn't worry too much. She looks dead, but she's not. Her body is using all the energy it can to heal."

"What if she stays like that forever?"

"Some people have stayed in a coma for years, others only a few days. Your aunt is super strong. She'll wake up sooner or later. I'm pretty sure of that, but I can't guarantee it."

"What if the beep in the heart machine goes flat while I'm in the room?"

"Have you been watching *Grey's Anatomy*?"

"*House.*"

"Even worse. You can hug her and kiss her, just do it very carefully. You don't want to mess up the IV. She'll be fine. I do it every day."

Since the first day after the surgery, Patricia had visited Claudia and quietly conducted business from her cellphone while she sat in what must be the most uncomfortable chair she'd ever used aside from the ones in school cafeterias, jury-duty waiting rooms, and the Mexico City airport. But since it was the only chair in the ICU waiting area, she'd hoard it with gusto. Every so often, as permitted by the nurses, she'd briefly go into the room and watch her sister lie in bed immobile, sallow, thinner than she already was, wishing for her to wake up, put some clothes on, and get on with her life. The surgery was in the past. The tumor had been dissected and analyzed in a lab that corroborated its benign nature. The fear of Claudia being incapable of breathing on her own had now dissipated. She had been disconnected from all life-support devices after Gabriel instructed the doctors to do so, and there she was, alive.

Patricia, Olivia, Keila, and Oscar took

turns going into the room, since they could stay with her for only an hour each day per ICU rules. But they promised one another never to leave Claudia alone, even if they had to keep watch outside in the hallway. The atmosphere got tense whenever Gabriel showed up. Thankfully, he'd gone back to New York to deal with lawyers on an intellectual-property lawsuit between two screenwriters, leaving Ramsay and Velcro at the Alvarados'.

Patricia found street parking (unheard-of in the vicinity of the hospital) and walked with Daniel the couple of blocks to the front entrance. The room was quiet, except for little beeping noises, an inherent part of the landscape. Claudia lay immobile in the semidarkness. Only a few rays of afternoon light came through the shades in straight beams and fell on the blanket that draped her. Daniel approached the bed and took Claudia's hand.

"Hi, Claudia. It's Daniel. I'm here with my mom. She's outside. They only let in one visitor at a time," Daniel said, in a whisper, so as not to disturb his aunt. "I'm supposed to tell you things, normal stuff, like if we were just talking. But we don't ever talk that much. I just wanted to tell you that I really like Ramsay, but I don't

235

think you've noticed. I also like Velcro. I hope you bring them when you come over to Bubbe's so we can play. And maybe someday you'll invite me to watch how they tape your show. I'm curious to see how they do it. If you make it out of here alive, we should definitely hang out more often."

Daniel had a few more things to say to Claudia: how much he was into her taste in clothes and how he'd like to have a Malibu beach party in front of her house and invite all his friends, but he stopped suddenly and ran out of the room and into Patricia's arms with eyes as big as moons.

"She squeezed my hand!"

Saturday, May 14th

So transparent was Olivia's house that you could stand outside one of the floor-to-ceiling windows and see the view on the other side right across the living room. At 7:17 A.M., just when the twins were having their breakfast in the kitchen, a mourning dove crashed against the sliding glass door and died instantly. Olivia would discover it later, its beak pointing sideways, its wing twisted and bloody. She'd hold it in her hands. She'd cry.

■ ■ ■ ■

"May Gray is not only a local climate phenomenon in Los Angeles; it's a state of mind," Oscar would mumble to himself sometimes, more so lately. He was well aware that depending on the weather conditions, it could take the form of a depressing marine layer over beach cities, annoying smoke from brushfires pushed by wind against the San Gabriel or San Bernardino Mountains, or a lingering cloud cover that tended to dissipate as the day warmed up. None scared him more than the smoke from a fire. He could guess how far away a wildfire was by the density of the smoke and the color of the haze. If a thin cover of ash lay on his car, he knew the distance was less than five miles, give or take. If he saw embers flying around, most likely it was time to evacuate. But on that day, an innocent marine layer covered the sky, and he sighed with relief.

That evening (last-minute unscheduled family dinner, no husbands), sitting at the head of the table with Keila to his right, an empty chair to his left (assigned to Claudia since birth), Olivia and Patricia in their respective chairs farther down, and Daniel at the far end, he wasn't sure what state his mind was in. The hand-squeezing incident was still the topic several days after it happened, and everyone had an opinion. Keila thought it was just an involuntary impulse, while Patricia assured everyone that it was the first sign that Claudia was healing. Daniel, being the recipient of the hand squeeze, spoke with the highest authority on the matter: "She communicated with me. I believe she wanted me to know that she is aware of everything that's going on and that she's recovering."

Oscar ate without his usual enthusiasm. On other occasions, he loved to dig into layer after layer of tamales de pollo smothered in salsa verde and Manchego cheese au gratin. But there was just too much turmoil in his head to allow himself to savor it. As far as he was concerned, Claudia's recovery had stalled. Overwhelmed by a collection of feelings — a mélange of hurt, depression, annoyance to the point of irritation, heck, outright anger, and what felt like boredom but was probably hopelessness — he decided he had all the symptoms of the May Gray phenomenon. He excused himself and walked out of the dining room, leaving his food untouched.

"See what I mean?" said Keila, pointing at the dining-room door, still swinging. "He doesn't care anymore. I've got a zombie husband."

"What if he's just sad, Mom?" Patricia came to his defense, reliving in her mind his warm embrace at the hospital.

"Yeah, he's probably worried about Claudia," said Daniel.

"I've been married to your dad for thirty-nine years, and the man who just walked out of this dining room has zero resemblance to him. So don't try to protect him. All he talks about, if he says anything, is El Niño this and El Niño that. Haven't you noticed?"

"Yes, Mom, we've noticed, we're not blind," said Olivia. "What have you done to help? Have you tried taking him to a psychiatrist?"

Keila wiped her mouth with the napkin and left the table without saying a word.

Thursday, May 26th

"I'm going to walk Ramsay. Come with me, Dad," said Patricia from outside Oscar's bedroom door.

"Tomorrow," said Oscar with his usual raspy morning voice.

"Eric is coming over tomorrow. I haven't

239

seen him all week. We're spending the weekend together. Let's go now."

"I'm in my pajamas."

"Throw something on."

Oscar came out of the room in sweatpants and a T-shirt, his abundant gray hair messy like an abandoned vulture nest, and followed Patricia to the street.

"We better not bump into the Sellys, what with your fashion statement," she said jokingly under a cloudless sky while she strapped Ramsay's leash to his fake diamond-studded collar.

Oscar smiled quietly, not giving a damn about his neighbors' opinion. Patricia, his baby, had been the one daughter whose company he cherished the most. They had an implicit alignment of the minds, never discussed, but always acknowledged by both of them.

They walked down the sidewalk quietly, side by side, stopping briefly to allow Ramsay to sniff the neighborhood's dogs' pee on every tree trunk of the jacarandas that lined the street. It was that time of the year when the blossoms fell to the ground and blanketed the streets of Los Angeles in exuberant shades of violet, as if wanting to add pizzazz to people's strolls.

"Look at this," said Oscar, pointing at the

ground covered in lilac. "It's better than any Hollywood red carpet."

"It's our very own purple carpet," added Patricia, gently pulling at Ramsay's leash.

"A magic carpet. It's a shame we don't get the jacaranda blooms in the fall anymore. I remember as a kid, they used to bloom twice a year. I wish Washington politicians felt the effects of climate change as much as the jacarandas do."

Patricia took her father by the arm and screwed up her courage. The conversation she was intending to have with him was long overdue.

"Something's eating you, Papi, we all know that," Patricia finally said as they turned the corner. "Mom is at the end of her wits, and you just cruise along, keeping everyone out. And it's not just what's happened to Claudia. This started way before the tumor. I really thought you trusted me. Want to share?"

Oscar knew that when Patricia wanted to get something out of him, he had no choice. That's just who she was; never gave up, never accepted no for an answer. He knew there was no way he could keep the orchard a secret indefinitely; at some point he'd have to come clean with Keila and his daughters. And Patricia was the only one in his entire family whom he felt it was safe to reveal his secret to. So after years of him enduring a paralyzing fear of being found out, the time had come. He stopped, closed his eyes as if he were about to plunge into an abyss, and uttered: "We might lose the crop."

There. It was said and there was no going back.

"What crop?"

"We have an almond orchard in Kern County."

"Wait, what?"

Once he started, Oscar confessed the entire situation to Patricia: the secret purchase of the orchard, the drought, and his fear of losing the entire family patrimony, his ancestors' inheritance.

"Your mother is going to leave me if I tell her about the orchard, and she'll leave if I don't."

Patricia listened quietly, ignoring the constant vibration of her cellphone in her pocket.

"You cannot tell anyone about this until I sort it out. Promise me, Pats."

"Promise."

After dutifully picking up Ramsay's poop and doubling down on her decision never to own a dog, she walked back home with Oscar. It was unfair to her, she thought, to

242

make her an accomplice, the lone person privy to family secrets: first Olivia, with her divorce under wraps, and now her father with the almond orchard. Next thing I know, my mom will be confessing to me that she has a lover, she thought.

Friday, May 27th

Keila locked herself in her studio, fixed her hair, and video-called Simon Brik.

"I wanted to see you," she said in an unusually tender voice.

"I'm so glad it's you. I've been worried about your daughter."

"She's still in a coma, but at least she's stable. I can't think of anything worse than losing my child. If she dies, I will die right after her."

"I wish I could assure you that she'll be all right."

"No one can guarantee anything at this point, not even the doctors."

"And you? How's your little heart? Are you taking care of it?"

"I am, but sometimes I have the urge to run to your gallery and look into your eyes."

"You know where the gallery is. Hop on a plane. Come and look into my eyes all you want."

"With a little encouragement, I would."

Keila realized that by saying those few words she had advanced her relationship with Simon a million miles toward the intimacy he always wanted.

"Oh, yes? Well, you certainly need a break from the terrible situation you're in. It's the only way you can persevere and be there for your daughter for the long haul. No one knows how much care she'll need when she recovers, and you'll need all the energy you can muster. I can be the island of peace you need right now to recharge. Just come for a couple of days."

"You're so convincing, it's scary."

"Do it."

"Maybe, but I don't think I can leave Claudia just yet."

"I know. It's just my hope talking."

After Keila hung up, she stared at her cellphone screen, realizing that she hadn't felt her heart thump, her stomach churn, her breath evaporate since she'd had a devastating crush on Aaron Bergman, a high school classmate who never even said hello to her. The adolescent feelings were like electricity, and unlike Aaron Bergman, Simon Brik was all hers. She launched the search engine in her computer and typed "LAX-MEX direct flights."

■ ■ ■ ■

Saturday, May 28th

The white sheets that wrapped Olivia that morning felt like a child's hideout, safe from the monster, the T. rex. She'd had a disastrous meeting with him the previous afternoon and had cried all evening. Between sighs and weeping bursts she'd managed to write down her feelings. It's what she did in times of distress. Seeing them spelled out on paper soothed her, even though they were infused with slander and rage. Still, she couldn't accept the scenario he had described to her and played the scene in a loop.

"I want you to be aware that Felix might get custody of the girls," said the T. rex, sitting behind his desk. Olivia noticed a family portrait of him, his wife, and three teenagers on the credenza against the window and wondered who'd be so brave or suicidal to marry this monster. "He'll bring out their near-drowning accident under your parents' watch as a reason not to entrust you with their care. He will probably demand that the embryos be destroyed, claiming that he cannot be forced into fatherhood. He could keep the house for himself or make you sell

245

it to get half the proceeds."

Olivia, trying not to break down in front of him, sat across the desk, quietly listening to his darkest scenario, suppressing whatever it was that was boiling inside of her.

"Under these circumstances, we have no choice but to go to court," he said.

"I refuse. That was my only condition when I hired you."

"If you don't accept my counsel, I'm afraid I will have to fire you."

"When does an attorney fire his client?" She raised her voice, shocked. "You said I could keep custody of the girls without having to escalate the legal process!"

After finally accepting the necessity of going to court, she had left his office defeated, and now she was hiding under the sheets, avoiding the sliver of sunlight that snuck through the drawn blinds and fell on the pillow.

She wasn't going to answer her cellphone, but it was Gabriel calling from New York.

"Did I wake you?"

"No. It's fine. I was just getting up."

"What's the latest on Claudia?"

"This is not a film project we're talking about here! Aren't you in touch with the doctors?" she asked, suddenly furious. "You're her husband. You're the one who should be informing us. You should be permanently lashed to her hospital bed. Instead, God knows where the hell you are that's more important."

"I've been swamped. I'm so sorry."

"Can you hear yourself talking? Your wife is dying! I just don't understand what's going on with you!"

She hung up the phone with a metallic taste in her mouth, as if she'd been sucking on a penny. It wasn't just that Gabriel had angered the entire family by giving the impression that he preferred his wife to be dead than disabled. Here she was basking in her own misery while her sister fought for her life. She got up, put on some clothes, and drove to the hospital.

Sunday, May 29th

Felix picked up the twins early in the morning to take them on a picnic to Will Rogers Park. Olivia prepared their bags with treats and sandwiches, bottles of milk, two changes of clothes, and several toys. For a moment she was tempted to include a sandwich for Felix, but stopped her impulse immediately. When she closed the door at 9:00 A.M., the house became silent, blissfully silent. Lola had gone home, so she had the entire house for herself to sulk and suffer with compulsion. She went to her bedroom, drew the drapes, and lounged in her bed for twelve hours, only to find that the refrigerator was turned off and everything in the freezer had thawed.

"Ha!" she said in a spark of realization. Why hadn't she understood what had been happening lately with her home's smart systems, their bizarre passive-aggressive behavior? Appliances mysteriously turning off on their own, devices acting as if they were alive. Was she too distracted by Claudia's medical crisis? The divorce? She was furious at her naïveté, at her lack of presence in the real world. No, her house was not haunted, her appliances were not out to get her.

She remembered the morning she woke up covered in sweat. She'd been having a feverish nightmare about Death Valley rattlesnakes creeping around the dunes, leaving their markings in the sand a few feet behind her. She had sat up and checked her forehead with the palm of her hand. Was she sick? Was a fire engulfing the house? She removed the soaked sheets, got up, and noticed that the thermostat was set at eighty-five degrees. Then a couple of days later, after a long drive from Westlake Village, where she was decorating a house, she'd come home to find her garden flooded with water, the irrigation system still going full force. Alarmed at the waste, she looked everywhere for the automatic-sprinkler panel to shut it off, but couldn't find it. She called the gardener, who came two hours later and fixed the problem by launching an app on his phone and shutting off the water with one click.

But the worst event had come the week before, and this is how it went down: At exactly 3:27 A.M., the live recording of Manowar's "The Dawn of Battle" began blasting in Olivia's ears. She jumped out of her bed, still disoriented and half asleep, and wondered if the neighbors were having a wild party. But the music was inside her house. She rushed to the sound-system panel in the living room and tried to turn it off, but didn't know how. Where were the buttons? She stared at the blank screen on the tablet attached to the wall and tapped it with her fingers, hoping an off button would light up. She wished Felix had installed the app on her phone. Why hadn't he taught her to use this equipment? Why had she never asked? Now it was acting on its own and pushing her to a state of madness. So much for smart devices. Within a minute, Lola walked in, holding the twins in each hand. The girls ran into Olivia's arms, scared, whimpering, covering their ears.

"What's going on?" yelled Lola.

The heavy-metal music was so loud Olivia could only raise her arms in disbelief.

"It's Felix's music! This is the stuff he listens to in his car!"

But Lola couldn't hear her. She took the girls out to the patio while Olivia tried to turn the system off. By 4:33 A.M., and only after listening to Manowar's "Kings of Metal," "Fighting the World," "Hail and Kill," and "Metal Warriors," she finally found a way to bring up an off button on the screen.

Now, she was in front of her thawed refrigerator cursing Felix in tears of anger and decided to save her rage for when he came back from the park.

"How dare you harass me that way? You're a monster! A creative one, I admit, but a disgusting man, nonetheless!"

The twins had run inside on Olivia's instructions to change clothes, as they were going for dinner later at Keila and Oscar's.

"What are you talking about?" said Felix, widening his eyes for effect.

"The heater, the fridge, the metal band, the sprinklers! Don't pretend you don't know. You've been manipulating the smart systems remotely just to mess with me. And the girls, I might add."

"You should thank me for bringing a little excitement to your life."

Olivia thought of saying "fuck you," but there were more fitting words to insult him, so she chose: "You subway rat, decomposing roadkill, subhuman specter, toenail fungus, blood-sucking leech, root canal gone wrong, pus-bursting zit, monkey cum, infected hangnail, sidewalk phlegm, underdeveloped penis, and yes, fuck you too," she calmly said before hearing Felix say, "Now, *that* was creative." She slammed the door, her chest cavity burning as if with fever.

Monday, May 30th

Because it was Memorial Day there were more visitors than usual at the hospital. The bustle of family members visiting their sick drowned the beeps and chimes of the vital-sign machines. Children raced along the hallways and nurses reprimanded them. Claudia's room was oddly quiet. No one had shown up yet except Eric, who stopped by early in the morning on his way to the airport.

"Who's my favorite sister-in-law? Huh?" he said, close to her ear, wondering if she was capable of hearing him. Just in case, he

251

tried to sound chirpy in a futile effort to lift her spirits. "I'm sure you're going to recover someday what with your off-the-charts spunk. Hang in there, warrior. I'll see you next weekend," he whispered, trying to mask the dread in his voice, not sure if she'd be there when he returned.

Claudia and Eric's friendship had flourished early on. He loved helping his sister-in-law around the kitchen whenever she cooked at the Alvarados', frequently advertising his French upbringing as if that alone qualified him to be the family food critic: *more butter, less salt, it's overcooked, nothing I haven't tasted, I'm not impressed, or this dish deserves a mention in Deliciously Ella's blog.* Claudia would humor him, finding his comments endearing. And as long as he volunteered to peel tomatoes, chop onions, pit cherries, and wash pots and pans, he was welcome in her kitchen.

Standing next to her bed, Eric studied his comatose sister-in-law, carefully allowing himself to feel the pang in his chest, a far worse pain than any acid reflux he'd ever felt before, worse even than a bleeding ulcer (not that he'd ever had one). He sent a small prayer into the sky not really believing it would ever make it to the appropriate deity and, teary-eyed, said his good-byes.

Eric had just left when Claudia opened her eyes. Tangled thoughts began to form in her mind. A dark shroud of confusion prevented her from realizing where she was or what had happened to her. She made a weak fist and felt her fingers coiling softly, touching her fingernails with her thumb. She lay on a bed; that was certain. A blanket covered her. Was that a hose between her legs? It felt warm and weird. She closed her eyes again. The beeps and chimes of machines suggested a hospital environment. Was she hungry? She didn't feel any pain. She wondered if she'd been in an accident, and tried to remember the details, but drew a blank. She thought random words in English and in Spanish. She mixed them up: sábana, bed, pipí, dark, tortilla con salsa. Yes, she was hungry. Then, after what could have been minutes or hours in which she moved her hands and wiggled her fingers, twitched her nose, opened and closed her eyes in the darkness, and felt her tongue sliding over her teeth, she heard a voice that she recognized and even felt a tender closeness to but could not pinpoint whose it was.

"Good morning, Clau. How's my lovely sister this morning?" said Olivia, not expecting an answer.

The slight touch of Olivia's cheek against

hers, a kiss, a sense of familiarity that she couldn't understand, prompted Claudia to whisper with much effort: "I can't see."

JUNE

Wednesday, June 1st

In typical June Gloom fashion, the month had begun with no sign of rain, just a dreary, overcast sky, confirming Oscar's fears: the much-hyped El Niño was a total disappointment. Los Angeles had recorded its driest five-year period in one hundred and forty years. That's what the meteorologist had announced on TV the morning of Memorial Day. But the most anticipated breaking news had come a few minutes later, when Olivia called to tell him that Claudia had woken up from her coma and that she couldn't see. He'd rushed to the hospital to find Patricia, Olivia, and Keila crowded around Claudia's bed, listening to the doctor's explanation.

"Her recovery will be slow. The loss of sight is temporary. She'll have blurry vision, but the optic nerve is intact, so it should take only a few days before she begins to focus. It's going to be an adjustment. There's still some swelling in her brain. She's producing quite a lot of fluid that will need to be drained through these little hoses inserted into her skull. She'll start very strict physical therapy as soon as she can eat a meal on her own. She's very strong, so I'm not concerned, but of course, time will tell as she progresses if there is permanent damage in other areas."

Friday, June 3rd

Two days later, Oscar was again driving to the hospital, thinking about what the doctor had said. What if he was wrong and Claudia's blindness was permanent? He parked right next to Gabriel's car, relieved and upset at the same time to find he had come back from New York. When he reached the lobby, he found him coming out of the elevator, so he couldn't avoid him.

"It's good to see you came back. Have you spoken with Claudia?"

"She won't talk, her eyes are closed, and she just breathes heavily. It seems there hasn't been much improvement since she woke up from the coma. What's the prognosis?"

"Didn't you ask the doctor?"

"I couldn't wait for him to come out of

surgery. I'm already running late for my flight back to New York. Will you keep me informed?"

"Listen, Gabriel, Claudia has her entire family watching over her; she doesn't need you, but I'm sure she'd want to have her husband around while she recovers. I don't know what's so important in New York that's keeping you from camping at the hospital day and night. I know I'd do that if it was my wife fighting for her life."

"I'll spend time with her next week. I promise you," said Gabriel.

Oscar said good-bye to his son-in-law and immediately, as Gabriel disappeared through the hospital doors, regretted not insulting him. He'd been too soft, too wimpy. He thought about Keila. What if she'd really been the one recovering from a coma? Suddenly he felt an urgent need to hug her with all his strength and never let go, but he knew he'd have to come up with a solution to his conundrum first. Such a failure he was, so deceitful. He caught himself just in time, before he sank into the deep well of self-pity that he visited regularly, and pulled out of it with pitiful explanations to himself for why he had bought Happy Crunch Almond Orchard in secret, why he'd kept it from Keila all these years, and why he wasn't confessing all this to her now. In truth, his behavior had been driven by pure fear. He realized he loved his wife more now than during their child-rearing years, which to him had been the best in the entire marriage. But he also concluded that he feared her just as much.

He walked into the dark room and made his way to Claudia's bed.

"It's me," he whispered. "Are you awake?"

"Papi," she said in a clear voice, extending her hand to touch Oscar's. "Don't ever leave me alone with Gabriel."

Oscar took Claudia's request as a call for help. He held her hand.

"What happened? Did he say anything mean to you? Did he hurt you?"

"I feel like shit. What's this on my head?" she asked, touching the dressing wrapping her head.

"You had a brain tumor, a benign one, the size of a kiwi," he explained, trying to downplay the impact of the news. "They took it out; it's gone. You're recovering very quickly! The doctors are very impressed. One of them is even writing a paper on your case."

"Ah, okay," she mumbled, not quite awake.

Desperate to feel useful, Oscar checked

the shunts inserted in her head to drain excess fluid, but they were dry.

"Something's clogged here. Where's the nurse?" He clumsily moved the shunts this way and that to try to get a better view. Not a drop. He ran into the hallway, yelling, "Nurse! Nurse! Something's wrong!"

By the time he reached the station he had lost his composure. "I'm calling you and you don't come! What if it's an emergency?"

"You don't have to get so worked up, Mr. Alvarado," said the nurse behind the counter. "Let's go see what's going on."

He followed her, half angry, half worried, into Claudia's room. He knew he needed to have the nurses on his side to get the best care for his daughter, so he made an effort to calm down.

"The shunts are clogged," he said. "And you weren't paying attention. Do you expect us to know what to do?"

The nurse checked the shunts quickly and said: "She's healing, getting better every day. That's why she's producing less fluid. Please don't panic like that, Mr. Alvarado. And next time, use the call button. We're right outside."

"I'm sorry," he said, feeling foolish.

"I'll be fine," said Claudia after the nurse left the room.

Later, after Claudia had slept for a while, Oscar sat next to her and gently brushed a strand of hair off her face.

"Have you eaten?"

"If you can call that mushy stuff they served me food, yes, I have. Even Silly Putty has more taste," she said in a barely audible voice, still feeble from her days in a coma.

Oscar saw Claudia's sarcasm as a good sign.

"Do you want me to open the curtains? It's nice out," he said, not paying attention to the fact that Claudia could not see.

"It's always nice out."

"People around the country tend to think so. East Coast people, people from the Midwest. They say, 'There's no weather in L.A. It's always seventy-two and sunny,' but that's inaccurate. Few people consider our five seasons to be different from one another, but they are. You know this. I know this, because we've lived here all our lives. Ah, but go ahead and tell this to someone back east. Our winter rainy season overlaps with our sunny and mild spring, then with our jacaranda season, our horribly hot late summer, and the Santa Ana season. That's five seasons there. Of course, some people in town would include the award season, but that's not climate-related unless the

Oscars' red carpet gets rained on. And then, what about the drought, the winds, the marine layer, the brushfires, the gigafires, the mudslides, the landslides, the flash floods, the atmospheric rivers, the heat domes, the Ridiculously Resilient Ridge, the very real possibility of a catastrophic ARkStorm, El Niño, La Niña, La Nada?"

"You're obsessed, Papi."

He held on to the curtain for a minute before dropping it. "You might be right. I'll stop boring you with all this weather talk."

Oscar held Claudia's hand, surprised to hear her call him "Papi," like when she was a little girl. She tightened her grip.

"You're starting physical therapy today, the nurse told me."

But Claudia didn't answer. She had fallen asleep again. Oscar tucked her in and left the room, finding Keila by the door, quietly waiting her turn to visit. Had she been eavesdropping?

"Claudia is sleeping. Do you want to get coffee downstairs?"

"I'll just stay here. Thanks," said Keila, a bit surprised by the invitation.

"I am trying," said Oscar, and left.

In the car, driving to Happy Crunch Almond Orchard, he wondered if they'd have to make special accommodations for

Claudia: a wheelchair, a ramp, or maybe even Braille lessons. She certainly wouldn't be able to live alone in Malibu while she recovered — if she recovered. How useless could Gabriel be? And then there was her puzzling request to avoid leaving her alone with him. He sure had behaved horribly throughout her surgery and recovery. He had meant to ask her what had happened between them, but he didn't want to pry. She still seemed so frail. He promised himself to oblige. He'd find out in time, for sure.

As he meandered around the dirt rows, he thanked each and every one of his trees, sometimes even hugging one and feeling its quiet thirst, its struggle for life. He stopped to caress the velvety shells hanging from the branches, hardening as the kernels formed within. He would have to irrigate them with scarce and expensive water. Would the weather change and bring rain in the next two months, before the start of the harvest? Doubtful. Drawing well water was out of the question. Not only was it expensive, it was unhealthy for the trees, with all those salts in the groundwater. And depleting the aquifers had already sunk the soil in the valley to alarming levels. He could not leave his orchard to die of thirst. Insects would populate the trees and spread to neighboring crops. He reevaluated his initial hope and realized he was reaching the point he feared the most: losing not only the crop, but the trees.

He returned to his car, thinking about the dark side of almonds, the killer side. If he could get ahold of and ingest the variety with the right kind of bitterness, he would be able to permanently solve the entire mess he was in and find eternal rest. Cyanide was not on his list of possible suicide means, but perhaps it should be.

Tuesday, June 7th
"You will lose the embryos and will have to sell the house to split the proceeds with Felix."

The T. rex's words went through Olivia's EarPods directly into her brain and bounced around inside, like a pinball.

"But the good news is that he agreed to let the court award you child custody," he added, his voice sounding distorted by a bad connection. "He can still see the girls on a schedule. It's up to you to accept this. If you prefer to continue paying me to challenge this, I'm fine with that. Your husband's attorney is happy to continue with the case, too."

Olivia hung up the phone, but called him right back.

"Okay," she said, blowing her nose and drying her tears with the same tissue. "I accept the terms."

Wednesday, June 8th

For the past thirty-three years, on the second Wednesday of every month, Keila got together with a group of friends to discuss a novel, a collection of short stories, or some other work of fiction. Her book club, endearingly named by its members The Sumo Team, was much more than a literary experience. It was group therapy, fashion consultancy, political analysis, career coaching, child-rearing and lately empty-nesting advice, and a gastronomy extravaganza. Sometimes they'd go for two or three months without agreeing on which book to read, but that didn't stop them from meeting at a different house each time and sharing their latest dishes and drama. This tight-knit group of eight remained the same over the years, having lost only one member, to breast cancer. Anyone aspiring to join was instantly rejected. In fact, people had stopped trying to get accepted and envied their activities from afar. The women also met between book club sessions to go shopping, or to have dinner in one of their homes, to which their spouses were invited, or in the case of those who were divorced or widowed, the occasional paramour. They organized a yearly fundraiser to finance tattoo-removal procedures, a service they provided free of charge to former gang members and ex-convicts who had signed up for rehabilitation at a nonprofit organization run by a priest in downtown Los Angeles. Every November, they congregated for Black Friday shopping, cramming into tiny fitting rooms and expressing their opinions.

"Don't even think of buying that dress. You look like a sack of potatoes," one would warn the other.

Telling the blunt truth with no filters was one of the most important rules in the club and was strongly enforced.

"I almost cheated on Oscar," confessed Keila to the group on that particular Wednesday, as soon as she walked in, bringing a Pyrex with huitlacoche crepes with poblano salsa, a recipe she'd perfected over the years. "If Claudia hadn't woken up from her coma, I would have gone to Mexico City to meet with Simon Brik. I already had my plane ticket."

Everyone knew who the main players were

in everyone else's lives. They had a phone chat group that kept them informed of one another's life details in real time, so there was no need to explain any further. Keila's friends, sitting around the table, began pouring their comments over the spread of huitlacoche crepes, taquitos, spinach dip, zucchini-flower quesadillas, and guacamole and chips.

"Don't cancel."

"Don't cheat."

"You said you'd give it a year."

"You need to be up-front with Oscar."

"Remember the Tarzan Principle: never let go of a vine before taking hold of the next one. I'd try things out with Simon before leaving your husband."

"Leaving your husband" were words Keila had never imagined she'd hear. She cringed when they floated out of her friend Betty's mouth as she chewed on a chicken taquito with crema and guac. The shock made her tune out the rest of the conversation, and as her book club members discussed the situation, talking all at the same time, she did a mental inventory of each instance in which Oscar had been assertive and helpful during Claudia's medical crisis. Bringing her a cake when no one else remembered it was her birthday certainly qualified as the gesture of a non-zombie. He had spoken with doctors, informed the family, made sure Claudia had plush pillows on her bed. She had to admit that he had made some attempts, however pathetic, to start a conversation with her, like when he offered to have coffee with her at the hospital and she declined. Many times he seemed to be about to say something but looked at her with sorry eyes instead. Lately she had awakened to his warm hand lightly caressing her shoulder over the pillow she'd placed between them as a barrier when he thought she was asleep. Not only was she failing to make good on her promise to her daughters to try to mend her marriage, but she was resisting all of Oscar's efforts. Worse even, she was contemplating an affair with Simon Brik. Was she abandoning her commitment halfway through the year?

By the end of book club, in which no one mentioned the book they'd read, Keila was lost in a jumble of thoughts. The wine had been particularly good that evening, so she drove home buzzed and confused and eager to call Simon.

Or not. Maybe. Damn.

Thursday, June 9th
The upcoming weekend was full of pos-

sibilities. Patricia was to pick up Eric at LAX the following day and drive up to Santa Barbara to spend a couple of days together. She lay in bed — house quiet, rooms dark — her hand distractedly reaching for her clitoris. She'd never really liked sex toys. Her fingers did a fine job in Eric's absence. But Eric wasn't on her mind that night, or the night before, or the night a week before when she had had impromptu sex with Benjamin in Minneapolis. Perhaps she was feeling giddy at the news of Claudia coming out of her coma and her attraction to her client prompted her to make the wrong decision. Funny, in all honesty, it didn't feel like a wrong decision. Her sex life with Eric had been more than satisfactory. She loved to fuck him, she on top, looking down to see his face contort with the pleasure of ejaculation. But in the past few days a feeling she had suppressed had risen to the surface, one that was far stronger than a craving and much more powerful than sex: she wanted warmth. She needed care. She missed the domesticity she had been brought up with.

This shift puzzled her, and she was unable to pinpoint an event that had triggered it. Having grown up watching telenovelas with Lola (unbeknownst to Keila), she'd developed an aversion to men who smothered women with their kisses and cheesy declarations of love. Of the many boyfriends she'd subjected to her chilly attitude throughout her high school and college years, she recalled the worst one, a sociology assistant professor in her senior year who had put his beating heart on the pillow of their lovemaking bed and set out to recite Hallmark-greeting-card-style poetry in her ear. Not quite down to the last stanza, she had quickly collected his clothes and shoes and sent him on his honey-dripping way. Eric was different. Cerebral. Calculating. If he ever felt he was melting with feelings of love, he masterfully concealed it. He agreed to her sexual demands and followed her lead. This was her unwritten contract and a major reason why she'd married him. But now she wished for what he could not provide and felt an explosion of despair inside.

Saturday, June 11th
The waxing crescent moon floated in the never completely dark predawn Los Angeles sky, like a fingernail clipping lost in the fibers of some old purple shag carpet. Olivia had been following its course for an hour. Unable to sleep, she had been spending

time outside, where she believed she could think more clearly. She lay on the hammock hanging on her terrace and took in the mild breeze. The divorce process was advancing faster than she had imagined when she first served the papers on Felix. Now she and Felix were waiting for the court to enter the judgment under the agreed-upon terms. How ironic, she thought, that she'd fought so hard to have a family and that the very fight was what had caused its demise.

After arranging a playdate for the twins and planning the rest of the day with Lola, who was taking them to get a haircut at the Yellow Balloon, a children's hair salon in Westwood, she left for the hospital. Olivia was the first visitor to arrive that morning and the hallways were eerily quiet. She had brought Claudia a box of macarons from a shop she loved in the Grove. She could never go to that mall without stopping to get some of those delectable French pastries.

"These are stale," said Claudia after nibbling on a few of them.

"I just bought them yesterday. Try the licorice."

Claudia put half a disk in her mouth.

"Nope. Tastes like air."

"How about this one? It's orange blossom."

She chewed slowly, trying to make out the flavor.

"Tastes like a rag," she said, and gave Olivia a piece to try.

"It's delicious. You're worrying me. Have you told the doctor?"

"I have and I didn't like his answer. It seems I have anosmia. I've lost my sense of smell and my sense of taste. My CN1 nerve was permanently damaged by the tumor. I didn't even know that fucking nerve existed."

Olivia considered the implications of what Claudia had just informed her of and sat on a corner of the bed.

"I know what you're thinking. Just say it," said Claudia.

"I'm sorry. I'm so sorry."

"History is full of deaf composers and blind painters. I don't see why there can't be a chef with no sense of smell or taste. At least my sight is coming back. If I trusted what I'm seeing, I could tell you I'm in a shower with the glass doors all fogged up. The doctor says it's expected."

Olivia extended three fingers in front of Claudia.

"How many fingers do you see?"

"Three. That's an easy one. Did you bring a pistachio macaron? Let me try it."

Olivia put the little green disk in Claudia's hand and waited for her to chew it.

"Nothing. It's like I'm chewing on cardboard. I don't know what's worse, having lost my sense of taste, or having lost Gabriel."

Was that a hallucination caused by the tumor, or had Claudia just dropped a bomb?

"What are you saying?"

"He has a lover in New York, Tammy fucking something, a lawyer at an oil company. I confronted him two weeks before I landed in the hospital. I thought you already knew."

"How could I know? No one told me. Does Mom know? How can anyone keep up with anything in this family!"

"I'm not sure. Didn't Gabriel tell you all? I told him I wanted to divorce him, which should have hurt, but the reality is that I wasn't feeling any pain. I really didn't care about his affair when he finally confessed. Maybe it was the effect of the tumor. I haven't been giving a shit about anything."

"That much I could tell. Just ask your Skirball Center client."

"But now it's starting to hurt. Not surgery,

but Gabriel cheating on me."

"I have to call Mom. Stay here."

"Not going anywhere," said Claudia with a droplet of sarcasm.

Olivia excused herself and walked along the hallways trying to imagine a future for her sister. It seemed to her that Claudia's life was playing out like a soap opera: the successful chef, the brain tumor, the coma, the loss of her sense of taste and smell, the end of her career, and now her husband cheating on her in the middle of her health crisis. It all suddenly came into focus, the fact that Gabriel was so interested in the possibility of Claudia dying before she regained consciousness. It was no accidental omission on his part, not telling the family about his lover, about Claudia's wish to leave him. He had to make sure no one knew Claudia had asked for a divorce, or he would have had a difficult time claiming her assets as his own.

Olivia called Keila and summoned her to the hospital. Then she called Patricia but could not locate her, so she texted her:

Call me ASAP. Fucking Gabriel cheated on Claudia. She wanted to divorce him since before the surgery.

?!?!?

We're meeting at the hospital.

Coming now.

Her next call was to Lola.

"Why didn't I see this?" said Olivia.

"All those trips. All the mystery. He sure does seem like a man who would do something like that, so suave and cool. But it's not your fault if you didn't see it coming. What is it with you girls? Why did you choose such crappy husbands?"

"I wish I knew, Lola." Olivia stopped and changed the subject out of profound discomfort. That was the key question she would have to ask herself later, when the fog of divorce finally dissipated from her mind. "I'll be back later, if you want to come to the hospital then. I know Claudia needs you."

"Of course."

Finally, Olivia called Gabriel, who surprisingly picked up at the first ring. "Don't you ever show your face around us again! You very well know why," she said, and hung up without letting him utter a word.

■ ■ ■ ■

Sunday, June 19th

On this cloudless ninety-six-degree Sunday, Olivia forced herself out of bed, through the record-shattering heat and into the cool confines of her car, and drove down the 134 to have breakfast with Lola. Olivia could have waited until Monday to tell her that her divorce process was coming to an end, but that morning she'd woken up with an uncontrollable urge to hide in Lola's arms, so she drove the twins to the bungalow that Felix had finally rented, dropped them off with an extra change of clothes, toys, blankies, and an emergency card with all their doctors' contact numbers in their bags, and sped downtown, not without first avoiding Felix's blank stare when he opened the door. No words were said. An exchange with a supermarket cashier would have been more cordial.

The street was populated with parked cars, some old and beat-up, others shiny and new. Olivia squeezed her minivan into the only available spot, half a block away from Lola's house, and passed through the elaborate wrought-iron gate. There was so much TLC concentrated in this tiny patio:

the bougainvillea that embraced the façade, the numerous pots with hydrangeas, lavender, hibiscus, and rosemary, the little fountain with the carved stone angel spreading its wings, the vegetable garden, the rows of corn. Lola opened the door before Olivia even knocked.

"That was quick!"

"The freeway was empty. I got you tamales."

"And I made chilaquiles with low-carb tortillas, just for you."

Once settled at the dining table, Olivia said, "The attorney just got the judgment notice on Friday. We're done. We're sharing child support of the twins, but I get custody; they'll be living with me. We each get to keep our business. We'll have to sell the house and split the proceeds."

Lola passed the platter with the low-carb chilaquiles.

"What's happening to the embryos?" she asked.

Olivia took her time to answer.

"The judge decided that he couldn't force Felix to be a parent. They'll have to be discarded."

Olivia hugged Lola tight, and in her arms, her favorite place in times of despair, Olivia came to the end of a life she'd imagined for herself, for the twins, for Felix, and for the embryos. In the minutes that the embrace lasted, she saw reflected in her inner eyelids the slides of a show that would never be projected, fading out as in a digital effect. No more could she wish for a family vacation, a road trip with the girls singing in the back seat and her riding shotgun, chatting with Felix about nothing important. Gone was the possibility of a quiet family evening in their living room, enjoying the girls' play, while cuddling with her husband on the sofa. What she might have lived in the future had vanished. How can I miss what hasn't happened? she thought, suddenly realizing she was in full bereavement for a lost life that had existed only in her hopes.

"Now go on and be with your dad," said Lola. "It's Father's Day, and as far as I can tell, he's being sorely neglected by all of you."

By the time she arrived at the Alvarados', Patricia had already prepared a brunch to celebrate Oscar on Father's Day — as Keila had refused to cook — and everyone was seated. On Claudia's recommendation, she had made curry chicken crepes, a simple frittata dish, and turkey bacon. The spread included a basket of corn muffins and other pastries that Eric had brought from a bakery on La Brea. But the table was half empty. With Claudia still in the hospital, Gabriel gone forever, and Felix at his bungalow, the festivity was mostly a mix of empty chairs and incomplete couples. In fact, the gathering was no festivity at all. All they could talk about was Claudia's impending divorce process. Oscar was meeting with a lawyer later in the evening and the family as a whole had to make some decisions and run them by Claudia.

But this was also Oscar's day, so he made the effort to be in better spirits than usual, if only to humor his daughters. He didn't deserve the acknowledgment. Only good fathers did. Perhaps he had been a better father before, when there were no secrets.

"Where's Felix?" asked Keila.

"He's in Oxnard with the twins. They're visiting his dad," Olivia replied quickly in front of an empty plate, her belly full of tamales and chilaquiles. She regretted not having thought of a believable explanation for Felix's absence.

But Keila didn't seem curious enough to continue the inquiry and moved on to the business of filling everyone's glasses. Eric had brought two bottles of Keila's favorite cava, a recurring gift that had quickly become a tradition with its corresponding expectations.

Olivia sat quietly passing the platters around, skipping Felix's empty seat. She imagined him reading the newspaper on a park bench while the twins played, half supervised, in a nearby sandbox, putting leaves in their mouths, getting sand in their eyes, and her mood soured even more. He didn't deserve the girls, not even on Father's Day.

She realized she could no longer keep her divorce from her family, but she had yet to come up with a strategy to announce it without infuriating her mother, given how advanced the process already was. And then there was Claudia's own ordeal. How much divorce could her family stomach?

Monday, June 20th

By Monday morning the Alvarados had united against Gabriel after a weekend of intense discussions, first by Claudia's bedside, and then at Keila and Oscar's home after the doctor asked them to leave and let Claudia rest.

Oscar hired a lawyer immediately and took charge of leading the strategy. Keila's surprise was evident, but she didn't say anything. Instead, she let him direct everybody, as he always had in the past.

Oscar didn't acknowledge his change in mood; he simply focused on the task of getting his daughter divorced as quickly as possible. But he did realize that any lingering thoughts of suicide had dissipated, so he silently thanked Gabriel.

By day's end, the lawyer had replaced all mentions of Gabriel in Claudia's will with her sisters' names and had gotten Claudia's approval to proceed. They had offered a clean deal in which Gabriel got to keep the New York apartment and his business, but nothing else. Claudia would keep the Malibu house, her cooking show, royalties, residuals, books, catering business, and anything related to her career, and no alimony at all. She'd also keep Ramsay and Velcro.

Tuesday, June 21st
Early in the morning, Oscar went outside to the shed where his work tools stoically accumulated dust to find a quiet moment to read the newspaper. Well, that was his reasoning, but on a more profound examination, he realized he was really hiding from the pain of watching Claudia's life crumble. He sat on the only chair and spread the paper over the worktable. Not one, but two wildfires had broken out at the same time:

280

the Reservoir Fire and the Fish Fire. He wondered how many thousands of acres would be scorched. In a few days the final tally would be published in the paper and Oscar would add the incidents to the long list in his Weather Events notebook, always hoping for zero fatalities. Sometimes unrecognizable bodies would turn up under ashes and debris, days or even weeks after cleanup crews combed the area.

He googled the satellite pictures on his phone, recognized the smoke and the burn scar on the surface of the Earth, and felt sorry for those people who might have lost their lives, for those who evacuated, for dogs and cats and wild animals running away bewildered and terrified. Everyone seemed to be suffering around him, coyotes and mountain lions immolated by raging fires, birds with ignited feathers as they flew their last flight in the red air. The images in his brain killed him with despair.

Wednesday, June 22nd
In the middle of all this, Patricia lost her Target client to a rival agency. She brushed the news aside and focused on helping Claudia get divorced. She could replace the account easily, but not now. Her sister needed her wisdom.

■■■■

Thursday, June 23rd

By Tuesday morning, a sheriff in New York had served the divorce papers on Gabriel as he was leaving his building to go to his Pilates class. A preemptive attack was the best way to proceed, according to Oscar.

To everyone's shock, the reply came on Thursday, so the family agreed to hold an emergency meeting at the hospital to advance the process as swiftly as they could. Gabriel claimed that he deserved to keep Velcro and the Malibu house, even though that had been Claudia's home years before she met him.

"Let him have the house," said Claudia. "I don't want to live in a place that reminds me of him. But Velcro is nonnegotiable. He loves me more than him. He has always slept on my side of the bed."

"Fine. We'll fight for Velcro. As for the house, let's sell it. There's no reason for you to lose it for emotional reasons," said Olivia. It pained her to not be able to share her own torment with her family, especially now that Claudia was going through it herself. How could she upstage her sister? But her comment didn't go unnoticed by Patricia, who gave her a knowing look across the room.

By the end of the day, they agreed to counter Gabriel's demand with the proposal to keep Velcro, sell the house, and split the proceeds 75 percent for Claudia and 25 percent for Gabriel.

Back at the Alvarados', Patricia and Olivia continued to discuss Gabriel's descent into the infra-world of jerks. How quickly he'd gone from ideal husband to concerned husband to absent husband and, finally, to the horrible person he now was.

"The monster was always there, just underneath the allure, under those fucking pink shirts he always wears," Olivia said, not quite in the room, thinking about Felix.

Exhausted from it all, Keila started the kettle.

"A cup of tila tea, anyone, to calm the nerves?"

Friday, June 24th

Claudia and Gabriel's last call went like this:

"I'm calling to let you know I'll agree to your terms. We can get this done very quickly," he said coldly.

"I see you can't wait to marry your lover. What's her name? Tammy? I have a collection of photos of both of you in *Variety* and

283

The Hollywood Reporter. Six red carpets! Eight screenings! And who knows how many more events that have not been reported by the media, how many more that happened while I was in a coma. You're so damn careless I even thought you were subconsciously screaming to be found out."

"Yes, maybe I was. But I didn't ask you to divorce me."

"I'm glad I did, and on my terms."

"Speaking of the terms, I still think I deserve to keep the Malibu house and the apartment in New York. I'm the one who is bicoastal. I need the two properties. Besides, you don't even know if you'll ever be able to live on your own again."

"I may end up being an invalid stuck in some assisted-living facility, but you can't even write a sentence and that's your worst handicap. You wish to be one of the writers you represent and worship, you want to be the storyteller being discovered, the one who concocts tales that send people to unimagined worlds, but you can't. You haven't got a single creative hair on your body and that's the one thing you'll never be able to acquire. In terms of talent, you'll always live in poverty. Get your own house in Malibu. And I'm glad I'm keeping Velcro."

■ ■ ■ ■

Camp was starting on Sunday, and Patricia and Daniel had just arrived in Lake Tahoe after a nine-hour drive from Los Angeles. Daniel would be spending the next two weeks with a group of LGBTQ-plus teenagers in the wilds. Daniel had found this summer camp. Patricia was surprised that it existed. She wished she'd had an opportunity like this to explore her own thoughts about sexual orientation as a teenager. She remembered a girl crush she'd had in seventh grade, a Guatemalan girl with a thick, long braid, and a wide smile, but in the end, her attraction to boys ended up pulling her in another direction.

As the camp's website explained, the goal was to create an environment where children could feel safe to express their thoughts, doubts, and feelings without anyone judging them, including questions of identity. How fitting, Patricia thought, that the camp would be located in Tahoe, on the shores of a lake split in half between two states, imaginary state lines dividing it lengthwise, and yet holding the same body of water.

"I bet we're going to go on horseback rides," said Daniel, thrilled.

"For sure. I saw on the website that you're also going to have campfires and hike with a bunch of kids your age. You'll put on a play that the parents are going to see at the end of camp. There's also going to be an art workshop, and a lot of other stuff. How cool is that?"

"Yeah. Cool."

"Are you nervous?"

"A little. No. A lot. Are there going to be many LGBTQ-plus people?"

"That's the group of kids this camp is for."

"I'm just wondering what kind of people fall into the plus sign after the Q. Maybe I'm one of those."

"You'll find out. I'm sure you'll learn a lot from this experience. Maybe you'll even be adding more letters to the acronym."

On arrival at the campground, on a wooded slope with a partial view of the lake, parents and children of various ages were ushered to the main cabin for a meet-and-greet.

"Welcome everyone! Our counselors, Tyler and Logan, are going to pass around some baskets with pronoun pins for you to attach to your clothes. Parents too! Please pick out the one that best describes how you wish to be referred to. Don't worry if you're not sure. You can always get a different one later on," said Coach Alex, a woman in her late thirties with a broad smile and sweet voice.

Daniel passed on the "They" basket, but he picked out a "He" pin and put it on his jacket's right pocket. Then he grabbed a "She" pin and fastened it on his left pocket.

"Can I keep both?" he asked Logan.

"You can do anything you want with those pins. Wear all three if you feel like it."

"Just these two."

After the orientation meeting, Patricia said good-bye to Daniel, and to convey trust in his judgment she gave him as little advice as possible. Of course he was going to brush his teeth. For sure he'd take care of his cellphone, avoid going in the lake by himself, and follow the rules and make friends. She didn't tell him, "Enjoy camp." Instead, she said, "Enjoy the journey."

Some of the parents left the campground together for an impromptu dinner at a nearby restaurant, but Patricia declined the invitation and went to town by herself.

Open mic was in full swing at the Divided Sky. The place was overcrowded past the legal limit, so she squeezed herself into a narrow space between two stools to order a mezcal at the bar.

"Are you into the smoky kind?" asked the man sitting on one of the stools.

Patricia drank a sip from her shot glass and took her time to answer.

"I do like the smoky kind, espadín, but if I can get some tobalá, I could sing all night."

"I'm Mexican, too," he said, guessing accurately.

His name was Jesús. He wore a man bun just like half the other men at the place, a flannel shirt over a dark blue T-shirt, and a pair of jeans that seemed one size too large.

"I knew you were Mexican by the way you pronounced 'mezcal,'" he said, preemptively answering a question Patricia had in her mind.

"I have to go," he said after the second round. "My friends are coming over. Want to join us?"

Surprising herself, she did.

Jesús drove along a dirt road into the forest and pulled into the driveway of a log cabin. Four other cars were already parked and loud music was coming out of the house, so Patricia ruled out the possibility of getting raped and murdered by a lone woodsman in a pitch-dark forest.

"My roommates and I have an art club every Saturday night and we invite a bunch

288

of people, some new and some regulars. We call it La Cabane Bohéme. Everyone brings an art project that needs to be completed by dawn."

"What's yours?"

"Mine is taking longer to build. It's a Trojan horse. I'm bringing it to Burning Man this year. I'm going to sleep inside. It's out back. I'll show it to you later."

Jesús's friends could have been the people from the bar, same kind of crowd. Everyone worked strewn about on the floor, as if they were kindergartners. One guy had brought a sewing machine and was busy putting together a vest made of shocking-pink faux fur. Another one was assembling a book using flattened cereal boxes and string. Yet another one in the far corner was painting a cartoonlike figure on a canvas leaning against the wall. Patricia could see the holes between the logs on the walls, some of them stuffed with pieces of old fabric or newspaper, but others clearly open, allowing the cool forest air in. She wondered how these people dealt with that in the winter months.

Patricia located a few half-empty bottles of alcohol on the kitchen counter and filled a shot glass with tequila after she removed suspicious fingerprints with her shirt. She found a spot on the floor, since the only couch available already had four people crammed one on top of the other, and sat next to a girl who offered her a drag of her joint. Taking a closer look, Patricia realized that these people were actually college students. Jesús's beard and thick eyebrows had disoriented her and she had failed to estimate his age.

"We just graduated last week," he said. "Most people are leaving town, but I'm hanging out here for a while. The Tahoe vibe is hard to resist."

Neither Jesús nor Patricia stayed in the living room to watch the art projects evolve. They spent the rest of the night in his room, where the rancid-smelling sheets badly needed washing and piles of clothes here and there resembled collapsed bodies. But the sex with Jesús was terrific; just as good as sex with Eric and with Benjamin. She added him to her mental catalog of ex-lovers: the Krav Maga instructor from Echo Park, the surfer dude from Windansea Beach in La Jolla, the silkscreen artist from Frogtown, and the landscape architect from Venice, all top performers. Those who didn't excel had been quickly forgotten. She thought about Claudia, about Gabriel and his lover, Tammy, and suddenly her hands felt sweaty.

Sunday, June 26th

As she drove back to Los Angeles the next morning, Patricia realized that somehow she'd known that what seemed an innocent question about mezcal would evolve into a night of sex and abandon. She had to admit that she had been looking for it. She loved Eric, but what kind of love was it? So much in their relationship was incomplete, but taking on a lover would only result in having an incomplete relationship not just with one man, but with two.

Then the call came from Keila.

"Olivia is getting divorced."

Tuesday, June 28th

Oscar wasn't running from the news of Olivia's imminent divorce, he thought. As he drove onto the freeway, he kept reminding himself that he had work to do at Happy Crunch Almond Orchard. As soon as he parked by the gate, he got busy with Los Tres Primos monitoring, evaluating, and fighting predator mites, peach tree borers, six-spotted thrips, protein-feeding ant colonies, and freeloading ground squirrels that could ruin his crop. And what about

291

nasty sons-in-law? For the millionth time he tried to switch back to the task at hand: the traps, the rodenticides, the protection of the delicate hulls that were about to split, but he concluded that Felix and Gabriel were the most dangerous pests and gave up avoiding the issue. Now he had two daughters whose married lives were unraveling and he couldn't help them, just as he couldn't help his almonds. Just as he couldn't help himself.

Not only did he have to save his crop, his orchard, but he had to earn money, he had to deliver. Claudia could tap into the proceeds of her royalties, but for how long? Would he have to help Olivia? Downsizing to a smaller house or an apartment would have been an option for him and Keila, but now with Claudia's situation, it was unlikely she could ever live on her own. And Patricia? She'd never lived anywhere else. Did he have the heart to kick her out? Could she be helpful in caring for her older sister? He realized how lucky he'd been all his life, never having to worry about money, and here he was, at sixty, watching his fortune wither in the hot, thin, dry California air.

JULY

The musty smell of standing water came from the flower vase at the center of Keila's dining table. Things had taken a turn for the worse in that tiny ecological unit: the dahlias were starting to lose their furiously red petals, which fell haphazardly onto the wooden surface, and their long, hollow stems were bending down in submission, accepting their inevitable death. Having been raised in Mexico, Keila knew that dahlias symbolized change, new life, and opportunities. But on that afternoon, she wasn't thinking about this well-known fact.

"But why? Why would you keep me out of this?" Keila asked.

Olivia bit her lip hard.

"You and Dad already had too much to deal with. I didn't want to pile it on."

"I could have helped you. And why was I the only one in the dark?"

293

"Only Patricia knew, Mom."

Patricia nodded from the other side of the table. "She wanted to protect you, Mom," she said.

"Protect me from what, my daughter's ordeal?" she replied to Patricia, then turning to Olivia: "I'm your mother. I am entitled to participate in all of your life's travails."

Olivia picked up a wilted dahlia from the table and squeezed it in her hand.

"I could have given you some advice that might have avoided this terrible outcome," said Keila, immediately regretting it. What authority did she have to give that kind of advice to her daughter? What was she doing to save her own marriage?

"What about the twins?" she asked Olivia, maneuvering around the subject. "Are you sacrificing their well-being, their family, for two embryos, two little buggers who don't have a life yet? And they'll have to be destroyed anyway!"

"They're not buggers. And they deserve a shot at life. Besides, the reason I wanted to end my marriage with Felix was not just the embryos. I ruined our relationship by pushing him too hard. It's my fault alone."

Keila wrapped her hand around Olivia's and decided that silence was the best reply.

Patricia kept quiet throughout the conversation, thinking that a separation from Eric would be out of the question. Her sisters had beat her to it, and she would just have to wait for a better moment, or work on her marriage. It bothered her that so many pleasurable things — or things that should be pleasurable — had been turned into work: "Are you still working on that salad?" she'd heard countless waiters ask her in the middle of a meal, prompting her to answer, "It's not work at all. I'm actually enjoying it."

"You better not be thinking about leaving Eric," said Keila all of a sudden, jolting Patricia back from her ruminations.

Monday, July 4th

Early in the morning Oscar had gone down to the garage to dig out a small American flag from the file cabinet where Keila kept her naturalization papers. He was now attaching it with tape to Claudia's hospital bed headboard.

Over the next few hours, the entire family paraded through Claudia's room, one after the other. Olivia brought her some gossip magazines, as her sight was improving quickly. Patricia gave her brand-new pajamas. Keila got her an arrangement of red roses with white and purple orchids. A group of her friends, mostly cooks, showed up with Independence Day goodies that she would not be able to taste, not even the yellowtail sashimi with ponzu sauce and jalapeño slices that she loved so much, from her dear chef friend Hiroshi.

"Sorry, man, tastes like rubber bands."

"I understand. No worries, I can give it to the nurses," said Hiroshi, walking away with the white Styrofoam box and chopsticks in his hands.

Up until that moment, Claudia had been sure that she'd be able to go back to work after she finished her rehabilitation. She had lost the palate to create new tastes, but she believed she would be able to rely on whatever she could remember. After all, the sense of smell was the sense of memory. She could still evoke the scent of the fresh cilantro from her mother's garden; how she crushed a leaf between her fingers, sniffing the fragrance in delight. Then her imagination suddenly became flooded by the pungent smells of a mix of chiles being ground together in the molcajete to make mole rojo. Those were her best childhood moments, when she could not leave Keila's kitchen, mystified by the unexpected flavors and perfumes that wafted from her pots and pans when she cooked her steamed nopales with onion and epazote, Hidalgo style; her huitlacoches with calabacitas and béchamel; her norteño tamales with black beans; her rabbit in chile ancho sauce; or her shrimp in pipián mole. And not just her Mexican recipes, but she vividly remembered her mother's Jewish cuisine, too: her home-baked challah bread, gefilte fish, holishkes, chopped liver, knish, rugelach, and her famous matzo ball soup.

At what point had she become an incorrigible voluptuary, finely attuned to the succulent messages coming from the outside through the windows of her body? She didn't know. Perhaps she had been born equipped with this talent, inherited from Keila. But she had it wrong about the sense of smell. It was the actual smells and flavors that brought about memories, not the other way around. Without real scents captured by her nostrils, without flavors enchanting or repulsing her taste buds, all she had were clear recollections of her past, but they felt flat and distant, as if seen behind a thick glass.

"I heard your show got canceled," said Hiroshi when he returned from the nurses' station. "I'm so sorry."

"Just residuals from now on, if that's

consolation," said Claudia.

"I'm glad I taped most of the episodes."

That bit of information gave Claudia's battered self-esteem a little breath of life. She might not be able to cook again, or even to write about food. What credibility would a chef who can't taste or smell have? But her work would transcend her, and that validated everything.

By three o'clock everyone had left the hospital to attend Fourth of July cookouts and pool parties around town in perfect seventy-three-degree weather, while Claudia stayed behind, in her hospital bed, wearing her new pajamas one size too large, and for the first time in her life, feeling sorry for herself.

Tuesday, July 5th

A thought, a persistent one, forced itself into Keila's mind as she dragged along the driveway two large trash bags full of red, white, and blue detritus and leftovers from the Fourth of July family cookout to dump in the appropriate color-coded trash bins by the side of the house: Why bother trying to save my marriage to set a good example for the girls, if they're getting divorced themselves?

■ ■ ■ ■

Wednesday, July 6th

Predawn freeway dwellers: Uber drivers taking people to LAX to catch the first flight out, territorial gym buffs rushing to get their favorite bike in spinning class, FedEx drivers starting their daily rounds, jardineros in their Mad Max trucks filled with tools and hoses and contraptions masterfully deployed to seduce the earth, someone else's earth, into beauty. These were the people sharing the lanes with Patricia that morning. She, too, was on a mission.

She pulled over outside the fertility lab where Olivia's cryopreserved embryos were kept and parked.

"I have an appointment with Dr. Keller to see if I'm a candidate for IVF," she said as she arrived at the registration desk. "Patricia Remillard, eight o'clock."

After a few minutes of filling out paperwork, she was called in where Mabel, the ultrasound technician, waited. She closed the door behind Patricia and spoke in a low voice.

"Is Olivia ready?"

"She's eager to move forward," said Patricia. "If we really want to do this, we need to move fast. We have very few days before the lab gets the court order. It's final now."

"Here are the prep meds and instructions," she said, as she handed her a plain brown paper bag. "Make sure you start taking them today and come back in a couple of weeks."

Patricia had befriended Mabel during the many fertility procedures Olivia had gone through. As her sister's treatments intensified and Felix lost all interest, she promised herself to always accompany her and hold her hand. It was during those multiple efforts and failures that Patricia and Mabel had started to go out after work. Patricia even had introduced Mabel to a copywriter from her agency. They fell in love and ended up living together. And now Mabel and Patricia had become co-conspirators in a scheme only they and Olivia knew about.

"I've got all the paperwork ready and set the eggs aside. Thankfully we have a new lab technician and I was able to get around her," said Mabel, reassuring Patricia. "We can't let this monster get away with discarding Olivia's embryos. Felix is such a sore loser. If he could have, he would have auctioned them off on eBay! You should have seen the ad he wanted to post. And he bragged about it to everyone in the clinic!

We had to tell him it was illegal. Unbelievable."

After the appointment and on the way to a meeting at Fox Studios, Patricia called Olivia.

"It's done. Mabel checked me and we're on track," she said into the phone's speaker.

"This is not right, Pats. We can't go through with this."

"What? Cold feet? After everything we discussed? You're not stealing your embryos; you're rescuing them. Think of yourself as the Robin Hood of fertilized eggs. It's like a mitzvah."

"I know, but it just doesn't feel right. And I want you to know how grateful I am to you for volunteering to carry the babies. Is there a better surrogate mom in the entire planet? No! But how are you going to explain your pregnancy to Eric? He'll think the babies are his! We really haven't thought this through."

"We'll figure it out in the next few days, you'll see. For now, I'm going to start taking the meds."

Olivia was right, Patricia thought. Eric was an unsolved hurdle. Or not. There was a high probability that by the time she showed a bump, he'd be gone from her life. But she couldn't disclose this to Olivia just yet. She called Keila.

"Where are you, Mom?"

"I'm at LAX. I'm off to Mexico City, last minute. I'll be working on a new show at the gallery. I'll be back on Friday night. What is it, honey?"

"Nothing. I just wanted to hear your voice. Wanted to thank you for birthing me."

"Oh, Pats. That's the sweetest thing you've said to me in a long time! I love being your mom, you know that."

"I do. Love you, too. Take care."

After she hung up, Patricia reached for the box of tissues on the floor and blew her nose. Somehow her visit to the doctor had brought about a forgotten feeling. She imagined herself wiggling through her mother's cervix, headfirst, and finding her way out of her vagina into a life so impossible to understand that numerous religions had been invented in the attempt to give it meaning. She pressed her teary eyes with the tissue and tossed it on the passenger seat.

Thursday, July 7th
A feeling of helplessness flooded Oscar's heart as he washed his SUV on the driveway, using as little water as possible. There

were still months ahead without a drop of rain and the reservoirs were hitting bottom.

He'd been missing Keila, the Keila he'd always loved. He longed to cuddle under the blankets as they used to and talk about unimportant things. A forlorn grimace settled on his face. He squeezed the excess soap from the sponge into a bucket and proceeded to caress the tire. How had his life come to this point? He remembered the day he met Keila in twelfth grade, an exchange student from Mexico with a smile that caused his heart to plunge into the depths of his guts. He could still recite from memory the carefully folded note passed down from student to student all the way to her hand in math class with a bold invitation to see *One Flew Over the Cuckoo's Nest*, a movie that would surely win at the Oscars. Then, as the school year progressed and his relationship with Keila solidified, they went to see Deep Purple at the Cal Jam II rock concert at the Ontario Motor Speedway and became regulars at downtown Chinese restaurants, unlikely venues where punk rock bands such as the Germs and the Weirdos played. At sixty, he was still a fan. Even after Keila went back to Mexico City the following summer, he'd still go by himself just to miss her while he listened to his favorite songs. How many letters crossed the border north and south before she said yes and returned to Los Angeles to marry him two years later, halfway through college? He rinsed the tires with a trickle of water from the hose and went inside to write Keila a note inviting her to the movies. He folded it carefully and threw it in the recycling trash can.

Nineteen hundred miles away, Simon Brik carefully unfolded the piece of paper that Keila had just slid across the restaurant table in downtown Mexico City. The only word, written in her hand, was "Yes."

"Are you sure about this?" he asked her, hopeful.

Keila nodded, her eyes locked on his.

"Then say it."

"Yes," she said without hesitation.

They skipped dessert, went to his apartment in the Condesa neighborhood, and as they reached the second-floor landing, Keila stopped.

"Maybe not." Her voice was almost a whisper, as if she were talking to herself.

"We don't have to do this, Keila, dear," said Simon, caressing her hair. "I can continue wanting you. I'm used to it."

After a long silence in which she allowed Simon to cocoon her cheeks with his hands, she said: "What kind of tequila do you have?"

Simon's 1930s Art Deco apartment occupied the entire floor; the walls were covered with art, the sofa populated by plush cushions, the lighting carefully designed to create a feeling of cozy sophistication. Keila focused on his collection to diffuse her nervousness. A Carlos Amorales gouache on paper here, a Gabriel Orozco on the opposite wall, an Iñaki Bonillas and a small, early Francis Alÿs over there, by the window overlooking the canopy of the park out front. Keila recognized several of her own pieces, some dating back two decades, before sculpture, when she was still painting. The old hardwood floor squeaked under their weight as they walked around the living room.

"Oh, look, that's a nice Dr. Lakra you have there," she said, pointing to a piece next to an antique armoire that had been upcycled as a bar and where Simon had just selected a crystal bottle of tequila.

"Art. It's my other obsession," he said, looking directly at her. No blinking.

They talked shop for a while, discussing the works of other contemporary artists as they drank a few shots. And sometime between ten thirty and midnight — neither would care to remember — Simon walked Keila to his bedroom and laid her on the bed.

"Isn't this a bit fast?" asked Keila.

"I've only been seducing you for more than two decades, but sure, we can slow down," whispered Simon in her ear. "I'll take you home."

Instead of leaving, Keila put her arms around Simon and pressed herself against him. He undressed her and cupped her still-supple breasts in his hands.

Their lovemaking was twenty years in the making, and yet it felt so new to Keila. That night, as Simon slept beside her, she wondered if this would be the first or the last time she'd sleep in that bed, with that man.

Saturday, July 9th

Of all the marathons that Claudia had run all over the country — Boston, Chicago, New York, Anchorage, Honolulu, Niagara Falls — there was one that gave her the most pride, not just for running it, but for breaking her own record: the incredibly challenging Grandfather Mountain Marathon in North Carolina.

But on that balmy seventy-five-degree Los Angeles morning, she was watching the marathon on TV in her pajamas when athlete Mike Mitchell crossed the finish line in first place. She turned off the TV and with a great deal of difficulty wobbled from her bed to the bathroom to pee.

Sunday, July 10th

Having flown into Tahoe on Saturday, Patricia made time for an overnight visit to her new and definitely temporary friend Jesús before picking up Daniel. Even many years later, in her old age, she'd always remember the forty-five-minute kiss and the whispers of desire in that log cabin in the woods right on the state line between California and Nevada. What was it with men in buns? It seemed to her so androgynous, so sexy. After breakfast — he cooked, not bad at all — they fucked some more, she on top, always on top. Then, she showered, lifting her toes to avoid touching the scum-covered tile, and drove her car to camp to pick up Daniel.

The campers' play, based on the novel *Middlesex* (abridged and adapted for teenagers), was a total triumph. It helped that two of the parents were working Hollywood actors and had volunteered to direct the kids. Not only that, they had financed the scholarship program for several of the campers whose families could not afford tuition. Patricia herself had pitched in, as had many of the other parents. It was a California thing to do and she felt proud to be a native.

Daniel spent a substantial portion of the flight back to Los Angeles listing for Patricia all the camp's highlights.

"I want to change my name," he said.

Patricia took the statement in and gave herself time to think about her answer.

"What do you want to call yourself?"

"Dani. It's Hebrew. It means 'God will judge.' It could be a boy name or a girl name."

"I like that. When do you want to do it? I can be your witness when we go to City Hall."

"Anytime this summer, but everyone can start calling me Dani now."

"What about your gender, Dani? Any thoughts?"

"I know that physically I'm a boy and I'm fine with that. But sometimes I want to do girl stuff. I feel more connected to girls, but I also want to hang out with boys. I really don't have to claim an identity. Alex says that I could consider myself gender fluid."

"And are you okay with this definition?"

Dani nodded and shrugged at the same time.

"What about friends? Did you make any?"

"Dylan's a great actor. Well, you saw them at the play in the role of Cal. Brook is cool. He's trans. But I think my best friend is Phoenix. She's from L.A. too. We're going to hang out. Will you drive me to Pasadena?"

"Of course. She can come over to our house too, if you'd like."

And just when the pilot said, "Ladies and gentlemen, as we start our descent, please make sure your seat backs and tray tables are in their full upright position," Patricia understood that her child was no different from the person he was before camp. She turned to Dani, his face pressed against the window to get a good view of the Los Angeles sprawl below, and wondered what kind of fate waited for him in this city of endless tract houses surrounded by yards with pools and detached garages, inhabited by dwellers who might or might not be as accepting of her child's gender fluidity as she was.

Monday, July 11th

It wasn't just that water was scarce. All that carbon dioxide, all those greenhouse gases launched relentlessly into the atmosphere were provoking irreparable changes in the

Earth's climate. What was going to be the consequence of this on water quality? Oscar looked around his backyard, standing on the keloid scar, and, making sure no one saw him, looked up to the infinite blue and extended his arms, palms facing the sky, and pleaded to his maker, whoever that was, for humankind to take some responsibility.

Wednesday, July 13th

Hull rot was the enemy right around mid-July. Oscar knew this and was ever more vigilant. He had to protect his Nonpareil almonds from rotting and was willing to do anything to procure a healthy hull split, that delicate moment in an almond's life when the nut finally flaunts its beauty. He had been shortening the irrigation time since early in the month to keep moisture at a perfect level.

This time, Aunt Belinda went along, a rare occasion. Her knee replacement gone wrong prevented her from venturing onto the uneven ground between the trees, but she was eager to discuss the business's finances with Oscar, and the SUV offered an ideal bubble of privacy.

"You'll have to tell her at some point," she said on the way to the orchard.

"It's not the right time," he said. "You

310

know Keila, how she overreacts."

"This is unsustainable. We already went over the numbers."

Oscar sighed. Aunt Belinda, his faithful manager, was sounding an alarm he didn't have the courage to hear. She'd always been the more levelheaded of the two. Oscar, always dreaming up new projects, not all of them sensible, ultimately acknowledged and appreciated her prudence. Her advice had prevented Oscar from making mistakes before, but never in a situation of this magnitude.

"Your papá José always listened to Mamá Peregrina," she said, referring to her parents and Oscar's grandparents. "And I inherited my mamá's knack for business. So, I'm telling you, be careful, Oscar. You could lose it all."

Oscar felt the weight of Aunt Belinda's words, how charged with family tradition they were, how strong a warning it was, but struggled to accept the advice.

"There's still a chance that we'll get more favorable weather. Let's wait this out for now."

Wednesday, July 20th
Patricia checked in at the fertility lab and

after a few minutes was called in by Mabel herself.

"Let's do this," she said, her adrenaline at full capacity. "We've got babies to make."

After scheming and scrapping a dozen options while barhopping around town and getting wasted, from going to the clinic in the middle of the night to stealing the embryos and performing IVF in some dark alley, Patricia, Olivia, and Mabel had agreed that the best way to go through with their plan was to do it in plain sight. So, Patricia had met with the doctor, confirmed that she was indeed a good candidate for the procedure, and scheduled her appointment like any other patient.

"Did you take your meds, your hormones?" asked Mabel.

"I did everything you asked," said Patricia. "Thanks for all those samples, by the way."

"Hey, I'm a stickler when it comes to prepping a uterus for embryo implantation, and two weeks is barely enough time to get it nice and ready. Are you sure you don't want even a little sedation?"

"No. I'll take the pain."

Had this not been a secret endeavor, Patricia would have live-streamed it to all her followers. Sharing her act of surrogacy on behalf of her sister would have been the ultimate experience, transparency at its fullest. But keeping it private offered a different kind of mystique, a rare privilege in these days of social media exposure, that she appreciated.

"We'll be done in no time. It won't hurt any more than a Pap smear."

Patricia changed into the exam gown and lay down on the patient bed, and as Mabel started the embryo transfer, she thought about her sister waiting at home. What they had just done was completely illegal and reckless, but it was divine. Earlier, Mabel had replaced Olivia's embryos with other ones that were to be discarded anyway. No one would ever know. Not the clinic. Not the judge. Not Felix. Especially Felix. In the Uber back to her house, she became convinced that she really only needed to deal with one person, and that was going to be a major challenge: Eric.

Thursday, July 21st

If this wildfire hadn't threatened to burn down the iconic Hollywood sign, it wouldn't even register: it scorched a mere eighteen acres right next to multimillion-dollar homes sprinkled here and there on the hill's sloping terrain. This particular fire caused chaos as drivers on the 101 rubbernecked

313

in smoke-filled air and tried to catch Insta-grammable photos. The slowdown, which happened during rush hour, reminded Angelenos that they'd need to get accustomed to an ever-extending fire season that caused the loss of billions in property, increased tragic fatalities, and forced evacuations. Among them, stuck in traffic, was Keila, who was busy practicing her Kegel exercises as she drove, worried about how relaxed her pelvic-floor muscles felt lately. She refused to have to wear diapers in the future and she'd already had a couple of little pee accidents.

By then she was resigned to miss a dinner date in Burbank with one of her book club friends.

"It's a disaster. I can even see a house on the hill burning right now. There are three helicopters circling around. No way I can make it. Let's reschedule. Give me a new date," she said, putting the phone up to her mouth as she spoke through the speaker.

She got off the freeway and turned around, taking surface streets back home in a *Blade Runner*–like atmosphere filled with smoke. It was as if God had sent the fires that darkened the sky to compensate for the eternal sunshine he had awarded the city. She thought of texting Oscar the photo she had taken, but remembered that she was angry with him. She thought of texting it to Simon, but she needed to put out that particular fire before it got out of control, so she put her phone away. A subtle feeling of remorse tickled her esophagus and instantly gave her heartburn.

Friday, July 22nd

The fuel was chaparral and brush, the cause, unknown. Oscar tallied yet another wildfire in his notebook with a squeezed heart: the Sand Fire in the Angeles National Forest, which broke out on a record heat day of 110 degrees. Would his beloved California become one huge, dark land scar to be seen from spaceships? On his way to the garage to check on the contents of their fire-evacuation suitcases, he wondered if there was anything he could do other than obsess about fires and landslides and dust storms. Yes, there was, but he'd been avoiding it out of sheer fear: he needed to make good on his promise to his daughters to mend his relationship with Keila, but every time he thought about bringing her flowers or surprising her with a dinner date, he'd restrain himself. He had the feeling none of those romantic efforts that had worked before would really make Keila welcome him in her life again. He'd already wasted half the year and hadn't made an inch of progress. He'd thought the way he'd handled Claudia's tumor crisis would help, but nothing softened Keila's stance. But, wait a minute, he thought: What was *she* doing to fulfill her share of their promise to the girls? And on his end, wasn't the orchard secret the single biggest obstacle to getting past this god-awful crisis?

Saturday, July 23rd
"Selling the embryos on eBay would still have made you a father. I thought that was the reason you didn't want to preserve them."

Olivia and Felix argued over avocado toast. It was their last breakfast at the kitchen table. The movers were on their way, and the house would be empty by day's end. Lola had come back after a weeklong vacation, and she now kept busy in the twins' bedroom, packing clothes and toys. Still, she could overhear most of the conversation, causing a spasm in her stomach.

"Don't forget to pack your tea," Lola said to Felix later in the kitchen, bringing out of the cupboard a gallon-size tin filled with leaves that Felix had imported directly from

316

India. "There's still enough here for another year."

Felix took the tin from Lola's hands and continued eating his avocado toast without even looking at her.

"You're supposed to say, 'Thank you, Lola,' " Olivia said pointedly.

Felix grunted, licked a blob of avocado off his lip, and said with his mouth full, "How do you know I wanted to sell them on eBay?"

"A mother knows everything."

"Bullshit. Someone at the clinic told you and I don't care. I'm not hiding anything. I did want to sell them and so what? Why let something of value go to waste?"

"I could have bought them from you if you'd asked me to make an offer," said Olivia with enough sarcasm in her tone for him to understand what she was really thinking.

"You don't get it, Olivia. Having more kids together would mean that I'd have to put up with you more than I already have to by co-parenting the twins!"

Olivia got up from the table, leaving half a slice of toast on her plate, and without saying a word continued putting stuff in the cardboard boxes that the moving company had provided earlier in the week. She had to turn around so Felix couldn't see her smiling. The thought of no longer having to deal with Felix soothed her. She'd have to seriously ask herself how she could have ever loved him, but this was a question she'd analyze later, months later, perhaps at a therapist's office. Right now, she needed to focus on packing the few things she liked that wouldn't remind her of him. Luckily, he wasn't interested in the pieces of modernist furniture they'd collected over the years, so she selected the Eames lounge chair, the Noguchi coffee table, the Børge Mogensen dining set, and the Hans Olsen teak table. She hesitated when she labeled this last piece with blue tape, indicating to the movers that it was to go to her storage unit, not Felix's. She knew it would bring terrible memories, but why not claim it now and overcome the negativity in the future? Everything must heal, she thought, even the furniture.

How ironic, Lola thought as she drove from Mulholland on the 101 South to East Los Angeles — a world apart only twenty miles away — that she was heading from an imploding marriage to one taking its first baby steps. Her friend Lucy's daughter, Jessica, best hairdresser east of the 5, was getting married this very afternoon to Yobany, the son of one of Lola's ex-boyfriends, who would surely be there with wife number three. Lucy had invited Lola as the God-mother of Cushion, one of the most coveted honors in a Mexican wedding ceremony. She'd bought a red, heart-shaped cushion with extra frills at a shop on Broadway that sold quinceañera gowns and wedding para-phernalia and had it personalized with the bride and groom's initials. The gold bands would be fastened with ribbons on the velvet fabric. Her job was to bring it to the priest at the right moment for the ring exchange.

Irritation welled up in her as she drove south on the 710. Why hadn't Olivia yelled back at Felix? Why had she ignored his insult? She cringed and tried to focus on the fact that Olivia's marriage was over, and she had a whole future before her where she could use the lessons learned. At least she hoped so.

She parked a block away from Our Lady of Lourdes Catholic Church and walked along the sidewalk, cracked by so many earthquakes, stepping carefully. High heels didn't go well with the terrain, but she had brought them along because they were a must at Mexican weddings. She straightened her dark purple dress with a sequined flower

319

pinned at her cleavage and discreetly pulled up her pantyhose.

She had a few minutes to stop at the altar in the courtyard to admire a tiled fresco depicting the famous moment when Juan Diego Cuauhtlatoatzin rolled out dozens of roses from his cloak, revealing the image of the Virgin of Guadalupe miraculously impressed forever in its fibers. She bowed respectfully, even though she wasn't much of a practicing Catholic, and hurried inside to get a good seat, right behind the bride's family's pews. That was the ideal vantage point from which to get an unobstructed view of the mariachi band.

As people trickled in, memories from her childhood, vivid ones, sprang up in her mind. Her parents had moved to East L.A. after being violently evicted in the early fifties from Chavez Ravine, a tight-knit Mexican neighborhood on the hills overlooking downtown Los Angeles where Dodger Stadium now sat. They had raised Lola and her older brother, Sebastian, there until they were killed in the bus accident, leaving the young man to take care of his sister, without making much of an effort, truth be told.

Lola had met Lucy on the first day of school, and the two had been friends since. They had grown up far from the sea breeze, miles above fault lines, where her neighbors favored tortillas over silverware and named their pets Chabelo and Tío Gamboín. They'd roam the barrio's streets lined with gardens behind wrought-iron fences and oleander hedges and hibiscus bushes, sometimes to run an errand for their mothers, other times to babysit for one or another aunt, or to get out of the house so their parents could fight at leisure, yelling and hurling dinner plates and pots and pans at each other across the room. Most of the time, they'd go just because.

Lucy had endured years of her husband Julian's philandering and maxing out credit cards; how many times had she said to Lola, "You're lucky you didn't get married"? But was it luck or a deliberate choice? Lola asked herself that question less often now that she was in her sixties, but sometimes, mostly during weddings, she thought about the numerous suitors she'd rejected, one of them Julian himself — years before he even considered approaching Lucy. Then there was Aurelio, a pasta chef at an Italian restaurant in Brentwood who cursed all day and smelled of garlic and basil; Hermenegildo, a mechanic who was mistakenly killed in a drive-by years after she dated him; Fernando, a plumber, who had failed to disclose the minor detail that he was married to another woman in Mexico, something she'd found out a month into the relationship. There had been others. Many. But she never needed any of them. Her life was full and it was all hers. She had no regrets.

The ceremony lasted almost three hours, with the mariachi band breaking into songs even where music wasn't called for: "El Milagro de tus Ojos" for the Entrance Rite, "Por Tu Amor" during the Gloria, "Si Nos Dejan" after the Opening Prayer, "Hermoso Cariño" right before the Liturgy of the Word, "Contigo Aprendí" after the Gospel, "Amanecí en tus Brazos" after the Homily, "Te Amo" for the Celebration of Matrimony and Exchange of Consent and Presentation of Gifts, where Lola had a starring role bringing the cushion with the rings to the priest. For the Communion Rite, the mariachi played "Mi Eterno Amor Secreto," and finally, "La Vikina" for the Recessional, the bride and groom marching out of the church followed by their bridesmaids in lilac gowns and groomsmen in pale blue tuxedos. Behind them, their families and godparents. Lola was one of the last to walk out. She looked spectacular.

During the Hidalgo-style banquet featuring caldo de oso, barbacoa de borrego, salsa borracha, nopalitos, and mole, one hundred and twenty guests sat around tables for ten according to the name cards on each seat. Lola's card was next to Leticia's, her oldest friend and next-door neighbor when she still lived with her parents in the rental duplex on Arizona Avenue. She'd come with Pedro, her new husband after her divorce from that god-awful womanizer Raúl Valverde. Other people wanted to spend time with Lola, so right after she finished her slice of wedding cake, she went from table to table to mingle and catch up with everyone.

During the dance in which Jessica, the bride, proved her chops as a hairdresser — she'd done her own updo, and after many swirls and extreme dance moves it remained intact — Lola sat down to catch her breath. Dancing reggaeton, salsa, merengue, mambo, rumba, quebradita, and norteña required stamina, and she had it after years of running after children, but there were just too many friends to dance with and she needed a break.

Lucy was making the rounds greeting guests when she stopped to chat with Lola.

"You're lucky you didn't get married," she whispered, casting a glance at her daughter and her new husband.

"I think you're right," said Lola, with Olivia on her mind.

Sunday, July 24th
The twins didn't seem upset at all. Staying at Bubbe's meant enjoying breakfast favorites like scrambled eggs with strawberry jam and matzo (left over from Seder and well preserved in the freezer to last the whole year), portable cribs to play in, and hugs and kisses from their grandparents. The only difference was that this time Mom was staying, too. Unconcerned about this unusual fact, they spent part of the morning in Oscar's closet, opening every other drawer and taking down his ties from the tie rack to make a nest to sit on. Dani (as all family members had been instructed to call Daniel going forward) had offered to babysit, so he sat on the floor and watched them pull out all the socks, belts, and wait a minute, what's that? He grabbed a half-filled pillbox from Andrea's hand and checked the label: Viagra. As with most everything else he didn't know, he looked it up on his cellphone's web browser and chuckled at the vision of his grandfather using erection enhancers. He quietly put it in the back of the boxers' drawer again, not without noticing that the medication had expired months ago.

■ ■ ■ ■

"Why did you let Felix list the house? He's an awful agent! And never mind the conflict of interest!" said Keila as she helped Olivia unpack the girls' clothes and organize them in the closet.

"I don't see the conflict, Mom. Aside from me, he's the only other person who wants to get the most money from the sale. And he agreed to split his commission with me. Hand me those pajamas, please."

"But he's quite the mediocre broker. He hasn't sold a house in over a year. In L.A.? Come on, give me a break!"

"Mom, we have more important things to think about, like how long I'm going to stay here. I need to find an apartment nearby with an extra bedroom for Lola."

"There's no rush. Take your time."

"It's temporary. Just while I find a place."

Keila wished Olivia and the girls would stay with her forever, but it was clear that this was not a viable option, even though she had enough bedrooms to accommodate everyone. She'd been in the United States long enough to understand that in this culture adult children living with their parents was unacceptable, unthinkable even.

She already had Patricia at home. Even with the excuse of helping her raise Dani, people found it odd, especially her friends from book club, who hinted every so often that Patricia should be able to live on her own with her son, or even better, with her husband. Everyone involved knew this was true. Patricia could very well afford to live independently, have her own place. But it was also a fact that everyone involved was happy with the current arrangement. Dani loved seeing his grandparents every day. Patricia could go on business trips or visit Eric up north without a worry, knowing trusted adults picked up Dani at school, checked homework, and supervised him when he had friends over. And Keila and Oscar had their youngest daughter around. Really, how bad was multigenerational living?

Monday, July 25th

"Dad, you might want to hear this," said Olivia, sitting at the breakfast table with Oscar, the *Los Angeles Times* in hand. "You know the Sable Ranch?"

"Are you going to tell me it burned down?"

"Oh, so you heard the news."

"It's a tragedy. The Sand Fire is destroying everything in its path."

"So many TV series and movies were shot there. All those film sets are gone. I liked *Invisible Man* with Chevy Chase and *Robin Hood: Men in Tights.*"

"I remember *The A-Team*. Great show."

"You're dating yourself."

Was that a profound feeling of daughterly love bursting inside of Olivia's chest? She suddenly understood, behind this otherwise banal Hollywood chitchat, the weight of her father's worries. Everything hinged on the weather. The way in which Earth spread heat and water all over its skin could save you or kill you, determine where you lived, whether your neighbor's house was spared from fire but not yours, if it blew away in a hurricane with you in it, or if you got electrocuted by lightning. She remembered the history lesson in high school about the mysterious Teotihuacan empire's demise most likely due to drought, followed by starvation. How many civilizations must have collapsed as a result of the weather? How many human migrations had been caused by famines? How many cultures annihilated by floods? And now this, in twenty-first-century Los Angeles. Her father's glorified barometer, his persistent weather-log entries came into focus with new meaning. Relentlessly watching the Weather Channel was not the behavior of a lunatic. What she'd understood up until then as an inexplicable eccentricity, an obsession that was jeopardizing her parents' marriage, was really a justified, fine-tuned alarm. Once the reservoirs that kept the city alive were depleted, would water become a precious commodity that only the wealthy were able to purchase at exorbitant prices to keep in their swimming pools converted into storage tanks? Or would there be a massive exodus? To where?

She reached for her father's hand across the breakfast table and held it tight. "I get you, Papi."

Tuesday, July 26th

Oscar was certain Keila wouldn't pass up his invitation to dinner at their favorite neighborhood taquería, Guerrilla Tacos, but she did.

"Sorry, I'm on the keto diet. No tortillas for me," she said, as she put on her makeup in front of the mirror in the bathroom.

Oscar knew this was a dumb excuse to avoid spending time with him, as there were numerous protein-based options, like fajitas (without the tortillas, of course), carnitas, chicharrón en salsa verde, guacamole. And why did she need to go on a diet if she was already slim? So he persisted.

"Let's give it a try, could we?"

"You never wanted to go to therapy. You think tacos are going to do the job?"

"We can go somewhere else. Italian? Japanese?"

"It's not the cuisine, it's you. I thought you were on the mend after Claudia's divorce, but you went right back to Zombieland."

"I'm trying, Keila, really. Please."

But Keila flicked her tablet's screen on to check the presidential-campaign polls, an obsession she'd developed over the past few months, and left Oscar wondering if his marriage really was doomed. She was wondering the same.

Saturday, July 30th

Valle de Guadalupe was Baja's hottest destination, and Patricia insisted on spending a weekend there with Eric so she could blog about it. The warmer, drier weather, courtesy of climate change, was a blessing for local winemakers and restaurateurs, and the place was teeming with gastro-tourists. As they drove Patricia's Prius down the highway (Eric's Tesla wouldn't make it through the desert without charging stations), she began noticing old car wrecks abandoned by the side of the road. Not five or twenty. Hundreds. All kinds of makes and models scattered about in the fields and ravines, most of them severely cannibalized to the point of being unrecognizable, empty carcasses. She asked Eric to stop so she could take a picture of a VW bus with graffiti on every side and no tires. Then they stopped to take a picture of a Country Squire station wagon, clearly from the seventies. What started out as a two-hour ride turned into a nine-hour photographic exploration of destroyed automobiles.

Hundreds of pictures later, Eric and Patricia arrived at their hotel in Valle de Guadalupe and went to bed still wondering what might have happened to the people involved in those accidents.

"It was probably more expensive to send the tow truck down to pick up the totaled car than to abandon it there," said Eric as he took off his clothes and lay faceup on the bed.

"It's definitely not good publicity for Baja," said Patricia as she undressed. "I'm sure tourists don't want reminders of how bad the road is."

And before she finished her sentence, Patricia mounted Eric, eagerly finding his penis between her legs and wrapping it tight.

A couple of orgasms later, and as the sun came out, they both agreed there was no point in waiting for a decent hour to start tasting wines. After all, Patricia already had a better story to blog about, with all those rusted metal carcasses still vivid in her mind. So they packed up and headed back home, cheerfully making up stories of how one or another car accident might have happened. There was one wreck that Patricia kept thinking about, but this one she would not share with Eric, not yet, as its story was still unfolding: their marriage.

AUGUST

It was crucial to keep the almond trees from defoliating prematurely.

"If we lose the leaves early, the flower buds are not going to grow fully and the nuts won't dry properly," his guru Lucas had warned Oscar when he bought the orchard years before.

On that hot August morning, as soon as Oscar got out of his SUV, Lucas greeted him with another warning: "We need to be very careful with the dust this year. That shit's our enemy during harvest."

As part of his greeting, Lucas offered Oscar a paper plate with two carnitas burritos his wife had prepared.

"They're a bit cold by now, but the salsa is really good."

They sat down under the shade of one of the trees to eat together, as they often did. This feeling of companionship with Lucas and his cousins only increased the pain of possibly losing the trees, but at the same time, it motivated him to soldier on. There was an orchard to be rescued. Farmworkers to protect. Family history to preserve. A marriage to be saved.

"We should definitely get a better sweeper this time around. We need to be able to adjust the head height with more precision," Lucas added, unaware of Oscar's fears. "Otherwise we're going to have dust all over the nuts."

As they walked among the trees checking for bugs and inspecting the almonds, Oscar noticed a certain anxiety among Los Tres Primos.

"What's that apprehension I'm sensing, Lucas?"

"We didn't want you to worry about us, but since you're asking, what do you think the chances are we're all going to get deported?"

"Our country can't afford to lose you," Oscar said with conviction, or so he thought.

Later, as he drove back to Los Angeles across Central Valley, he saw dozens of small groups of workers, many of them undocumented, he knew, planting, growing, and harvesting such a spectacular cornucopia of fruits, vegetables, and nuts — a plethora of agricultural products, enough to feed half the country. No, he thought, they'll be safe, but something in him knew he might be wrong.

Tuesday, August 2nd

In her nightmare, a recurring one, Patricia saw herself as a fourteen-year-old girl in tears, being interrogated by a police officer. Even though he was speaking, no voice came out of his mouth, as if the sound had been muted in this movie. But she knew what he was asking. Over and over again. "Did you give him consent?" "Were you pressured?" "Did you explicitly tell him to stop?" "Were any of you drunk?" "Did he use a condom?"

She woke up with a hole in her insides and went to the bathroom, disgusted and dizzy, but could not vomit. Having those dreams lately worried her. Wasn't this event from her past already dealt with and forgotten? Why was it coming back? She went to bed again in the semidarkness of her room, opened her laptop, and launched the search engine, her go-to place for answers.

Wednesday, August 3rd

Los Angeles was developed as a horizontal city so its image could be projected in glorious Panavision. That was Patricia's personal insight about her hometown as she drove down Olympic Boulevard to the hospital. She made a mental note to share this thought on Instagram along with a photograph of the sprawl she'd recently taken from the Griffith Observatory with an unusually clear sky devoid of smog, fire smoke, or marine fog, the L.A. trifecta of air quality. She'd go there oftentimes just to remind herself that because she lived in the wealthiest city of the wealthiest state of the wealthiest country in the world, she had been bestowed with the ultimate responsibility: to thrive in her endeavors many times over on behalf of all the immigrants who hadn't been given the chance.

She pulled her phone out of her bag during a traffic light, dialed quickly, well aware of her dangerous habit, and left a message requesting an appointment with a therapist she'd googled.

When Patricia arrived, Claudia was showered and dressed and had already packed her suitcase. Her vision was back to normal, although it still fluctuated at times, distorting the outside world and making her squint.

"Put the discharge papers in your backpack," she said to Patricia. "I don't have any space left in my bags. Let's go."

In the car, Patricia noticed how pale, sickly, and thin her sister looked. The months Claudia had spent in the hospital had brought out her cheekbones and sunken her eyes, making her resemble a cubist portrait.

"As soon as you feel better, let's get a spa treatment," she said.

"Yes, let's do that sometime," answered Claudia, uninterested. She looked out the window and into other people's cars, wondering how much of life she'd missed. Here was an obese guy in a red Mazda, pushing forward on the steering wheel like a granny sitting on the toilet. There was a guy in a white BMW, his left arm hanging out the window with a big bling-bling watch screaming to get robbed. And over there was a woman in her black RAV4 Toyota sticking her finger up her nose. What was she expecting to find in there, a little appetizer to hold her over until lunchtime? Oh, and look, three people riding in the same car? In L.A.? Perhaps she hadn't missed much of life, Claudia thought. She knew it would be interesting, even with her condition. She could walk with a cane and was quickly regaining strength and range of motion in her legs, but her doctors had confirmed that the noticeable limp in her left leg would be permanent. There was no way to repair the damage the tumor had caused to the frontal lobe of her brain.

Exhausted from the car ride to Oscar and Keila's house, she slowly made her way upstairs to her bedroom and plopped on the couch in front of the bed. Patricia hauled her bags up, and with Keila's help, she began to unpack pajamas, sweaters, socks, slippers, and tennis shoes.

"What's this?" asked Keila, astonished to find a stethoscope in her hand.

"And this?" Patricia had just dug out a blood-pressure cuff from a snarl of underwear in the suitcase.

They went on to unpack two wrinkled pillowcases with the hospital logo in blue; a landline phone, cord and all; an oxygen flowmeter; a wall clock; a universal TV remote; a brand-new box of latex gloves, medium size; a nurse call button; a pair of reading glasses; several slip-proof socks still sealed in their pouches; and a pulse oximeter.

"What?" asked Claudia when she finally saw all the loot sinking from its weight into the bed's plush comforter.

"This is a good sign, sis."

Claudia was as shocked as her sister upon

being presented with the evidence of her theft, stuff that clearly didn't belong to her but had come out of her suitcase.

"Exhibit A," said Patricia with a grin, pointing to the array of items. "For better or for worse, you're back to your old self."

Thursday, August 4th

Precisely at 11:47 A.M., when the day was hottest (eighty-four degrees was his guess), Oscar walked along Van Nuys Boulevard in Pacoima, an old neighborhood in the northern San Fernando Valley, thinking about Claudia. If she could not work as a chef anymore, if her income consisted only of the residuals from her canceled show, something that would surely dwindle over the years if not months, if she was not going to get any alimony from Gabriel, how was she going to support herself? Would he have to take care of his daughter? Would he be able to if he lost the almond orchard? He had always admired her spunk and drive to succeed, a very fitting attitude for a first-born, but wondered if she had lost that part of her personality. She seemed so frail now, so helpless.

He examined the commercial storefronts, taking notes in his mind: fast-food restaurants; churches in former movie theaters;

pawnshops and check-cashing and money-transfer businesses on every other corner under the relentless August sun. He passed big soundstages where Hollywood magic was surely being created and snaked in and out of residential side streets, observing life in the different houses he came across. Most of the people he encountered were Latino. They were his people, and he felt right at home.

When he was in high school he had promised himself to walk all the neighborhoods of Los Angeles in order to be able to understand his city in all its complexity. As he continued to fulfill his goal over the years, he realized that the exercise would prove impossible. In every area he got to roam, he'd confirm what he already suspected: there were hundreds of cities within his city, each telling a different story. He'd need several lifetimes to understand its many incarnations. One of them, the most obvious one, perpetuated by many out-of-towners, was the entertainment mecca, with streets and parks named after movie stars, familiar locations, and neighborhoods banned by the film industry due to shoot burnout. People who knew little about L.A. imagined everyone walking around with a screenplay soggy with sweat under their armpit. This was the birthplace of Hollywood, after all. But in truth, Los Angeles was whatever you wanted it to be, and that was thanks to the constant influx of immigrants arriving with their dreams, not only from other countries, but from other states within the nation. Even its famous palm trees came from somewhere else. He imagined a reality show host selling Los Angeles to a live audience: "Are you a surfer dude hitting the waves? You'll fit right in. How about a hipster starting a gluten-free cookie brand or a new church? Of course. And is there a place for a young family raising small children? You bet. How about a retired couple wanting to play bingo all day? Indeed. High-powered executives? Yes! Lawyers, doctors, agents, and managers? Best place to thrive. Gym buffs, starlets, chefs, yoga teachers, students, writers, healers, misfits, trainers, nurses? Right this way, please. Are you into cosplay, improv, porn, Roller Derby, voyeurism, cemetery movie screenings, food truck drag racing, AA, relapse, rehab, open mic, plastic surgery, wine tastings, biker meetups, karaoke, clubbing, S and M, or escape rooms? Come on over!"

Every race, religion, nationality, gender, sexual orientation, and food preference was well represented within Los Angeles County, and this is what Oscar loved most about his city; how it welcomed everything and everyone. It was true that History had spared it from centuries-old clan clashes, like the Battle of Glen Fruin in Scotland; it hadn't been the epicenter of horrendous religious massacres, like the Crusades, the Hundred Years' War, or the Holocaust; or lived through ghastly battles, like the one that took place in Verdun, France, that produced one million dead young soldiers, their destroyed bodies strewn about the battlefield. But in its young history, Los Angeles had had its own share of human hurt, drama, and bloody events, from the Spaniards' Indian exploitation, to the U.S. invasion when it was still part of Mexico, to the Chinese Massacre, Japanese internment, and even uprisings as recent as the Los Angeles Riots in 1992. Sadly, when tourists visited Los Angeles's special landmarks, riding on roofless tour buses under a scorching sun, all they'd hear was things like, "This very place is where the Terminator rips out the punk's heart."

He reached his SUV and with a snort snatched the parking ticket from under his windshield wiper (one more for the collection), then drove off to Happy Crunch

Almond Orchard, where his beloved trees waited for his embrace. But on arrival, he realized someone else was already hugging his trees. A bride and her groom were striking romantic poses for a photographer who seemed to be directing the shoot in the middle of Oscar's orchard. At least these people were not as intrusive as the dirt bikers zooming through the rows, kicking up dust and rattling the trees with their godawful engine noise, as had happened before. But still, these lovely people were trespassers and they had to go.

"Hello, excuse me. I will have to ask you to leave. This is private property and you're disturbing the almonds."

"I'm so sorry," said the bride. "There was no one here."

"It's past four. My guys have gone home to rest, but that doesn't mean this place belongs to no one."

"This is a once-in-a-lifetime opportunity," said the bride. "We're almost done. Could we shoot a couple more shots and then we'll leave? I promise."

"This isn't even the best time of the year to take pictures! You should have come in the early spring, when the trees are blooming. Now, that's a sight for the ages," he said.

"We hadn't even met in the spring! It's not easy to time when love arrives," said the groom, giggling.

Or when it leaves, thought Oscar.

"All right, but just two more," he said. How could he deny these young people a morsel of happiness?

"Can you hold this light reflector for me?" asked the photographer, handing Oscar a flexible, round moon of silvery canvas. "Angle it this way to get the afternoon sunlight on the bride's face."

That's some chutzpah, Oscar thought, but at the same time he followed orders, moving the reflector this way and that as the shoot continued. Here was a new couple, fresh and tender and promising, ready for the future, while his daughters' marriages unraveled. So much for so-called once-in-a-lifetime opportunities. And what about his own? He'd have to come clean, confess to Keila about the orchard, and hopefully save his own marriage. He knew flowers and a love letter would not cut it.

Harvest season was a few days away. He'd wait.

Friday, August 5th
With the news fresh in his mind — officials had just announced that the Sand Fire had

343

been fully contained after scorching 41,432 acres — Oscar entered the numbers in his log and put it back in his nightstand's drawer. He knew there would be more fires, less water. L.A. had grown so much as to encroach on its surrounding deserts — Palmdale, Victorville, Palm Springs — and its mild Mediterranean climate, the one that had convinced the original Angelenos of El Pueblo de Nuestra Señora la Reina de los Ángeles de Porciúncula to settle here, was now in jeopardy. The city owed its existence to William Mulholland's construction of the Los Angeles Aqueduct, which brought the city's water supply from Owens Valley hundreds of miles away. But had that been a reasonable strategy? Without its own water, was the growth of the megalopolis he lived in justified? If L.A.'s access to water faded away, would the city become another man-made atrocity engulfed by sand, like the neighboring Salton Sea, a terrible mistake of death and pestilence?

He went from one gloomy thought to the next, this one more pressing, urgent, a recurring dread that upstaged the wildfire's final and horrific acreage count, one whose outcome he had the possibility of controlling: he couldn't stop wondering how he could support his daughters about to start a new life at home. What if they lost their home to fire? Where would they live, now that Claudia was back at home? And Patricia. And Dani. And Olivia and the twins. And hopefully Keila.

Saturday, August 6th
This was where things stood at the Alvarados' on that Saturday morning: Keila and Oscar kept the master bedroom and the adjacent sitting area where Oscar watched the Weather Channel. Keila had considered for some time asking him to move to the TV room couch, but now with the girls back home and after her promise to try to mend things with Oscar, she listened to her better self and stayed put, at least while she figured out how to erase from her mind her night with Simon. Olivia and the twins had settled — temporarily, as she had emphasized to Keila — in Olivia's old bedroom, large enough to fit the two portable cribs arranged lengthwise below the window to form a choo-choo train of sorts. As soon as she arrived, before unpacking suitcases, she set out to rearrange the furniture to her present-day liking, wondering how she could have lived in that room for so many years without minding the bed's orientation. In her own defense, she had

only learned Chinese geomancy after she'd moved out and gotten married, so she forgave herself and proceeded to put her stuff away. Dani, who had lived in Claudia's old bedroom since early childhood, moved to the boudoir across from the sitting area. "Cozy" was his polite way to describe its small size. In order to fit the bed in he had to remove the shelf where he kept his toys and donate his dinosaur collection; the Legos; numerous cars, trucks, and motorcycles; most picture books; all stuffed bunnies and cute animals (except Mr. Monkey, who was actually a bear); and the dehydrated piranha embedded in an acrylic cube that his mother had brought from Brazil at his request (but which gave him countless nightmares that resulted in him running to sleep with her in the middle of the night). Patricia stayed in her own bedroom, simplifying the already complicated logistics. Later that evening a thought came to her, and she wondered if it was scary because it was supposed to be scary, or if it really was scary: She'd always lived in that room. She'd never lived anywhere else. She was twenty-eight years old.

Claudia, on the other hand, had left for college, promising herself never to go back home, no matter how much she had loved growing up there. It had been part of her plan: to become fully independent in all areas of her life. So much for that, she thought as she straightened the pillow on her armchair. The initial idea had been to set Claudia up in Lola's room next to Keila's studio by the detached garage in the back of the garden so she wouldn't have to use the stairs, but ultimately she decided she'd stay in her own bedroom. "I can handle the stairs," she said, not sure if she really could pull it off on a daily basis. So, Lola was pleased to get her old bedroom — with plenty of privacy and a nice view of the garden — where she had slept for years on weekends while the three sisters were growing up. It took Keila several hours to move the artwork and materials she had stored there to a corner of her studio to make room for Lola's things. As much as Keila hated clutter, she loved having a full house.

Monday, August 8th

A stream of urine bathed Patricia's pregnancy test. Within minutes, two well-defined pink lines appeared in the tiny screen of the stick. Patricia held on to the sink for balance. She could not tell if she was made light-headed by the news, or if this was the first physical sign of her gravidity. She composed herself, wrapped the test in tissue, and got in her car, leaving the driveway with a tire screech.

Olivia was in the middle of passing stucco inspection at a construction jobsite high up in the Hollywood Hills. Standing on the scaffolding with the inspector, she saw Patricia park her car on the curb and get out wearing a Gioconda smile.

"I need to speak with you in private. Now!" said Patricia as she started to climb the ladder to reach her sister.

Olivia asked the inspector for a few minutes of privacy and he obliged, puzzled, making his way down to the sidewalk.

"I have this for you, Olie."

Patricia dug in her backpack for the pregnancy test and put it in Olivia's hand.

"A baby!" she yelled.

"Maybe twins!"

Olivia held up the test stick to the sunlight and started jumping up and down on the scaffolding. Patricia followed suit, kissing her sister, and dancing and yelling incomprehensible shrieks of joy without minding the fact that they were on a precarious contraption of planks and pipes.

Downstairs, as the scaffolding perilously shook and wobbled with the weight of the

Alvarado sisters, now joined forever in motherhood, the inspector looked up at the scene dumbfounded.

"Women," he mumbled.

Sunday, August 14th

"It shouldn't be so hard. You already speak some decent Hebrew," said Keila to Dani over a hefty brunch of pancakes and bacon.

"But we're not even that religious. We eat carnitas! We could just skip the Bar Mitzvah altogether and no one would care," said Dani.

"It's not just about religion. Your grand-parents were Jews, I'm a Jew, your mom is a Jew. It's identity we're talking about here. Do you feel Jewish?"

"I guess so."

"When asked, what do you say?"

"That I'm Jewish."

"There you have it. Even if we don't go to temple, we are who we are. I already made you an appointment with Rabbi Nebenzahl, our go-to rabbi for all things Jewish. He's Reform, so it will all be fine. When the whole thing is done, you'll be glad you did it."

"Can we hire a cool band to play at the party? Poetic License played at Ezequiel's Bar Mitzvah."

"Why don't you focus on the importance of chanting Torah and what the whole ritual means to you for now? We can discuss the music later."

Wednesday, August 17th
Some called it a fire whirl. Others, a fire-nado. But what triggered the evacuation of eighty thousand people on the outskirts of Los Angeles really came to be known as the Blue Cut Fire. Oscar watched the news in horror as the historic Route 66 diner, the Summit Inn, burned to the ground while nearby residents fled. It took thirteen hundred firefighters, four VLATS — known among laymen as very large air tankers — three super-scooper planes, and fifteen helicopters to contain the blaze. Oscar thought about all those evacuees leaving behind their photo albums and passports and pets. Dogs were easy to round up, but cats? In the last family evacuation drill just a few days before, Velcro had run from everyone's haste and hid behind the stove, a place impossible to reach, even with a broom. Had it been a real fire emergency they would have had to leave him behind to burn with the house. You can't run around looking for your cat when the flames are licking your roof.

■ ■ ■ ■

Thursday, August 18th

Putting the leash on Ramsay was the easy part. Getting Claudia to change from her pajamas and make her way outside was a nearly insurmountable ordeal, but Olivia drew patience from the heavens and after substantial convincing was able to take her sister and her dog for a stroll around the block for the first time since the surgery.

"But I'm not picking up after him," said Claudia. "I'm an invalid."

"Nice try, but I'm not enabling you," said Olivia, handing her the little roll of plastic bags.

Although Claudia had healed faster than her doctors had anticipated, the discrepancy between her physical recovery and her state of mind was notable. She had stopped complaining about pain in her leg, but when dinnertime came, she'd drink a protein shake standing by the fridge and go to her room without saying a word to anyone.

"We miss you at the table, sis," said Olivia as they walked along the neighborhood, strollers and nannies abounding. This was West Los Angeles, after all.

"Why should I torture myself watching

you all enjoy your food?" she said as she shambled along the uneven sidewalk.

"Maybe because we want you to participate in the conversation?" said Olivia, trying to alleviate her sister's bitterness by making her feel needed. "There's a lot going on these days, and we could sure benefit from your insights. Make use of that big part of your brain that's intact."

"Let's go home. I'm tired."

Sunday, August 21st

On the very day that Olivia's house went on the market, six offers came in. A couple with five children made the most attractive offer. All cash. No property inspection or contingency period. No repairs request. No title report. No appraisal. One-week escrow. This sounded like a dream real-estate-deal scenario, but it wasn't: Felix had purposely undersold the house.

"Why?" asked Olivia in disbelief, immediately regretting not having gotten involved in the sale process. After all, she'd thought, Felix was the real estate expert. But why was she so naïve? What made her believe that Felix would not undermine himself in order to hurt her, if that was what he did while they were married? Why did she even marry him in the first place? That was a question with a very long answer, one that would require perhaps years of self-examination. Claudia would say to her things like, "You're Felix's mudroom mat." Perhaps keeping that image vivid in her mind when analyzing her behavior during her marriage would be a good starting point.

"Why would you undersell the house?"

"Take the cashier's check and go live your little life. I got the same amount you did and I'm not complaining," said Felix as he showed her an identical check, this one written in his name. "And just so you know, the new owners are going to demolish the house and build a Tuscan villa."

A Tuscan villa? Now, that hurt even more than finding out Felix had practically given away their home. She'd seen these houses pop up everywhere on the Westside; most of them seemed too large for the lot, built with the same ready-made floor plans, the same sad color palettes, and all resembling a Disneyland set.

Doing the numbers later that evening, Olivia realized that Felix had sold the house for way below market.

"He did it out of spite. He couldn't help himself. All he wants is to fuck you over," said Claudia.

"But he hurt himself, too. What an idiot. I

353

was counting on that money to buy a condo."

"You didn't supervise him. I get it. Smart people do dumb things, but that was more than dumb. Now you'll have to stay here until you save up."

Thursday, August 25th

Rape is not sex but violence; her rapist wanted to have control over her; he didn't act out of lust, but power; she's not a victim, she's a survivor. That was the mantra Patricia chanted aloud to herself as she drove her Prius out to Thousand Oaks that morning, hoping to believe it by constant repetition. Traffic was especially damnable, but the time sitting in her car allowed her to continue percolating the insights she'd arrived at during the three weeks since her return to therapy.

An hour after she headed east out of the city on the 101, she reached her exit, turned left, and took a small road down a canyon. Although she was a seasoned hiker, she'd never been to that part of the outskirts of Los Angeles. She promised herself she'd bring Dani with her someday to explore those trails and climb those boulders, but made a note to do it soon before that area succumbed to some future inferno. She was grateful to live in L.A., where, fire permitting, she could go snowboarding on Big Bear's slopes in the morning and surfing in the Santa Monica waves in the afternoon; or have a fancy Sunday brunch at some hip hotel and then go hiking in the mountains after that. For now, she'd focus on the beauty of her surroundings while they lasted. It helped soothe the anxiety that had spiked since she started having nightmares.

After another twenty-five minutes on a dirt road (who drives an hour and a half to see their therapist?), she arrived at the ranch where Irene waited for her in cowboy boots and a Stetson hat. The cottage sat in a womb of steep slopes covered in chaparral: sand verbena, maidenhair fern, our Lord's candles, and woolly blue curls. Inside, the living room was furnished with cozy sofas and pillows and throws and an oversize ottoman with two small trays on which to set mugs with hot chocolate. Photographs of horses and Irene's Ph.D. diploma hung from the walls. She offered Patricia a cup of chamomile tea and both women walked outside.

Farther along on a dirt path, they sat at a picnic table under the shade of a berry manzanita tree and spent some time going over the previous session's insights.

Exploring her past, Patricia had realized that most of the men she had had relationships with had been physically distant or emotionally challenged in some way, including Eric. Two of the guys she dated in college transferred out of state, a plan she'd known from the get-go. Another one was on the brink of getting married. What was wrong with them? Or was it her? She knew Eric would not move to Los Angeles, and from the beginning he had happily accepted her condition to live separately. Now she yearned for closeness and didn't know why she was starting to feel different.

"Let's spend some time with Big Boy now," said Irene.

They walked a short distance along the path until they reached a round pen where a few horses gathered in small groups around a couple of bales of hay.

During the first session and on Irene's suggestion, Patricia had named an Appaloosa horse Big Boy. He was her other therapist. She was immediately drawn to his spotted coat; he reminded her of a giant Dalmatian. He seemed not so feisty as to inspire fear, but with enough character (and a thousand-pound body) to command respect. But when Patricia first approached him, her unspoken message to him was *I call the shots,* which didn't go well. She rushed forward to pet him and Big Boy retreated, startled, raised his head, and turned his ears backward.

"Remember that Big Boy is a prey animal. He can spook at anything that feels the least bit threatening," said Irene in a kind and patient voice.

It took Patricia the entire session to understand that if she was to develop a solid relationship with him over the course of her equine-assisted therapy, Big Boy had to be treated gently.

"You'll need to start looking straight into his eyes," said Irene. "Make him feel comfortable around you."

Patricia changed strategy and tiptoed toward Big Boy. When he didn't move, she slowly raised her hand to touch his muzzle, knowing he could very well bite her fingers off, but he let her, still seeming a bit suspicious. Then, she caressed his face softly and slid her hand along his cheek as if ironing it. Starting to get carried away, she tangled her fingers in his mane, and that's when she noticed that Big Boy had his gaze on another horse shuffling its hooves on the soft footing not far from where she was.

"That's Mamma over there, the lead mare," said Irene. "Big Boy is asking for permission to be petted. It's fine. Go on."

Unsure of the potential results of this kind of therapy, Patricia had decided to let herself follow Irene's instructions.

"For our next session, give this question a thought: Why do you always have to be on top when having sex?"

Patricia said good-bye, got into her car, and drove back home with the question burning in her mind.

Saturday, August 27th

Claudia's house was so clean and tidy that *Architectural Digest* could have come in with their photographers and gotten print-ready images without having to move a single knickknack. Even though Claudia had never been her favorite among the Alvarados — too self-absorbed, not really empathetic, quite a little scoundrel if you asked Lola — she now felt profound compassion for her. No one deserved to have a brain tumor of any size, be it cherry or papaya.

She finished later than she expected and drove down PCH to the 10 toward East L.A., where she'd been invited to a barbecue with childhood friends. As she saw the last vestiges of the Westside in her rearview mirror and passed downtown to her left, she smiled at this thought: Freeway exit names like Centinela, Sepulveda, La Cienega, La Brea, Alameda, Santa Fe, César Chávez, Soto, bound the City of Angels' dwellers, East and West, North and South, to the Mexico of her ancestors whether they liked it or not, regardless of their race, beliefs, political affiliation, or ethnicity. She cherished the language her parents taught her, playful, harmonic; listened to Latin songs on the radio every morning; knew all the Spanish stations' drive-time DJs by name. The airwaves were American, and not. The city was American, and not. And she loved it just like that.

When she arrived at the cookout, a little late, Los Barón de Apodaca blasted out of the speakers on opposite corners of the patio where the hosts had set a long table composed of three tables of different sizes joined together under a bright pink table-cloth. A *zarape* along the center went from one end to the other. The barbecue coals were already red hot and the mounds of carne asada sizzled on the grill along with bunches of pearl onions and chiles torea-dos. She greeted a multigenerational assort-ment of guests who were dancing and mill-ing around — thirty or so was her estimate, most of them old friends from the neighbor-hood. There were Ana and Mateo standing by the cooler, married the year before on the ferry to Catalina Island surrounded by waves and dolphins (and a few seasick guests). Over there, under the shade of the jacaranda, Elena, the little sister of her friend from elementary school, fanned her menopausal sweat. Lola greeted Don Flavio and Doña Carmen, grandparents of three girls she had babysat for on and off when she was a teenager. She noticed a couple of boys grabbing handfuls of chips, dipping them in guacamole and dripping it on the floor, everywhere. Tempted to scold them, she scanned the patio for the parents who were obviously distracted, but decided against saying anything. She wasn't on the job, after all. She finally bumped into Amanda, the hostess, as she was bringing out a large skillet with nopalitos sautéed with tomatillo salsa and a palm-leaf-woven chiquihuite, surely brought from Oaxaca, containing a stack of warm blue corn tortillas wrapped in a cotton towel.

"How can I help?" offered Lola, kissing Amanda's cheek.

"Lola! So glad you're here! Put fresh ice in that bucket over there and bring out more beer. It's in the fridge, please. Oh, and the molcajetes with the salsas; they're on the counter. Can you spread those out on the table?"

Lola went inside to find another group of friends bunched together, deep in gossip. Paco, Gonzalo, and Hugo, middle school classmates of Lola, called her over. She joined.

"Look at you, guapa!" said Hugo, checking her out. "Every time I see you, you look younger."

"Oh, stop it," she replied, enjoying the compliment. "Help me bring out the beer."

As the afternoon turned into the evening, Lola and her friends laughed. They helped. They went out to the patio. They ate. They danced. They ate again. By midnight, Amanda had twice replaced the trash bags from the big bins where people threw used paper plates, beer cans, napkins smeared with salsa. Lola said good-bye to her friends and drove home with a full belly and a heart overflowing with happiness.

Sunday, August 28th
"I'm not even sure if I'll ever need any of this stuff again," said Claudia.

She pointed at her rarely used sculptural dining table for twelve designed by Joseph Walsh, at her Mario Bellini modular sofa, at her Raúl Baltazar hanging above the fireplace mantel, at her Pininfarina corner sofa outside in her patio by the pool.

"And look at all this shit!" she said, walking into the scullery adjacent to her dining room where she kept her Georg Jensen silver trays, serving dishes and flatware, table linens, and dinnerware sets for twenty-four bought specifically for dinner parties she never organized.

"Should I put it all in storage? Or just have an estate sale and get rid of it all? What do you think, Olie?" asked Claudia.

"Estate sales are for when people die. I wouldn't use that term. It's too depressing," said Olivia, turning her attention to Andrea just as she dropped a Baccarat crystal ashtray, sending shards all over the floor.

"I guess I won't have to pack that one," Claudia chuckled.

"So sorry! Where's your vacuum cleaner?" Olivia said, picking up Andrea so she wouldn't get cut. "Girls, go play in the other room. There's nothing you can break there."

As Olivia vacuumed the floor, Claudia yelled over the noise, "I feel dead sometimes."

"You've been through so much, Clau, give yourself some time. I can understand why you may be feeling dead, but you need to make a plan for the future. If there's a plan in place you'll feel more in control, like you always have," said Olivia, after she shut the vacuum cleaner.

"Control is an illusion," said Claudia, resigned.

Olivia wasn't a seasoned pep talker, but Claudia seemed to have picked her to hold her up and cheer her on, so she did, for hours on end. They'd sit in Claudia's bedroom, like when they were girls, and talk about their divorces and Claudia's recovery. "At least Gabriel is gone, out of your life. I have to deal with Felix all the time. It's sickening," Olivia would say, just to make Claudia feel better.

But now, other important decisions needed to be made, and Claudia was asking for help.

"Why don't you send everything to storage? You never know if science will invent something that will restore your sense of smell and taste and then you can go back to your old life, minus Gabriel, the prick," said Olivia as she took her phone out and started taking pictures of the different rooms in the house.

After they finished, Claudia said good-bye to her stuff and rode with Olivia and the twins in Homer, the minivan, back to her

parents' house with an empty belly and a
heart filled with dread.

Sunday, August 28th

"He was never someone you'd notice. At
school, he seldom said hi in the hallways;
mostly he just stared at people. I didn't even
realize he was at the party that night. A
bunch of us were smoking in the pool
cabana and when everyone went back inside, I stayed behind to look at the moon. I
remember it was full. Then he came out of
nowhere. What was a junior doing hanging
out with a freshman? I had no idea what he
wanted. He sat very close to me. He didn't
say much. Not that I can remember. He just
pounced, like a beast. It was over very
quickly."

Patricia, her eyes a well of tears, blew her
nose with a tissue and continued: "I don't
know why I never told you all this."

Olivia, who was sitting next to her in the
kitchen, held her tight and said, "I don't
know why I never asked you."

Thursday, September 1st

Monthly meetings with Aunt Belinda were increasingly devastating. At eighty-seven, with advanced arthritis and zero ability or interest in using a computer, she was a numbers prodigy, and the numbers were bleak.

"You can't get another loan to pay for the harvesting machines and the farmworkers' salaries," she told Oscar.

"What if I get a little more from the house equity line?"

"You're maxed out, dear. Remember you used most of that money to pay for the bees during pollination season? And you've been buying overpriced water."

"Have you included the money that we're going to make from the sale of the almond hulls?"

"That's coming next month. I don't think we'll find anyone in the dairy industry who will prepay for the hulls."

The decision was there, right in front of him, but Oscar had yet to face it. He knew that his only option was to pull out the trees and plant a more water-wise crop. But this meant spending money he didn't have, unless he used the harvest money, his livelihood, his only income.

"You can't use the money from the harvest to get rid of the trees and plant something else. You need it to pay for your family expenses," said Belinda, as if she were reading his mind. "Especially now, with all the girls living at home."

"I could ask Patricia to contribute more than she already does, but I'm not sure if Olivia can help out. And the money situation with Claudia is still uncertain; I'd never ask her for the money she will get from the sale of her house. That might be the only source of income she'll have left."

Oscar went home after making Belinda promise, once again, not to tell Keila about the orchard. As his accomplice since the beginning, she'd been lying to Keila about the family's finances and helping him find resources to fund the orchard during the drought. But this secret had to end. He would have to be the one who told Keila, and it would have to happen before harvest.

■ ■ ■ ■

Saturday, September 3rd

The moving van, proudly sporting a bright blue logo on its side that read SABRA HAZAK MOVING, was parked in the narrow driveway in front of Claudia's house. Four men jumped out deftly, bringing down dollies and blankets. Patricia and Olivia had already packed up their sister's stuff, carefully following her orders as to what got packed where, and now Oscar was standing by the front door to supervise the move to a storage facility, the same one where Olivia's belongings were being kept.

The house had been sold to an entertainment lawyer, the kind whose job is to babysit their rock star clients, following them around and paying for whatever damages they inflicted during their stays in hotel suites and venues.

"I have the designer coming tomorrow with a crew of painters. Will the house be empty by then?" he asked Oscar after he maneuvered his Porsche into the tiny space next to the truck.

"Oh, for sure," said Oscar. "We'll be out of here this afternoon. In fact, here are your keys."

Oscar handed him the house keys after he removed a silver ring with a round pendant that had Claudia's initials engraved, a gift he'd bought for her at Tiffany's when she published her first cookbook.

The lawyer took the keys, said good-bye, and left. Oscar held the key ring tight, so tight that the edge of the silver pendant dug into the skin of his palm. Was it anger? Sorrow? Shame? His daughters' lives were falling apart, and yet they faced their new reality with dignity. What a coward he was. He looked up at the cloudless sky.

Sunday, September 4th

Early in the morning, when squirrels hop from branch to branch looking for cats to tease and mourning doves coo the loudest and people are home sipping their coffee and reading the paper, Oscar walked out of his house and paced around on his porch. This time, the whipping boy that paid for his mistakes was a flowerpot. He kicked it until it broke like a piñata and the potting soil and the hydrangea spilled onto the staggered brick floor. He didn't have a Kleenex on hand, so he used his shirtsleeve to dry his snot and tears.

■ ■ ■ ■

"I really do like to be on top when having sex. This way I can control the pace when I ride the guy," Patricia said, as she settled at the picnic table with Irene. "That's my answer."

"That's it? Let's elaborate. Is there anything else you'd like to say about the idea of control?"

The first thought that came to Patricia's mind was why hadn't she asked herself this question before if the answer was so obvious?

"It's not just the pace or the rhythm. I feel more comfortable when they're vulnerable. I think I've been trying to keep myself safe this way. And I do it to remind myself that having sex is my prerogative. Cowgirl, reverse missionary, face sit, sidesaddle. Doesn't matter. I'm in charge of my own pleasure. And you know what? Men comply. Some even like it. At least the men I choose."

As she heard herself speak, she realized that she'd been looking for men to control during sex, men who made little or no attempt to achieve the intimacy she now

369

longed for. And not just sexual intimacy, but the delicious kind that domesticity provides. She imagined having her own apartment somewhere in Echo Park where she'd spend hours intertwined with her husband on a plush sofa saying little nothings to each other while Dani did his homework in his room.

"When can I go for a ride with Big Boy?"

"You won't while you're pregnant. Your work will be on the ground for the next few months. You've got quite a way to go. Be patient. For now, you'll need to start making some decisions."

Friday, September 9th

Just landed.

ok see you outside the terminal ma choupinette

Eric had asked Patricia to discuss on the phone whatever she had to say that was so important. She didn't have to fly out to San Francisco in the middle of the week. But she had refused to say anything until they were together, face-to-face, not on Face-Time.

The ride home was particularly stressful.

Not much was said.

"SFO was a madhouse today."

"Yeah."

Eric brought Patricia's carry-on bag up the stairs and into the bedroom. The bed was made and a small vase with fresh red tulips had been lovingly placed on her nightstand. She noticed.

"What's going on? What's all this mystery about?" asked Eric, plopping down on the bed, intrigued.

"I have to tell you this in person, that's why I'm here. I'm hoping to have your full support. I'm sorry I didn't consult with you first but I needed to do it, regardless. I'm pregnant with Olivia's embryos."

It took Eric what seemed hours to react. He propped himself up with a pillow and stared at Patricia's flat belly, looking for some physical sign.

"I don't get it. Why didn't you tell me?"

"Because I knew you wouldn't agree."

"Damn right!" he said, trying to control the volume of his voice. "This is a decision that we should have made as a couple."

"But really, Eric, we don't do chores together, we don't run errands, we don't watch TV, we don't even have a joint bank account or share our salaries. Are we a couple?"

"I thought we were," said Eric, anticipating a reply he didn't want to hear. He rubbed his nose insistently and combed back his hair with his fingers.

"I made this decision on my own because I don't see us together down the line."

"Are you saying we should separate?"

"Divorce."

Eric swallowed hard and then, surprised, said unexpected words, especially coming from a professional futurologist.

"Fuck, I didn't see this coming."

"I'm so sorry."

"So you believe our marriage was a mistake. Is that what you're saying?"

"I don't. It has been wonderful on many levels, but I now want things you can't provide. It's not a flaw, so don't feel guilty. I want a dad for Dani; I want someone to spoon with every night."

Eric looked in the direction of the tulips to avoid Patricia's gaze.

"I could be more present, more tender. We could even try being kind of married, Pats," he said, trying to save something, anything.

"We've been kind of married."

"You're right. If we wanted this to work, we'd have to make major changes. But if I'm honest with myself, which I am, I

372

wouldn't know how to deal with Dani and with your pregnancy."

Patricia sat on the bed next to Eric and held his hand.

"Will you forgive me?" she said softly.

"How can I? A pregnancy in which I'm not involved and a request for divorce, all dumped on me in five minutes? It's too much for anyone to take in, Patricia. I can't produce forgiveness while you wait. It's not a burger delivered from the drive-through window."

Whenever Eric called her Patricia and not Pats she knew she was in trouble. "Will you at least consider it?"

"I don't know yet." He was about to caress her hand with his thumb, but restrained himself. "Are you keeping the babies?"

"No. They're Olivia's."

"And Felix's, I suppose. Does he agree with this?"

"That's another thing I want to discuss with you."

"I don't like where this is going."

The room began to feel stuffy and small. The tulips wilted in front of their eyes, their stems becoming flaccid.

"Let's get some fresh air. I'll explain."

Eric drove to Kearny Street in silence, found a parking space, and he and Patricia started a steep descent down the Filbert Steps among lush gardens. Overhead, a flock of wild cherry-headed parrots swooshed by, squawking.

"These parrots have lived on Telegraph Hill for years," Eric said finally. "It's an entire colony. They mate for life, you know."

"A lot of bird species do. We should learn from them," said Patricia, with a bit of sadness and, was it envy?

"It'll have to be next time, I suppose."

"Even if you never forgive me, we don't have to hate each other."

"Of course not."

"Why should we?"

"I could give you one reason to hate you, for sure, but I know how much you love your sister — even more than you love me, obviously — and why you decided to help her bring those babies into the world without asking me first. I'm not holding it against you."

They stopped their descent for a moment and Patricia tenderly traced the bridge of Eric's long nose with the tip of her finger, as he pulled back.

"Will you be okay with our new relationship?"

"Which relationship?"

"Divorce. It *is* a relationship."

"It's just that I was really comfortable with our marriage."

"We don't have to have a big rupture. We could still get together once in a while."

"But isn't that against the rules of divorce?"

"Everyone is entitled to write their own divorce rules. I'm very much anti-acrimony, and I think you are too."

"Indeed."

They kept climbing down the steps, crossing paths with a few tourists, some holding binoculars, perhaps hoping to get a closer look at the mate-for-life parrots.

"Did you do this behind Felix's back?"

Patricia nodded, biting her lower lip.

"I thought so. Oh, shit."

"Shit is right. Felix doesn't know we did this. He might never find out."

"I have the feeling you're about to start a lifelong family farce."

"Truth is, we still haven't sorted out that detail and now you're making me very nervous."

"I've always loved your wildness, Pats, how you use your impulses to deal with shit, but this is damn reckless, this is so topsy-turvy, so *sens dessus dessous*!"

When they reached Embarcadero at the bottom of the hill, they took an Uber back to Eric's car, drove home, and fucked all night.

Sunday, September 11th
"Because my bubbe said bar mitzvah is about identity."

"Right, tell me then, Dani," said Rabbi Nebenzahl. "How do you identify yourself, first and foremost?"

"Gender fluid," said Dani with newfound certainty, not realizing that he had just come out to his rabbi.

"I was framing the question in the context of religion," stuttered Rabbi Nebenzahl in his thick Jewish accent.

"Then I'm a gender-fluid, nonpracticing Jew with a Catholic grandfather and a Protestant stepdad."

Needless to say, Dani's first Bar Mitzvah session didn't go so well, even according to the standards of a Reform rabbi.

Monday, September 12th
"Don't even try to give me a present," said Keila as soon as she woke up.

Oscar was still sleeping on the other side of a king-size pillow that Keila placed between them every night as a meager divider.

"What are you talking about?"

376

"Today is our fortieth anniversary, in case you forgot."

He sat on the bed and looked at Keila, her hair a bit messy, but just as beautiful as day one. The air felt dry and crackly and so did Keila.

"I thought about it yesterday, but I didn't dare get you anything you could hurl at me."

"Well, I don't want gifts, anyway. We're not in the mood to celebrate. It's September already and this is going nowhere. We're failing our daughters; you're going to fail them," said Keila at the same time she asked herself if it was she who was refusing to acknowledge his efforts.

"Then let's go for birria tomorrow," said Oscar. "Let's go out on a date and give it a try."

Keila felt a hairline fissure appear in the wall she'd built around her to keep Oscar out.

"I'll agree to go downstairs with you and make some quesadillas tonight. That's all. And don't remind the girls about our anniversary. I don't need a party. If I'm lucky, they won't remember."

Countless times during the past few weeks, Keila had relived in her mind the night she spent at Simon Brik's apartment. She hadn't returned to Mexico City, she'd

377

been ignoring his calls and deleting his texts, as if that could erase her betrayal. Every time Oscar came to her showing his efforts to mend their marriage, her guilt became more intolerable. Why was she rejecting Oscar's attempts? Was she afraid he would see through her, figure out what she'd done?

Thursday, September 15th
"I want you to hear me out. Please don't interrupt, don't say anything until I'm finished," said Oscar in front of the mirror in his closet, among old ties and worn-out sweaters and raincoats he hadn't used in years. He'd been practicing his speech since three in the morning, motivated by the quesadilla dinner a few nights before in which he and Keila had been able to produce small talk for twenty minutes. But when he heard Keila downstairs preparing breakfast he realized he had no more time to rehearse. This was it.

When he walked into the kitchen he found his entire family having coffee and juice, enjoying their scrambled eggs with matzo and strawberry jelly. Suddenly he felt the weight of having everyone back home again, a feeling both wonderful and terrifying.

He had to stay focused on his goal: tell

Keila about the almond orchard. He waited for Claudia to start her physical therapy in the living room, Olivia to take the twins to Mommy and Me, and Patricia to go to work. There was no going back.

"I want you to come with me, Keila. I need to show you what's been happening with me all this time."

"Oh, is it something outside this house?" she asked with a hint of sarcasm, putting the last plate in the dishwasher.

"Please get ready. Wear comfortable shoes. I'll wait out front."

Once in the SUV, Oscar drove down Olympic Boulevard, turned right at Cotner Avenue, and got on the northbound 405.

"We can talk about it now, or we can wait until we get there. It's your call. We're a good three hours away."

"Let's get this over with," she said, shocked to be so cool now that she was about to get her long-awaited answer.

"Agree. I want you to hear me out. Please don't say anything until I'm finished."

Keila was surprised at Oscar's assertiveness, a trait she loved but hadn't seen in over a year.

"I'm listening."

Oscar took a sip of tila tea from his thermos. Outside, the freeway traffic dwindled as they left the city.

"Remember that place where Claudia and Olivia took a defensive-driving course when they were first learning, the Buttonwillow Raceway Park?"

Keila nodded, intrigued.

Oscar took his time to continue. This was it, the moment he'd been dreading for so long. Saying the very words that had kept him awake, tossing and turning in bed, for years was now in his immediate future, which was now. He quickly glanced at the Magic Mountain's roller coasters on the left, a sign that they were past Santa Clarita and approaching Castaic. They were a metaphor of his current emotional state.

"So, what about Buttonwillow?" she said.

"Well, we are owners of a beautiful almond orchard right over there, west of it, toward McKittrick in Kern County," said Oscar finally, putting an end to years of a torturous secret. Whatever came next was anyone's guess, but be it for better or for worse, it was a consequence of his doing and he'd own it.

"Since when?"

"Seven years."

"So, I've been in the agrobusiness totally unbeknownst to me. Great. Is this the reason you've been a zombie?"

"Please let me finish. It started out really well. In fact, the first couple of years the business yielded quite a good profit. But almonds are a thirsty crop and with the drought I've had to make extra investments to irrigate properly, and now production is as low as it has ever been on that piece of land. On top of that, I couldn't plant more than half of the property. The other half is on very windy hills, unsuitable for almond trees, what with the delicate blossoms that can blow away. And to make things worse, the almonds' price per pound has gone down. I'm not going to bore you with the details. The fact is that I'm in debt. The rains are not coming. I'm not sure I can continue supporting the orchard. And I've been feeling awful for not telling you about this business."

"I should have had a say!"

"I know. But every time I came to you with a business idea you dismissed it. I'm not blaming you at all. This wasn't your fault. I made this choice on my own. I couldn't help it. I wanted to put the money to good use. And I loved the trees. When you walk among them in bloom with honey-bees buzzing around, foraging for pollen and nectar, you feel like you're in a mystical world. Just think about this next time you put an almond in your mouth: a bee had to pollinate its blossom for you to eat it. That's how miraculous it is."

Oscar stayed on the 5 toward Stockton at the intersection with the 99 toward Bakersfield and accelerated to drive ahead of a semitruck snorting dark fumes.

Keila tried to stay quiet and listen to every word Oscar said. This was a difficult exercise for anyone with strong opinions, more so since it involved her directly, more so since this was the very reason her marriage was crumbling away. She should be furious, but as she heard Oscar's explanation, something strange happened: she began to feel a timid compassion toward him. Yes, he had kept this endeavor a secret; yes, he should have gotten her blessing. But at the same time, she hadn't been as open as she should have been when he proposed business ideas. Instead, she resorted to sabotaging his endeavors. Why?

At some point along the 5 Freeway, Oscar took an exit, approached a dirt road, and eventually reached the orchard.

"Welcome to Happy Crunch Almond Orchard."

Keila let out a laugh. "Is that the name of our business? Did you come up with it?"

"What's wrong with it?" asked Oscar, a

382

bit insulted.

"It's too funny. That's all."

"Don't you like it?"

"It's so incredibly silly I love it."

It was hard for Oscar to understand what he was feeling. How could he? Relief was a sensation as distant as undiscovered planets. He had imagined Keila erupting in anger, slapping him, biting him, kicking him, and pulling out his hair. He was willing to take the beating, a well-deserved one, but it didn't come. Instead, she laughed. So, he chuckled hesitantly, got out of the SUV, and went around to open the door for her.

As they walked toward the rows of trees, he held her hand. She let him. How long had it been since they touched each other? Keila's fingers felt long and bony in Oscar's, and a sensation of warmth traveled all the way to his chest, making it heave. Forgiveness could not be attained so easily, not from Keila. But he recognized her reaction as a good start, so he gave her the grand tour around the property without letting go of her hand.

Just a few days before and against Aunt Belinda's advice, he'd gotten a ninety-day credit from a loan shark at an obscene interest rate and hired a machine with an extended arm that was now clamped to a tree trunk and was vigorously shaking the almonds off the branches, leaving a wall-to-wall carpet of nuts on the ground.

"The pickup machine is coming next week to haul the almonds away. We could come back to watch, if you'd like. It's the culmination of all our efforts."

"Well, if Happy Crunch Almond Orchard is my business too, I should get involved, the girls should get involved. Have you told them? Am I the only one who's been kept in the dark?"

"Only Pats knows, and only very recently."

"That's the next step. You have to tell them. Understand? You owe it to them. They need to get involved, even if it's at the very end of the season."

The very end, indeed, Oscar thought, but not just the end of the season. How was he going to tell Keila now that there might not be a future harvest, that they might lose the trees? One thing was his secret; the other was his failure.

Friday, September 16th

No sign of rain was the Weather Channel's ominous message that morning. Oscar sat in his chair in front of the television, remote in hand, ready to fall headlong into climate-induced despair, when his phone chimed. A four-word text from Patricia appeared in the family group chat: "I am divorcing Eric."

Sunday, September 18th

"Copycat," was Claudia's comment at the dinner table.

After Oscar lectured Patricia about the awful way she delivered her decision to divorce Eric (you don't just text news as important as that), and after she explained herself (I was going to give you further details in person), she called for a family dinner to discuss the issue.

"I'm not being a copycat. It just so happens that the whole thing unraveled around the same time as your own marriages; I had to wait my turn," said Patricia, a bit offended.

"And how are you feeling?" asked Olivia.

"I'm good. Eric and I are on the best terms. We decided to transition into another relationship, not sure what it's going to be like, but a positive one for sure. In fact, he wants to talk to you. Hold on."

She pulled out her cellphone and got Eric on the screen.

"Hi, everyone." He waved his hand, smiling. Patricia panned her phone around the table so he could see her sisters and her parents.

"Hi, Eric. We're all here talking about our divorce," explained Patricia.

"Have you told them about the party?"

"Not yet. Go ahead."

"Well, Patricia and I decided to host a party to announce our divorce," said Eric. "A small one, just close friends and family. Can we have it at your place? We could rent a venue, but we really want to keep it intimate. Claudia, could you recommend a caterer?"

Had it been an audio call instead of a video call, Eric would have thought that he'd gotten disconnected, since no sound came out of anybody's mouth.

"Hello? Can you hear me?"

"Yes," said Claudia, breaking the awkward silence. "Mom, is it okay for them to have their party here?"

Keila nodded with apparent discomfort.

"Of course, but I still don't get why you kids want to get divorced if you're so amicable."

" 'Amicable' is the key word, Mom," said Patricia. "Are you going to support us in our decision or not?"

"Look, Pats, I hope you understand that it's not easy to digest three divorces in the same year."

"Then don't ask why or how," Patricia

said. "Don't make assumptions. Don't investigate. Trust us. It's what's best for us. Just know that Eric and I will be fine."

"Don't think you're going to get rid of me that easily," said Eric, suddenly reminding everyone that he was still on the video call.

After Patricia's cellphone went around the table, everyone saying good-bye to Eric, blowing kisses and air hugs, and after everyone had started eating, Oscar said to his daughters, "You know, I'm actually angry right now and I want you all to hear what I have to say."

Keila stopped cold. Was Oscar recovering his assertiveness?

"When your mother announced to you back in January that she wanted to divorce me, you rejected her decision forcefully and with zero validation of her feelings. And yet here you are, divorcing your husbands, all three of you, and you expect us to support your decisions without question. I know you are each doing it under different circumstances, I get it, but by the way things have turned out, I sense a double standard here and I want to hear what you have to say about it."

Keila, for once, found herself speechless. It took her a few seconds to realize that

Oscar was right. All of a sudden she needed an apology from her daughters, for her and for Oscar.

After what seemed a long silence, Patricia said, "Mom, Dad, I'm so sorry! I've been so selfish. We never really asked why you were at odds, why Dad's behavior was so terrible that you wanted to split up. We just acted like little kids."

"Yes, Pats," said Claudia. "All this time we were demanding that Mom and Dad make up while we were busy messing up our own marriages. That's so sick. I feel terrible myself. But, if I can say so, Mom, Dad, you're really giving it all you've got. I see a lot of progress. I really hope you stay together, but only if you want to. No more pressure from us. It's really not fair."

Olivia took her time to answer. Holding back tears, she finally said to her parents, "All of our lives you guys have taught us what a good marriage should be, even during these difficult months where you humored us and gave yourselves a chance, but we've failed in ours. We all married the wrong guy to start with, and even though we succeeded occasionally — well, the twins are proof — look at us; we're back home licking one another's wounds, leaving a trail of debacles behind. I think we asked you to stay together because we loved your marriage more than we loved ours."

Keila reached across the table and took Olivia's hand, causing her to weep, now with abandon.

There, it had been said.

Monday, September 19th

"Why did you even get married?" asked Dani, puzzled, fluffing his pillow.

"That's a question I'm asking myself. Maybe I don't think things through, I'm finding out. I'll have an answer for you soon. I'm working on it," said Patricia, sitting at the edge of her son's bed. "Eric is a good man, but he's not the right man for us. That's why we're divorcing."

"We don't need a man, or a dad. Or do you?"

"Question number two. I might not."

"I like Eric, but I hardly ever see him. I wonder if I'll miss him."

"He's still going to visit sometimes."

"That could be cool. Can I borrow your iPad?"

And with Dani's question number three, Patricia realized that her divorce from Eric was not really an issue to be concerned with. Not for Dani anyway.

Dani came back into bed with Patricia's iPad.

"There's more news. This one you might really like," she continued. "I'm going to have a baby."

"What?" Dani put down the tablet, puzzled.

"Maybe two."

"Wait, but why, if you don't love Eric?"

"It's complicated. Eric is not involved at all. I'm carrying Olivia's embryos, the ones you've been hearing about over dinner. She doesn't have a uterus anymore, so mine is the next best thing."

"Wow. So they'll be my brother-cousins?"

"They'll be Alvarados."

"That's so sci-fi."

"Olivia and I will be raising them together, like we've raised you. We'll be sister-mommies. But you can't tell anyone just yet. Promise?"

"Promise."

Patricia took a deep breath and got up to leave. "Fifteen minutes and the lights go out, okay?"

Tuesday, September 20th

Invites to Patricia and Eric's divorce party were sent out on the same day they hired a mediator.

"Eric and I are using the same guy," Patricia said when Olivia offered to refer her lawyer. "We've agreed on everything. So, why should we have separate representation?"

"But my lawyer's a T. rex. He can help you sort out all your assets," Olivia insisted.

"You mean my shoe collection? My car? My devices? I don't own anything. I don't even own a frying pan. I have no need for monster lawyers. Eric keeps his stuff and I keep mine, as simple as that. What I really need is a caterer. Claudia is not being helpful."

"Let's call her chef friend Hiroshi," said Olivia, abandoning the T. rex idea.

After making a few calls and finalizing the party, Olivia and Patricia spent the rest of the afternoon drinking coffee and eating cookies in the kitchen. By the time they'd rescued some leftover chicken from the fridge, dabbed it in mayonnaise, and nibbled it to the bone, they'd already covered all kinds of gossip, except the Big Issue that was uncomfortably wedged between them.

"I'm afraid to ask you if the pregnancy had anything to do with your decision to divorce Eric."

"Of course it did, in a good way. Everything was resolved in the end. You really need to work hard to have a good, solid marriage, and neither of us is prepared for that, let alone a family. It's nobody's fault. And we're open to some kind of relationship, whatever it is."

"What a relief, Pats. At least one of us has had an amicable divorce."

"Right. There really is no acrimony between Eric and me. And as for the embryos," she said, rubbing her incipient belly, "we did it!"

"Yup," said Olivia, unsure if keeping the truth from Felix was the best way to handle the situation. Secrets have a tendency to come out eventually, in unexpected and nasty ways.

Wednesday, September 21st
Would she ever be able to get rid of the cane? The more her physical therapist told her she would fully recover, the more Claudia's fear intensified. She'd lost something. What was that part of her brain, now obviously damaged, that had always made her so plucky? Now not only her step but her personality was wobbly. When Olivia wasn't home, Claudia would text her repeatedly with big and small wants and needs: "Could you stop by the pharmacy to pick up my meds?" Or: "I need a better pillow."

Or: "Do you love me?"

Olivia complied dutifully and lovingly, storing away any resentment that had resulted from years of enduring her sister's bullying and criticism. She humored Claudia's neediness and dismissed it, not quite convincingly, as temporary.

She'd recently noticed that Claudia had been camping at the dining table for days, typing away on her laptop. Was she binge-shopping? Online dating? Applying for a job? On that afternoon, her curiosity brought her to glance at her sister's screen. Startled by Olivia's presence, Claudia hastily shut her laptop.

"Are you watching porn?" asked Olivia, taken aback.

"Of course not."

"Then what are you hiding?"

"Nothing. It's a personal project."

"Right. It's none of my business. I'm just curious."

"You're always going through my stuff!"

"I only did it that one time years ago!"

Olivia remembered that day very well. Keila and Oscar were going on a scuba-diving trip to Tulum and left Claudia and Olivia with Lola. Patricia hadn't been born yet.

"Take very good care of your new glasses.

They cost a small fortune and you already lost a pair," Keila warned Olivia right before she and Oscar left for the airport.

That very evening, Olivia carefully cleaned her glasses and set them on her nightstand before going to sleep. To her shock, the next morning they had disappeared. Puzzled, she looked everywhere over the following two weeks, including in Claudia's closet and drawers, to no avail.

"Mom's going to kill you for losing your glasses. I bet she's going to ground you for a year," Claudia would tell Olivia with a sneer.

Olivia was sure that her sister was hiding them somewhere. It was a classic Claudia maneuver. She'd torture her at every opportunity, and Olivia would agonize over the threat of punishment.

Of course, the glasses surfaced mysteriously on Olivia's nightstand the day Keila and Oscar returned from their trip.

Now, years later, standing in front of her frail sister tightly hugging her laptop against her chest as if it were a CPR rescue lifesaver board, Olivia felt a warm rush of compassion flow through her.

"No need to show me your personal project," Olivia said.

"I will, when I'm ready."

■■■■

Friday, September 30th

Los Tres Primos waited at the Happy Crunch Almond Orchard entrance gate for Oscar's SUV, their hats' inner bands wet with the sweat of labor. When they finally saw the cloud of dust swirling around on the road announcing the car's arrival, all three of them straightened their shirt collars and wiped their faces as if choreographed.

The first one to step out of the car full of Alvarados was Patricia, followed by Dani.

"*Shanah tovah*, Mrs. Alvarado," said Lucas.

"Happy Rosh Hashanah!" said Dani without asking himself how these Mexican farmworkers knew how to greet them in Hebrew on this holiday.

"You're Los Tres Primos! My dad said you're going to tell us about the almonds," said Patricia with a wink, as they knew she knew and were in on the surprise for her older sisters. "I'm Patricia, but people call me Pats. This is my son, Dani," she said. She shook their hands, their callused skin hardened by years of working the land.

"Grandpa says you are masters at growing almonds," he said, hoping to corroborate

395

Oscar's assertion.

Lucas blushed and smiled at his cousins.

"We make a good team," he said, and Saúl and Mario nodded in unison.

Olivia helped Claudia step out of the car and reached for the cane so her sister could maneuver the uneven terrain. Then she went to the back of the minivan to get the twins out of their car seats.

"Don't go very far, girls. I want to be able to see you at all times," said Olivia, quickly scanning the rows of trees for potential danger.

As expected, Diana sprinted to the east and Andrea to the west, and without waiting for any sort of instruction, Lucas went after one and Mario after the other, bringing the girls back to Olivia within minutes.

"So sorry, they've never been in the countryside," said Olivia, embarrassed, feeling the need to explain.

"That's what the open land does to city kids," said Saúl. "They can't help it."

Oscar watched the scene as he unloaded the picnic basket and the cooler, taking them to a long wooden table that Los Tres Primos had prepared on Oscar's request, clad with a flower-patterned plastic tablecloth and set with enamel dinnerware brought from the cousins' home. A small vase with wildflowers picked that morning at the Carrizo Plain served as a centerpiece.

"I'm not telling you where we're going. It's a surprise," he'd told Keila, his daughters, and his grandchildren days before when he invited them to celebrate Rosh Hashanah at a mystery location.

"So, we're not going to temple, right?" Patricia had asked Oscar with a veiled, conspiratorial smirk, knowing that a surprise visit to Happy Crunch Almond Orchard would be the way Oscar revealed the secret to his other daughters.

"We'll just have to miss it." Keila suspected where Oscar wanted to take his family, so even though she considered herself a "twice-a-year Jew" and enjoyed the prayers and songs at the synagogue on Rosh Hashanah and Yom Kippur, she didn't make a fuss about skipping it this year.

On the way, Oscar announced that they were to have a picnic at an almond orchard, and they were to meet Los Tres Primos, the almond experts, so they could ask questions about the nuts. With a little encouragement from Keila, everyone humored him, as they hadn't seen him so excited about anything in a long time.

As soon as everyone sat to start lunch and commented on the beauty of their surroundings, Oscar said, in ceremony: "How many years since we had a family picnic? I can still see Claudia and Olivia flipping a quarter to decide who would break the piñata."

"And what about the time Pats got chased by a swarm of wasps in Big Bear?" said Claudia, interrupting her father.

"I'm sure you remember this one, too: the time you made us tortas for that beach day at El Capitán and we all got sick," said Patricia, still mad at Claudia for making fun of her after the wasp attack, years before.

"Well, this is also a very special picnic," said Oscar, trying to redirect the conversation toward his big announcement. "I wanted to bring you here as a surprise because this land, these trees, and the hills you see over there to the east, they're ours. I bought this paradise a long time ago after I sold the land in Silicon Valley, and I bought it behind your mother's back, so I want to ask her again to forgive me today, in front of you."

Keila stood still, her eyes fixed on Oscar.

"And I also need to apologize to you all for behaving as horribly as I have," Oscar continued. "For a long time, almonds have been our family's livelihood unbeknownst to you, but the drought has driven the orchard into the ground, which is why I've been obsessed with the weather. Now we're broke, in debt, and it's possible we might lose the proceeds of the crop. I just had to share this dreadful secret that's been killing me."

"I'm speechless, Dad. What did you gain from all this deception?" said Claudia, still in shock.

"I thought I could prove to you that I shared the ability of our ancestors to become a great steward of the land, to collaborate with nature making something beautiful and delicious, and not telling your mother gave me the freedom to act alone and try my luck at agriculture, but I was wrong. I'm not the farmer I was hoping to be."

"I'm sure you must have felt awful, keeping this secret and watching how it has driven Mom away," said Olivia, trying to understand. "You could have picked Yom Kippur to come clean, but any day is a good day to repent."

"If I may say with respect, Oscar" — Keila spoke in a low voice — "I know how much you admire your ancestors, but you're not being fair to yourself by making comparisons. Don Rodrigo Alvarado and Doña Fermina de la Asunción Ortega received the

399

land grant from Governor Figueroa because he was a friend of Don Juan Bautista de Anza. The key word here is 'received.' They didn't start out at zero."

"Neither did we."

"Fair enough, I know, but you didn't just sit on the part of the land you inherited; you tried to grow the wealth for us, for our daughters. I will help you and we will come out of this slump. We're not done yet," said Keila with teary eyes.

"Yes, Dad. We will help too," said Olivia, who had been instantly enamored with the land.

Patricia was silent, until Claudia noticed: "Aren't you going to say something?"

Patricia wavered for a moment, turned her gaze at the plates of food on the table, and said: "I already knew about the orchard."

"How did you find out? Why were we in the dark?" said Claudia, annoyed.

"All I had to do was ask. You never seemed to care about why Dad was so sad and worried all this time."

"Hey! Stop now. Don't point fingers," said Oscar. "All of this is my fault and no one else's. I want us to look to the future. My appeal to you today is that we work together as a family to try to save Happy Crunch Almond Orchard."

The explosion of laughter startled Oscar. "What did you call the orchard?" asked Claudia.

"Happy Crunch?" said Olivia in disbelief.

"You don't like the name either?" said Oscar, a bit offended.

Keila laughed with her daughters, delighted to realize that they also found the orchard's name preposterous, but she was determined to defend it just because it included the word "happy" and she was ready to feel happiness again.

When the initial shock subsided, the Alvarados and Los Tres Primos shared the picnic that Oscar had prepared, starting with slices of apples dipped in honey, one of Dani's favorite dishes of the traditional Rosh Hashanah meal. The potato kugel was so good that Olivia suspected Oscar had bought it at Canter's Deli instead of making it himself, but she decided not to comment. Then, instead of sweet brisket, Oscar brought carne asada, a far tastier choice. Mario fanned the flames in the firepit by the side of their picnic area and heated the meat, the rice, and the tortillas for everyone. There was no gefilte fish or roasted asparagus, but the refried beans and the sliced poblano peppers with sautéed onions were perfect sides for the main course.

Not far from where they sat, a harvester was busy vacuuming the nuts onto carts to get them ready for distribution.

"After that machine over there is done," explained Lucas, "we'll be sending the almonds to a huller to clean the crop and separate the shells from the hulls. Nothing goes to waste. Shells make great livestock bedding. Cows love to eat the hulls, and the whole world eats our almonds. Next time we see the nuts they'll be at the grocery store."

Dani raised his hand, as if in a classroom.

"What happens to the trees?"

"Under normal circumstances, that is, if we weren't going through a bad drought," explained Lucas, "the trees spend the winter in a sort of downtime. Then in March we've got the bloom. That's Don Oscar's favorite time. It's when all the blossoms come out. In June we get the kernels. That's the time I like the most. And at the very end of the cycle, in September, is the harvest. It's when we're the busiest, but we don't care. It's the big payoff, when all our work gets rewarded."

"But what happens to the trees now that there's the drought?" Dani insisted.

"That's a decision your grandpa has to make," said Lucas, his brow creasing.

"We'll have to wait and see what the weather brings," said Oscar, trying to hide how horrified he was at the idea of having to pull out the trees.

No one understood better than Los Tres Primos the decision Oscar had to make. Oscar had told them already that there was no more money to prep the trees for the winter downtime. They knew Oscar had taken bank loans against the orchard to pay for water and was on the brink of defaulting on them. Not only did they fear he could lose the trees, but the entire orchard, the land, which he'd used as collateral on the big loan.

"I have something to say," Keila interrupted the almond lesson. "Before we finish these delicious figs with cream, I want to come clean myself."

"You have secrets too, Mom? What's going on with you guys?" asked Claudia.

"Your father didn't tell us about the almond orchard because I spent years sabotaging his business ideas. I was so angry! And I didn't know why I felt so resentful. Now I know I've had this thorn stuck in my heart for being excluded from his ancestors' trust. I wasn't seeing everything your dad has given us, all that love and attention and care. I've been an idiot.

"I'm so sorry."

Oscar held Keila's hand and let his wife's words lodge in his brain for future understanding. Claudia started packing the leftovers in silence. Olivia hugged her mother and wiped a tear from her cheek. In the aftermath of Keila's declaration and as everyone was getting ready to leave, Patricia quietly checked in Claudia's handbag and, not surprised, pulled out an enamel plate that she put back on the table, right in front of her sister.

"Goddammit, are you stealing from the farmworkers, klepto?"

OCTOBER

For the third time since their breakup, Felix brought the twins back to Olivia's early.

"Another date?" asked Olivia, regretting it at once.

"It's not your business what I do or who I go out with, so stop."

Olivia grabbed the girls' little backpacks from his hand and closed the door, holding her breath. What do I care? she thought.

She had been thinking and rethinking a plan that was still vague in her brain. She was terrified by what Felix might do if he found out the truth, that Patricia was pregnant with the embryos that were supposed to have been discarded.

She shut the door quickly as if that would blow the problem away and hurried inside to hide under the sheets. That little space had become her thinking shrine. Surely a brilliant idea would pop into her head like magic. She waited. And waited.

Thursday, October 6th

The money from the sale of the crop came in sooner than Oscar had anticipated. Just in time to keep the bankers satisfied, and to hire the tree-removal and grinding service. His trees, only eight years old, could have yielded crops for another twenty years. What a waste, he repeated aloud over and over on the way to the orchard.

They were very busy, the executioners of his beloved trees. They'd told Oscar on the phone that morning that they'd have to schedule him for the end of the month, which was fine by him. He had yet to collect some more money from the sale of the hulls to dairy farmers, which would go to pay down more debt. When all was said and done, he'd have no money left, and no trees.

Such a farmer he'd turned out to be. A fraud. A failure. A flake. A featherweight. A flop. A fucking fool. He tried to find another fitting word starting with the letter "f" but couldn't come up with one. He'd have to sit down with Los Tres Primos and Aunt Belinda and consider his options, but before then, he'd lay it all bare in front of Keila. She had offered to help. She needed to know that they'd soon be losing the

406

trees, if not the entire orchard. Enough subterfuge.

Saturday, October 8th and Sunday, October 9th

Ninety-two degrees for an outdoor party. Not bad at all. Patricia and Eric had hired one of Claudia's caterer friends to serve at the soiree after Hiroshi declined, explaining he didn't have the manpower to serve forty-seven guests. Performing at the top of her game, locally famous DJ AlleyCat, in fishnets and stilettos and bleached cornrow braids crowned with a sparkly kitty-ears headband, spun fast-paced sets, all vinyl — garage, electro, funk-punk, reggaeton, mashups, whatever — to the thumping crowd on the dance floor that covered most of the Alvarados' lawn. There was even a three-tier cake with dark-chocolate frosting, absent the sugar bride and groom on top. Patricia made a special effort to look dazzling, wearing a black dress that seemed to have been painted on her skin.

Aunt Belinda quietly wondered whether Patricia and Eric's marriage, which seemed passionless to her, had meant anything to them, or if they were just conducting their split with dignity and grace? She took a swig of champagne and thought about her own marriage. Losing her husband to cancer early on had been a blessing of sorts. She'd often say, "Every married woman deserves at least ten years of widowhood." If he'd lived, would she have left him? Or would she have braved a contentious marriage? The answer was evident. She attributed it to the times. In her day, you endured it till the very end and that was that.

"If you thought we were going to return the wedding presents, you're mistaken," joked Eric during his speech before several dozen people, some of whom had flown down from San Francisco for the event. "But we are untying the knot and wanted you to be the first to know. Please don't take sides. We both love you all, and since Pats and I will remain friends, there's no reason for you to choose one or the other. Cheers!"

After a robust round of applause, the party went on until daybreak, when the last guest, a pothead friend of Eric's, zigzagged across the front lawn and boarded an Uber with the help of the driver.

Patricia and Eric collapsed on her bed and slept until early afternoon on Sunday.

"Let's wrap this up," said Patricia when she woke up.

"What are we wrapping up?"

"Our marriage."

"Oh, I get it."

Patricia turned over and mounted Eric, but this time swaying tenderly, as if she waved good-bye with a silk handkerchief.

Something had changed. The way she had learned to approach Big Boy at the horse pen, quietly, slowly, her gaze fixed on his in complete communion, had taught her that she didn't have to call the shots, and that even though he was many times her weight and could hurt her if he wanted to, he wasn't in command either. That in order to find the little space where intimacy flourished, they'd have to aim for reciprocity.

Later, while getting coffee down the street, Eric asked, "We're ending our marriage, but that doesn't mean we're not going to see each other again, right? You said to me that we'd be writing the rules of this divorce. I said in my speech that we'd stay friends."

"You tell me. How do you envision our friendship?"

"I just want to leave the door open for possibilities, you know; maybe later we could do a triad with someone else."

"As in a thruple?"

"Something like that. Or even a V."

Patricia took time to answer.

"If you believe polyamory might work for us, then I suppose that can stay on the table for the future. We'd have to see where we are in terms of relationships. Right now, I just want to focus on my pregnancy. Do you have anyone in mind?"

"Not really. Just thinking out loud."

"Sounds intriguing, but at this point I don't see how that kind of arrangement would fit into my life now," she said, motioning to her abdomen.

They left the coffee place and walked to Patricia's house. Eric got his suitcase and called a car.

It didn't feel like good-bye.

Meanwhile, Oscar and Keila drank a glass of cabernet in the lounge chairs in the backyard, facing the keloid scar. Rental tables, chairs, and soiled linens sat by the gate waiting to be picked up.

"Great party," said Oscar, afraid to start a conversation he'd been practicing in front of the mirror (by now a habit) for the past few days. This was not about the loss of the orchard, or about their daughters' divorces, or their particular drama. This was a far more crucial matter and he needed to deliver a pristine message to his wife if he wanted to save his marriage.

"No need for small talk. I know what you really want to say."

"You do?"

"I don't read minds; don't freak out. I heard you rehearsing in your closet."

Oscar had to laugh.

"Well, then. You know what I want, what I've wanted all along. What do you say?"

"I say yes."

Oscar got up and sat next to Keila on her lounge chair. He put his hands on her cheeks delicately, as if holding an injured dove, and kissed her. Upstairs, unbeknownst to them, the pillow that Keila had placed between them in bed for the past two years morphed from a snarl of concertina wire into a giant marshmallow of love.

Wednesday, October 12th

How fitting that Oscar and Keila picked Yom Kippur to announce to their daughters that they had decided to stay together.

"So, here we are this evening," Keila announced in a soft voice to her three daughters. "You demanded that we work out our problems and asked us to give ourselves a year to decide if we were staying together or not. We already processed this as a family, thank you again for your apologies. And now, I'm happy to report that we are indeed staying together, not because you asked us, but because we want to. There's still a lot of

411

forgiving to do, though."

"And it's not just between us, your mom and I," Oscar added. "We believe you deserve an apology, at least from me."

"It seems to me that you'll need to start by forgiving yourself, Dad," said Patricia.

"Agree," said Olivia.

"Forgiveness is as much for the one being forgiven as it is for the one forgiving," said Oscar. "So, let's forgive each other, let's forgive ourselves, and let's get on with our lives. We have too much to do as a family and we're going to need one another's help."

"Oh, you bet we will," said Claudia.

As the family sat around in the living room, Velcro on Claudia's lap, Ramsay on Olivia's, the twins in the other room, playing with Dani and Lola, it became clear to each of them that a cosmic mandate had brought them together again in the house of Rancho Verde.

"Time to break our fast. I'm starving. Who wants deviled eggs?" said Keila, looking at her watch.

Friday, October 14th

Even without looking, as he woke up the next morning, Oscar recognized the symptom that had become uneasily clear under the sheets: the hairs on his arms and legs were standing like passengers on a platform waiting for a train. He feared he'd engage in a stupid argument with someone (last year was a neighbor; the year prior, the gardener). He'd refrain from driving the car, since there was an increased probability of getting involved in some road rage situation. He knew this meant he needed to stay out of Keila's way. His first order of business would be to separate Ramsay from Velcro, locking them in different rooms of the house to avoid a confrontation between the pets. He also needed to put away the lounge chair cushions and make sure the patio umbrellas were secure. The Santa Anas were back.

Funny how they meant different things for different people, he thought, as he shut the bedroom window tight. For Patricia, a Santa Ana wind day was a bad hair day. For Oscar, it was a hundred-mile-per-hour disaster electrifying the air and wreaking havoc. Over the years he'd seen those nasty winds fuel devastating wildfires with massive property destruction and countless fatalities. He'd watched jacarandas falling on top of cars, crushing the people inside. He'd avoided driving over fallen palm tree branches spread all over the city streets. He'd helped homeless people chase after their tents. The Santa Ana winds were a Los Angeles season in themselves. He waited for it with dread.

When Keila came back in one piece from her weekly shopping, this time at the farmers' market in Echo Park, Oscar sighed with relief.

"Some of the awnings on the produce stands blew away. One pipe from the structure hit a woman on the head. Look!" Keila showed Oscar a bloodstain on her scarf. "I held her until the paramedics arrived. I was standing right next to her. It could have been me."

Oscar hugged Keila tight and cursed the Santa Ana winds before going on to curse the drought, the fires, and a long litany of weather events that had preoccupied him to the point of obsession in the past years. How could he have neglected the woman he now held in his arms, and focused instead on the weather, something he had absolutely no control over? He had risked losing her for what? Almonds? It was indeed better than losing her for peanuts, but still, not worth it at all.

Later, at precisely 11:58 P.M., the order to evacuate came loud on everyone's cellphones, jolting the entire family out of bed.

As previously rehearsed, they automatically engaged in their wildfire emergency action plan: Prepacked suitcases at the front door in four minutes flat. Ramsay in his carrier, barking away. Backpacks with laptops, hard drives, chargers, passports, medications, cash, all ready to go.

Oscar looked out the window and saw in horror an orange glow spewing tongues of fire lighting up a dense cloud of smoke behind the neighborhood's treetops. Patricia snapped a few shots with her phone and quickly caught up with Olivia, Lola, and the twins, who were already at the foyer. Keila held Claudia's hand as she went down the stairs.

"Where's Velcro?" asked Claudia, in a panic.

"We don't have time to go looking for the cat," yelled Oscar.

"I'm not going anywhere without Velcro," warned Claudia, and sat on the stair landing, crossing her arms in rebellion.

"Everyone! Find Velcro! Now!" ordered Oscar, thinking about his constant fear of losing a cat to a fire.

The frantic search took twelve excruciating minutes. Dani, the hero of the night, finally found him and pulled him out from under an armoire in the family room.

"I've got him!" he yelled while everyone ran to Oscar's SUV.

"Get the kitty litter box too!" yelled Claudia from her seat to Dani, who ran back inside.

Once they were fleeing down Sunset Boulevard, suggestions as to where to go started pouring in:

"The Rancho Verde Recreation Center is open for sure," said Keila. "Last time we evacuated there it was pretty good, everyone was super nice, considering the situation."

"Yeah, they were handing out free Krispy Kreme doughnuts," said Dani.

"We could go to a hotel this time. My sous-chef Alicia gave me a list of hotels perfect for evacuation: pet-friendly, kitchenette, in-suite sofa beds," said Claudia, pulling out her phone to look for the list. "I'll pay for the rooms."

"How about if we go to the house I'm remodeling? It's empty. The only problem is that the toilets aren't installed yet; we'd have to use the Porta Potty," said Olivia.

Patricia checked her text messages and announced, "Hey, my friends Don and Laura are hosting an evacuation party. They've got plenty of sleeping bags. Some people are there already."

"Come to my house," said Lola finally. And that's where they all went.

Saturday, October 15th

Like a natural extension of her plentiful arms, Lola's house cradled the Alvarados with the warmth of familiarity. She'd had them over for parties or just for simple visits many times in the past. Claudia and Olivia settled in the second bedroom. Lola took the twins into her bed. Keila got the sofa and Oscar the easy chair. Patricia and Dani picked the space under the dining table. Ramsay favored the kitchen floor. Velcro inspected every nook and cranny of the premises all through the night, meowing in a what-the-hell-am-I-doing-here tone.

It's really up to the wind whose home gets destroyed by the fire, Oscar thought, his eyes wide open, staring at an old leak stain on Lola's living-room ceiling. Would their house be spared, again? He thought about the small Carlos Almaraz drawing he loved so much hanging in a frame in his living room and imagined it being engulfed by flames. Funny: he realized he didn't care. Everything he truly loved was with him, right there, safe in that little house.

Following LAFD updates while having breakfast (Lola prepared her special chilaquiles recipe for everyone and Keila made tila tea to calm the nerves), Oscar had learned that the fire was moving toward the coast, pushed by ferocious Santa Ana gusts, precisely in the opposite direction from Rancho Verde. But that wasn't cause for relief. Hundreds of homes were in the path of destruction. And embers were known to fly around and land on shingle roofs miles away from the inferno. That's how unpredictable the fire was; the way it decided to dance with the wind determined who was spared and who lost it all.

By midafternoon, Rancho Verde was cleared of danger and residents were allowed back into their homes. As they entered the house, Keila looked around with new eyes, as if it weren't her house. Everything seemed foreign. While her husband, daughters, and grandchildren went straight back to their daily routine, she wandered from room to room making a mental inventory of the things she and Oscar had bought over their forty years of marriage: the antique cabinet where she kept the stemware, her red sofa, the Murano lamps they'd bought in Italy years before, her sculptures, her china. And so, before nightfall, both Oscar and Keila reached the same conclusion in different ways. "It's just stuff," she said to herself.

Sunday, October 16th

Outside, the gusts of wind ruffled the palm trees with enough mischief to worry Patricia. She put on a pair of jeans and a sweater and went out to secure the barbecue-grill cover that the merciless Santa Anas had blown over to the ground. She wiped a thin blanket of ash off the table. She took a deep whiff of the smell of smoke that still lingered in the air and went back into the house to find Keila posting a 2016 calendar on the fridge.

"It's from a PETA and LAFD joint initiative. It came in the mail with my donation's receipt; it just turned up now that I reorganized my studio," she said, admiring the pictures of handsome, bare-chested firefighters holding rescue kittens and puppies in their pumped-up arms for each month of the year. She turned the empty pages of months past and opened it on October. "We can still use the last three months," she said. The featured fireman was a strong Chicano with eyes the color of honey. He was smiling at the camera and was rinsing a cute mutt in a tub of soapy water. The photo caption read, "Laundromutt."

419

Keila took a green Sharpie and wrote on November 10th: "Teeth cleaning, 9:00 am."

Patricia took a red Sharpie from a mug holding markers of all colors that her mother had just produced from who knows where, one for each member of the family, and entered on November 16th: "Ultrasound — bring Olie."

She turned around and hugged Keila.

"Our family calendar is back!" she sighed, delighted.

Monday, October 17th
Rain!

The water pounding on the roof sounded to Oscar like a standing ovation. He thought about the firefighters still putting out spot fires and chasing embers around nearby neighborhoods. The drought had killed more than sixty million trees throughout the state since January. Luckily, his almond trees would likely be spared from being engulfed in flames, as the roads helped stop the fires, but still, he'd seen the valley blanketed in ash and smoke from wildfires in faraway forests. Almost seven hundred thousand acres in the wildland-urban interface, where the city met foothills covered in brush, had been burned by wildfires. He knew the numbers well. He had kept them meticulously in his log as the proud pyro-geographer he believed himself to be. Was this rain the beginning of the end of the worst drought in California in over a thousand years? The muddy stream meandering along the yard toward the drains said so, but there was no way to make sure. This could well be just a little tease, courtesy of climate change, the little jester.

He'd have to keep a precipitation log, but the rain gauge he'd installed in his backyard had been knocked over and broken by two fighting (or copulating) squirrels three years ago. Not that he had needed it. But now, he'd have to buy a new one, so he threw some dry clothes on, grabbed his raincoat, which had been relegated to the very back of his closet, and drove to a nursery he liked in Torrance.

Because it was the first rain in over a hundred days, the roads were slick with oil: the perfect condition for hydroplaning. Worried about accidents on the road, he listened for the SigAlert report on the radio and sure enough: a multivehicle crash on the eastbound 10 Freeway had caused a two-hour delay on the morning commute. A rig had jackknifed on the northbound 405 at Jefferson Avenue, blocking three lanes. An ambulance was still at the scene. He was glad to be going south, but knew it would take at least three times longer than usual to reach the nursery, what with all those people rubbernecking as they passed the accident on the opposite side of the road. Several other crashes on surface streets were reported, but most were out of his way. The meteorologist had said that the rain wouldn't last long, and the temperatures would rise again to the hundreds by Thursday. Why bother buying a rain gauge? He might as well turn around and go home, he thought, but the sliver of optimism he still had made him continue on his quest.

Wednesday, October 19th

Ordinary Wednesdays didn't go like this. Oscar had spent most of the morning searching for the right words to describe his reality, words that would help him accept it and communicate it to Keila. In the end, he concluded that there was no fancy way to say it, so he delivered the news to her as bluntly as he could:

"We have no more money to invest in the orchard. It's as simple as that. And we still have significant debt. The rain we've had so far has fallen in the wrong place. Kern County is still dry. We'll have to sell our land."

Keila, who was still decluttering her studio, stopped cold and sat down on the red love seat, patting the space next to her with her hand, motioning to Oscar to sit down.

"First of all, the part I like best about what you've just said is the word 'we.' Second, have we considered leasing it? There are other farmers nearby who might want to work the land," said Keila, not sure if it was a good idea.

"We could. But if we lease it, all the income would have to go to pay debt. How are we supposed to live on no income? And then we have the girls living at home again. There's no way we could sell the house and downsize now."

"Give me a few days to think."

Friday, October 21st

This morning, as a result of the recent rain, Patricia felt entitled to extend her shower to a full five minutes so she could think. She rubbed her still-flat belly, looking for a sign of life. Inside of her, one or hopefully two tiny hearts were beating too faintly to be noticed by anyone. The fetus, or baby, depending on who you asked, would soon be an Alvarado, but it would be just as much an Almeida, and Felix had to know. Or not.

She thought about Dani. Half of him had come from the boy who had raped her, but thankfully he never showed any interest in the baby. It would be best if she and Olivia could find a way for Felix not to care about the pregnancy. She'd need a lot more shower time to come up with a plan, but for now, she allowed the last few drops to fall on her skin like a mystical absolution.

Monday, October 24th

Claudia had stayed up, watching rain droplets slide down her window while she wrote on her laptop.

"What's it about?" asked Olivia in the morning. "I assume you're writing something, your recent medical experience, maybe?"

"I'm not sure yet. Just doodles, I guess."

"Like a novel?"

"God no! Sounds too daunting. What I'd really like to try is to write a TV pilot."

"And send it to Gabriel under a pseudonym?"

"Ha. Wouldn't that be hilarious? But fuck Gabriel. Don't yank me out of my creative zone by mentioning that creep. I do think I have a knack for telling stories, though."

"So, when can I read what you wrote?"

"Now. But don't be cruel with your comments."

Tuesday, October 25th

The Mexico City airport was, as usual, a disaster. Too small for the number of people that passed through it; too old and cheaply built; too many poorly planned additions that had turned it into a tortuous labyrinth. Still, Keila loved the I'm-finally-home feeling she had every time she arrived. She navigated the airport deftly; she knew it well. She got in a taxi and went home to drop off her suitcase and then straight to see Simon Brik.

"I'm leaving. I'm no longer going to work with your gallery," she told him as soon as she sat down at his desk.

Simon didn't seem surprised. He offered her a glass of sparkling water. She accepted it.

"You've made up with Oscar and want to stay away from the temptation of a possible relationship with me. Am I correct?"

"Yes."

"You've been announcing this with your silence."

"I'm done, Simon. It's not healthy. It's never been. Thank you so much for so many years of support. You helped my career tremendously, but it's time to say good-bye."

"I have a few of your pieces in storage. Is there a new gallerist I should ship them to?" he said, resigned, not even trying to hide his sadness.

"Just send them to my studio. Thank you."

Keila leaned across the small desk, kissed Simon on the cheek, and walked away. She was happy the break had been so quick and efficient.

At home, in her parents' house, she roamed around the rooms and felt lonely and small. Perhaps she could list it on short-term-rental apps. Or she could lease it to someone who planned to open a boutique hotel, like the many that had sprung up elsewhere in Polanco. With six bedrooms and six bathrooms, it surely qualified. She considered the possibility of opening a bed-and-breakfast, but this idea required capital she didn't have, and her full attention was hard to provide from Los Angeles. Any of these initiatives would help alleviate the cash problem she and Oscar were in. On the other hand, along with the house she would be giving up all the memories that it contained. The thought of it felt like treason.

She took an Uber to the cemetery and went straight to her mother's and father's graves. After clearing them of weeds, she posed the question point-blank: What should she do with the house?

She waited for an answer from her mother, but this time she didn't hear her voice.

Thursday, October 27th

Patricia and Eric met at a bar in the Arts District, the kind of joint meant for social interaction where the noise from people talking makes it impossible to converse. Their marriage was officially dissolved, and they were toasting the future. Negroni for Eric, Virgin Mary for Patricia.

"Can I touch?" asked Eric, and without waiting for permission, he put his hand on Patricia's belly.

"It's too soon, dummy. Wait till the fifth month and you'll feel all the kicks you want," she said, laughing.

Eric turned serious, as if he had something important to say.

"You know, this thing with your pregnancy could go south fast if Felix finds out the wrong way that you're pregnant with his embryos."

"I know, but we still don't have a plan. Any ideas?"

"The more I think about it, the more I believe this scheme could work only if we were living in Telenovelaland. How long do you think you can sustain this farce before he finds out and sues the shit out of you and Olivia?"

Patricia caught most of Eric's words in spite of the bar's sea of chatter and music. She filled in the rest by reading his lips, a skill she'd acquired in noisy venues and restaurants during college. She had to give him credit for thinking straight, the only one with a level head in what was looking more like a mess with no solution. She took a swig of her drink, having sworn off plastic straws.

"I can offer this," Eric added, looking at her without blinking. "If asked, I will say, which is totally true, that our divorce had nothing to do with your pregnancy."

Friday, October 28th

What's with this end-of-the-month traffic? It was that day of the year when monsters, witches, and creatures swarmed the streets demanding candy. Even though Halloween proper was on the thirty-first, it was customary for children to go trick-or-treating on the previous Friday, right after school. Olivia had just dropped off Diana (a little Frida Kahlo, unibrow and all) and Andrea (a little Amelia Earhart with helmet and goggles) after collecting a sizable amount of sweet loot around the neighborhood. Lola was to give the twins supper while she took Claudia to the doctor for her follow-up appointment as she always did.

When they got home, Patricia was already waiting for them.

"Hurry up! We'll never find parking," she said.

In the car again, this time Patricia's Prius, the three sisters barely fit wearing their costumes: Claudia was dressed as C-3PO. "I can walk like I'm holding a potato in the crack of my ass without faking it," she'd said. Patricia had decided to go as R2-D2, but her legs stuck out of the cylinder in place of wheels, which broke the illusion. Olivia had chosen Princess Leia and was still attaching the cinnamon-roll faux hair twists when they arrived in West Hollywood.

"It's acceptable that we're all going together, but we didn't have to pick out our costumes from the same movie franchise," Patricia had said when her sisters revealed their choice for this year's Halloween parade in West Hollywood.

"It's not like we planned it," said Claudia. "See? We have a sisterly connection. We should embrace it."

"Parking spot!" yelled Olivia.

■ ■ ■ ■

Saturday, October 29th

When Keila arrived home from LAX, she found Oscar up on a ladder fixing a gutter that had come loose from the stucco and hung by the side of the house. He noticed Keila standing a few feet away, still holding her carry-on suitcase.

"You're back! How long have you been standing there?" he said, surprised.

"I like watching you work on something you'd abandoned."

"All the gutters are clogged with dead leaves. I'm glad I checked. Gotta prepare for the rains. How was Mexico?"

"Brik & Spiegel won't represent my work anymore; I just fired them."

"I hope you're making the right decision; Simon has been your gallerist for so long."

Keila had decided not to share with Oscar the reason she had parted ways with Brik & Spiegel Gallery. She had fretted over the issue during the entire flight to Los Angeles, and by the time the plane landed she had convinced herself that telling him about her lifelong flirtation and one-night affair with Simon would only damage her marriage after their having barely survived its worst

430

crisis. But when she found Oscar in the backyard cleaning out the long-neglected gutters, she felt a need to be honest. Why perpetuate a history of secrets?

"The truth is, Simon has spent the past twenty-some years pursuing me, not just as an artist, but as a woman. And I slept with him. Once. Very recently. I was angry with you."

Oscar came down from the ladder and looked at Keila for an infinite minute. Of the myriad thoughts that his brain produced at warp speed, one question stood out: Would he be able to live with this information? He checked his feelings and realized he wasn't surprised. There was no rage, no horrible feeling of betrayal. No humiliation. Just Keila, there, telling her truth. He saw in front of him a field of wildflowers waving in the mild wind of a clear day and felt clean, transparent, new. So, holding on to this image and before he changed his mind, he kissed her long and tenderly, not even trying to avoid soiling her clothes.

"I know. Welcome home, love," he said, and started rolling her suitcase into the house.

Sunday, October 30th
Right before Keila's homemade cajeta flan

431

and after her legendary chicken with pistachio and chile poblano mole, Patricia called for silence, clinking her glass with the edge of her dessert spoon. She had news.

"I'm pregnant."

It took only an instant for Claudia to recover from the shock to reply: "But you just divorced Eric!"

"It's not Eric's. I'm pregnant with Olivia's embryos and Felix doesn't know about it."

There. She'd said it.

No one comprehended what they'd just heard Patricia say, so blunt and jarring, like a sudden hailstorm in midsummer.

"Why would you girls do this?" Keila's voice expressed surprise, dread, and delight all at once. "Didn't the judge order the embryos to be destroyed?"

"We weren't going to let an Alvarado go to waste," said Patricia. "We'll just have to find a way to deliver the news to Felix. He needs to know I'm pregnant, just not with his and Olivia's embryos."

"Why make up a new secret that can haunt us for years to come?" said Keila.

"Well, this year we've proved that we're good at keeping secrets."

"What if he finds out? He can very well sue you!" Keila warned Olivia.

"It'll be worth it."

432

"This was highly irresponsible, girls, and we don't know at this point what the consequences will be, and there will be for sure, ugly ones, but I have to say this: now that it's done, we have to stick together and raise that baby with all our love."

"Are we having twins?" said Oscar, now thrilled after the initial shock.

"We don't know yet, Dad. But however we handle it with Felix, Olivia and I are going to raise our kids together as sister-mommies," said Patricia.

Suddenly, Claudia, who had been quiet throughout the entire revelation, got up from the table, lunged her napkin in the direction of Olivia, and stormed out of the dining room.

"Claudia!" yelled Olivia. "What's the matter? Come back!"

Olivia ran after Claudia, followed by Patricia into the kitchen. Claudia stood by the peninsula, furious.

"What's going on?" asked Olivia, puzzled.

"You stole the embryos from the fertility lab?!?"

"Yeah, I guess we did," said Patricia, suddenly realizing the enormity of what they'd done.

"Don't you ever, ever call me klepto again!" she said, and as she released her anger, her screams turned to laughter and she hugged both her sisters, who were still processing her reaction.

"How could I steal something that's mine?" asked Olivia.

"Half yours!" corrected Claudia. "Deal with it."

Oscar and Keila watched Claudia's outburst from the kitchen door, calibrating the magnitude of the news. When they all calmed down and as they all settled back in their seats, it suddenly became clear to Oscar that the heart was not a pie. If it were, slices would become thinner with each new baby. He could feel his heart growing to make room for the new addition or, better yet, additions. He marveled at this revelation, and just as he proclaimed, "Let's celebrate!," the rain began.

Monday, October 31st

The IronWolf 700B, a fifty-ton behemoth of a machine, waited for the Alvarados at Happy Crunch Almond Orchard, its steel rototiller fangs on alert, its engine snorting impatiently. Nearby, Los Tres Primos discussed with the University of California Cooperative Extension adviser and the machine's operator the multiple advantages of using this novel method to remove almond trees instead of the traditional multistep process that ultimately turned the trees into wood chips.

Asking around at UCLA, her alma mater, Patricia had come across this new method, contacted the researchers who were helping roll it out to the industry, and negotiated with them: the Alvarados would volunteer the orchard so the university could conduct a demonstration for the students, free of charge to Oscar. They were to remove the entire orchard. Cheaper and faster methods were being experimented with, using other machines like the horizontal chippers, but given Oscar's financial situation, no speed or cost could beat a free tree-removal service, so he canceled the service he had initially hired.

When the Alvarados arrived, a few dozen students were already there, clustered around the IronWolf, ready to watch the formidable feat that was about to take place.

Diana and Andrea had stayed home with Lola, but Dani was allowed to skip school. Wearing his Imperator Furiosa Halloween costume — the top half of his face stained with charcoal, his left arm covered in a tin contraption resembling a mechatronic prosthesis — he climbed on the IronWolf's roof and, playing the part, yelled incomprehensible words while wielding a stick with his one able arm.

"Is it safe for him to be up there?" asked Patricia to the operator as she took a picture of her son with her phone.

"This is not a high-speed battle rig. It'll be like reenacting the movie in slo-mo. He'll be fine. Just ask him to wear these protective goggles."

He climbed into the IronWolf's cab, gave Patricia a pair of goggles, and revved up the engine.

"Ready, Mad Max?"

"Not Mad Max, I am the true fearless heroine, Imperator Furiosa!" yelled Dani, thrilled.

No one else among the Alvarados seemed to share Dani's excitement. In fact, the atmosphere was somber and anxious, as if they were about to witness someone getting burned at the stake.

The beast's fangs, accustomed to crushing ice and rock, started rolling. Its road wheels began to turn the tracks that slowly crunched the ground beneath like a panzer relentlessly and unapologetically climbing over war rubble. As the machine pushed the first tree over, Keila watched with horror as it devoured its trunk and branches, ripping it entirely into shreds, mulching it and incorporating the bones and guts back into the soil, all within one minute.

"I can't watch this anymore," said Keila, after an entire row had been obliterated.

"I was waiting for someone else to say it first," said Claudia, who was sitting on a folding chair she'd brought from home.

"This will go on for a whole week. I think we've seen enough," said Olivia.

"Fascinating, worth sharing on social media, but I'm ready to get out of here; it's too depressing," said Patricia, still documenting the process with her phone's camera.

Oscar found it harrowing to see his beloved trees disappear under the crusher, but he endured it stoically as part of his self-imposed punishment. What he could not tolerate was to watch Keila suffer.

"Let's go, then," he said, relieved as well.

437

NOVEMBER

Tuesday, November 1st

Early in the morning, after she clipped her fingernails short (no pretty manicure for clay artists), Keila brought in a large box and set it on the worktable with some tools she had ordered online and a few glazes that she wanted to use on her next project. But as she organized the new materials, she decided to discard the idea that she had been developing of families clustered together and replace it with a more pressing one. Having watched the almond trees being mutilated and digested by that mechanical monster had stirred fears that she needed to portray in her work. She cut open the plastic bag that contained a puttylike dark brown clay block and kneaded it as if it were dough. Then she flattened a portion of it on the table with a rolling pin and loaded an extruder with the rest of the material to produce several clay cylinders and coils of different widths and lengths. Later, she molded the material with her fingers to resemble torn branches, broken tree trunks, hopeless twigs, sad wood chips, and desperate root snarls. As she worked on the elements of her future installation her anger intensified. Why was she just now starting to worry about the drought? Why hadn't she understood Oscar's obsession with the weather? Her dismissiveness had prevented her from seeing the truth. She only had to read the news, listen to her husband, visit Kern County, and watch the crops suffer to accept it. Now she had the need to unite her voice with the ones of those who cared about the Earth, to express a message so urgent and vital that denying it would be a mortal sin. She'd join Oscar in his quest, in her own way, through her art. She'd create clay installations of destroyed forests, melting glaciers, expanding deserts, flooded coastal cities, burn scars seen from space. She'd be a warrior for the planet. For home.

Thursday, November 3rd

There was definitely something there, in that little story that Claudia had written. Olivia was not a literary critic, but she did enjoy reading more than anyone in her family and was able to discern if a piece was decently composed. It was, in her view, well told, a bit heavy on the dialogue, but it felt colloquial, natural, and that was not easy to accomplish, let alone by someone who had only written cookbooks. But the subject matter bothered her to the point where she considered throwing the pages in the trash bin, out of her sight, mostly because she recognized the event and it made her anxious.

In one of the scenes, the main character, a famous chef, was driving along the freeway in her convertible car speaking with her assistant on her cellphone. The dialogue went like this:

"Hey, sorry, I had to hang up," said the chef. "A police car was following me, but he got off the freeway so we're good now."

"No problem. Everything all right?"

"My nieces had an accident in the pool. They fell in. I'm on my way to the hospital. Write down this menu in case there's a funeral and we need to cater it: the squash-flower mini tamales, the grilled lobster tail skewers with tamarind dipping sauce, the silver-dollar quesadillas with chilorio, the scallop ceviche tostadas from Culiacán, and check on our tequila inventory. Don't buy anything just yet. Let's see how this develops. Shit! Missed the fucking exit! Can't talk and drive. Call me later."

In the story, the nieces die.

Tuesday, November 8th

The day ended in mourning. Like a majority of Angelenos, Oscar went to bed with a debilitating stomach ache. The life his people had worked so hard to achieve was no longer possible, all their sacrifices in vain. Would recent immigrants be deported immediately or held in limbo? He wondered what would happen to Los Tres Primos and their families, to so many farmworkers who fed the country with their backbreaking labor. He tried to sleep but was kept awake through the night by a profound sadness. He knew there wasn't much he could do for all the Mexicans who would suffer the wrath and bigotry of the newly elected president of the United States. So he wept.

Wednesday, November 9th

"Should we move to Mexico City? We still have my parents' house. It's large enough for everyone to come with us. We could bring our girls and our grandchildren and settle there. Not many people have that choice. We should feel fortunate."

"No. I refuse to be bullied out of my country by anyone."

Thursday, November 10th

When Keila first migrated to the United States years before, she was told that in this country anyone born in the United States could become president. She took this assertion as a hopeful sign that she was going to live in a real democracy where every election was clean and every vote counted. She quickly developed a profound pride, knowing she was a tiny thread in the great American fabric. But on that morning, as she sat at the dentist's and her hygienist asked her question after question that she could not answer with her mouth open and full of cotton balls, she remembered what she'd been told. Yes, anyone could become president. What she hadn't been told was that this applied literally to everyone. She worried that the new president would project his wrecking ball toward long-standing institutions and wept silently.

"Am I hurting you? Want some more anesthetic?" asked the hygienist.

Monday, November 14th

"I'm starting school in January. Writing school."

Claudia made her announcement to Keila, Oscar, Olivia, and Patricia at Hiroshi's Japanese restaurant. Hiroshi sat at the table with them for five minutes before going back behind the sushi bar. He had been visiting Claudia often during the past few weeks. Although he had been clear with her that he didn't believe eating large amounts of wasabi would bring her taste buds back, he still humored her and served her little plates full of the cone-shaped green paste. This night was no different, and as she put them in her mouth, one after another without breaking a sweat, she explained her reasons for going back to school.

"I can't be a cook anymore. I'm not going to sit at home all day moping around. I need to help Mom and Dad around the house. I'm bored. I'm done focusing on my recovery. I need a creative outlet."

She could have continued to produce more reasons but decided that the ones she'd offered were enough to convince her family that she was sane and sound and still worth something. There was one more reason she thought about, but kept to herself: she hoped to wrack Gabriel, fucking Gabriel, with envy.

■ ■ ■ ■

Wednesday, November 16th

When Patricia's first ultrasound at the seventeenth week of her pregnancy showed two shapes side by side on the blurry screen, the doctor, an Asian woman in her forties who seemed just as thrilled as the Alvarado sisters, said: "Twins! And look here, this one's a boy! That's his penis!"

"He's certainly going to make someone happy with that!" said Patricia.

The little protuberance coming out of a larger mass disappeared quickly, morphing into another image: two tiny flickering lights.

"Those are their hearts, beating."

"What's that?" asked Olivia.

"That's one of the babies sucking on his toe, and it's also a boy!"

Olivia burst into tears. "We'll raise all five kids together," she said to Patricia, sobbing, trying to make out the shapes of her babies as they came on the screen.

Neither of them was thinking about the future complications of such a venture; they were too excited to see the embryos turned into babies, alive, healthy. But later, in Olivia's car on the way to pick up Lola and Diana and Andrea at the park, they discussed

444

the scenario that likely awaited them.

"There's nothing special about our arrangement. How many war widows throughout history have done the same thing?" said Olivia, seeking to reassure herself.

"Right. It's totally normal. We can definitely take care of five kids between the two of us. Who needs dads?"

"We do have Dad around. He can be the father figure."

"Yeah, for sure."

"And Mom can help."

"And Lola."

"And Dani. He's almost all grown up now."

"Claudia can be the crazy auntie."

"I don't think she's much of a baby person."

"She'll be a better influence when they're older."

"As long as she doesn't teach them to steal stuff," said Patricia with a hint of dread in her voice, aware that these babies existed as a result of a theft.

"Where are we going to put their cribs?"

"In my room, of course. Diana and Andrea are already sleeping in your room."

"Right. Plus, you'll be breastfeeding them."

"Oh, shit. I hadn't thought about that."

445

"You could pump milk into bottles, and I can take care of the night feedings so you can sleep."

"We'll take shifts."

"We'll have each other's backs on everything. We've both been through it already, with Dani and the twins."

"Except when they throw up. I can't deal with that."

"Are you saying I'll be assigned to vomit duty?"

"Please."

"All right then, you'll be the diaper changer."

"I feel I'm getting the raw deal here."

Friday, November 18th
Keila's pieces arrived from Mexico City in well-packed crates. Simon had sent them along with a nice, but impersonal, note. Nothing else. Keila stored the packages in the garage without opening them. She didn't see this delivery as the end of something, but as a beginning. She went into her studio, opened her laptop, and searched for "art galleries in downtown Los Angeles."

Saturday, November 19th
"Guess what? Your aunt Pats is going to have two baby boys! They're in her tummy!"

446

Olivia told Diana and Andrea as they were getting dressed and packed up to spend the weekend with Felix.

"Is Uncle Eric going to be their daddy?" asked Diana.

"No. Uncle Eric is not your aunt's husband anymore. Remember the party where he said good-bye to you? Now she found someone else to have the babies with: Mr. Sperm Bank. He's going to be the daddy."

"Oh," said Diana, half interested, when the bell rang.

"Your dad's here. Let's go."

The seed of the Great Family Farce had been planted.

Sunday, November 20th

Nothing could be accomplished in Los Angeles. The weekend had been ruined. Beaches were empty. Parishioners had skipped Mass. Brunch reservations had been canceled everywhere, even at indoor restaurants. No cookouts. No swimming. No volunteering. No jogging. No errands. The streets were a mess. Traffic was unbearable. A winter storm had moved into the city. A flash-flood watch had been issued for last season's burn areas. It was time to rejoice. This was the official arrival of the rainy season they'd been praying for.

When Felix showed up at the Alvarados' front step that evening, with him and the twins soaked, Olivia asked Patricia to start a hot bath for the girls and handed them to her. As she was closing the door, Felix stopped her.

"I hear Patricia is pregnant," he said.

"Right."

"I guess she doesn't need a husband."

"I guess not."

"I wonder how that's going to sit with Eric."

"Eric has no say."

"Diana understood the father was some Mr. Sperm Bank, can you believe it?" he chuckled.

"What isn't there to believe?"

"So cute, her innocence."

"Yes, that's funny," said Olivia dryly, holding her laughter. "You can't say anything around these kids."

Monday, November 21st

Oscar hadn't rejoiced the previous day. He had watched the rain hitting hard on the pavement, creeks by the curbs quickly disappearing into the storm drains, frantic windshield wipers, dripping umbrellas, people running for cover. He should have been elated. This was the most anticipated rain in years. But instead, a horrible thought overcame him as he looked down from his bedroom window on his flooded garden: Had he destroyed his almond trees in vain? Had he acted too soon? Was the drought over? On that morning, when the lawn was still wet and squirrels were still shaking the water off their fur, he fell on his knees and banged his head on the windowsill.

Tuesday, November 22nd
It took weeks for Keila's clay pieces to dry, what with all the humidity. But now they were finally ready for the kiln, so she carefully set them inside and turned on the gas. "This is not environmentally friendly," she said aloud to herself. "I'll have to replace this kiln with an electric one. It won't have the same result, but we all need to adapt."

Wednesday, November 23rd
An erotic netsuke figurine twisted into a knot was what Keila saw when she walked in on Claudia and Hiroshi, who were having sex in her bedroom, her legs up in the air, his body sideways, wrapped around her torso, and more arms than she could count.

"We need to find another place to fuck," said Hiroshi after Keila apologized and shut the door.

■ ■ ■ ■

Thursday, November 24th

"Well, our prayers were answered," said Oscar, standing at the head of the table as he started his traditional Thanksgiving speech in a ceremonial voice. "We're getting more rain than we can handle. That's a very positive turn of events. God knows how much we need it here in California. I'm thankful, but I think we could have saved the trees, had we waited a few weeks."

"What a mistake! Pulling those trees out!" wailed Claudia, slamming her fist, barely missing the plate in front of her.

"We didn't know it was going to rain so much! It's not Dad's fault," said Patricia, coming to Oscar's defense.

"I'm not saying he did it on purpose. It's just that the timing was so fucked up. Now what?"

"Stop right now!" shouted Keila. "We don't need to fight over this, let alone question Dad's decision. It's Thanksgiving and we should be focusing on the good."

Everyone remained silent.

"Well, I'm going to start," Oscar said, clearing his throat. "This hasn't been an easy year for anyone sitting at this table, but together we've survived a near-drowning experience, an estrangement, a brain tumor, three divorces, embryo theft, a wildfire mandatory evacuation, and the loss of our almond orchard. But it's not over. We need to work together as a family to compensate for those dark and powerful forces that are working against harmony in our country and on our planet."

"I propose we develop a list of actions we can take to counter this trend. Anyone up for it?" said Patricia.

Everyone raised their hands and waved as if trying to catch butterflies.

"Ditch plastic bags!" said Dani.

"Ditch plastic bottles," said Claudia.

"I've already given up straws!" said Olivia.

"Me, too," said Keila.

"Ride-sharing to the extent possible!" said Claudia.

"That's a tough one in L.A.," said Keila. "We won't be able to wean ourselves so easily out of our cars."

"I'm getting an electric car when I sell my TV pilot," said Claudia, still uninformed about the difficulties of selling intellectual property in Los Angeles.

"I pledge to design and build energy-efficient homes," said Olivia.

"I won't flush the toilet unless it's absolutely necessary," said Aunt Belinda, surprised at everyone's sudden expression of disgust.

"I'll join marches against anti-immigrant policies," Oscar chimed in.

"I want to propose something more radical," Patricia said. "Let's all go vegan together. No more meat consumption equals a more compassionate and kinder world for animals and fewer methane emissions," she said, standing up for emphasis, looking for a nod, a yes, a let's-do-this. But instead, the omnivores sitting around the table stared, salivating, at the steaming turkey on its platter, its skin perfectly crispy-browned, and the huachinango a la veracruzana — the fish's glassy eyes staring lifeless at the ceiling — not a holiday dish, but one of Keila's most popular from her vast repertoire.

"C'mon, guys, commit!" she said, frustrated.

"I don't mind. I'll join. Everything tastes the same to me anyway," said Claudia.

"Why don't we eat now and commit later?" said Keila. "Pass me the huachinango."

Friday, November 25th
When faced with the option, Patricia much

preferred Cyber Monday to Black Friday. No driving anywhere. No crowds. Better deals. More stuff to choose from. But this time she went along to the mall just to humor Olivia and to supervise Claudia, who insisted on tagging along, explaining that she should also have a say on what kind of cribs the new babies were going to get.

"We're just going to see what's out there," said Olivia.

"Then let's not go," said Patricia. "The whole point is to get the discounts. If we're just going window-shopping, let's turn around and go on a different day when there are fewer people."

"If you don't want to buy baby stuff now because you're afraid of another miscarriage, let me tell you, Olie: this time it's not your uterus. The babies are safe," said Claudia from the back seat of Patricia's Prius.

Claudia's words landed on Olivia with a loud thud, as if someone had dropped a batch of stones on her, the smooth Mexican river pebbles, like the ones used in landscaping, paths, and driveways. Her sister was right. But why had her blunt statement hurt? Wasn't she elated about Patricia's kindness in carrying the babies for her? As Patricia sped down Santa Monica Boulevard toward Century City, Olivia closed her eyes and kept quiet, trying to listen to her feelings. Yes, she was elated for the gift of motherhood in her impossible circumstances, but a sense of loss overpowered her joy. She forced herself to acknowledge it all, opened her window, and yelled into the onrushing air, "Accept the good!"

DECEMBER

Friday, December 2nd

It was a Santa Ana day, again. The eighty-mile-an-hour winds whistling through the canyons and passes said so. Inflatable Santa Clauses, reindeer, and assorted holiday decorations flying away from rooftops and lawns said so, too. Patio furniture and umbrellas getting thrown off into swimming pools, small cars trying to stay in their lanes on the freeway, and pedestrians on the lookout for falling palm tree branches — all of that indicated that the Santa Ana season was in full force. Patricia's hair, usually groomed, was now an unruly tangle, a toy for the wind to play with, when she arrived at the restaurant and gave her car keys to the valet attendant. She would have looked for street parking as she often did, but she was running late to her lunch with Benjamin, her Target ex-client.

"We're shooting a commercial on Monday, but I wanted to fly down early to see you," said Benjamin.

"Well, that's awfully nice of you, considering that your team gave the account to another agency."

"It wasn't my decision, Patricia. I always admired your work and loved seeing you at the office. Maybe we can spend the weekend together?"

"Whoa! This is a little abrupt. We haven't seen each other since we had sex in June. A lot has happened. I divorced Eric, and now I'm pregnant with my sister's embryos."

"That's all? A social media ace turned into a divorced surrogate mother."

"One doesn't exclude the other. Follow us on our new joint Instagram account: @2.mommy.sisters."

"I don't see you in a few months and all this happens?"

"Right. And as you can imagine, I'm not dating anyone right now. Who knows? Maybe in the future. But at this point my world is Dani, my job, my pregnancy, my sister Olivia, and my mom and dad, who just made up after a long, dark period."

"Well, then, let's toast to that world of yours that seems as full as an infinity pool."

"I'll have a virgin mojito."

Sunday, December 4th

Felix sounded unusually apologetic when he delivered the news to Olivia. The Alvarados' doorstep had become their habitual meeting spot when he dropped off the girls on Sunday evenings. The sisal mat on the floor didn't really mean it when it spelled out the word "Welcome." Not for Felix. But this was where they talked, always briefly and, as of late, strictly about the twins' issues. He took his time to hug them before they rushed inside to have supper with Keila.

"Wait, don't close the door just yet. I need to tell you something important," he said to Olivia, who had already taken a step back into the house. "An opportunity came up; it's work-related. I don't know how to say this. You won't like it: I'm moving to Vancouver. The real estate market is insane over there with all those foreign billionaires buying mansions and penthouses."

Olivia couldn't wait for him to be gone.

"How do you envision exercising your visitation rights?"

"That's the thing. I might not be able to," he said in a tone that Olivia understood as

457

contrite. "But, please, let's avoid making this a big deal. Let's keep it out of the courts."

Hiding her delight, Olivia staged a measured angry response.

"So, you're abandoning your children. It doesn't surprise me. You never wanted them." She stopped there so as not to make him change his mind and stay.

"I understand why you're mad at me. I know this means the responsibility of raising the girls falls mostly on you."

Not that it changes anything, thought Olivia. She remembered the few instances when he actually had assumed that responsibility, albeit reluctantly: once when she had to travel to Houston for three days to evaluate a property and he stayed home to look after the girls, and the other when she tripped over a hose in her backyard and broke her ulna. He watched the twins for two days while she was in the hospital getting her arm put back together.

"I'll try to come and visit them during the winter. It's low season for Realtors over there."

"You do just that," she said, trying to sound cold and upset.

"I'm sorry for doing this to you."

As if we needed him, thought Olivia,

shutting the door without saying another word.

The neatly arranged funeral pyre involved logs, branches, sticks, and twigs made of bisque clay. On top, a crackled Raku ball dipped in cobalt glaze with iron blotches resembled Earth. A bloodlike pool of red glaze oozed out from underneath the entire structure. She lifted the kiln shelf and set it carefully on the table next to other similar pieces depicting the planet in various scenarios: in a freshly dug-up grave hole, on a mortuary embalming table, its foot sticking out from under a white sheet with a morgue toe tag that read EARTH, and a tombstone with an engraved epitaph that said HERE LIES EARTH. I WARNED YOU.

"This must be your best series so far," said Oscar, standing by the door, startling Keila.

"You scared me!"

"So sorry. I'm impressed by what you're doing."

"I'm not sure that portraying Earth's death is the right message. It's not really about saving Earth, but about saving life. Earth will ultimately be fine; it will continue on without humans and other species. It

459

has already survived five mass extinctions. It's the Sixth Great Dying that I'd like to get across. I might have to rethink all the pieces."

"You're so right. That's what some people don't see."

"And yet, it's clear to me that we're stuck in our California bubble talking to ourselves, the converted. We make movies based on the science, we create art based on research, we come up with evidence as clear as a melting glacier, but all we hear back from the other side, if anything at all, is 'We don't believe,' as if we were talking about a religion."

"It's not about beliefs. It isn't faith-based. It's fact-based."

"And then there's the other thing I'm realizing: my work is useless as a megaphone. How many people can be exposed to the message in an art gallery? It's such an elitist medium. I like to work with clay, and I will continue to do so, but I also need to join the cause and fight."

This was the Keila Oscar loved. He felt a rush of fascination flooding his entire body, making him dizzy. There she was, his wife of forty years in her dark brown bob, her characteristic strand of gray hair falling down the side of her face, showing him the way with her clear head, her convictions. He approached her slowly, removed her leather apron, her clay-stained T-shirt, her bra, and ran his hands along her collarbone, her bare shoulders, down her breast, then traced her areola with his index finger, making a quick stop on a tiny freckle that was about to climb up her nipple.

"Count me in," he whispered before kissing her.

Keila pushed him on the red sofa and kissed him back, reaching for his belt buckle.

Friday, December 9th
On the way to Hiroshi's restaurant, Patricia, who was deftly maneuvering her Prius in the god-awful early-evening traffic down Olympic Boulevard to give her sister Claudia a ride to her dinner date, said: "Stop judging my driving!"

"I didn't say anything," said Claudia, sitting in the back seat so she could stretch her leg.

"I'm looking at you in the rearview mirror. You're giving me the eye again. Stop it!"

"Okay, okay, but I'm about to throw up back here."

"Next time take an Uber."

The two sisters kept quiet, but as Patricia

crossed the Bundy intersection she said: "I found one of the new pacifiers I bought in your room. Care to explain?"

"What were you doing in my room?"

"Getting your laundry bag. But that's irrelevant. You promised me you wouldn't steal again. Why do you do it? You have the money to buy what you want. And even if you didn't, it's illegal, unethical. Is it just because you can?"

Claudia squinted and wrinkled her forehead as if she were looking directly at the sun. "But you stole the embryos."

"The embryos are half Olivia's. It was a rescue operation. Now, stay on topic, this is important. Is it the thrill of getting caught? Do you find it exciting?" added Patricia.

As Patricia made a left on Lincoln and headed toward Pico, she heard a small voice coming from the back seat, the voice of her oldest sister, now a reprimanded little girl: "I'm addicted. I need help."

Sunday, December 11th
The weather forecaster on the TV screen, a Korean woman in a tight skirt and high-heel pumps, reported in a vivid tone that a heavy downpour was imminent and that Los Angeles was experiencing its wettest year in God knows how long. More than

462

fourteen inches of rain since October was clearly a record for the city. It was more than 200 percent of the typical rainfall in any given year. Not that anything was typical anymore.

As soon as the traffic report began, Keila put down her glass of wine and looked out the window. Sure enough, rain was starting to fall hard. It was 8:07 P.M. She wondered, with trepidation, if there would be news in the morning about a landslide, about houses tumbling down muddy hills along the coastline, or a flash flood sweeping cars and trees away. If all went well and there were no tragedies, for sure roofers all across the county would be crazy busy patching leaks like the one they'd just discovered in the garage.

"Oscar?" she called.

"I'm already writing it down in my log. I'll check the rain gauge in the morning," he replied from the bedroom in a muffled voice.

And all of a sudden, in this otherwise uneventful exchange, Keila and Oscar, one in front of the TV and the other in their closet, came to realize that they inhabited the same world again.

■ ■ ■ ■

Monday, December 12th

"I have another secret," Keila said to Oscar, simply and bluntly. They were having sushi at Hiroshi's restaurant for the third time in the past two weeks, compliments of Hiroshi himself.

Oscar dropped his chopsticks but recovered quickly.

"You're kidding, right?"

"When I went to Mexico City to fire my gallerist, I put my parents' house on the market. I got a call from the broker this morning. It just sold."

"Why did you do that? It's all you have left from your parents. You love that house."

"Yes, but I love the equity even more."

"I don't get it."

"I decided not to tell you until it was a done deal. You wouldn't have wanted me to sell it."

"You must have a good reason, I suppose."

"Indeed. We're using the money to get out of debt and to start a new business. I already registered the name; it's my turn now: 'Happy Sunshine Fields.' "

■ ■ ■ ■

Hiroshi Mukai had landed in Los Angeles from Osaka a few years back, lured by the freedom to create Japanese dishes without constraint. He had worked in an okonomi-yaki shop in Dotonbori and eventually felt restricted; with the exception of fugu, which did require years of training, he wanted to make takoyaki, kushikatsu, yakiniku, tempura, udon, soba, even sushi, but his clientele's expectations prevented him from delving into these other dishes. He'd heard that in California you could have all of it under one roof if you felt like it, so he packed up and set up a tiny four-table restaurant on a nondescript corner of Pico Boulevard, which meant it could well have been on any of its hundreds of corners, as the entire street was by definition unremarkable. The full length of it was sprinkled with dry cleaners, pet-supply stores, repair shops, jewelers, mini-malls, nail salons, kosher meat markets, and small restaurants just like Hiroshi's, offering different kinds of cuisines from every other country on the planet. Here were the Mexican restaurants with delicacies from Oaxaca, Puebla, Mexico

465

City, Tijuana, or any number of states and cities south of the border. Over there were the Ethiopian joints, the Italian, French, Salvadoran, Korean, Guatemalan, Greek, Chinese, Argentinean, Peruvian, Brazilian, or Indian, depending on the neighborhood the street happened to be crossing through.

He soon discovered that Americans, not the hard-core foodies, but Americans in general, were far more inclined to try sushi than any other Japanese dish, and some even believed that that was all there was. "It's the taco syndrome," explained Claudia when she and Hiroshi discussed the issue. "Ask most people and they'll tell you that Mexican cuisine is just tacos, nachos, quesadillas, burritos (which aren't even Mexican), and guac and chips. In the case of Japanese cuisine, it's all about sushi and tempura. So sad," she sighed.

"I believe in the Angeleno sense of adventure when it comes to Japanese food. I won't despair," he said. "There's no need to impose California's foodie culture on everyone else. Gastronomic proselytism is not what I do."

And so their conversation went, a succession of erudite insights about food culture, ping-ponging all night with the sole purpose of impressing each other.

466

In the beginning Hiroshi had settled in the back room, setting his futon on the floor among crates of food and sacks of rice. The living arrangements were supposed to be temporary while he made enough money and developed a sound enough credit history to rent an apartment, but as time went by, he could no longer see himself anywhere else, so he stayed put and enjoyed his full-immersion, round-the-clock culinary lifestyle. It all fit perfectly, until his sous-chef, holding a knife in one hand and a fillet of salmon just delivered by the fishmonger in the other, walked in on him and Claudia as they were in the middle of performing a complicated sex position.

"We need to find another place to fuck," she said.

In one of his letters to his parents (yes, Hiroshi still wrote letters longhand and mailed them by post across the Pacific Ocean) he told them that he was dating an American woman four years older, and divorced. The reply came back drenched in dismay (weren't there any single, young, Japanese girls in California?), but he ignored their concern and continued pursuing Claudia.

Claudia, for her part, was delighted to be pursued. For a while after the surgery she had believed herself to be damaged goods. But Hiroshi quickly changed her thinking. And she changed his. "You could add to your sushi rolls ingredients like chipotle, corn, nopal cactus leaves, Cotija cheese, papaya, manguitos con chile, Tampico habanero salsa, poblano pepper, whatever," she'd say, sitting up on the futon. "Go crazy; you don't have to be so orthodox."

"Move in with me," he said.

Claudia took her time to reply to Hiroshi's proposal. Of course, he wouldn't mean move in with him to the back room of the restaurant. They'd have to get a proper place; an apartment with some natural light and a bed she could get up from. The futon was definitely a challenge. But those were easy accommodations. There was something else that prevented her from accepting Hiroshi's invitation, as much as she was falling headlong for him, and it took her a long minute to realize it.

"I won't leave my sisters. Not now. Maybe not ever."

Friday, December 16th
Rained hard. All night.

Saturday, December 17th
The loud thud woke everyone up. It was

468

5:23 A.M. and the Alvarados quickly jumped out of their beds and gathered in the TV room, as it was the previously agreed-upon safe spot in case of an earthquake. But there was no shaking.

"What was that about?" asked Oscar. "Wait here."

He went downstairs and looked out the window to discover that the Sellys' old eucalyptus tree had fallen across the backyard. The fence and the lounge chairs were squashed underneath, and the treetop was spread over the keloid scar and the other neighbors' hedge.

After delivering the news to everyone, he suggested they all go back to sleep.

"Another Santa Ana wind casualty," he said stoically.

"It could have fallen on top of the house," said Patricia.

"But it didn't," said Claudia.

Back in bed Patricia wrapped herself with the comforter but wasn't able to find the security she needed. For the first time she felt a strange angst. She was carrying her sister's babies, the bump now evident, and the responsibility of this commitment suddenly crushed her. She'd have to stay away from peril, avoiding car accidents and falling trees.

■ ■ ■ ■

Sunday, December 18th

Back in Kern County, Oscar and Keila went to visit Los Tres Primos to say good-bye and to celebrate their new endeavors. As soon as the word got out, several farms had offered them jobs, but they only accepted the one that had proposed to hire all three of them together as a team.

Keila and Oscar arrived bearing an assortment of foods: Keila's mole coloradito from Cuicatlán, tamales de elote, empanadas de morilla, and salpicón de cazón, brought in several reusable containers, a couple of beer six-packs, and an orchid plant in a terracotta pot. Lucas had insisted on hosting them for lunch, and they in turn proposed a potluck, which Los Tres Primos agreed to cheerfully. Mario and Saúl, who lived nearby, were already there with their respective wives and their children.

Martha, Lucas's wife, was still in the kitchen steaming a large pot of tamales over two burners, but that didn't stop her from getting the party started. Bottles of beer were handed out. A bowl of chips and guacamole appeared, and the volume on the radio tuned to the local Spanish station was cranked up. A framed poster of the Virgin of Guadalupe hung high on the living-room wall, along with the kids' graduation pictures, some wearing braces, others beautiful smiles. Half a dozen small appliances occupied the kitchen countertop, next to a traditional stone molcajete. A colorful zarape was draped on the easy chair next to a sparkling Christmas tree tucked in a corner. The oversize TV was tuned to a football game in full swing: the Philadelphia Eagles against the Baltimore Ravens.

After the sun set, after the Ravens won, and after many hugs and kisses, the Alvarados left Lucas's home with a full belly and a sad feeling.

Monday, December 19th
"You really shouldn't write autobiographical details involving our family," said Olivia; outside, an unheard-of forty-one degrees. "It's been bothering me; I had to tell you."

She poured herself another cup of green tea to warm up and looked Olivia in the eye, sitting across from her in the kitchen peninsula.

"I'm so sorry if it's irritating to you, but I can't commit to that. I can only write what I know about and my family is what's closest to me. It really does spark creativity."

471

"Why did you have to kill off the twins?"

"It's more dramatic."

"Why don't you write a memoir, something we can all live with, which is the reality of our lives?"

"Our life is boring."

Olivia let out a loud "Ha!"

"It's got to be more dramatic. I want this story to be a television series. That's the most profitable genre these days, aside from the ransom note, which I won't get into for obvious reasons. Cutting letters out of magazines . . . it's a pain in the ass."

"Then write a television series based on us but stick to the facts."

"Where's the fun in that?"

Wednesday, December 21st

The people that Claudia now saw as the characters in her yet-to-be-written television series got in Oscar's SUV and headed to Kern County. Even in cars the Alvarados respected a well-established seating arrangement, always in birth order, survived by numerous uprisings throughout the years started by Patricia (why do I have to sit behind Dad where there's no legroom?), then Olivia (the middle seat is the worst; there's no place to put my feet), then Claudia (when Mom's not in the car I get

472

to ride shotgun because I'm the oldest). Dani was allowed to sit anywhere in the third row, and when the twins arrived, he decided to sit bookended by the two car seats, picking up pacifiers and toys from the floor and managing their feedings, as the good babysitter he was.

Oscar, at the wheel, wondered that morning if he'd have to replace his SUV and get a mariachi-band van or one of those little tour buses that circulated all over Hollywood with sunburnt tourists to accommodate the new set of twins that were on the way.

After three stops, one to take Andrea to the bathroom, another to buy strawberries by the side of the road, and one more to allow Patricia to throw up, they arrived at what had been Happy Crunch Almond Orchard.

"I know it's a sad sight, this barren land," said Oscar as they all got out and were stretching their legs. "But I want you to see it as a clean slate. Your mom and I have moved on and are looking forward to the future. So, welcome to Happy Sunshine Fields!"

Oscar expected loud laughter from his daughters and was not disappointed. After a series of jokes, Olivia asked: "So, what crop are we planting?"

"We're planting acres and acres of solar panels," said Keila, proud of her literally brilliant idea. "We'll be harvesting sunshine."

And, as if on cue, it started to rain.

Thursday, December 22nd

As soon as the proceeds from the sale of the Mexico City house came in, Oscar and Keila spent most of the morning at the bank paying off the debt, sending hefty severance-pay checks to Los Tres Primos, and opening accounts for their new company, Happy Sunshine Fields, LLC. The world was quickly moving away from fossil fuels and into clean energy. There was no going back, and Oscar and Keila knew this.

Back at home, a crew was furiously cutting and hauling away the trunk and branches of the fallen eucalyptus, as they'd promised to finish by end of day.

"It would have been nice to plant windmills," said Keila, back in the car and on their way to lunch, again at Hiroshi's. "Imagine an army of giants creating power out of air. It's so poetic."

"I've thought about it, but our land is not suitable, except maybe on the hilly side. We'd have to partner with a bunch of

474

neighboring farms. Definitely a much more complicated operation. I'm very happy with our decision to go for solar."

Friday, December 23rd
"We're a bunch of weather wimps; we can't even stand a little rain," said Claudia, driving for the first time since her brain surgery in the middle of a superstorm, just the kind that holiday shoppers did not need, not in the open malls all over the city.

"We're not used to it, give us a break," said Patricia, nearly hypnotized by the fast-paced windshield wipers waving at her, as if they were a new invention. She'd heard Claudia was on her way to do some Christmas shopping and decided to go along to make sure she didn't put anything in her purse without paying for it, now that she had started therapy to treat her kleptomania.

"You've never lived outside of L.A.," said Claudia with authority. "New York winters? Now, that's real weather."

"I've spent a lot of time in Minneapolis. I know weather. But what I'm saying is that everything's relative. People on the East Coast, the Midwest, they're used to extreme cold, tornadoes, hurricanes, just as we're used to drought, extreme heat, fires, and

475

flash floods. So don't weather-wimp me," she said.

"Look at that idiot! Move it!" Claudia yelled as she passed a slow Honda and a couple of cars stalled out in high water that ran down the curb. "I'm just saying, we pray for rain, and when we finally get it, we're miserable."

"That's L.A. for you."

Sunday, December 25th

After a hefty brunch composed of Christmas Eve's leftovers — Keila's salted bacalao, romeritos, and huauzontles filled with quesillo — the family gathered in the living room, sitting on chairs and on the floor next to the Christmas tree surrounded by boxes of all sizes wrapped in colorful paper. Nearby, on Keila's mother's cabinet, a menorah still held the little stubs that had once been pencil-thin candles.

Outside, the rain was coming down, hard and persistent.

Dani was the first to open his gift, a guitar. The twins followed, pulling a stuffed unicorn and a bear wearing a blue ballet tutu out of their respective packages. Claudia got a monitor for her desk, Olivia and Patricia got two beautiful baby cribs, and Oscar and Keila got a weekend at a spa in

Palm Springs. This could have been an ordinary Christmas morning at the Alvarados', but it wasn't.

The new 2017 calendar had appeared posted on the refrigerator's door a few days before. Keila had custom-ordered it online and had personalized it with a different family picture for each month. Patricia flipped through the pages to find that a photo of the twins coming home from the hospital was featured in January; there was one of Oscar staring out the window in February; a family shot, minus Claudia, during Easter brunch in March; Patricia and Dani, sweaty and dusty, on a hike in April; Claudia on a hospital bed surrounded by Keila and Oscar in May; a selfie of Olivia and Oscar on Father's Day in June; another selfie of the three sisters unpacking Olivia's stuff at the Alvarados' in July; Dani on his way to Sunday school in August; a family shot with Los Tres Primos at the Rosh Hashanah picnic at Happy Crunch Almond Orchard in September; Dani dressed as Imperator Furiosa right before the almond trees got pulled out in October; a picture of the family at the Alvarados' table over Thanksgiving dinner in November; in December, a group shot of the entire family standing on the barren land that would become their new venture, Happy Sunshine Fields.

How arbitrary is the measure of time, Patricia thought. Earlier that morning, after everyone had opened their Christmas gifts, they sat in a circle on the floor and shared their New Year's resolutions, as if the turning of the calendar offered a clean slate, as if every struggle, crisis, or project could be resolved by the end of the year, only for fresh challenges to arise come January. She thought about her parents, having just barely made amends. What kind of new drama would 2017 bring to their marriage? How would they launch their renewable-energy business? What kind of crisis lurked just beneath the surface waiting to pounce at the least expected moment? And Claudia? Venturing into a whole new career, a writer in the making, still recovering from the consequences of her brain tumor. What awaited her in her writing class? Would her new relationship with Hiroshi lead to marriage? She rubbed her belly and wondered if her pregnancy would be complicated, if the babies would be born healthy, if Olivia would allow her to co-parent as they had agreed. Would the Alvarados continue living together in the house in Rancho Verde, or would they go their own ways? Would the house burn in a fire? Her family's stories were never neatly wrapped up at the end of the year. They just went on, and it felt good, this continuum. There were so many unknowns, so many loose ends; there was so much to look forward to and so much to dread. No wonder fairy tales ended with ". . . and they lived happily ever after." Once all the conflict got resolved, the stories became boring. There was not a morsel the storyteller could leave for the reader to imagine. What else could be told?

Patricia reviewed the entries that had been posted already for the month of January 2017. There was Oscar and Keila's meeting with investors for the solar farm on the seventeenth; Claudia had entered the word "write" along a long and overoptimistic Sharpie line covering the entire month; Olivia was taking the twins to a birthday party on the twenty-first. She took the red Sharpie from the mug next to the fridge (her assigned color) and entered "First Lamaze class" on the twelfth and "Dani's orthodontist appointment" on the fourth. Then she noticed an entry from Keila on the tenth: "Mammogram at Dr. McLean's."

"Mom? Isn't your yearly checkup with Dr. McLean in May, around Mother's Day? You put it down on the calendar in January."

Keila was busy putting away a stack of

plates in the cupboard, but stopped to reply, "Ah, yes. I want to get this little lump in my left breast checked. It's the size of a pea. It's probably nothing."

"Nothing?" gasped Patricia, alarm bells clanging in her head. "You can't wait until the tenth! We have to see the doctor now! And why didn't you tell us?"

"First, it's Christmas. Try finding a doctor. Second, I didn't want to ruin the holiday. I was going to tell you tomorrow."

"What kind of priorities are those, Mom? For God's sake! First thing in the morning we're all going to the doctor's office, whether we have an appointment or not. It's Monday. Someone should be there to take care of emergencies. And you better tell everybody else now."

As Patricia and Keila entered the living room, where the rest of the family picked up shredded pieces of wrapping paper, boxes, and bows to throw in the trash, she announced: "Mom has something to tell you. Listen up!"

"I don't think this is cause for alarm," said Keila in a minute voice. "I found a tiny lump in my breast and I'm going to get it checked. That's all."

Oscar's blood seemed to drain into his gut. A feeling of nausea made him hold on to the back of the sofa so as not to fall.

"When did you feel it?"

"Just a couple of days ago," said Keila, waiting for a scolding for not sounding the alarm immediately.

"What are we, strangers? Didn't we have a right to know as soon as you found out?" he said, in a raspy voice, terrified, angry, confused, in shock.

Claudia and Olivia rushed to hug Keila in solidarity.

"It's going to be all right, Mom," said Olivia. "Even if it's cancer, the chances of survival are huge these days."

"Don't say the word!" yelled Claudia.

Oscar wobbled away to the backyard, engulfed in denial, and stood in the middle of the keloid scar under pounding rain. How long did he stand there, soaking wet, his mind a jumble of thoughts, conjuring possible outcomes for Keila, for himself, for his daughters? What a way to end the year, and what a way to start the new one.

A few minutes later, Keila and the girls rushed out to the backyard, skipping puddles, protected by an oversize valet umbrella, and gathered around Oscar, the whole family hugging one another to avoid getting wet. And at that very moment, Oscar realized that in all the uncertainty that awaited the people that he loved the most, a single thing was undeniable: never before had his family been such a tight knot of love.

ABOUT THE AUTHOR

María Amparo Escandón is the author of the #1 *Los Angeles Times* bestseller *Esperanza's Box of Saints* and *González & Daughter Trucking Co.* Named a writer to watch by both *Newsweek* and the *Los Angeles Times*, Escandón was born in Mexico City and has lived in Los Angeles for nearly four decades.

The employees of Thorndike Press hope you have enjoyed this Large Print book. All our Thorndike, Wheeler, and Kennebec Large Print titles are designed for easy reading, and all our books are made to last. Other Thorndike Press Large Print books are available at your library, through selected bookstores, or directly from us.

For information about titles, please call:
  (800) 223-1244

or visit our website at:
  gale.com/thorndike

To share your comments, please write:
  Publisher
  Thorndike Press
  10 Water St., Suite 310
  Waterville, ME 04901